The Legacy

A Tale from the Realm of the Blind

William Wilkin

Bell Street Publishing, LLC

Published by Bell Street Publishing, LLC,
7360 Middlebrook Circle,
Nashville, TN 37221-6545

Copyright © 2020 by Bell Street Publishing, LLC

ISBN: 978-0-9903164-9-7

First Published in the United States, 2020

Cover Art:
Digital Painting: James W. Wilkin
Graphic Design: Matthew A. Stone

Contents

Acknowledgements

I owe an immense debt of gratitude to several people who have contributed substantially to this book's artistic integrity.

There are my two sons, James and Matthew Stone.

James contributed the digital painting on the cover which captures as I never could my vision of the sense of the book. He also made a number of graphic design suggestions that are incorporated in the cover design and interior of the book.

Matthew Stone made manTy suggestions for the layout and design of the interior as well as completing the cover layout.

My wife, Lou, contributed in both obvious and subtle ways to the completion of the book. She is a Spanish teacher and has extensive experience editing and correcting texts – both student and professional. Any remaining grammatical and spelling errors must not be accounted to her. They proceed from my eccentric ideas about the value of deviating from standards occasionally to accurately portray a state of mind or emotional content. A subtle way that she supported the completion of this book was her endless patience with those eccentric ideas.

In addition, she was willing to endure the many, many times that I worked into the early morning hours pursued by my characters who insisted on telling their stories at the most inconvenient hours.

She has always been emotionally constant in the shifting winds of our lives throughout the long thankless years of the struggle to bring these stories to print. Bravo Lou!

Preface

The first days of school after my return was as difficult as they were for most students. In one way, it had seemed that only a summer holiday had passed, but in another, it felt like years had passed.

We humans were blackmailed into helping destroy the Souls aka ghosts. I was hardly home again when I had to go to school and teach Wendt's classes. I managed to sneak some time in with MY family on the odd weekend when I didn't have a crushing weight of homework to do.

However, eventually, I began to have a little time to do a few nice things purely for me. Aurora and I went shopping in Diagon Alley one Saturday. One Sunday afternoon I totally splurged on a visit to Desdaemona's hair salon. Besides a new "do", I had my nails done (something I never did for myself), and had my hair streaked with purple! That was on Halloween week. It was the closest that I ever got to a disguise for Halloween.

Later, around what Wendt thought of as Thanksgiving, I was having lunch in London with my husband, Ed. He asked a question that provoked thought. "I think that Wendt did some writing. He might have written some stories based on his little adventures. Maybe you should think about doing that with your adventure."

I was disturbed by the idea at first, but before the lunch was over I admitted to him, "That's capital! Of course, I couldn't publish it. The Ministry made me sign a non-disclosure contract." I hesitated as I remembered that meeting.

The final meeting that we had with the Minister of Magic, the head of the Department of International Cooperation, the head of the Auror Office, and a few other bureaucrats like Ginny Weasley was hideous. The Minister had started politely, "My dears, I want you to know how very, very grateful we all are for the part you played in the battle against the Souls."

I was flattered, but at the same time, I was disturbed by the way they saw our role. I wasn't alone. Aurora and Nicholas Brahms were also disturbed by the way the Ministry chose to see our role. Nicholas spoke instantly. He said, "I don't think you understood our report. We didn't see ourselves as being at war with the Souls, but instead, we were trying to broker a peace between them and the Pak from the beginning throughout the mission."

The head of the Department of International Cooperation, Fred Orbison, said, "You see. That's exactly what we don't want people thinking. Our heads would be on the line if we admitted to saving the Soul worlds."

That comment sparked a lengthy, heated debate about what people would think. On one side were Pam Moertl, the Minister of Magic; Orbison; the Head of the Auror office, Richard Ryan, and the head of the Wizengemott, Richard Broward. That thought sparked a memory. Traditionally, the Minister of Magic was also the head of the Wizengemott. After the terrible misuse of that power by Minister Fudge, there had been a change of law that forbade the same woman from holding both positions.

On the other side were Ginny Weasley, an Auror; Aurora Brahms, the Astronomy Professor of Hogwarts; Nicolas Brahms, a Muggle and owner of a computer security consultancy called Last Resort; Dudley Dursley, a published author and apprentice to the Maintenance Engineer of Howarts (Argus Filch); and me, Mrs. Jamie Brewster, the second English Literature Professor of Hogwarts. Of course, we didn't have much influence, but it was good to have the advantage in numbers.

There were basically three positions held by one or another of the members of the group:

- Even though the Souls were intrinsically evil, we maybe shouldn't go out of our way to commit genocide, but if someone else wanted to do it that was just fine.
- No one should ever commit genocide, but it wasn't our

duty to be the Aurors of the Galaxy.

- No one should ever commit genocide, and if we had an opportunity to prevent it, we should.

Moertl spoke for the first group. She pointed out, "Everyone on the Earth falls into one of two camps. There are the people who were infected by the Souls and remained aware—at least part of the time. They virulently hate the Souls and are ready and willing to exterminate them.

"Then there are the ones who were unconscious the whole time and awoke to a changed world months later. They may not hate the Souls for what happened to them, but almost all of them have dear friends or relatives who were awake while they were infested. They may not go out of the way to wreak vengeance on the Souls for themselves, but they would support genocide if it came down to a choice—so long as they didn't have to do it themselves.

"We would be remiss in our duty if we didn't honor the wishes of both groups. We will be seen as traitors if they ever learn the truth of what you did."

I was about to speak when Nicolas Brahms entered the debate. "That isn't the whole story. When the people awoke, they found a very different world. There was no one who was malnourished. Almost everyone who had diseases were either cured or well on their way to cures. That includes cancer victims. You wizards don't appreciate how devastating these diseases that you have cured or at least ameliorated are. I've talked to real Muggles. Hell, all my relatives are Muggles. They may not love the bloody Souls, but a lot sure are thankful for the improvements they brought. I have a brother-in-law who had pancreatic cancer. He had lost sixty pounds, was racked with pain, and was expecting to die in a few months. When he awoke, he was alive! If you don't think that made him and his family happy the Souls had come, you're crazy." There was no doubt which group he was in.

Broward was no doubt in the second group. He said, "Of course, we can't commit genocide or even consciously help some one do that, but you went way beyond what you were officially authorized to do."

Ginny snorted and said, "Officially authorized! Sure, they weren't officially authorized to prevent genocide, but I was in on the early meetings. We sure were hoping they would." There was some quibbling, but no one opposed that idea.

Eventually, Moertl forced us to the next agenda item. She said, "We have to get you all to do the Unbreakable vow to keep what happened on your mission confidential."

I asked, "When does the vow end?"

Moertl replied, "Why, never, of course."

Aurora sneered, "Like we'll take that vow anytime soon."

Moertl replied, "You'll take it right now—like it or not."

Nicholas asked in a very calm, soft voice that I suspected hid fury, "And just how will you force us to do that?"

Moertl's mouth opened and then snapped shut. She looked over at Broward, who nodded almost imperceptibly. "Why, we can send you to Azkaban for breaking the official secrets act." She turned to Broward for confirmation.

He said, "While technically the official secrets act is only a Muggle act, it has been used by previous wizard administrations to prevent the revelation of secrets that would be harmful to all wizardkind and even Muggles, as in this case."

I stood and declared, "What! Hiding behind Muggle skirts to approve suppressing freedom of expression!"

Ginny took my arm and pulled me back into my seat. She whispered, "I don't want you locked up in Azkaban." She then whispered even more softly, "You know why." She was right, of course, I did know exactly why.

Nicholas said, still in his controlled calm voice, "I'd rather eat gruel in Azkaban than make such an oath."

Moertl looked in turn at each of us who had been on the mission. Each nodded silently. She sighed and muttered, "Why is it always me?" Then she made an offer, "What if it is not the Unbreakable, but just an ordinary promise that you won't make this public for . . . say ten years?"

I said decidedly, "No."

She sighed again, "Five years?"

That presented me with a difficult decision. If I wanted to publish this, it would have to wait more than five years. I said, "No."

She said, "Come on, I'm being very reasonable."

Dursley, who was sitting next to me, patted my shoulder and said, "Even if you don't, Wendt probably will."

I grimaced at that and said, "OK. Five years, but not a second longer."

Moertl released a long held breath and looked at the others. They all nodded agreement. She then said, "Done and done. Very well. On to other business. . ."

□□

That had been my first experience with government censorship.

I carefully answered Ed, "I like the idea of writing that kind of story. I have a problem with the story that you have in mind. I sort of promised not to write anything for a few years."

"Unbreakable?"

I shook my head. He nodded and said, "Good."

I went on, "However, Wendt might have a story or two that he's not written but has—let us say—notes about. I might be able to . . . oh . . . ghost-write I guess would be the right word."

Ed was very interested, "What kind of story are you talking about? Something that I'd never heard of?"

I wasn't sure myself. As far as what Wendt had involuntarily shared with me, I'd had a policy of pretty much keeping myself to myself. This was such a fascinating prospect though that I couldn't help being attracted to the idea. "I'm not sure. I have a sort of tickle in the back of my head that makes me think there may be a story that would be worth writing."

"Then I really want you to write it."

"I'll have to see if I can find any notes that Wendt might have made on it."

□
□□

I didn't really do anything about it for a while. Term final exams were coming up, and I wanted to do some lesson planning for the next term before looking seriously. Then one day, I was looking for Wendt's lesson plans for the 2nd term of 4th year english lit. I pulled a loose leaf notebook off the shelf that I thought had 2nd term lesson plans. When I opened it, I discovered that it had a hand-written manuscript that completely filled it. Its title was *The Inheritance*.

I couldn't help myself. I started to read it. At first, it almost sounded like a diary, but I quickly realized that it was an account of events that I'd never heard anything about in the *Prophet* or any Muggle newspaper. I forced myself to put it down before I'd finished two chapters. The fact that I'd never heard anything about it seemed to indicate that its publication must have been blocked by some non-disclosure agreement. I put it back on the shelf and swore that I would not look at it again.

I went back to lesson planning, found Wendt's real lesson plan notebook, and finished my lesson plans. I swore to myself that I would not touch the story again.

The Christmas Holiday began. Before it did, though, Ed asked me, "What about it, Jame? Did you find a story? Will you publish that story? Or at least finish it for the family?"

I blushed at the thought of the desire that I felt to do what I had refused to do earlier. I really did want to do it. I paused long and hard in thought as I worked through the balancing forces in my head. On one hand, I really wanted to know what happened myself. The story started slowly, as most of Wendt's did, but I had begun to see a ghost, faint and shimmering, of where he was headed, and I wanted to follow that specter. On the other hand, it was his story. It was probably based on real events that some government authority wanted suppressed. How could I publish it with integrity? I temporized, "I don't think so."

That night I couldn't let the idea go. I slept fitfully and sometime in the early morning hours awoke, my heart racing with the idea of reading it. I slipped out of bed and went down stairs to the hearth. I stood on the hearthstones trying to summon the courage to do what I'd said that I wouldn't. Then I stepped into the hearth with a handful of floo powder and walked out in my office.

I walked to the bookshelf, scanned the shelves for the notebook, and put my fingers on it. This was my Rubicon. I stood in my nightgown, my hands shaking with desire.

I pulled the notebook off the shelf and sat on the sofa. I lovingly opened the cover and paged through it one page at a time, not wanting to pass where I had left off by accident. I found the very page. I turned it and began to read. I finished the chapter. I closed the notebook. I returned it to the shelf, hoping no one would notice that I'd disturbed it. Silly, I know, but I still felt guilty. Then I returned home and slipped into bed hoping that Ed had not noticed my absence.

In the morning, Ed showed no signs of being aware of my guilty secret.

Then Christmas came. I had a wonderful time at home with my family. We visited the in-laws on Boxing Day as we had before. The dinner and gift exchange went so much better than they had that one time before I married into the family.

Toward the end of the evening after most of the aunts and uncles and cousins had left for home, we were sitting around the fire. It was a cold evening out. My mother and father-in-law were snuggling on the sofa near the fire. Ed and I were snuggling with Sissy on the rug nearby.

Sissy said, "This is a perfect night for a story. Does anyone know one that I've not heard a hundred times."

Her grandfather started to say, "How about *Babbity Rabbity* . . ."

She snorted and said, "I've heard that at least a million times." Then she turned a little whiny and said, "I want something new. You know—like those stories that Professor Wendt used to write—something about the Souls or something like that."

Ed said, "You've got Wendt's old office. Did he leave behind any stories that he didn't publish?"

I took a deep breath and thought, "Bloody hell. I'm going to get back at Ed before the night is over for putting me in this spot." Then I said, "Actually he did. I read a little of one. It sounded interesting. Of course, I only read a little of it. That's all I could tell you. Maybe that's all I should tell you."

Sissy kept going with her whiny voice, "Oh, do! Please!"

I sighed. "I suppose I'll have to now that I've mentioned it."

Everyone seemed happy. Sissy almost swooned, "Oh, goody!"

I said, "Well, you'll have to give me three minutes to floo over to my office to pick up Wendt's draft of the story." Everyone nodded enthusiastically. "Now, before I leave, you'll all have to vow to never share what I read with anyone outside this room."

Sissy went back to her whiny voice. "Not really? *Unbreakable?*"

I said, "Of course, not."

Everyone swore, and I stepped into the hearth in the room. After, I returned, I started, "The day began for teachers at Hogwarts as it always did during a school term. The winter term had just begun a week before. . ."

⌗

The return to the normalcy of the second term of Hogwarts allowed me an opportunity to set aside thoughts of *The Inheritance* for a while. Just as absence from a lover allows one to think of other things than one's overwhelming desire for him, the day to day of school allowed me to forget my desire to publish this story for a while.

Then one day I was grading parchments when a thought crossed my mind. The story was mine as well as Wendt's. I could write it from scratch in my own style. I had not made any promise to maintain confidentiality. That thought decided me. I would write and publish. My first act was to rename the story to *The Legacy*.

Ballard

The day began for teachers at Hogwarts as it always did during a school term. The winter term had just begun a week before. The Great Hall has some of the finest cuisine in the world. Even those who have spent most of their lives teaching at Hogwarts can hardly fail to appreciate the variety that the House Elves bring to every meal. This morning, the featured entrée was a soufflé that made me think, "Is there anything that a Frenchman would not do to get this for breakfast?"

I said as much to Minerva. She smiled and said, "Just another day in paradise."

It was not a meal that I relished after an owl landed on my plate with a small note grasped tightly in its beak. It seemed to think that the item of mail was its property because it refused to relinquish it even though I was obviously the intended recipient. I tried several stratagems to get it to let go, including finally offering it some of the incomparable pastries of the chefs who lived below our feet. I hoped that it would open its beak to sample the delicacy that I was offering it and thus allow me to wrest the letter from it. It had a single mind, though, retaining the letter.

To my relief, I realized that someone was standing over my shoulder. That someone was my bed-mate hardly an hour before. She held out her hand and with the other scratched the monster under its chin. It promptly released the note and it fell into my hands. She picked up the tidbit that I'd been attempting to use to bribe the thing. She gave it a toss high into the air. The fiend leapt from my plate with a flapping of wings that cleared my plate of what food was left. It soared into the air, captured the last edible part of my breakfast, and flew off with it.

"How do you always get those things to do what you want them to?"

"You have to be a witch."

I smiled. It has always been hard for me to stay mad at my wife for long – even before she was my wife. "Thanks."

She sat in the empty chair beside me. By this time, everyone at the head table had left my neighborhood, hoping to avoid the consequences of any misstep with an owl post that I might have. She leaned over to try to see what my letter had to say.

I glanced at it. I immediately handed it to her, "Well, Minerva, I wouldn't want you to strain your lovely eyes reading MY letter over MY shoulder."

She just nodded. She didn't even bother to give me a quick kick to my shin. She chuckled at her coup and demanded, "Guess who wants to meet you and me after breakfast tomorrow morning at 11 AM."

"Oh, I don't have to guess. I finished the note before handing it to you. It's my favorite SAS Major. I just don't understand why he wants to meet us at Heathrow. Why not somewhere in London?"

The Head gave a quick glance around and gave me a quick peck on my cheek as she stood. You'd think that we were still lovers trying to keep our relationship from the rest of the school. Everyone knew that we were married and some people were offended that I had the inside track to information about the school. It was pointless. There was no such thing as "inside tracks" with her when it came to Hogwarts.

She had already made for her first class. She insisted on having a Transfiguration Class at the earliest class period. I was happy to leave that privilege to her. I was also happy that my first class usually was not until 10 AM.

□

The note had said that we should be at Heathrow at 11 AM sharp. We were also to meet a pair of Americans arriving on American Airlines. As usual, when we were going somewhere, I'd insist on traveling by Muggle conveyance if possible.

Minerva was saying, "We have to disapparate in any case. Why not disapparate directly to Heathrow?"

"Because I'm getting tired of disapparating into a stall in a woman's WC. Why not go into a dark corner of a Tube station somewhere close to Heathrow?"

She squinted at me and then shrugged and said, "Why not?"

"Look, I don't ask for that often, but . . ."

She stared at me again, "OK. I agree already."

"You agree?"

"Certainly, it's a reasonable request."

I was thunderstruck for a moment, but I quickly recovered and said, "Yes. Let's go. Now. Before you change your mind." I eagerly held out my hand. She took it in hers, and I was suddenly staggering on a train platform.

She was still holding my hand. "Happy?"

I smiled, "Infinitely – whenever I'm with you."

She smiled at that. Then we started looking for the side of the platform that would take us to Heathrow.

We arrived and began looking for a chauffeur at the baggage claim carrying a placard that read, "Ballard". We found him soon enough. He seemed to be looking for us as well, for he approached us and said, "Are you looking for Lt. Colonel Parker?"

I nodded and he said, "As soon as Ballard and his companion arrive, I'll take you all to the limo where Lt. Colonel Parker's waiting for you."

Apparently the flight was a bit early because two Americans approached, and the taller introduced himself as Ballard – Adam Ballard. I started to introduce Minerva and me, but he insisted that we wait until we were in the limo. They collected their luggage, and the driver led us out to the limo.

He opened the door for us, and we found that we all had real seats except for Lt. Colonel Parker who was sitting on a jump seat. He simply started with introductions. Indicating the man we already knew as Adam Ballard, he said, "This is Adam Ballard. He's Under Assistant to the Director of the National Science Foundation of the United States. His companion is Phil Harris – on special assignment with the FBI."

He then turned to us. "This is Professor Minerva Wendt – the Headmistress of a public finishing school. Her companion is also a professor at the same school. They are the people that I told you about."

Harris said, "Before we say anything more, we need to get to a secure site."

Lt. Colonel Parker smiled and said, "We're headed for one of the most secure locations in England. There are few places that your secrets would be safer."

Harris asked, "#10? A military base?"

"Oh, much more secure than that."

Harris raised his eyebrows.

Apparently, Parker had given the driver the destination before any of us had arrived. The driver proceeded without hesitation or guidance from Parker. As we reached central London, I had a suspicion where we were going. When he pulled to a stop, I was sure. I was so sure that I immediately got up and opened a door before the driver could.

I beckoned our guests to exit through that door. The driver by this time was out and was giving me a sour look. I suppose he thought I was usurping his privileges. Maybe I was, but I knew that we'd waste some time explaining why we were here, and I didn't want to waste any more time than absolutely necessary.

Ballard exited next and looked around but had no comments. Harris was out but was clearly suspicious. He asked, "This is your high security destination? Is it a safe house?"

Parker was out and answered for me. "Not this spot but nearby. Please bear with us for a few minutes." He led the way down the little byway that lead to our destination. I have to admit that he was good. Minerva was the last out, and she followed with full deference to everyone else – including not admitting to any knowledge of where we were going.

Parker led us almost to the exact point that we needed to be. He turned to the small party and said, "Here we are – I think. Minerva will assist us at this point. Please, Mr. Ballard and Harris, each take one of Minerva's hands."

Ballard balked, "I don't see anything here – not even an entrance to the building."

Parker just smiled indulgently, I suppose as he would with a small child who was objecting to going home from an outing to the park.

Minerva was used to dealing with recalcitrant children. She simply said, "Come now. I'm not asking you to swim the English Channel. Just take my hand for a minute."

Parker nodded, and the two took her hand. Harris gasped and Ballard squinted at the sudden appearance to him of the entrance to the Cauldron and its sign. Perhaps he wondered how he'd missed the two objects. Of course, Parker and I only saw what seemed to be an old iron post with some cobwebby stuff attached and slight darkening of the brick wall.

Minerva was reaching the end of her patience with the two holding her hand. "Come now. My hands are full. Would one of you please play the gentleman and open the door for us."

Harris jumped at that and stepped forward. He must have opened the door because he, Minerva, and Ballard disappeared in that instant.

A moment later Minerva reappeared shaking her head resignedly. She held her hands out to us. Neither Parker nor I hesitated to take one and I beat Parker to the door and opened it for us.

We almost knocked over Ballard and Harris. They were standing just inside the door gaping at the interior. I have to admit that at first sight it does appear that one has stepped into the 17th Century. Ballard commented as much. He went on, "This is your safe house?"

Parker answered, 'Oh, no. This is just a way station on our way to the safe house. But it is a good stopping point to let you two get your bearings. It's only polite to the establishment to have a drink while we talk."

As he said that, the proprietor came over from behind the bar and asked what we'd have to drink.

Parker seemed to want to prove his mastery of this situation, immediately ordered, "A fire whiskey, please."

Tom, the barman, then turned to our guests, "My name's Tom. Whom do I have the pleasure of serving?"

I stepped into the void and simply said, "These are two guests of ours from America – Adam and Phil." At the mention of his name, Harris bristled but he must have realized that he had no way of calling back what I'd said. He just frowned at me.

Harris recovered quickly and said, "I'll just have a bourbon."

Ballard looked around the establishment and said, "I'll have whatever you've got on tap."

I glanced at Minerva. She said, "Oh, your house white would be good, Tom."

He nodded and turned to me. "I'll just have a butter beer." Tom stared at me but didn't object. Parker led us over to a quiet table near a corner.

When we were seated, both Ballard and Harris were anxious to ask questions. Ballard won the competition. "Just what is this place? That was a good trick with the invisible entrance. How did you manage it?"

I thought that it would be good for Minerva to have to answer a difficult question, so I just looked at her. She gave me a dirty look and said, "I know that Professor Wendt loves explaining things. I think he should answer that question."

I decided to fall back on Socrates. "Before I talk about this place, I'd like to know what your explanation is."

Harris looked at Ballard as I had looked at Minerva. Ballard glanced around the hall. "This is strange. Any high-tech entrance like we went through would be available only to defense agencies or high end criminal establishments. I don't see how this crowd would be

13

present in either. It just looks like a common pub to me."

Just then, Tom arrived with our drinks. Ballard noticed him and apologized, "I hope you won't take offense at my thinking this is a normal pub."

Tom smiled and said, "If you're paying customers, none taken."

I took the hint and pulled out my purse. "Tom, here you go." I gave him three ten-galleon coins. "There should be something there for you to have a round on us."

Tom nodded and went back to his bar. Meanwhile Harris asked, "Just what were those coins you paid him with?"

I said, "Ten-galleon gold coins. This is not a common pub."

Harris snorted and said under his breath, "You can say that again."

I went on, "It's a pub for magicals, run by magicals. You are among a privileged few Muggles to have seen the inside of it."

Ballard laughed. "Magic? Well, that would explain the entrance. Good joke."

I smiled, "Are you sure it's a joke? Look behind you at the portrait on the wall."

He turned and the portrait of what appeared to be a lady in a black shawl nodded to him and even winked.

When he turned back to us, his words said, "That's a neat trick." But his voice said, "Oh, shit."

Parker re-entered the conversation by suggesting that we move on to Hogwarts, where we could talk in a really secure place. I agreed. "This next trick will convince you that we're serious.

"We're going to move on to Hogwarts." I looked over at Minerva and said, "Don't you think my office would be best? I don't want to startle them too much."

She looked over at the two and said, "Calling the Cauldron a common bar! They deserve to be startled seriously." She hesitated and added, "Oh, I suppose your office would be good."

I went on. "OK. It's going to be pretty much the same procedure. You and Harris will take Minerva's hand. We'll all walk over to the fireplace. One of the two of you will take a small handful of dust from the little pot next to the fireplace. Why not you Ballard? Anyway, all three of you will walk into the fireplace. Then, whoever has the dust will hand it to Minerva who will throw it down." They looked at each other and got up together as though on cue. They did take Minerva's hand and walked toward the fireplace.

When they got close, I said, "Oh, one more thing – close your eyes and prepare to be a bit queasy when you open them."

Minerva looked back and said, "You Muggles are all so namby-pamby." She turned back to the two and said, "Just step out of the fireplace when we arrive and don't touch anything or go anywhere until the rest of us arrive."

Ballard gingerly picked up a little of the floo powder. After they'd stepped into the fireplace, he muttered, "This is so stupid." But he gave the floo powder to Minerva who threw it down and said, "The Office of Professor James Wendt." There was a burst of green flame, and the three seemed to spin as they disappeared.

After they'd gone, Parker said, "Those wizards do seem to have bizarre ways to get around."

I nodded, "Bizarre and unpleasant."

A moment later, Minerva reappeared in the fireplace and held out her hands to us. I enjoyed holding her silky skin. Parker got the handful of floo powder, and we showed up in my office.

□□

I took over as host. "Please pull up chairs to my desk. Mr. Ballard, why don't you take the red leather?

"You are now in the second most secure office in the UK, I think."

Harris confidently added, "After Downing Street"

I simply replied, "No." That surprised him but nobody objected to my statement.

Harris looked over to Ballard, "Well, Adam, this is your show. Go ahead."

Ballard looked around the table. "Have you got any water?"

I slapped my forehead, "Apologies. I've not been the best host. Yes, we have bottled water. I also have something stronger – if you wish."

Ballard wanted bottled water as did Parker. No one else wanted anything yet. I went to my bookshelf. There was a drawer in it where I kept bottled water, glasses, etc. I pulled two and asked if anyone wanted glasses. None did.

Minerva asked, "Would you like the water chilled?"

Parker allowed that he did. Minerva got out her wand and did a silent spell. The bottle didn't look any different, but it had definitely cooled in my hand. I handed it to Parker. He opened it and the release of pressure triggered the crystallization of part of the water in the bottle. Parker commented, "Neat."

I replied, "I know. I used to put bottled soft drinks in the freezer and tried to time it to get exactly that effect. Usually, they either froze

15

completely or weren't cold enough."

Ballard and Harris were both impatient to get on. I sat. Ballard picked up his brief case and pulled a small key from his pocket. He used it to unlock the briefcase. From the briefcase, that seemed to be bulging with files, he drew a Mac Book Air.

He started to open it. I interrupted him. "Sorry, that won't work in here."

Ballard chuckled, "But this is a Mac. It just works." He pushed the power button but nothing happened. He looked over at Parker, "I suppose that's why you asked me to bring hard copies of everything?"

Parker just nodded. Ballard's face fell and closed the Mac. He put it back in and pulled a manila folder out. He turned it so that Minerva and I could read it easily. It said, "PFC Reynaldo."

I offered to turn it so that everyone else could read it, but Harris and Ballard shook their heads. Parker could read it fairly easily, so I left it lying where it lay.

Ballard leaned back and said, "Open it."

Inside there was an 8 x 10 head and shoulder shot of a soldier in desert fatigues who had wavy, short black hair, and an expression on his face that could be generously called a smile. I studied it a moment and shrugged.

Ballard spoke:

"This is PFC Reynaldo. His last duty assignment was in Iraq near the border with Syria. He was a spotter."

Minerva's smile turned to a frown and then a question seemed to be forming on her lips. I stepped in. "Minerva doesn't keep close tabs on the Muggle world."

Harris interrupted, "You've used that term a couple of times. What does it mean?"

Minerva quickly answered, "Non-magicals."

I went on. "There is a war going on in Iraq and Syria at the moment. The States aren't involved much except for close air support."

She interrupted, "What is that? Surely, they don't need any help keeping the air up?" She chuckled at her little joke.

I soldiered on. "No, they don't. It means that the States are using airplanes to bomb the Suni's. The war is between two Muslim factions, the Shia's and the Suni's."

She interrupted again, "And the States are taking sides? Why?"

"Well, this particular group of Suni's want to start Armageddon." I braced to answer the next question, but apparently Minerva knew what Armageddon was. I continued, "But the leader probably really just wants to rule the world, ushering in the age of perfect Muslim Sharia law."

She stared at me a moment as I gave her another chance to interrupt. "Now, for close air support to work, you've got to have people on the ground to direct the airplanes exactly where to attack. Otherwise, you're as likely to kill your own people as your enemy's."

She nodded at that. Ballard took that as his sign to proceed. "A little over two months ago, Reynaldo was involved in an IED blast that should have killed him. Besides having some minor wounds, a fragment of shrapnel penetrated his skull and imbedded itself in his right temporal lobe.

"His was air evacuated to a hospital in Ryad, Saudi Arabia, where he was treated. The attending physician gave him a fifty-fifty chance of living. He did survive and was sent on to the Poly-Trauma unit in San Antonio, Texas.

"In Ryad they'd not removed the fragment. They'd left it for a top neurosurgeon in the States.

"In San Antonio, the surgeon gave him a 10% chance of full recovery after the operation. In any case, he expected that it would take three months to a year for him to have as much recovery as he was going to have.

"The next day, the patient was pretty weak but could sit up and feed himself. The day after, to the complete surprise of his surgeon, he insisted on walking. The surgeon allowed him to walk with assistance to the loo aided by a nurse.

"The nurse became disgusted that she had to accompany a man who was obviously at least as able to get around as she was. The next day, the surgeon reluctantly allowed him to walk to the loo on his own, and when he requested to visit the hospital library, he allowed that as well."

Minerva asked, "I suppose he wanted to read the newspaper or a magazine?"

Ballard gave a mirthless laugh, "No. He went to the bookshelf and found a couple of college level physics texts and started to read them."

I asked, "I'd expect a hospital library to have medical texts and maybe biology, but physics?"

Harris answered, "Oh, the Polytrauma unit in San Antonio is part of a large VA facility. It is certainly the only one in the US. It may be the only one in the world. They have the texts that you expect but also have a wide variety of others."

Ballard went on, "Anyway, he never checked any books out of the library. The only way that we know what he was reading was that first day in the library, the librarian had to shoo him out at closing time. She

17

noticed that he had three books open at the time. There was a general physics text, a text on electromagnetism, and a text on general relativity. She was a very observant librarian.

"Anyway, that went on for a couple of days. By this time, the surgeon reports that he was tempted to release the man back to active duty, but he decided not to. He feared that a relapse might happen. He decided to keep the man in for observation for a month.

"Reynaldo began using the computer in the library to access the internet. He used the library's access to journals to begin reading original research in physics and chemistry. He was reading articles in *Physical Review, Physical Review Letters, Journal of High Energy Astrophysics* to name a few. We have a complete list. The computer's archive has been searched. We could give you a list of the articles but I doubt they would help you understand what he was doing. They certainly haven't helped us.

"By the next week, he was doing nothing but reading. One day when the librarian shooed him out, he asked if he could borrow a tablet to use when the library was closed. The librarian liked him and decided to loan him her work tablet informally.

Ballard paused to frown. Then he went on. "I said that he did nothing but read. That's not true. The surgeon had scheduled a fair amount of time in physical therapy for him. He hadn't followed up to cancel it after it became obvious that Reynaldo didn't need physical therapy. Reynaldo kept the appointments anyway. Shortly, the physical therapist was letting him do his own routine under her supervision. His workouts went far beyond anything that would happen in real physical therapy—unless it was physical therapy for a circus acrobat. After a few days, the therapist just let him do what he wanted to on his own."

Ballard took a deep breath as though steeling himself for what he was about to say. "It was during the third week that things got strange."

Minerva had been drinking some bottled water when he said that. She practically choked and finally said, "Things hadn't been strange yet?"

Ballard shook his head, "No. One day early in the morning, Reynaldo returned the librarian's computer tablet.

"Later that day, he . . . well . . . when he didn't show up for physical therapy, the therapist thought there might have been something wrong. He never missed a reserved time, but she didn't report it. Finally, that night, when the nurse came by to check on him, he still wasn't there."

Minerva asked, "He went for a walk and never returned."

Ballard gave another of his humorless chuckles, "I guess you could say that. We don't know what happened exactly, but I can tell you this. We think that the librarian was the last person to speak with him in the VA facility."

Here Harris cut in, "I guess I should take up the story now. We believe that he just walked out of the facility."

Minerva asked, "I've been in the hospital a time or two. They always have you wear one of those embarrassing gowns. Surely, he didn't walk out in one of those."

Harris, who seemed to have a bit more sense of humor laughed, "No. Not that it would have been impossible. The facility and grounds are huge, and patients very frequently walk out of the buildings to smoke since smoking is forbidden in buildings. But we're pretty sure that he was wearing civilian clothes.

"That same day, one of the surgeons—not Reynaldo's—discovered that his suit was missing from his locker. The lockers have combination locks, and staff can also use a padlock of their own. This doctor used a Master lock that uses a key. When he reached his locker in the early evening as he went off shift, his locker seemed undisturbed. However, when he opened it, he discovered that his street clothes were missing BUT all his possessions from pockets were still in the locker. That included wallet, all ID, money, credit cards, house keys, handkerchief, you name it."

Minerva nodded, "Well, he was a considerate thief anyway, even though he was a thief."

Harris shook his head, "Less so than you think. Two days later, a letter arrived at his office. It was postmarked at a nearby post office. Inside, there was a single sheet of 8 ½ by 11 stationery, apparently from his bank. There was a brief handwritten note. It simply said, 'I hope this covers the cost of the suit.' It was unsigned. There was not a return address."

Minerva who sometimes gets impatient, "AND??"

Harris imperturbably went on, "AND, five crisp new one hundred dollar bills.

"We traced the bills. They had come from the Fort Worth Western Currency Facility. We really didn't need to, though. We discovered that Reynaldo had gone into a branch of his bank at about 2 PM on the day that he disappeared and withdrew almost all his money from his checking and savings accounts. In total, it amounted to more than $4300."

I asked, "If he stole someone else's clothes, how did he prove who he was?"

Harris frowned, "Not as hard as you think. He walked up to a teller and told her that he didn't have his ID with him – it had been stolen. He wanted to withdraw some of his money.

"He told her that he knew his account number and password as verification."

"She was reluctant to do it when she saw the amount of the withdrawal. She called over one of the assistant managers of the bank. They went into her office.

"Reynaldo was perfectly calm and reassuring. He wasn't in a hurry. He explained his situation.

"The manager decided to pull up a photo of him from their computer files. They matched, although when we interviewed her, she remembered that he had a small bruise on his forehead. She asked him details of his address and other identifying information. Of course, he supplied those without a hesitation.

"She apologized for the inconvenience. He was very gracious and assured her that she'd done the right thing.

"He walked out of the bank with the money and hasn't been seen since – as far as we know."

Minerva said, "This is amazing, almost miraculous, but why are you involved, let alone us? After all, people disappear every day."

Ballard said, "A couple of things. First, I forgot to mention that all military personnel are tested at induction. The tests include the standard Stanford-Binet IQ test. Reynaldo's IQ was measured as 118. Definitely above average but not spectacular.

"Shortly after surgery, it was measured again – more for thoroughness than anything else because IQ almost never changes throughout one's life. His IQ measured after the operation was 182."

Minerva said, "Shit. They made a mistake."

Ballard answered, "Well, they were surprised enough that they decided to give him a different IQ test. It was pretty close, measuring 190."

I asked, "And the other was?"

Ballard picked up the skein of the story, "Well, Reynaldo wasn't the . . ."

Parker asked, "I'm in the military. I know that we don't try very hard to find AWOLs. Did you?"

Harris said, "We didn't try very hard – even later, but in the last couple of months we've been trying – hard. We took photos and tried to find how Reynaldo got out of San Antonio. No luck. We've gone nationwide now. He's number 9 on the FBI's ten most wanted. We've not heard a peep."

I interrupted, "There was another reason."

Ballard nodded.

I went on, "Let me guess. Somebody from Iraq got a head wound. It was serious. He was transferred to San Antonio. He was operated on. He recovered quickly. He started studying . . .'

All through this, Ballard was nodding placidly. Then when I reached this point and was saying, ". . . studying physics," Ballard shook his head.

I echoed, "No?"

"No. He started reading Molecular Biology and Genetics. At least, that's what we think he started reading. We don't know in as much detail, because he never tried to stay in the library after it closed.

"But in a few days he asked the librarian about borrowing her computer tablet. She agreed."

Parker asked, "Did he start using the library computer like Reynaldo did?"

Ballard said, "No. And that bothers me." He then reached into the brief case again. Out came another manila file folder. He tossed it down on top of Reynaldo's. It said, "Cpl. Hadley." He then nodded at me, and I opened the file folder. Inside was a photo of a young man. I wondered if he were even twenty. He had fair hair and skin and a bright smile on his face. He was wearing a dress uniform.

Ballard went on, "As you guessed, the rest of the story is pretty much the same with a couple of important exceptions.

"First, his use of the tablet was to study the subjects that I've mentioned. But toward the end, he started reading Information Technology as well.

"Second, the librarian started putting two and two together and got a couple of dozen. Borrowing her tablet was unique enough that she did a little checking and discovered that Hadley had the same sort of injuries as Reynaldo had.

"She went to the head of surgery and expressed her concern about what might happen to Hadley."

Parker interrupted, "Did they both have the same surgeon?"

Harris said, "Yes, they did."

Parker went on, "Strange that he didn't notice, don't you think?"

Ballard said, "I don't care at this point. The head of surgery did care and had the nursing staff come in to check his room every two hours—day and night. They weren't to disturb him or wake him, just make sure that he was still there. Also, there was a standing order at the nurse's station to note when Hadley left the unit and to ask him casually where he was off to."

Parker asked, "What came of that?"

Ballard said, "One morning he returned the librarian's tablet to her. She asked him if he didn't want to use it any more. He just smiled and said that he'd have to see.

"That day, nothing seemed to happen out of the ordinary. But the next day, the evening meal tray was still there untouched."

Harris said, "We interrogated the nursing staff. They all swore that Hadley was still in the room the previous day, watching television. They had no idea that the meal tray was untouched. The nursing station did not report that he'd left the floor."

I was feeling frustrated, so stood. I began pacing and asked, "Don't you have security cameras?"

Harris said, "The VA hospital is a low security facility. There are security cameras in the elevators and the main entrances. That's pretty much it. We did a little analysis on the floor plans. There was no way that he could have left the floor without passing the nurse's station, but once he'd gotten past there, he could use the stairs and an emergency exit to leave without being observed. BUT, no one saw him off the floor. That isn't unusual. How many complete strangers could you identify in a hospital full of patients and visitors?" He was kind of steamed himself.

I said, "OK. Maybe no one saw him leave. I suppose he stole someone's clothes."

Ballard shook his head. "That's another thing that scares me. No one lost their shirt. I can't believe that a patient could walk away and board a bus without someone noticing that he was wearing a hospital gown."

Parker asked, "I suppose he showed up in a bank to withdraw his life's savings?"

Harris didn't seem any happier than Ballard when he said, "No. He just dropped off the face of the earth. As far as we know, he left without pocket change. He never stepped into his own or anyone else's bank. That is what really scares me."

Parker said, "Why. He must have just robbed someone."

Harris said, "We can't know for sure. But I don't think so because what I really believe is . . . "

The scary thought just occurred to me, and I said dully, "He had help. Reynaldo."

Harris nodded and said, "At this point, the VA started looking for the both of them seriously – sending out Military Police."

I said, "You still weren't called in, right?"

Ballard just nodded.

Everyone was silent. Ballard pulled another manila folder from the briefcase. He tossed it on top of Hadley's. It read, "Staff Sgt. Connover." I opened the file. It showed the photo of an African American, probably in his 30's. He was on the verge of being heavy-set. It might have been muscle, though. Ballard went on relentlessly.

"Connover was in the motor pool of a unit in Iraq. He was walking along the perimeter fence of the base where he was posted when an IED exploded." Ballard hesitated and said, "I think I'll leave out the common threads of the story. You've heard them twice. But Connover's case is a little different yet.

"By this time, the staff at San Antonio were not going to be fooled a third time. They set a 24 hour watch on his room. There was also a guard stationed at the nurse's desk in the ward."

Ballard, slapped his knee, "Oh, yes, Connover studied metallurgy."

Minerva asked, "What about the librarian? Did Connover ask for the loan of her. . . what did you call it?"

I supplied, "A computer tablet."

Harris answered, "No, he didn't. He walked into the library, got a temporary library card and borrowed all two metallurgy texts that they had in the library and a graduate level physics text."

Parker asked, "Why didn't you prevent him from borrowing books? That's what I would have done."

Ballard said, "When Connover showed up, the DOD decided . . ."

Minerva asked, "The dod?"

He said, "Department of Defense. Anyway, they decided that they needed outside help. They did that while Connover was still on his way to San Antonio."

Harris said, "That's where I came in. The DOD got us to put the two of them on our most wanted list. We did some investigation at the VA, and while Connover was still there, we decided to call in the NSF."

Parker asked, "But they didn't get to your level right away did they, Mr. Ballard?"

Ballard shook his head. "No. I didn't get involved until Connover walked out of the facility. . ."

Parker interrupted, "Did he overpower the guards?"

Ballard shrugged, "No, he just walked out. Like the others."

I asked, "And still nothing on security cameras?"

Harris said, "We had added more security cameras – in the halls on his floor and especially the stairwells. We also added them at most of the exits. But no joy. He somehow didn't show up on any camera. The tech boys think that the extra cameras were so new that there were still bugs to get out of the system."

23

I wanted to know, "When was the last time that he was seen on a camera?"

Harris said, "He just thumbed his nose at us. He went down to the library to return his library card to the librarian and thanked her. He then walked back to the elevator bank, got on an elevator, arrived at his floor, got off and entered his room. That was the last that anyone saw him."

Ballard summed up. "We have no idea how he got out."

Parker said, "No idea how he got out?"

I asked, "So, when did you decided to come to us for help?"

"Everything that we talked about had barely happened when Minns showed up."

I asked, "Another veteran of Iraq."

Harris answered, "Yes. We got started investigating seriously. The first thing we did after reviewing," he pointed at the pile of files, "we decided to look for commonalities among the cases. We requested the pieces of shrapnel that had come out of the men. Unluckily, they were all discarded except the most recent."

I was getting anxious to find out what it showed, but Harris hesitated. "We took it to the FBI crime lab. The shrapnel was one of the strangest things that they'd ever come across."

Then he did something odd. Rather than pull a photo out of the file in front of us, he reached in his pocket and pulled out a small plastic bag. He opened the seal, reached in, pulled out a small piece of metal, and tossed it to me. I caught it but was not sure that I had until I squeezed it in my hand.

I said, "Well. . . " I held it up to my eyes. "It feels too . . . uh . . . light." I was comparing it mentally to the bullets for my Glock. The cartridges were about the same size and had a nice heft when you held them in your hand. This thing was practically as light as air.

"Right. Its density is about a tenth that of water."

I exclaimed, "How is that possible? Is it hollow?"

"Not exactly. We couldn't explain it. So we transferred it to Ballard's group at the NSF. Tell them what you found."

Ballard pulled out another file folder. It said, "Lt. Minns." I opened it and found a photo of an officer in Khaki. His eyes had been focused on the camera as though he could see the people who would later look at his photo. They weren't unfriendly, certainly not malevolent, but there seemed to be a mild strength in them that wouldn't be shaken by adversity.

Ballard was saying, "Another IED. Same base. When he arrived at San Antonio, he recovered the most quickly from his wounds. Harris set two dozen agents on guard continuously. They placed video cameras in his room and replaced the ones in the hall outside his room. You might as well look at his EEG although you're not going to see anything spectacular, I think."

I asked, "Do you have EEG's for all of them?"

"Sure. For the moment, this is as good as any of them to look at."

I flipped the photo and there they were. All four of them looked much the same, but the similarity hadn't robbed them of their exotic nature.

Ballard went on, "We examined the piece of shrapnel. Harris only gave you a hint of just how strange it is. It's by far the strongest metal sample we've ever tested. We cut off a small fragment to do a scan with an atomic force microscope. We couldn't dent it with a diamond saw. Eventually we used an industrial laser. We discovered that we could use a standard Electron Microscope to get a good look.

"I included one photo underneath the EEG." I flipped it, and what I saw didn't look strange. It was a regular pattern. Exactly what I'd expect from a crystal.

Ballard said, "Not very impressive, eh?"

I nodded, knowing that I was stepping into a logical trap. He said, "Well, look at the scale at the bottom of the photo." There was a short line with the label, "One micron."

I thought a minute. "But this structure is mostly empty space – lots of empty spaces."

Ballard nodded, "Right. That's why it's so light. Those empty spaces are large enough to contain very complex molecules."

I didn't know what he was driving at, but he seemed to think that was a sinister revelation. He was going on, "As soon as I saw that, I wanted to meet this Minns. I caught a plane for San Antonio immediately."

Minerva asked, "What was he like?"

Ballard leaned his head back so that it was almost staring directly at the ceiling. Then he returned his gaze to us. "Not at all what I'd expected."

□
□□

Ballard had been thinking about what the first thing he'd say to Minns throughout the flight to S.A. What do you say to someone who might be twice as smart as you – whatever that meant? How did you keep from revealing how frightened you were of him?

During the cab ride, he was still composing a first sentence to say to him. Seven seconds – the amount of time it takes most people to form a first impression. Of course, he would spend some time talking with Minns' doctors and nurses before seeing him. Maybe they'd give him an idea.

The doctors were unhelpful. They talked about his amazing recovery from a terrible head wound. They talked about his bizzare EEG. They talked about his amazing IQ. They were worthless.

The nurses were better. They all liked him. He was polite, unassuming, even funny at times. All of them seemed ready to go out on a date with him if he asked. They all said that he was easy to talk with and seemed genuinely interested in them.

Ballard was even more frightened of him than he had been after seeing the reports and the photo of the shrapnel section.

He finally decided that he'd just introduce himself and ask Minns the questions that he really wanted answered. Who knew—maybe he'd actually get a useful answer.

The second day after arriving he finally decided that he couldn't prepare himself better than he had already for the meeting. He practiced his first three questions in front of a mirror in a men's room on the first floor for the last time and went to find the elevator up to the ninth floor.

As he went, he tried to see how many of the guards that Harris had placed that he could spot. He was pretty sure about one person in the waiting room on 9 and he'd seen a couple of people in the Main Lobby that he suspected. There was an obvious guard immediately outside Minns' room. The guard glanced at his ID badge and nodded. He stepped back from the door and placed his hand casually on his sidearm.

The guard let Ballard open the door himself.

Inside the room was a standard bed with all the monitors that are standard in modern hospitals. There was a large window facing the parking lot. The standard stuffed chair was facing the window, and Ballard could see a newspaper extending slightly into his line of sight. The man in the chair said, "Ah." He rose, turned, and walked to Ballard extending a hand to shake.

As he did this, he said, "It's good to finally meet you Mister Ballard."

The surprise shown on Ballard's face. Minns immediately noticed and said, "Don't be surprised. Your reputation precedes you. The nurses are quite impressed by you. I think Beth wouldn't mind it if you asked her out for drinks after work." Minns' easy smile didn't waiver. They shook hands briefly, and Minns went on. "Would you like to sit? I can only offer my chair, but you're welcome to it. I can take the bed. I'm afraid they've removed all the rolling office chairs from the 9th floor."

Ballard was finding it both easier and harder than he'd expected. This Minns could easily monopolize the conversation if he let him, but his easy manner would make it less difficult to ask the hard questions coming up. He replied, "I'd prefer to stand. But please sit if you like."

Minns surprised him by accepting the invitation. He sat in the armchair, seemingly completely unconcerned with anything.

Ballard unconsciously leaned against the bed and took a deep breath. He knew that was bad body language, but he couldn't help it. He began, "Are you aware how lucky you are?"

Minns smiled that disarming smile, "You mean that I'm still alive?"

Ballard nodded, and Minns continued. "I've been told that a few times. I was unconscious during most of the worst of what happened to me, so I'm not particularly aware of my luck."

Then he said, "Or maybe you mean my sudden windfall of intelligence?"

Ballard said, "That too. Do you feel smarter?"

Minns shook his head almost regretfully, "No. I don't. Oh, I suppose I solve the crosswords quicker than I used to. But, I almost wish I did feel smarter. It's so disappointing to have a gift and not really sense it."

Ballard took the plunge into dangerous territory, "Are you aware that you're not the only person who's had the same kind of experiences?"

"Really? You mean, the wounds, the IQ change?"

Here was real danger. He didn't want to reveal anything – just learn the limits of Minns's knowledge. "Yes."

Minns's answer was as casual as any other. "No."

Ballard was afraid that Minns would ask how many, but he didn't. Ballard turned to his next question—another fraught with danger. He walked around the room trying to find something that could make the question seem less pointed. He noticed a book on the window sill. He glanced as casually as possible at the title, *Civilization and It's Discontents,* Sigmund Freud.

He asked, "Freud. Are you thinking of psychoanalysis? I hear that everyone should undergo it at some time in their lives."

Minns was as casual as ever. "Oh, just something I noticed in the hospital library and decided to glance at."

Ballard tried another dangerous question, "How do you occupy

27

your time during your recovery?"

Minns said, "Oh, I eat the excellent food, do a little reading, oggle the pretty nurses."

"Ever have any temptation to discharge yourself." He regretted the question as soon as it was asked. He didn't want to put the idea into Minns's mind. and he certainly didn't want to suggest that he was concerned about the possibility.

But Minns yawned and said, "Why in the world would I want to leave this paradise. I'm well fed, have plenty of reading material and, . . . uh . . . well, you know."

Ballard almost laughed aloud. Minns was perfect. He felt like Minns was playing with him. He was also sure that there was something going on inside Minns head besides a smart, very smart man. He decided to make one more try. He'd try leveling with Minns. "Well, you know, your predecessors walked away from this hospital. Do you have any idea why?"

Minns looked directly at Ballard and said, "No."

Ballard left Minns. He found himself having to fight the temptation to run to the elevators. He waited a seemingly interminable time for an elevator to arrive and rode down to the main floor. There he walked into the lobby and dialed Harris's number on his cell phone.

When Harris answered, Ballard skipped all formalities, "This is Ballard. Double the guards on Minns. Do it now." It was indicative of his seriousness that Harris didn't argue. He just said, "Right."

Parker asked, "What happened to Minns?"

Ballard sighed. "He walked out of the hospital—just like the rest."

I asked, "What about video? What happened?"

Ballard said, "No one saw him leave. His nurse that day swore that she couldn't believe that he'd just leave without telling her.

"We analyzed the recordings from all the video cameras in the hospital. God, I wish I could show you the video we put together."

Minerva cleared her throat, but I spoke first. "Actually, you can." I added hastily, "Not here but we have a building separated from the Castle where there isn't any magic, and electronics work pretty well."

Harris exclaimed, "This is a castle!"

Minerva shrugged and said, "Yes, what were you expecting?"

He just shook his head.

I stood and said, "Come on, let's go see if the BG is at home?"

Harris started to ask something and just closed his mouth again. We left my office and walked down the main hall, past the Great Hall. I was happy we weren't going through there. Explaining the transparent ceiling would just slow us down. We went out the main entrance, and I led them off toward the Shrieking Shak.

It was a long walk, but no one complained. We arrived. Ballard was somewhat put off by the rough exterior. "Are you sure we're at the right place," he asked.

I opened the access door for the digital lock and entered my code. The door unlocked, and I led the party in. They were much happier at the interior than the exterior. It was paneled in Mahogany, and the floors were hard wood. We went up a floor to the main Control Room. It had once had half a dozen people watching the monitors, but now it just had one occupant, the Boy Genius.

He turned and asked who our guests were.

I introduced Harris and Ballard. I decided that he would pick up the gist of what was going on quickly enough if we just proceeded on our business. He just asked what he could do for us.

Ballard accepted my simple introduction of the B.G. without comment.

I asked the B.G., "Would you just provide some juice for this gentleman's laptop and watch some video with us?"

He smiled his wicked "finally some real business" smile and said, "Oh, let's project it up on the big screen." It wasn't a question, just an announcement of what he was going to do.

Ballard opened the laptop, pushed the power button and was pleased to see the monitor light up. He quickly had opened the Quicktime app, and after the B.G. hooked him up to the projector, we saw the video that he'd promised.

It started with a view of Minns's room. Minns glanced toward the camera,and the view went black. Ballard provided running commentary. "There's no more video from the room. We don't know how he disabled it."

Next, we saw Minns walking down the 9th floor hall. Somehow, all the guards and nurses and doctors seemed to find something very interesting to look at as Minns approached them.

There was even video in the elevator. Harris said, "We tracked down all the people in the elevator. Nobody noticed anyone in the elevator that matches Minns's photo."

On the main floor, Minns walked toward the back of the hospital. The cameras followed him back to a door. He took it, tried to turn the handle, which didn't budge. He then manipulated the handle in a way that I couldn't make out. The door opened, and he entered. The view remained unchanged.

Harris gave color commentary. "We didn't have a camera in this property room. Minns' uniform and a few personal belongings were stored there. There was a man on duty at this time. We interviewed him. He claimed that no one had entered the room or taken Minns's things.

"We've not edited this video out because we want to show you how fast this operation was."

A few seconds later, the door opened again and Minns walked out, now wearing a khaki uniform. He was one of a number dressed that way. He continued down the hall, arriving at a loading dock. He actually looked at a manifest from one of the trucks in the loading dock, and then walked up to the cab, and apparently said something to the driver.

Harris went on, "The driver actually remembers Minns slightly. But he didn't remember what Minns said to him. The cameras at the back of the building don't have complete coverage, but it doesn't matter because—as you'll see—he eappears in a camera covering the parking lot."

You could clearly see him walk out an open gate from the parking lot. He crossed the street and within a couple of minutes, a city bus drove up, and he apparently got on it.

"And that is the last that we've seen of Lieutenant Minns."

Minerva asked, "And none of your men reported anything out of the ordinary?"

Harris answered, "Nope."

Parker asked, "What did he study besides Freud?"

Ballard seemed bored as he reported, "Oh he studied experimental psychology and finance."

The B.G. asked, "I suppose that he cleared out his accounts and hasn't used any credit or debit cards or cell phones."

Harris glumly reported, "No to clearing out his accounts. We have no idea where any of the four are or how they're supporting themselves."

The B.G. whistled, "There are four of them?"

Ballard said, "Depressing isn't it?"

The B.G. replied, "Depressing? It's as scary as hell."

Ballard commented, "Well there you have it. Most of the rest of the story is Harris'."

Harris nodded and said, "I approached some contacts that I have in the NSA."

Minerva harrumphed, "What is it with you people and acronyms. I suppose NSA stands for Network of Stupid Assholes."

Harris' lips compressed into a thin line, "That's easy for you to say. I'd like to see you do better against these . . . these . . . people." Apparently he couldn't come up with a better word.

He went on, "They listened and told me that there was someone who had been very helpful in defeating one of the greatest threats that our nation has faced.

"I asked what that threat was. All they would say is that the name was Tom Riddle. I've never heard of him. My contacts absolutely refused to say anything else.

"Of course, they did give me your name, Wendt, and said that I could contact you through Colonel Parker. I contacted him. He referred me to the Home Office. They gave me an introduction to Parker and here we are.

"You are the best bet that we've come up with. Do you have ideas?"

The B.G. said, "Wait. Before we brainstorm, I need to get the rest of the facts."

I insisted that I summarize in order to test how well I'd absorbed everything that we'd heard and seen. I probably cut the presentation time by a third. The B.G. sat and just nodded his head through it all. He didn't stop me once for a question. I had begun to wonder if we were boring him.

When I stopped for breath trying to think whether I had forgotten anything, the B.G. stopped nodding and spoke. "Do you have the electron microscope image here?"

I shuffled through the papers that had come out of Ballard's briefcase and found the photo. "Here it is."

The B.G. studied it for a minute or two, holding it close to his eyes a couple of times.

"How old is the fragment of shrapnel?"

Ballard looked to Harris who stared back. Ballard asked, "What do you mean, 'How old'? I suppose that it was made in some little local refinery recently."

The B.G. laughed. "That was not made locally. I want to know how old it is."

Ballard scratched his head that was beginning to bald. I thought that I could see why. "But how can we figure that out? It's made of iron and lead, not some radioactive material that decays."

He nodded, "Lead. Good. You can date that by looking at the ratio of isotopes. Your technical people surely realize that."

Ballard's face colored a bit. "I didn't think of it."

"Well, get on the phone to them and find out."

Harris objected, "The phones don't work here."

The B.G. rolled his eyes. "Does the laptop work?"

Harris blushed this time. "Right."

Ballard got on his cell phone and spoke briefly. "I know it's the middle of the weekend. When you go into work tomorrow get an age on the shrapnel shaving you've got. . . Yes, yes. Isotope ratios. Read up on it. As soon as you know, give me a call. Leave a message if I'm out of range of cell towers. Yeah. Good night to you, too." The last sentence sounded sarcastic.

The B.G. had been rummaging around in the papers while Ballard was on the phone. Harris looked nervous, but he was in our house, and here we call the shots.

The B.G. muttered something to himself and then asked, "Do you have digitized data of these EEG's? "

Ballard thought a minute and said, "Yeh. Let me do a little rummaging in the laptop." He worked the keyboard and mouse.

Meanwhile, Minerva said, "It's dinnertime at Hogwarts. I'm going to eat. Anyone else who wants to eat, come now."

We all discovered that we had gone through most of the day without a meal and dinner would be welcome – especially those of us who knew Hogwarts cuisine. Minerva opened the door and exited followed by most of us. I noticed that Ballard and the B.G. were still bent over his laptop.

I asked them, "Well. Have you decided to fast today?"

Ballard said, "I'm on my way in a second."

The B.G. mumbled, "Don't wait. I've got an idea that I want to run down."

I shrugged and waited for Ballard to finish transferring some files to a flash drive that the B.G. had provided. We walked out, and I commented, "You are in for a real treat."

"I'm hungry enough to eat possum. Anything would seem like a treat to me."

When we arrived at the Great Hall, Minerva was already at the head table and had apparently said her graceful word for the evening. The tables were already heavy-laden with the delicacies with which I have never become jaded.

There were a couple of empty seats at the end of the head table— apparently saved for Ballard and me. I led him there. We were about to dig in with gusto when a raven-haired beauty approached the table.

She walked around to the other side of the table and knelt down so that she would be at eye level with Ballard and me. Her face was squeezed tight with fury. I tried to temporize, "Professor Brahms, allow me to introduce you to Adam Ballard. He's a guest and . . ."

She was furious. "Don't YOU introduce me. What have you done with Nick?" She paused for breath and said, "I know. You've given Nick a new toy, haven't you? You gave him some puzzle that is more important to him than eating or . . . or . . . well, what is it?"

She then turned her attention to Ballard, "It's you, isn't it. You brought this puzzle for him to waste time with and get into trouble over. Didn't you?"

His jaw had dropped, and he was trying to come up with something to say. She just stood up disgustedly. "Well, as soon as dinner is over, I'm going back with you. I'm bringing poor Nicky a plate of cold, plain food. AND I'm going to find out why you're wasting his time."

Ballard asked, "Is she always that . . . uh . . . irritable?"

"She's become more possessive than when she was dating me."

Ballard puzzled over that for a moment and then said, "Don't you mean when you were dating her?"

"Oh, believe me, I was not dating her, but she most certainly was trying to and occasionally succeeding at dating me."

Ballard shook his head and after a few moments of pure culinary pleasure commented, "I see what you mean about the food here. It's great."

I grumbled, "Yeah, if you survive to enjoy it."

⊞

After dinner, I said, "I guess we don't have any choice. We've got to go back to see what the B.G. is up to and take Aurora with us."

I rounded up our happy troop, and Ballard asked me, "Aurora is Professor Brahms' first name?"

"Yup."

"She's Nick's wife?"

I supplied, "Yup."

"Yeh. I see."

We trooped off to the Shrieking shack. On the way, Harris asked, "What does this Boy Genius or Nicholas or whatever his name is do?" The emphasis was definitely on the "do."

"Well, right now, he's doing computer security consulting. He's got a couple of banks and several government departments as clients. They seem to be very happy with what he's done for them. None have been broken into – as far as we or they know."

Harris nodded and asked, "What's his company?"

I shrugged, "The name's something like Corinthians Associates."

Harris became excited, "You mean 'Corithian Associates'?"

"Yes, I guess."

He said, "Of course, I know them. He's it?"

"Oh, he has a couple of associates from the bad old days when Tom Riddle was around."

Ballard stared at us, "Tom Riddle? Who the hell is that?"

I sighed. "Well, it's a long, long story and I really don't want to go into it now. Let's just leave it that he's the magical version of Hitler."

By this time, we'd reached the shack. Aurora, who was clearly in a hurry, ran up to the door, popped the keypad cover, and keyed in the code faster than eye could follow. The door clicked unlocked, and she flung the door open, ascending the stairs three at a time.

I said, "There's no real hurry to get up to Nick's office. I'm sure Aurora would like a little 'face time' with him." No one objected so we took our time strolling up the stairs."

We arrived and miraculously found that Aurora had her arms around Nick's neck and was administering a pleasant kiss. She reluctantly released him and said, "Don't keep me waiting for dinner again."

She looked around at us and said, "Well, haven't you ever seen a woman kiss her husband before."

No one commented, but Nick smiled broadly and said in a little sing-song voice, "I've got a surprise for you." He then turned on the projector and went to his laptop. Of course, I wasn't surprised that he had a surprise for us. From the first that I knew him, he had surprises for Minerva and me.

He began explaining his surprise. He is probably the only person that I know who has to explain his surprises. I even recall Parker commenting once that somehow a surprise that has to be explained isn't maybe really a surprise.

In any case, he began as the projector warmed up. "I thought I noticed a peculiarity in the EEG data that Ballard provided, so I imported it into a simple database and did some data analysis on it. I've extracted the results of that analysis and loaded it into a spreadsheet so that it can be visualized in graphics.

"First, let's look at the EEG's—both before and after the strange change that came over these four men." The projector had warmed up, and the wall was lit by four graphs. Each pair had its graphs in different colors. Reynaldo was red, Hadley was green, Connover was blue, and Minns was black.

"Notice how chaotic the 'after' EEG looks. I decided to do a Fourier analysis of all of them."

Minerva asked, "What's a Fourier analysis?"

Nick sort of stared into the sky and finally said, "I don't know how to explain it. Anyone want to make a stab?"

Ballard cracked a smile and said, "Let me try.

"Minerva, you know how when you listen to someone's voice, say while they're singing, you can tell if it's high pitched or low. You can maybe even hear individual notes?"

She nodded but seemed suspicious, "I guess so. Sure."

"Well, that's your brain doing a Fourier analysis of the sound that your ear hears. It's just that this isn't sound; it's electric waves."

She rolled her eyes and said, "Somehow, I knew this was going to get back to ekeltricity sometime."

Ballard squinted at her, "Did you say, 'ekeltricity'?"

She just replied by saying, "Never mind. I understand."

I wasn't so sure, but I was not going to express my doubt of her understanding. I'd been there before, and it wasn't fun.

Nick took that as settled and continued, "Here's the result. You'll see that each of the 8 EEG's now has a simple list of Fourier component strengths. It's hard to see as lists of numbers, but if we graph them. . ." The screen changed, and then there were a set of bar charts. "It's easy to see that all of the before EEG's have only a few large Fourier components and they're at low frequencies. The 'afters' all have large components at high frequencies."

Then he went on to another single graph. "This is putting all the four graphs of 'afters' together on one chart. Does anyone notice anything strange about this?"

Minerva raised her hand, "All the low frequency bars are different, but the high frequency bars are all pretty much the same for all four men."

Nick beamed and said, "Light bulb!"

He went on, "Now, let's just remove the low frequency jumble." The next graph just showed the high frequency bars. They were all almost identical heights.

"Now, let's do the inverse Fourier transform on these four bar charts."

Minerva kicked my shin and whispered to me, "What does that mean?"

I whispered back, "He's going to let you see the way the waves would 'sound' without the low frequency jumble. It's like taking the singers in a choir who can't sing very well out of the choir."

The screen now showed something that kind of looked like a simple wave pattern but it seemed to have gaps. I asked, "What are the gaps?'

Nick beamed again. "The problem is that we're seeing the graph on a white background. Where all the points for the 4 men fall on the same point, they combine to white. They disappear against the white background. Now let me show you that on a black background."

When he showed that latest chart, I heard somebody whistle. I might have done myself. The wave form showed clear and simple. It was clearly high frequency and regular. Most of it was white, although there were some sections that seemed to be colored. Nick was explaining, "If we had perfect data, I think the entire waveform would be white, but the imperfect data resulted in some spots where the 4 waves don't line up perfectly."

Harris asked, "Just what are we looking at?"

Nick laughed. "That's my question. What are we looking at? I think that the low frequency components that we removed were the brain waves due to the individual men's normal brain activity. But the high frequency part of each man's brain activity is not really his. It's identical across all four men. I think it represents one mind. Now, my question is 'Just where did that one mind come from?'"

That statement silenced everyone. Ballard asked, "Where do you think it came from." Before Nick could answer, Ballard provided his own answer.

"The only thing that the four of them had in common was the strange shrapnel that each carried in his brain for a while." He hesitated and quickly said, "That metal had great cavities in it that could contain. . . must have contained . . ."

Nick nodded encouragingly, "What?"

"Some sort of RNA or DNA."

Nick wasn't smiling any more. He spoke softly but in the silence that ruled the room, there was no problem hearing him. "I think it would be a good idea to find out where that shrapnel came from and what's in it."

Now, the silence thundered for a moment. Then several conversations began at once. I couldn't make out any except the one that I was having with Ballard. I asked him, "Have you tried to find the source of that metal?"

He answered over the din, "Not really."

Minerva has many talents, but one that really shines out is her ability to gain control of a room of unruly, immature youths. She showed that. It didn't take her long to quiet the room. Her Scottish brogue was coming out. I recognized that as a danger sign and immediately silenced Ballard and me. The rest followed suit quickly.

She spoke in her best school-marmly tones. "Gentlemen, Mr. Ballard and Mr. Harris, you came here for a reason besides amazing us with your inability to understand the gravity of the situation. What is it that you want us to do?"

Ballard stood and said, "Well, our original idea was to ask for help in finding the four AWOL's. But these developments require more than that, I think."

No one else noticed, but I saw Nick rifling through the photos out of Ballard's files. I saw him eye the scanner in the corner lovingly. He immediately snapped to when the question of finding people was raised. He looked like a school boy who's got the answers and is anxious to demonstrate. He could hold back his excitement no longer. He actually raised a hand and said, "Mr. Ballard.

"I can help with that. I've got this nifty pattern recognition system. I've used it to find all sorts of people in video from security cameras and the like." His enthusiasm was hard to resist.

Ballard did, "That sounds helpful. We should talk later about that and we'll see where you need to start looking. But it's a big world and these people could be anywhere."

He turned to the rest of the group and said, "I think now that it's more important to find the source of this strange metal and learn who manufactured it and how. How can you help us with that?"

Harris nodded and said, "I can get the boys – and girls." He added that quickly after noticing the expression on Aurora's face, "in the FBI lab to research the manufacturers of exotic alloys. Somebody's got to be advertising this amazing stuff."

Ballard said, "I can get our scientists searching the literature. Whoever made this must have published somewhere."

Nick asked, "What are you going to do when those don't turn up anything?"

Ballard asked, "Do you have an idea?"

"Why not ask the people who made the IED's?"

Harris seemed to be starting a snappy comeback when Ballard silenced him with a look. He said, "That's not impossible. We'll get hold of the NSA and see if they can give us some leads."

Harris finally had his say, "I wish you luck interrogating the people you find."

37

I glanced at Minerva, and she nodded back. Then I said, "I think that we might be able to help with interrogation, don't you think so, Minerva?"

She nodded. "Yes, we'll have to make some preparations but if we have some latitude in what we're allowed to do. . . "

Harris's lips curled a little, "I don't think that we can allow anything cruel or unusual."

Minerva said, "I promise that we'll not harm anyone physically or put them through any pain."

Harris's lips uncurled and he said, "Good luck." I think it was a genuine wish.

Ballard agreed and finished the night for us. "Look, I'm absolutely beat, and I would be even if I hadn't flown for ten hours getting here this morning. Let's call it a night and talk over breakfast."

No one objected. We all walked back to the castle. I offered my office to Ballard and Harris. It had an attached bedroom and the sofa in the office itself was pretty comfortable. One of the staff had slept there for weeks on end and declared it was as comfortable as his normal bed.

Harris asked where I would sleep. I replied, "Oh, where I always do. The Head and I are married, and I always spend the evening in bed with . . ."

She interrupted and said that they had as many details as they needed or deserved. Everyone else slept in their own beds.

Sunday morning came earlier than I liked. I refused to get up in time for breakfast. As it turned out, I wasn't the only one. Harris and Ballard had slept in until almost 10 AM.

I went up to see how they were doing. They'd barely gotten out of bed when I arrived. Ballard asked if they'd missed breakfast. Of course they had, but I had good news for them.

"If you're hungry, we can go down to the kitchen. The staff is always happy to provide a snack on special occasions."

They agreed, and I led them down to the dungeon levels. I had been giving them a heads-up on what to expect in the kitchen. "The staff is sort of unusual. As a matter of fact, you've probably never seen anyone of their species before."

Ballard shook his head as if shaking a pesky mosquito away, "I could have sworn you said 'someone of their species.'"

"I did. They're elves."

Ballard sighed. "I suppose I should just let things unfold and see what happens. But I have to ask. Do they speak English?"

I shrugged. "It's definitely a second language for them but you won't have any trouble understanding them or they you."

"OK. Open the door. How bad can it be?"

We went in. The kitchen, of course, was like you'd find in any large restaurant. We had only taken a few steps in when the chef approached us. He asked, "Professor Wendt, were you missing breakfast again?"

I shrugged. He said, "You are missing a wonderful quiche."

I nodded and asked, "Could you do an omelet?"

"Of course. For you and friends?"

I nodded again. Meanwhile Ballard and Harris's were staring openly.

"Please be sitting at the table." Kretur indicated a small round table in a corner. As he spoke, chairs flew through the air to the table. "We'll have the omelets up in a minute."

Harris looked around the kitchen at the buzz of activity preparing for lunch. "Why aren't most of those, those . . . " He searched for a word and failed. He just said, "wearing anything like real clothes?"

I too struggled for words and finally settled for, "It's a status thing." I didn't elaborate that the ones without real clothes were technically slaves.

Harris shrugged as though it was just what he expected. Before our omelets arrived, there was another arrival. Two old friends approached our table.

"You've been sleeping in." The speaker shook his forefinger at us, 'Too much of the hair of the dog?"

We all stood, and I did introductions. "Mr. Ballard and Harris, this is our Head Janitor."

Mr. Filch interrupted, "Now, now. Facility Engineer. This is my apprentice, Mr. Dursley."

All I could do was to invite them to join us. A house elf ran up with a couple of extra chairs. He asked, "Are you wishing omelets too?"

Filch said, "Yeh, yeh."

Filch sat and said, "Of course, Mr. Dursley is The Mr. Dursley, renownified author."

Ballard opened his mouth – I suppose to object that he'd never heard of him – but held his piece.

Filch was going on, "You probably just don't recognize him because of the bad photo on the back cover of his book."

39

Harris gulped and said it. "What book is that?"

Filch stared at them as though they were Martians just landed on the White House lawn. "You've never heard of the memorial edition of *Advanced Potionmaking*?"

Harris only said, "Oh." He wisely decided to let that dog lie undisturbed.

Fortunately, our omelets arrived, and we were occupied with more pressing issues.

After the edge was off our hunger, and we were no longer leaning into our meals, Ballard followed up on the book, 'Who does the book memorialize?"

Filch appeared to be preparing a new blast, but Dursley got in first. "Why, it was the best potion-maker that Hogwarts has ever had as a Headmaster, Severus Snape. He was in a way my mentor even though I never met him in my life."

Ballard probably would have pursued further, but I decided to deflect the conversation onto safer ground. "Mr. Dursley, have you and Stephanie set a date?"

"OH, no. Her parents insist that we wait for her 23rd birthday. It seems too far off to set a date. But, Stifie would have loved to have been in your wedding."

I said, "I'm sorry. I wasn't going to invite every Hogwarts graduate to be at my wedding."

"You didn't listen. She wanted to be part of the wedding. She wishes that we could have gotten married along with you, the other Professor Wendt and Nick and Professor Aurora."

I couldn't help laughing. "Well, I wasn't going to invite every pair of lovers in Hogwarts to get married with us either."

"It's OK with me. I need the time to get used to the idea that Stiffee really wants to marry me."

Ballard seemed bemused by this conversation with people he'd only just met about people he'd never heard of before. I was trying to think of another way to turn the talk when Minerva appeared at the door. Filch must have noticed my preoccupation with something behind him. He turned and noticed Minerva when she was half-way to us. He cackled, "Ah, Headmistress, did you sleep in too?" Even from behind his turned back, I could tell that he was trying to execute an exaggerated wink.

Minerva pretended not to hear his comment. She addressed me, "I should have known you'd be down here with your drinking buddies. If you'd been at breakfast, I could have told you that I'd arranged for lunch to be served to us in the Teacher's Lounge. That will allow us to talk without fear of being overheard."

She turned to go and then spun around back. "Oh, just one more thing. We're eating at 1PM sharp. Don't be late." That command was obviously delivered to everyone at the table.

Ballard nodded slowly. "She is direct when she wants to be."

"Yeh. If you'd like to take a walk around the grounds, feel free to. Just stay out of the forest." I thought a second. "And stay out of the dungeon." After another moment, "You could go to the library, but don't talk above a whisper."

Harris nodded. "I would like to walk the grounds. Are you busy?"

"Oh, I've got to shower, shave and think. Not necessarily in that order.

Ballard and Harris managed to find the Teacher's Lounge on their own. The rest of us were there well before 1PM.

Besides the people I expected, Sally showed up. That didn't surprise me. She was Minerva's executive assistant after all. But what did surprise me was the appearance of Filch and Dursley just after Minerva arrived at spot on one PM.

We'd all stood for Minerva, but Filch took it as due to his appearance. "Don't stand for me. I'm hungry as a horse. Let's dig in."

Minerva observed, "I'm afraid you weren't invited, Mr. Filch."

His response was pure Filch, "Oh, that's all right. Mistakes will happen." He then took a seat at the table that had been set for us. Dursley took Filch's arm and tried to suggest that they'd do better closer to the food in the kitchen.

Minerva, just shook her head at Dursley and said, "That's alright Dudley. It might even be a blessing to have a down-to-earth viewpoint at the table."

Harris just shook his head and said, "This is not a secure meeting."

I replied, "Really, it could not be more secure. It's here in Hogwarts with some of the most talented witches and wizards present." Filch's face perked up at that.

Harris gave up, and Minerva called the lunch meeting to order. The food appeared magically on the table. There was a selection of fresh fruits, vegetables and several types of sandwiches – Corned Beef on Rye, Reuben, Chicken Mayonnaise, etc.

As we ate, she laid out the situation as she saw it. "We have several abilities that you need to help you solve your problem." Ballard

41

appeared ready to speak, but she cut him off. "As I see it your problem is that you're afraid that these people are about to do something nefarious or even fatal. You want to find the,m and you want even more to find out who or what is motivating them.

"We have talented people who can do those things. If any of them walk in front of a video camera that's connected to the Thing of Internets, the B.G. will find them. I can interrogate people and squeeze the truth out of stone. When I'm finished, you'll have the truth, the whole truth and nothing but the truth. Wendt can . . . well . . . I don't know for sure what it is that he can do, but somehow things always seem to come out right when he's working a problem. Aurora knows science backwards and forwards." That, of course, was an exaggeration, but when Minerva gets wound up, things sometimes get stretched a little.

Ballard shrugged, "I guess you've got all the bases covered. How do you want to be included in the team we've put together?"

Minerva had thought it out already and she said, "Easy. Nicholas stays here with his computers and looks for people on the sly – as always. Aurora stays as his consultant.

"James and I stay ready to go to wherever you want us to interrogate someone."

Harris said, "Very neat. No one moves, and you can all do your more or less normal jobs?"

Ballard nodded, "We need you to be available on a moment's notice. You and Wendt need to be at our headquarters so we can all move at once."

Minerva seemed unmoved but I knew that she was considering. "All right. But this can't go on forever."

Ballard just shook his head.

Just then Sally Harker, Minerva's executive assistant stood up and delivered an ultimatum, "You can not leave me behind. You've tried that before, and it just doesn't work. Either I come along or this school turns into more of a chaotic mess than you've ever seen."

Minerva looked murder at her, but I know what Minerva looks like when she means murder, and this wasn't it. She gave in.

Ballard objected, "Wait a minute, I've got a say in this."

I shook my head vigorously, "No, you don't. We put together the team, and if you don't like it, you don't have it."

Sally whooped and said, "You tell him boss."

That caused Minerva's murderous gaze to turn to me. I hastily corrected, "I'm not your boss."

Sally just said under her breath, "In a pig's eye."

That seemed to settle things. Of course, we worked out details like when we would arrive in Washington, with whom we'd be contracting, where our office would be. The answers were Wednesday next, the NSF, but our offices would be in the J Edgar Hoover building – somewhere in the basement.

⌗⌗ ⌗⌗
⌗⌗ ⌗⌗

There was one more detail to work out. That evening, Minerva invited Professor Slughorn to her office for drinks after dinner. I was there, of course, but so were Sally and Ballard.

Slughorn walked into the office and nodded politely at Sally and me. Then he noticed Ballard. He looked back and forth from Minerva to me to Sally to Ballard and started backing out the door. Minerva didn't miss that for a second. "You come right in, Professor."

Slughorn cursed under his breath and then said, "You are not dumping this god-awful job on me again." He looked around at the company again and said, "You're taking Sally with you, aren't you?"

He looked at her and said, "Coward. You're the only person who keeps this ship afloat and you're leaving!"

She smiled and said, "Afraid so, guv."

He accepted the drink that Minerva had been holding out for him the whole time and sunk into an armchair. The only thing he asked was, "How long?"

Ballard answered, "We don't know." At that Slughorn moaned. "But we want it to be quick every bit as much as you do."

Slughorn stared into his drink and said dispiritedly, "Easy for you to say. You don't have to try to keep order in this insane asylum. Every underage wizard trying his hand at transfiguration and disapparation and curses and who knows what all – it's a wonder that I survived the last time."

Ballard asked, "There was a last time?"

Slughorn answered, "Oh, yes. Something that was all hush-hush, and nobody could know where they went, what they were doing, or how to get hold of them.

"When does the sentence begin?"

I answered, "We fly out on Wednesday morning. But I think we'll go to the Leaky Cauldron the night before."

"Oh sure, I'd get out as soon as possible too."

The conversation sputtered to an end. Slughorn finished his drink and said goodnight.

Washington

We had argued about how to get to Heathrow from the Cauldron. She won that one. I had to accept disapparation to a loo in Heathrow. At least it was the Men's loo.

We hadn't flown in several years. Minerva's patience was tried to the breaking point – almost. Having to take off her shoes was the next to last straw. Fortunately, we didn't reach the last straw.

She remonstrated with the security person, "But do you see those tiny flats. There can't be anything dangerous in them."

After the first couple of rounds, they summoned a security woman who commiserated with her, "I know ma'am. I have the same problem when I fly. There just isn't any reason to it." That mollified Minerva enough to let us finally get past the scanners and on to our gate. The flight was full. We were in coach, but Ballard had at least seen to it that we had one window seat.

After we were finally in the air, Minerva was quite contented. She reminisced about our various air travels of the past. "Do you remember when we went to Washington? That trip was so romantic."

I scratched my head and said, "I think we didn't fly that trip. Wasn't it by port key into Arlington Cemetery?"

"Yes, it was so romantic."

I agreed that the bed and breakfast that we stayed in was romantic. She had her arm looped through mine and had intertwined our fingers. She was really in a sentimental mood.

Then I remembered about that trip. "Yes, Washington was very romantic and fun. But it seems to me that after Washington, I was attacked on the train to New York. And I was in the hands of sadists masquerading as doctors." Then the real indignity of that trip occurred to me. "And you spent lots of time with that Archie . . . Archie . . .

what was his name? Oh, yes. Griffin. Archie Griffin."

Her eyes dropped, and I knew that I'd hit home. Finally she said, oh so softly, "Yes, he was very very charming." But I couldn't bring myself to press my advantage. We just left it at that and enjoyed most of the rest of the flight, her arm holding my hand softly.

Our landing evoked her usual complaints about the dangers of flying compared to—oh say—slydiving.

When we had retrieved our luggage from the carousel, we were the ones greeted by a chauffeur with a placard reading, "Wendts." Minerva smiled and said, "I never tire of seeing that word – Wendt WITH the 'S'."

□

The ride to our hotel at the Watergate complex was uneventful. Minerva complemented Ballard for picking a good hotel. Privately, I thought it was much more likely his secretary.

The next morning, there was supposed to be a chauffeur waiting for us, but Minerva wanted to disapparate to the FBI building. I decided I needed to humor her as much as possible so I didn't complain – much.

We arrived in the service drive for the building and walked around to the front. We entered and found that we had to go through a metal detector before we could reach the information desk. I shrugged and walked through after emptying my pockets.

That was perhaps my first mistake. One of the guards asked me to open the purse. He was dead serious and no jokes about the "cute" purse.

I froze for a moment and could only think of what would happen if I opened the purse and they found my loaded Glock. The purse was an old gift from Professor Dumbledore. Its interior is very large while the exterior was much like any coin purse. It can only be opened by its owner. From the outside it always appears to be empty regardless how much is inside. When I'm traveling, inside it I normally keep money (both wizard and Muggle), my Glock, ammunition for it, and anything else of value that I want to keep safe. Then I regained my composure and tried to nonchalant it. I said, "Really?"

The guard just nodded and let one hand rest on his service pistol.

I tried to decide whether I should look back to Minerva and appeal to her.

Then a familiar voice said, "Wendt, why didn't you wait for the limo? You're late. Don't waste our time." It was Harris. He pulled out his ID and flashed it at the guard.

"Special agent Harris. What's the problem here? They're already late for a meeting."

The guard didn't look away from me, and I swear that he grasped the handle of his pistol. "Mr. Harris, this gentleman won't open his purse for me."

My eyes turned to Harris and I tried to put as much appeal in them as I could muster. He didn't seem to react, but he glanced at the purse and said, "That thing's as flat as a fritter. There isn't anything in it." He then turned to me and said, "Come on."

The guard was still not satisfied, but he released his grasp on his pistol and took a step back. I walked toward Harris who held out a hand and shook it.

Minerva and Sally went through uneventfully. They x-rayed their purses and nothing suspicious showed up. I don't know what they made of the wand but they seemed to not pay any attention to it.

The four of us walked down the hall past the information desk and around a corner. Then Harris, without looking at either of us, asked in a casual voice, "What was in the purse?"

I answered, "Well, sir. I think it would just be better for everyone if I didn't tell you."

He nodded and said, "That bad, eh?"

I didn't say anything.

Harris took us to a guard station where we were photographed and issued ID's. Minerva used the lanyard that they offered and hung her ID around her neck.

I commented more than half seriously, "Quite becoming with your grey suit. I don't remember your having a grey suit."

She smiled, "There are still things you don't know about me."

I'd have made a snappy remark if Harris weren't still with us. He took us to the basement and opened a door to a dingy little room. It had two computers. He pulled an envelope out of an inside pocket and handed it to me. "This contains your signon credentials. Memorize and burn."

Minerva asked, "Don't you mean, eat?"

Harris just went on unperturbed, "I imagine one of you knows how to use a computer."

I raised my hand and said, "Yo."

"Good, teach your partners. Check your email regularly. There's an internal phone directory in one of the desk drawers, but if we need you for an interrogation, I'll probably call or find you. Otherwise, it will probably be boring for a while.

"Your badges will let you in where you're allowed to go – which isn't many places.

"We have a short standup status meeting in my office every morning at 9. Please come. You may not have much to report, but you should keep up with what's going on in the team.

"Questions?"

Sally asked, "Where's the caf?"

Harris was puzzled a second. "Oh, you mean the cafeteria?"

I nodded.

He answered by turning and saying, "Come on, I'd like a cup of coffee anyway. I'll show you."

That was the last significant event that day for us since the status meeting had already happened.

□□

The next day, Friday, was almost as exciting as this one. The status report was brief. It consisted of everyone;s admitting that there were no new leads and, really, no old leads to follow up on.

Ballard showed up that day for the status meeting. It turned out that he usually called in and listened in, but this time he actually put in an appearance.

After the standup, Ballard suggested that we go to the caf for coffee. This was the REAL status meeting. He asked us if we hadn't had anything from Nick.

I answered, "No. You've got the wrong idea about him. When we were looking for Riddle it took weeks to find him, and we only had England to search."

Ballard frowned, "You mean it might take months?"

I could only shrug.

Harris asked, "Who was Riddle?"

Minerva started to say something, but I interrupted and said, "Sorry, Minerva. That's too long a story and not really relevant, I think. Let's just say that he was a terrorist who was so underground that most of the British government didn't even realize that he existed."

Harris snorted, "Well, I sure didn't."

"Great." Ballard turned to Harris. "Any advance on finding the bomb-maker?"

Harris had to disappoint Ballard too. Meanwhile, there was some sort of disturbance at another table where a couple of people were

47

reading a paper, and several others were looking over their shoulders. They seemed to be laughing.

Minerva asked, "I wonder what the joke is?"

Sally got up and walked over and looked over a shoulder looking over a shoulder. What she saw was a page 3 story. A glance didn't make her laugh. She looked around and found that there was a small stack of papers by the checkout. She went over and bought a Washington Post.

When she got back to the table, she opened the paper to page three and folded it over so that almost the only thing showing was one article. The headline was *ISIS loses half a Billion*. There was a subtitle, something like, Robbers Are Robbed.

We all scanned the article silently. Then Harris broke out into a laugh himself, "Well that's poetic justice for you."

But neither Ballard nor I was laughing. He said, "You don't suppose . . ."

I nodded. "I think that we may just have found one of the genii."

Minerva nodded too. Harris gave us a crooked look. "You don't mean to say that you think one of our boys had anything to do with this heist?"

Sally smiled, "I think that we just got our first good lead."

Harris said, "I'll get hold of the NSA people and see what they know about this."

□
□□

We were riding across the river to Langley with Harris and Ballard. Sally asked, "I suppose we can't take any souvenirs back with us from the CIA?"

Ballard just rolled his eyes, and Harris didn't react at all. We were passed in. Our FBI contractor badges didn't have much influence, but I was careful nowadays to carry my purse in my briefcase. When security people x-rayed the briefcase the purse didn't show up at all.

I suppose that Harris would have shot me himself had he known that I carried a loaded Glock into the CIA headquarters. However, no one was the wiser.

We were conducted to a Conference Room that they called the War Room. There were lots of flat screens and projectors. The CIA analyst who ran the presentation for the Deputy Assistant Director for ISIS was the one who did most of the talking.

"OK. What you're about to see officially we don't know anything about. As soon as the theft from ISIS was known to us, we re-purposed a satellite to photographing the site where ISIS's gold repository had been.

"The very first day, we hit the jackpot." Then he advanced to the next slide. He seemed to think that it was a doozy, but nobody reacted at first.

Sally was the first to say anything. "You know those little blobs grouped around the building kind of look like people." She hesitated and then said, "Except they all seem to spread out on the . . . ground."

The analyst said, "Bingo. They're spread out because . . ."

Sally went on, "They're all dead."

He said, "Exactimento. Whoever knocked over the bank didn't leave any witnesses."

Minerva gulped and asked where the Ladies' Loo was. The analyst gave her directions. She got up slowly and then sped up as she left the room.

Ballard asked, "You don't know who did it?"

"No, we're trying to trace the gold. There aren't that many dealers who will handle large quantities of hot gold, and you don't get much hotter than ISIS's gold." He added, "Maybe, we'll give him a medal."

I asked, "Just what kind of a force would you have to have to attack that stronghold?"

He leaned back in his chair and thought a moment. "If we were doing it, we'd fly two, three dozen special forces in at night in stealth helicopters and catch them by surprise.

"If you didn't have that, then you'd need more forces." He turned to his supervisor who just nodded.

"What about four soldiers on foot or in a truck?" I asked.

They just laughed. Minerva re-entered the room.

Minerva said, "If you find the dealer, we'd like to talk with him."

The Deputy Director shook his head. "Look. When we find him, we'd like to ask him a few questions ourselves, but it's going to be hard to get to talk with him and harder still to get answers. He's probably in the Middle East, and it may not even be that easy to get into the same room with him. Leave the heavy lifting to us."

Minerva would not be dissuaded. "You haven't seen me interrogate someone."

Harris nodded, "I'd cut her some slack here. I know that it sounds crazy, but she does come with some good cred among our contacts."

The Director sighed, "We'll let you know when we think we've got a good suspect, but we won't help you go find him or talk with him."

Harris's jaw clenched, but Ballard didn't seem troubled. He said,

"Don't worry. We'll handle that."

□□
□□

The rest of the afternoon went smoothly, although Minerva seemed a bit off her normal gate. It was hard to put your finger on it, but she didn't offer to disapparate us back to the FBI. That was unusual. Nothing much happened until we were most of the way through the afternoon.

I was reading the *Times* of London online, and Sally was reading something on her computer. She whistled and said, "Guess what! We've got a meeting tomorrow afternoon."

I asked what the subject was. Sally answered, "You must already have gotten the meeting notice. The scientists have got the age of that bit of shrapnel. They'll be issuing their report. We're all invited to one of the Conference Rooms."

Minerva asked who was on the invitee list. There were the usual suspects here and a couple of the scientists.

Sally said, "What about Nick and Sinistra? Surely he should be in on it."

Minerva asked, "How can he be? He's in Scotland." Then she answered her own question. "Oh, yes. Telephone."

Sally suggested that we do a video-conference. "After all, he was the one who requested it."

"Seems reasonable, but we'll have to get Ballard to sign off on it." I added.

She went ahead and forwarded the meeting invite to Nick and Sinistra.

□□
□□□

That night, I tried to initiate foreplay but Minerva was not interested. Then, when we went to bed, after we kissed, she promptly rolled over on her side facing away from me. I wondered what I might have done and tried to go to sleep.

After a while I noticed that her shoulders were heaving slightly, and I heard a faint sighing. I placed a hand on her side and kneaded it gently. She broke out into full-fledged tears and sobs. I waited.

She pulled the hand around her but still didn't say anything. The sobbing stopped, and she said, "It was that awful picture today."

"Yeh, I wondered why you left the Conference Room. You're usually not squeamish."

"It just. . . just . . . reminded me of that awful night when Valdemort attacked Hogwarts." She broke into sobs again, and then she described it. She'd never talked about that night before. Her use of Valdemort's name after years of using his real name, Tom Riddle, showed how disturbed she was.

There were Deatheaters everywhere. Beams of red and green criss-crossed throughout the castle. One moment in a lull I thought that some fly on the wall would think that Christmas were here. But this Christmas the gifts were mangled bodies, crushed skulls and lifeless figures on the ground.

I saw the Lupins fall together in what looked for a second like an embrace. Then the scene broke, and they were just bodies falling to litter the floor of the castle. Deatheaters and Order of the Phoenix members don't look that different when they're on the floor. The blood is the same color. The ashen cheeks – I think that I'll never forget those cheeks as long as I live.

The dawn came, and the reality of those bodies crushed us. The sunlight left no doubt that the bodies were real bodies, that the lips would never laugh or cry or talk or kiss again, that the broken arms would never be set, that the names would never be heard again except at a memorial service or in our recollections on a cold winter night.

That dawn saw Potter defeat Valdemort, but it was followed by full light when we had to put bodies, so many bodies, in the body bags that the Royal Marines provided where they would wait for relatives or friends or us to claim. It took a week before the last of those hideous bags disappeared.

I had my own memories to deal with. That night that she was remembering, I had been in an old warehouse in London. I'd almost killed her and all the others, both those who survived and most of those who'd died that night. We'd neither of us talked about that night before. I wasn't sure that I could tell her what I'd almost done that night.

Her sobbing had stopped, and her body relaxed. We were both

exhausted – she by what she'd said and I by what I'd not said. She pulled my arm about her a little closer and I moved the rest of me closer to spoon her. Sometime that night we'd both fallen asleep and when we woke, we found that we'd rolled and changed position, but she pulled my arm around her again and said, "Let's just lie in a bit longer."

We did.

⛶ ⛶

The next afternoon, we had gathered in the Conference Room in the basement. There were introductions. There were the three of us, Ballard, Harris, the Director of the FBI Crime Lab, and a scientist who worked there. Sally had set up the projector and connected us with England via Google Hangouts. The three frames of Hangouts showed us, Nick and Aurora, and the PowerPoint. The PowerPoint slide showed the main points of the results of dating the sample of shrapnel.

The scientist was speaking, "As you can see, the main result is absolutely incredible. The age of that sample is 13.52 billion years with an error bar of 0.07 billion years."

Aurora certainly found it incredible. "That's impossible! How could it possibly even be a third of that number of years?"

The Director was patient. "I know. We didn't believe it ourselves. We repeated the measurement three times. They were all consistent within a couple of tens of million years."

She was not to be put off so easily, "Did you re-calibrate the mass spectrometer."

The scientist was a little indignant himself, "Of course, we did. We ran several tests with samples of known age. They included at least two lead samples. One was from a bullet that had been manufactured recently and another was ore that was known to be a little over a billion years old. Everything checked out.

"We had two different teams run those checks. They all agreed within experimental error."

Aurora got up and paced back and forth behind the still-seated Nick. Meanwhile Harris asked, "Why is that so incredible?"

I gave an answer, "Well, I'm not a professional astronomer like Aurora, but I do know that the Universe is only slightly older than that – maybe a couple of hundred million years."

Harris pushed on. "So, if it had tested 19 billion years, that would be a problem, but so what if it's younger than the age of the Universe?

And, are you so sure you know the age of the Universe that accurately?"

Aurora really had her dander up now. She swung around toward the camera and said, "Yes, we do know the age of the Universe that well. I don't have time to give you several physics courses on Cosmology, the Big Bang, General Relativity. So you'll just have to trust me that we do know that."

She wasn't satisfied with that but went on, "There isn't anything on Earth or in the Solar System that's within 10 billion years of that age."

At that point, Harris asked the scientist and the Director to leave the room and go to their offices. "If we need more information, we'll call you on my phone and ask you to come back."

She waved her hands expansively and said, "There might be some stars within a hundred thousand light years that are that old, but there isn't any lead in any of them, and even if there were, I'd sure not want to meet the person who could pull it out to make this shrapnel."

She started to rise, and then sat, and then got up to stay up. She started walking back and forth and talking as she walked. It didn't all come through too clearly because she was facing away from the camera a lot, but her practically shouting made up some for that. "Look. Where to begin? All right. First, the only way that lead gets made is in Supernova explosions. It takes a hundred million years or so for stars to get old enough to Supernova. So that lead was made about 200 million to 400 million years after the Big Bang. The star that made it formed about 100 million to 300 million years after the Big Bang. Do you know what that means?"

Harris didn't say anything for a moment and then said, "Were there any stars then?"

Aurora showed real surprise. "Right, that's a great question. Were there any stars then?" She went ahead to answer her own question, "We think that the first stars were really strange. They might have formed as early as 100 million years after the Big Bang, but probably a little later.

"Here's the thing. When those stars formed, there wasn't anything but hydrogen and helium. They probably were giant stars hundreds of thousands or even millions of times larger than the sun. It took so much matter to form stars that they were probably separated by giant stretches of space." She flung her hands wide again.

She stopped for breath and maybe to organize her thoughts, but no one dared interrupt her. She was like a force of nature – irresistible. It was hard to believe that she'd wanted to snare me but hadn't succeeded.

She went on, "Here's the deal. Time." She hesitated, "There's not enough time.

"Let's add it up. The first stars start forming – 100 million years. The first stars go Supernova – another 100 million years. The cores of the stars blasted out, cool,, and condense into small bodies – another, Oh God, I don't know – say another 20 or 30 million years. Another star forms – say another 100 million years. While that's happening, the little bodies with the lead in it accrete into planets or large asteroids. The interiors melt and the metals separate and form cores of solid metals that cool. Then the asteroids start colliding and breaking up, exposing the solid metal cores – say another 50 or 100 million years."

She threw her hands straight up into the air and shouted, "Bingo." She calmed down a little and went on. "We're already up to 400 million years and we're not done."

Ballard, who'd been nodding approvingly throughout, asked, "Why aren't we done yet? What more do you need?"

She turned sly now, "Yes. What more do we need?" She looked around to see if anyone would provide an answer.

No one here did, but next to her, her husband raised his hand and said, "Oooh! Oooh! I do."

She looked down at him and asked, "Really?"

"Sure. Do you want me to tell?"

She shrugged and said, "Go ahead. Why should I hog all the fun?"

He leaned back. "You've all been forgetting what that shrapnel is like. It's not exactly in a naturally occurring form. It's in a highly unusual crystalline form that had to be intelligence-made."

Despite her promise, she took up her story again, "And how long does it take to develop intelligence?" She hesitated and said, "I'll give you a hint. How long did it take here on Earth?"

Ballard said, "Over four billion years."

She had a self-satisfied look on her face, "And where do we get an extra four billion years to play with?"

Harris definitely had a troubled look on his face. "What's your solution then?"

Aurora sat and said simply, "I don't have one."

I had a comment, "We're dealing with really high intelligence. Maybe it developed really quickly."

Everyone looked around at each other. Sally summed it up, "Then we're dealing with Super intelligence from somewhere across the Universe?"

Ballard said, "Looks like."

Harris tried one last time, "Isn't there some other interpretation that makes sense?"

Sally said, "Well, if it makes you feel better, it could be a super intelligence from across the galaxy in the last few million years trying to fake us into thinking that they're from across the Universe 13 billion years ago."

Harris asked a question that I hadn't expected. "Is any of this actionable?"

It took a minute for us to re-orient ourselves to this shift in topic. I gave my pat answer to questions like this. "I can't think of an action that we can take based on this right now, but I sure wouldn't rule out the possibility later."

We went around the room and to England. Nobody had any ideas.

We were dismissed. When we got back to our basement office, Sally asked, "Do you really believe that those things were made thirteen and a half billion years ago by a super-intelligent race?"

Minerva turned her gaze on me and asked, "Yes. What do you believe about that?"

I sat and unscrewed the top of the water bottle that I'd brought to the office in the morning. I took a drink. Everybody knew that I was stalling for time, but that was OK. I then spoke, "I know just enough about astronomy to be dangerous, but everything I know fits in with what Aurora had to say. Given what we know, it may be very unlikely, but it's the only possibility that I see."

Minerva said, "Well, Sherlock, if that's true, shouldn't we be trying to find the source of that shrapnel."

I said, "We are."

Sally answered, "I know. I mean shouldn't we REALLY be trying."

"I guess so. I'll talk to Ballard about it."

I did talk to Ballard. He agreed, but he insisted that we just had to let the military keep working on it.

However, the day after next, we got a break. At the morning standup meeting, Harris announced that the CIA had found the gold dealer. He was located in Beirut.

That was good news, but what followed was a struggle over who would go, if anyone. Harris was reluctant to let anyone go to try to interview him.

We finally ended up in another meeting at Langley. We all went—

Sally, Minerva, Harris, Ballard, and me. Harris had said that we had to convince the Agency (as the CIA calls itself) that we could take care of ourselves and actually get some useful information out of the dealer.

We didn't know what to expect, but I was sure it would be something that we would have no hint of in advance. Neither Harris nor Ballard had any ideas.

We arrived in our limo. I'd brought my briefcase—just in case. We were directed to a Conference Room where we sat and waited. Someone whom we'd never seen before entered and said, "We're going to give you a field test. You're to come with us. We're going to a detention unit where we have someone for you to interrogate."

We all stood but our host shook his head. "Only the Wendt's."

We exited the Conference Room, and our host led us down the corridor to an elevator. We went to the B2 level. It turned out to be an underground garage. There was a Humvee into which we were invited. The host rode with us.

I asked him. "Where are we going?"

He said nothing. We went along for several minutes. While we were driving, an idea occurred to me. I looked over at Minerva, and I said, "You should use some of your interrogation skills on our host?"

He didn't say anything.

Minerva stared at him a moment and then said, "You know, I think that would be a good idea." She gazed at him a minute and then sneezed. She excused herself and reached into her purse for a handkerchief. She used it to blow her nose and then put it back in her purse.

She smiled and I could see why. Our host had relaxed, almost to the point of closing his eyes. They were barely more than slits. She then began a seemingly innocuous conversation.

"We've not been formally introduced. I'm Minerva Wendt. What's your name?"

He simply said, "Robert Engle."

She went on. "I'm a teacher. What do you do?"

"I'm the control for our East Lebanon agents."

She started to ask, "What are their names?" But I interrupted her and she said, "Never mind. Where are we going?"

In a perfectly flat tone he said, "We're going to Andrews Air Force Base."

I wanted to see if he would answer me, so I asked, "We're going to board a plane?"

"Yes."

"Where is the airplane going?"

"Guantanamo."

Minerva frowned a question to me. I suppose it was "what is Guantanamo?" We'd handle that later.

She went on, "What's the test we're going to take?"

He hesitated a few seconds, "We have an ISIS member who we think knows who and where the bomb-maker is. We want you to find that out."

I nodded and asked Minerva if there were anything else that we should know. She just shook her head. I said, "You won't be able to tell anyone about this conversation. Do you understand?"

"Yes."

I said to Minerva, "You can release him." I added the question, "*Imperius*?"

She just nodded.

By this time, we'd pulled up next to a small private jet. We were ushered aboard. As soon as we were on, the pilot came over the intercom and said, "We're going to take off momentarily. Please fasten your seat belts. You may smoke if you wish, but no moving around the cabin until the seat belt light goes off."

With no further ado, we taxied out onto a runway. They must have been holding traffic for us because there was no hesitation through the whole process. We taxied, turned onto a runway, and, without slowing in the least, we accelerated and were in the air in a few seconds.

There were no other passengers. Engle got up even before the seat belt light went off and said, "You can make yourself drinks at the wet bar, and we have some snacks. The flight should be about three hours."

Minerva asked, "Why is this ISIS person in Guantanamo, wherever that is."

Engle grimaced and said, 'Guantanamo is on the island of Cuba. It's illegal to use some of the interrogation techniques that we use in the US. So, we do a lot of it at Guantanamo."

Minerva nodded and commented, "Strange. Things are legal outside the States that aren't inside."

Engle grimaced again but didn't say anything.

There were more than snacks in the wet bar. They had a refrigerator with various sandwiches. There were chocolate fudge brownies. There was a plate of fresh fruits. We made a little lunch about an hour before our arrival time.

We landed and were hustled into a Humvee for the ride to a low squat building. It was surrounded by a fence and had a gate with a guard post. We were passed in and escorted by an armed guard in addition to Engle. We entered the building, which was not air-conditioned. There was an empty room with a rough table and a couple of chairs. It was warm and humid. Minerva asked Engle if the prisoner understood English. He replied that he had a decent understanding, but that there would be a translator present for several reasons: to make sure that he understood the question, to speed the process up, to catch any muttered statements that might shed light on the answers. Minerva just smiled.

Another guard entered, preceded by a man in orange fatigues. The guard pointed at one of the chairs. He took it. Then a soldier wearing khaki fatigues entered and sat. He invited us to sit. We all took seats around the table opposite the ISIS prisoner.

The soldier in khaki introduced himself. "I'm Tom. I'm the translator. You've already met Bob. He's got questions for you."

Bob handed over to Minerva a list of questions on a folded-up piece of paper. She glanced at them. Then she put the paper on the table and opened her purse to get a pen. For a moment I was afraid that she'd bring out a quill, but she didn't.

The prisoner looked completely relaxed.

Tom said, "Don't let him fool you. He's tough as an old shoe. Ask your question. I'll translate. We may use something to encourage him when he clams up."

Minerva said, "Don't worry. That won't be necessary."

Tom rolled his eyes.

Minerva started, "Well, Mr. Khali, where were you stationed most recently?"

The translator turned that into a lengthy question. I looked a question at him. He said, "I had to put in a little profanity. He won't know we're serious without it."

Before he'd finished saying that, the prisoner started speaking. Tom's jaw dropped, and he asked the prisoner something. The prisoner seemed to repeat what he'd just said.

Tom looked over at us. "He just said that he was stationed at Tikrit but he'd been at Tal Afar before." He paused and said, "He doesn't usually answer right off like that—even if it's a lie."

Minerva said, "That's not a lie."

Tom nodded and added, "I know."

Minerva scanned down the list of questions. "Let's just cut to the chase. Who is the bomb-maker?"

Tom shrugged and said something. This time it was quick. Just as quickly the prisoner answered. Then Tom looked over at Engle, "Can I let them know?"

Engle asked, "You think he's not lying?"

"I don't know."

Engle responded, "Let's not take chances. Don't."

Minerva then asked, "Where is he located."

The prisoner didn't wait but spoke immediately in Arabic. At least, I thought it was probably Arabic. I was tempted to look the question at her, "How did he know?" But I was afraid to have Minerva reveal anything of her abilities."

Engle asked, "What did he say?"

Tom said, "Since I'm sure that you all heard it, the town Mosul. That's what he said – at least part of it. I think you and I have to have a talk Engle."

Engle nodded. He picked up the sheet of questions, glanced at it, and said, "Ask one more question. Number 11."

He handed the sheet back to Minerva but she shook her head, "I remember what it was." She then turned to the prisoner and asked, "What happened to the gold?"

He hesitated, and then said a brief phrase followed by a long statement that seemed too forceful to be anything but a diatribe. After a while he wound down, and the translator shook his head.

Engle said, "I didn't catch all of that but I'll translate what I think you need to know.

"In simple terms, he said that the guards didn't resist hard enough. There were some mentions of dogs and vermin but I'm not up on my colloquial Arabic enough to give you a good translation."

Minerva reached into her purse. Engle sent the prisoner back to his cell. We left the building. On the way back to the airplane, Engle said that he was satisfied. We would fly back, and the CIA would arrange for us to get to see the dealer. However, they make no promises beyond that.

By then it was late afternoon and we took off, facing into the sun. After about an hour into the flight, Engle went into the pilot's cockpit and spent an hour there. When he came back, he had more information for us. "Tomorrow we'll have another meeting to discuss your approach to the dealer. We may be able to help you get an audience with him."

That was the last that he would say for the rest of the flight. When we landed at Andrews it was pitch dark. Our chauffeur was there waiting for us. He dropped us directly at our hotel.

When we arrived, we found a welcome committee in the lobby. There were Ballard, Harris, and Sally.

They all asked the same question at once. "What happened?"

Minerva shrugged, "They flew us to Guantanamo. There was a prisoner there that they wanted interrogated. We asked him some of their questions. I guess they were satisfied. They told us there'd be a meeting tomorrow to plan our approach to the dealer."

Harris was surprised. "We'll invite ourselves to your room to discuss this further."

Minerva said, "Look, I'm bushed. This was a long day. Let's hold it for tomorrow."

Ballard said, "I agree with Harris. We need more discussion before we go to Langley tomorrow."

When we were back in our room, we offered drinks, and everyone had something. Minerva and I had a Dewars. Ballard had a Michelobb. Harris had nothing – not even water. I don't remember what everyone else had.

Harris started the questioning. "We gather they had a tough case that they wanted you to interrogate. Who was it and what did they want to know?"

Minera really was tired. She just nodded in my direction, so I took the question. "They had someone whom they thought knew who our bomb maker was. He seemed to. We asked him who he was and where he was. He gave answers."

Ballard was excited. "Where is he?"

"Mosul."

Ballard went on. "That must mean that they're going to try to get him for us. That would be a real break."

Sally asked, "Was that all?"

Minerva seemed to be revived by the drink. She answered, "No. They wanted to know about the robbery – what happened to the gold."

Everyone hung on her next words. But she disappointed them. "He doesn't know. He just knows that ISIS leadership was pretty bloody mad about losing the gold. They all thought the guards should have fought harder."

Sally expressed all our thoughts when she said, "They were all dead. What did they bloody want?"

On that pleasant note, no one could think of anything else to say besides, "Good night."

There was a ringing in my head, it kept getting louder, and then resolved itself into words, "Come on, we've got to get going."

I mumbled something like, "Well, give me a kiss to energize me."

"I'll energize you all right."

We had a little tussle on the bed. My goal was to get Minerva under me, and hers was to get me on the floor, where I'd have to get up – even if it was just to get back into bed. Her idea sort of worked, and mine did too. She was under me, on the floor.

The tussle had wakened me completely. "OK. OK. Knowing you, I'm confident that you've already showered."

"You know it."

I was hoping I could buy a little time for a few winks while she showered, but she had anticipated me. I was in the bath, did my usual 5 minute shower, and was dressed in another 10. She was still working on her hair, but had finished tightening up her bun before I could get my fingers in it. I commented, "You know me way too well."

She just smiled wickedly at that, and we went down to the lobby for the complimentary breakfast.

We reached the office by disapparation, rather than the subway. So we arrived a couple of minutes early. In our office, Sally had already logged on to her computer and was reading emails. She informed us, "We got a meeting notice – 11 AM at Langley."

We arrived and were led to our usual Conference Room. The same analyst was warming up the projector when we arrived. It appeared to be only him this time.

When the projector was warmed up, he started in. "OK. The dealer's name is Mohammed Bagdadi. He has a shop in Beirut. He is a registered dealer in gold and does a respectable business above board. He clears between a million and two million Euros a year lately.

"Below board, he is the second biggest gold dealer in the Middle East. He probably is in the top five world-wide." During this discussion, a photo of a well-built olive-skinned middle-aged man was projected on the screen. He had short hair that tended to curls.

The analyst was going on. "He's got a small army to protect his

61

interests if a client turns unfriendly or he just wants to stiff him.

"Don't cross him if you can avoid it. We WILL NOT give you backup. You're on your own once we deliver you to his place of business.

"We have a translator and contact who will get you there. He'll identify himself by a code word – Mosul.

"You'll need a cover story to get you in to see him." At this point, he reached into his brief case and drew out a purse that looked a lot like mine.

As he moved it, it jingled slightly. He opened the draw string and dumped its contents onto the conference table. It looked like a pile of small irregularly shaped gold nuggets. He asked, "Do you know what those are?"

Sally picked up one, felt it, and then shivered. She nodded and said, "Those are gold fillings." The analyst nodded and she added, "Jewish. From the Holocaust."

The analyst said, "Perceptive. We got them from the Holocaust museum, but you have a different story.

"You found a lost horde of German gold, including these fillings. You need a dealer. Don't be too quick revealing that information. Hesitate as much as you can. Make him pull it out of you. You have another three hundred kilos of it. Let him have this sample. No strings attached. It's not part of the deal – just to prove that you're really rolling in it.

"Of course, don't make up a place that you found them."

"That should get you in. I know that Engle said you were a wiz at interrogation, but you won't be sitting in nice friendly Guantanamo surrounded by armed guards – or at least your armed guards."

"Remember that you can bail out at any time – including now."

We all looked at each other. Minerva, Sally, and I had been in much tougher spots than this. BUT, we hadn't had much choice at the time. No friendly advisor had said, "You can bail out any time – including now."

Among people who have been through those kinds of things more than once, there is an understanding that lets you communicate without words – even without looks, almost. This time, we all looked at each other, and we were agreed. I said it for the three of us. "No, we're not going to bail."

The analyst just said, "Good. Let's get down to details." He pulled a folder out of his briefcase. "These are your tickets. They are fully refundable, so you can change them at any time without penalty." I noticed that they were first class tickets. I supposed that gold dealers travel that way all the time.

"We tried doing research on you all. You have some history, but you've got big gaps in the last couple of years. That's good. It will make Mohammed less suspicious.

"We've got you a reservation at the Crowne Plaza Beirut. It's a four-star hotel and should be safe from anything short of ISIS.

"Oh, one last thing. We're not bankrolling you--other than the gold. Make sure you've got money, credit cards, etc."

That would not be a problem for Minerva and me.

He looked around as if trying to look for visual cues of anything he might have forgotten. He didn't find anything and said, "Good luck."

I put the folder and gold in my briefcase and we left Langley happy to be away but not particularly happy about what we would be soon facing.

Beirut and Beyond

We started our trip east auspiciously. The weather was beautiful, and the first class accommodations were great on the 747 from Dulles. It hadn't been so great trying to talk Sally into staying behind and coordinating all our wide-flung activities.

She did have a point. There were three tickets—one had her name on it. Minerva used to hate flying. Now she only despises it. In the past, we used to try to get her to try the window seat. Now I just take it. Minerva got the window seat for this flight, and I was determined to get some advantage from yielding my aisle seat for it. Sally has never liked the window seat, so she was happy to sit across the aisle from our seats. We could talk and even have a food fight (we didn't).

We changed planes in Rome. The last leg was short, and we were acutely aware that we would have to be on the ground in the Middle East shortly.

I had begun to appreciate the view expressed by the main character in the movie, *Up in the Air*. He was only happy when he was flying. He thought he was safe, pampered, and entertained. I was ready to settle for just safe, and that was about to end.

The rear wheels of the jet touched down, and the shudder that went through the plane was the knell of the end of that safety. The front wheels touched down, and it was over. We'd passed the point of no return, and we were completely committed.

Sally verified that. "Well, here we go."

□

We slowly migrated from the safe, comfortable, even fun environment of the Boeing 747 to the interior of the secured, air-conditioned section of the terminal.

We reached the immigration section. The officer checked our passports and stamped them with entry visas. Were we there for business or pleasure? My brain screamed to say, "Neither." For how much pleasure would there be running down this dealer and risking our lives. But business? Minerva and I were teachers. Sally was an executive assistant.

I just smiled and said, "I hope to do some sightseeing."

We reached the baggage claim. Each of us had a bag in addition to our carry-on. I took Minerva's and mine. We reached the luggage check. This was the last barrier between us and our fate.

The immigration officer asked, "Anything to declare?"

"Nothing."

He opened my luggage and found clothes, and my shaving kit. He asked to see my briefcase. Opened, it revealed laptop, a newspaper, pen, a pad of paper and my purse.

He riffled through the contents and noticed the purse. He asked, "What's in the purse?"

I shrugged, "Nothing. I brought it for any fragile souvenirs. It's padded."

He shrugged. "Hope you find something."

We walked outside the terminal. There were several cabs lined up. All three of the cabbies were out, shouting at us. I heard someone say the word Mosul – not shouting. I looked around to see who it was. Minerva took my arm and led me over to him. He was leaning against his cab.

Sally asked him, "Why are you here?"

He smiled, "I hear you want to deal some gold."

She asked, "Where do we deal?"

He asked, "Mosul?"

The three of us looked at each other, and there was that unvoiced agreement. I said, "Let's go."

As soon as we were on the road, the driver asked, "I recommend the Crowne Plaza Beirut?"

That further confirmation of his knowledge of us was reassuring – mostly.

He went on, "Baghdadi is out of town for a couple of days. You

65

should probably enjoy the sights. I'm available to you. I'd be happy to be your tour guide."

Sally asked, "Is this business on the side or part of the service?"

He sounded truly offended, "Oh, you must let me show you Beirut. I would not dare to touch money."

I nodded. "No. We couldn't allow you to waste your valuable time with us. We are only humble servants of the greater good."

He smiled. "Well, perhaps we can work something out."

"What do you recommend seeing?"

He enthused, "Oh, the Beirut National Museum is unequaled. You should see the Corniche. The Omari Mosque is necessary too. It was once the Cathedral of St. John."

We drove a little while, and he said, "If I may make a recommendation to the ladies." He proceeded immediately with the recommendation. "I would advise when you travel in public, that you completely cover. The current garb is fine for the airport, but you should obtain more modest attire if you don't already have it. The shop in the Crowne Plaza will have many fashionable styles that will be modest but attractive."

That raised another question in my mind, "We must go together to see Baghdadi. Any ideas?"

That clearly disturbed our guide. "If you must go, of course, dress modestly." He thought a moment, "It might help if both ladies go. It suggests a harim. Of course, they should be silent and always stand behind the gentleman."

I nodded.

The driver told us his name, Mahmud. He asked, "Do you have the gold?"

"Yes, it's . . . " But I was interrupted.

"I don't know where it is. I don't want to know anything about it. When you go to see him, he will insist that you prove that you are not wasting his time. Give him the gold as a gift. He'll test it and its authenticity.

"Above all else, don't go in armed. That will spoil the deal and might cost you your lives."

I nodded.

We arrived at the Plaza. Mahmud carried in our bags and made a point of publicly reminding us that we had hired him to guide us tomorrow morning.

After he left, we checked in. The clerk said, "Gentleman and ladies, I would not recommend using a cab driver to serve as tour guide. The hotel can connect you with a number of reputable, registered guides."

I nodded politely but said, "I have a good feeling about him. We'll try him tomorrow and see how it goes."

The clerk showed his consternation. "But sir, I really would advise . . ." I interrupted him with a motion of my hand. He simply ended, "Allow me to provide our list."

I allowed, and we carried off his list of approved guides to our room. We were all checked into a single suite. It had two bedrooms. One had two queen size bed, and the other a king-size. We debated who would get which room.

Sally asked, "If we're supposed to be your harim, shouldn't we all be in the one with the king-size?"

Minerva gave her a glare that would stop a charging rhino in its tracks. Her comment to me was, "Any more talk like that, and we'll take the queensize and you'll sleep by yourself."

Minerva and I ended up in the King-size, and Sally with the two queen-sizes.

⊓⊓

The next morning, we went to have breakfast in the hotel cafe. Mahmud was waiting for us in the lobby. He thought that we'd probably had breakfast in bed – who knew how many beds – and we'd be ready to go immediately.

"I'm sorry Mahmud. You'll have to wait for us to have breakfast in the cafe."

He took the disappointment well. He told us that he'd be waiting outside in his cab. We felt a little guilty about making him wait. We rushed through a breakfast of fruit and assorted pastries.

We found him standing outside his cab. It was a slow drive to the Museum. The temperature was very temperate – low 70's. The skies were cloudy, but it wasn't dank.

Again, Mahmud let us out. We entered the museum on our own. It was a tour of local history, which goes back a long ways in the Middle East. We finished the Premier Etage by early afternoon. Sally was reaching her limit on ancient history. And as a matter of fact, I was pretty close myself. So we decided to go have a leisurely lunch and not come back.

Mahmud took us to a western restaurant – Chili's. He was fascinated with it, and we insisted that he join us. I'd never eaten at a Chili's before. It turned out to be a Tex-Mex based in Dallas, Texas.

67

Neither Minerva or Sally had had real Tex-Mex before, so it was sort of a foreign restaurant to us all.

Mahmud found the spicy entrée that he selected to be well within his tolerance. He commented on how well Minerva and Sally fit in, dressed in local modest attire.

After lunch we returned to the Hotel. On the way, Mahmud took a little detour from the straightforward route. At one point, he said casually, "Don't look too hard, but on the left ahead, is Baghdadi's establishment." As we drove along, he said, "I'm going to count down. When I reach one, we'll pass the establishment."

Then he started his count, "Five. Don't turn your head. Four. . . Three. . . Two. . . One." We looked at it out of the corner of our eyes. There was a sign hanging over what appeared to be a steel door. There were no windows, no bars, nothing out of the ordinary for the block.

After we'd rounded a corner, he said, "Tomorrow let's go to the Corniche.

The next day, the Corniche was more interesting. For, though the Museum was beautiful architecturally, and the ancient art contained in it was also beautiful in a way, the Corniche with its long, active waterfront and multitude of food vendors was easier to waste time in.

We didn't have formal meals that day – not even breakfast. Mahmud talked us into eating at the Corniche. The day had nothing outstanding in it, but it was a joy to be able to really be the tourists that we were pretending to be.

That night when we went to bed, Minerva wanted to make love. It seemed like bad Karma to me. It was as though we didn't expect to survive to make love again. But we did eventually lose ourselves, if briefly, in the joy of giving each other pleasure.

The next day, we had breakfast in the Crowne Plaza, and for a change Mahmud joined us.

He gave us his final recommendations, "Go mid-afternoon. But before afternoon prayer. For Allah's sake, the ladies must remain silent, subservient, in the background. Don't try anything 'cute' or 'funny'. Just ask to see Baghdadi. Give them your gold as proof of your bona fides. If he doesn't see you, just leave."

He thought a minute and added, "Don't lie to him except when you absolutely have to. He has resources and can check your claims. Just tell him the least that you can get away with.

"Ask your questions. When he doesn't answer, go away wiser."

I promised that we would take his wisdom with us. He sneered at that.

After breakfast, we went back to the room and had our final counsel of war.

We debated how to use the two spells that we intended to use. We finally ended up with the following script for the encounter:

- We get into the inner sanctum.
- Once in, on my first signal (baseball fastball signal), Minerva imperiouses the guards in the room.
- Later, when I think best, on my second signal (baseball curveball signal), Minerva imperiouses Baghdadi.
- Next, on my third signal (baseball slider signal), Minerva uses the Mufliatto spell so that anyone listening in to what is happening won't know that we're interrogating Baghdadi.
- Next, Minerva releases Baghdadi on my curveball signal.
- Then, she ends the Muffliatto spell on my slider signal.
- Then, she releases the guards from the imperious curse.
- We leave with Baghdadi's blessing and his information.

Simple but not necessarily easy to accomplish.

Minerva removed her wand from her purse, removed the handle, and taped the resulting thin wand to the inside of her left thigh. She claimed that to work, it only need be in contact with her skin somewhere. She did that in Sally's and my presence. There was not the slightest hint of sexual innuendo in the act. We were all scared silly by the precaution.

We had a simple lunch of olives, almonds, and bread. Then we met Mahmud in front of the Crowne Plaza. He drove us to the entrance to THE street. He stopped the cab and turned to us in the back seat. "You can still bail now if you want."

We all shook our heads, and he drove forward. He stopped in front of the entrance to Baghdadi's lair. We got out, went to the door, and attempted to open it. It was locked, but there was a button close to the doorknob. I pushed it.

We all hoped that no one would answer, but an answer did come quickly. A tall slender man with the darkest, straightest hair that I'd ever seen answered the door and respectfully invited us in.

The interior was paneled in some dark wood. There were display cases showing various gold jewelry, ornaments, and even plain ordinary bullion.

Our host asked what he could do for us.

I answered. My companions remained respectfully behind me and uttered not a peep. "We understand that Messier Baghdadi buys and sells gold at competitive prices."

Our host nodded. "Which do you wish to do?"

"Sell."

He nodded. "I would be pleased to help you." His English was urbane and almost without accent.

"I would prefer to directly deal with Messier Baghdadi."

"Of course, it is his establishment. However, I am fully authorized to execute any trade that he would, I assure you."

I sighed as though I tired of the endless talk. "Please give Messier Baghdadi this sample of my wares as a courtesy. This is only a small fraction of what I have to deal."

I withdrew my purse from my pocket, opened it slightly, and poured out the gold nuggets onto the palm of my hand. I then neatly turned them over onto the glass display counter in front of us.

Our host looked at them as though they had come from another planet. He picked up one gingerly and examined it with a jeweler's loupe. He then pursed his lips and said, "I must consult my superior. Please wait." He turned to go and then turned back. "How much more do you have?"

I nonchalantly said, "Three hundred kilos."

He turned wordlessly and left the room. It seemed like a half-hour, but I think it could hardly have been fifteen minutes. He returned and said, "Please follow me."

He led us through a door and into a dark corridor. He opened the second door on the right and asked us to make ourselves comfortable. "There is chilled bottled water in the refrigerator. You can also mix yourselves a drink at the bar. Please allow a few minutes for Messier Baghdadi to meet with you.

I was not going to drink or eat anything here and neither of my partners seemed inclined to either. It was not more than five minutes when two guards entered the room. They approached us and without a word administered a quick, efficient frisk of all three of us. I was worried that they might notice the wand, but apparently they didn't or maybe Minerva imperioused the one who searched her before she was examined.

One left the room for a minute. A short, wiry man with grizzled hair that was beginning to turn grey entered the room with the guard who had left.

"I apologize that I find it necessary to use such unpleasant precautions, but occasionally people in my business are disappointed by our business partners."

I said, "I understand completely."

"Please sit, Mr. . . . "

I supplied my real name. "Mr. Wendt. And do I have the honor of speaking with Messier Baghdadi?"

He nodded. It seemed obvious that the courtesy of a chair didn't extend to my companions. It occurred to me that he might regret that oversight later. But he had begun speaking, "Mr. Wendt. The samples of gold that you provided have been verified as 18 carat gold. They appear to be . . . well . . . to be indelicate, they appear to be fillings. Just where did you obtain them?"

I nodded as though I completely expected the question. "I won't tell you what my source is, but I will admit that they are fillings and they come from a horde accumulated by the Nazi's and never captured by the Allies in World War II."

He laughed, "Real Nazi gold. That is ironic. How many western movies feature the recovery of Nazi gold? And yet I think that none ever has been."

I shrugged. I also gave the fastball sign. "Well, it really doesn't matter if this is the first or not, does it?"

He shrugged too. "I suppose not. But you really do have another three hundred kilos?"

I nodded and gave the curve ball signal. The figure slumped slightly in his chair and his gaze seemed to extend into the distance. Now came the real test. I answered, "Well, I really might not, but it doesn't matter, does it?"

The mechanical answer, "No", came back. I gave the slider signal.

"And, you'd be happy to answer all of my questions, wouldn't you?"

"Yes, of course."

"Good." I reached into my pocket and pulled out my cell phone. "I'm going to show you a couple of pictures. Please tell me if you've seen any of these men before."

I pulled up the photo folder and showed him the four photos that Ballard had given us. He denied having seen the first three, but he said, "Yes. The last."

I nodded. I guess I wasn't surprised but still it was electrifying to hear it. I hoped that my companions weren't showing any signs of excitement. I continued the questions, "What was the connection?"

Baghdadi shuddered, "I bought some gold from him."

"How much?"

He hesitated as though in calculation and said, "About four

71

hundred seventy million Euros at the current price of gold on the open market."

I had the hardest time keeping from whistling, although I doubted that anyone could hear me besides the four of us around the desk.

I went on, "Tell us all about the sale."

Baghdadi shuddered again. But he began.

About eleven days ago, the man you showed me, came into this room to bargain – like you. He gave my associate a small ingot of 24 carat gold, weighing about one kilo.

Of course, we took precautions and invited him in here. He was very persuasive. We eventually settled on three hundred twenty five million Euros for the price. I agreed to deliver to him four thousand US Treasury bills of one hundred thousand dollar denomination that could be cashed by anyone.

He didn't require any particular precautions. He agreed to meet me at my location. He said that he would come alone, driving a truck that he would turn over to me. It would contain the gold. I would supply a brief case with the Treasury bills.

We made our usual preparations for this sort of swap. I brought half a dozen associates. They were well-armed. The meeting was for 1 AM. We arrived at the site far into the desert. We arrived before sunset and examined the area. We had night vision goggles. We were prepared for anything. If the Lieutenant arrived with forces, we were ready to fight or retreat.

As the sun set, the air chilled quickly. The sky was clear and there was no moon. The stars were as bright as I had ever seen. They were cold, and a chill crept into all of us as we waited. It had nothing to do with the air.

We were on edge, and little differences blew up into arguments. Raiza put his prayer rug down at sunset. Ahmed tripped over him in the dark, and there was a scuffle.

I was on the verge of calling the deal off that night.

But there was a lot of money to be made.

The hours crept along. Finally, someone shouted, "Vehicle coming."

I heard a motor, but the madman was driving without lights. Raiza laughed, "He'll run off the edge of the road and kill himself. Hey! Maybe we won't have to pay him at all."

But he didn't. He pulled up next to our Humvee and got out. He walked directly to me and said, "It's all in the truck."

I grunted, "Somebody turn on lanterns." They did.

I said, "Raiza, check it out."

He let down the tailgate of the truck and took someone with him. They opened a couple of crates. They were marked, "Shovels." They pulled out a couple of ingots. They performed tests. Someone sawed a couple of ingots in two. He reported, "Solid gold."

Once someone had tried to cheat me by selling lead ingots coated by a thick layer of gold. They sawed another ingot from a different crate. It was solid too.

They were opening other crates and checking, but I wanted to get away with the gold quickly. I told the Lieutenant that he could check my payment. Ahmed brought up the briefcase and handed it to him.

He took it and placed it on the camp table. He flicked the latches and opened it, nodding as he did. He picked a bundle of T-bills up and hefted it. Then he said. "You're short. We agreed on 4000. This is 3500."

Of course, I was expecting this. I gave my usual reasons. "It was harder than I expected. The price I can get for the gold is not as good as when we talked. I had to bribe more officials." I shrugged.

The Lieutenant looked me in the eyes and said, "We had an agreement. You'll send the additional 500 to my hotel tomorrow."

I laughed, "What will you do? Go to the police?"

He looked up at me again, and I cursed under my breath. Did he think he could just come to my house and tell me what to do? I sneered, "Leave while you still can. Thirty-five hundred is a lot of money."

Then he said something I'd never heard anyone say, "I need the four thousand. You'll send it tomorrow."

This impudent dog! Did he think he could threaten me! I slipped into Arabic in my anger, "Do you think that you can dictate to me! You come alone and unarmed. I don't even need my boys. I could gut you myself, you pig!"

I reached down to my boot and pulled my knife from it. I would show him. He was standing beside the camp table where I was sitting. I got up, raised the knife to his throat, and applied pressure. A trickle of blood appeared.

But it was my blood! I was holding the knife at my carotid artery! The trickle of blood I felt on my throat!

He said in perfect Arabic, "I think that you'll find that the only person you can cut with that knife is yourself."

73

I could feel the pressure that my hand was placing on my throat. I dared not speak a word. The pressure increased, and I realized that the slightest move or word spoken, and I would bleed out before I could reach a hospital.

In the mildest tones, the Lieutenant simply said. "Be sure that your payment reaches me tomorrow."

I resisted the temptation to shiver. The pressure on my throat lessened slightly and I mouthed without saying, 'Of course."

He reached out his hand to shake. The knife fell from my hand and I convulsively extended my hand. He took it and shook. With that, he turned and walked off into the night with the briefcase.

One of my boys, said, "You dropped your knife." He bent and picked it up. He extended it toward me. I couldn't touch it. I was afraid that I'd do something with it. He noticed the trickle of blood on my throat. "Oh! You nicked yourself.

"Anyway, you showed him. He took his money and left."

They had all been in the truck checking the gold. My voice was hoarse. "Yeh."

I got into the Humvee and got my phone out. I called one of my bankers. "Yes, it's me! Mohammed. I need a loan from the bank."

The voice on the other end asked, "How much? A couple of million?"

I could hardly get the words out. "Fifty million Euro's." There was a chuckle at the other end. I added, "Bearer bonds."

The voice on the other end said, "Seriously?"

I could hardly choke the word "Yes" out of my throat.

There was a long pause. Finally, the voice said, "I could manage 30 million, but the interest rate would be high. It will cost you 50 million, and I'd expect payment within a month.

I gulped but could say no more.

The rest of my crew were driving the truck to my warehouse. My driver got into the Humvee and, seeing me on the phone, chuckled, "Making your next deal already." He continued his inane chatter but I didn't have time to interrupt. "He's crazy. Walking away into the desert. We'll probably find him a few miles down the road. You'll have your money back."

I was sure that we wouldn't. I paid no attention as he started the engine and drove off. I called my next prospect.

I spent the rest of the night and day search for the next 20 million Euros. I finally found it and arrived at the Lieutenant's hotel at 10:30. He was in the coffee shop. As I walked into the hotel, he approached me and said, "Good to see you."

I handed him the briefcase. He hefted it and said, "I see you have some smaller T-bills in here."

I almost choked wondering if he would object that they weren't all 100,000 dollar T-bills. But he only said, "That's acceptable." With that he walked out the front door of the hotel.

I walked to the front desk. I asked the clerk, "The man who just left the hotel."

In a bored tone he answered, "Yes."

"What room is he in?"

In the continued bored tone he answered, "I couldn't tell you that, Messier."

I took his arm and pulled him around to face me. "Do you know who I am?"

The clerk's eyes widened, "I'm sorry, Messier, I didn't realize whom I was talking with. The gentleman who just walked out of the hotel doesn't have a room. I've never seen him before."

In the guard room of Baghdadi, one of the guards jostled the other. "I don't like this. I can't understand what they're saying."

The response was a bored, 'Oh, nothing's going on. They're just talking business. No one's made any threatening gestures or even moved."

"I tell you I don't like it. They've been talking so long."

"The guards in the room aren't bothered, why should you be?"

'It's just not natural. The negotiations never last this long. The Knife never talks this long."

The other guard took a more careful look at the video screen. "Nothing's happening. Maybe the guest is a sports fan and they're talking football. Keep your eyes on them. If anything funny happens go in there and get fired for interrupting."

I had been listening to Baghdadi's story for nearly an hour. I was sorry that Minerva and Sally had to stand through the whole thing, but it was about time to finish up. Baghdadi had finished his story.

I asked, "Do you know anything about what Minns did with the money he got from you?"

The monotone answer was, 'No."

Then another question occurred to me, "Why do you always call him the Lieutenant?"

Baghdadi hesitated and then said, "That was the name that popped into my mind when I first saw him."

"Did he ever call himself that?"

"No."

"All right. We're almost done. We didn't reach a deal, but you like and respect us and hope for business in the future. You won't remember any details of what we talked about. Do you understand that?"

"Yes."

I gave Minerva the curve-ball signal. She apparently did something because he suddenly sat up straighter and focused on me. He said, "I'm sorry that we can't do business this time, but I hope you'll consider us in the future."

During this speech, I signaled slider. I couldn't tell if she'd done it, but it probably didn't matter. Baghdadi stood and extended his hand. We shook briefly and I turned to Sally and Minerva and said, "Let's go ladies."

As we approached the door and the guards, I gave the fastball signal. They came to and stuttered a moment deciding what to do. Baghdadi said something sharp in Arabic. Then,the two opened the doors, and we walked through. When we reached the door to the store-front, someone from the other side opened it, and we strode through and on to the main entrance. A guard unlocked the entrance, and we left.

None of us felt exactly safe yet, especially since we didn't see our guide. I put my hand in my pocket to get out my cell phone, but just then the cab turned a corner and headed toward us a little faster than I really thought was advisable in the narrow street that had several cars constricting clearance even further.

It pulled up. The doors unlocked, and Mahmud hissed, "Quick! Get in!"

We didn't have to be urged. As soon as we were in, but before the doors were closed, he sped off. We were all silent until we turned a corner. "Allah be praised. Did you get what you wanted?"

I was about to answer, but he immediately repented the question, "Never mind. I don't want to know."

He went on, "I took the precaution of breaking into your rooms and packing your luggage."

There would have been shrieks of protest if we weren't all so surprised. He went on, "You've got to get out of town. We're going straight to the airport. Do you all have your passports?"

We were shaken but we said that we did.

"Good. You need to exchange your tickets for the earliest flight out. It doesn't matter where it's going as long as it's Europe or America. DO YOU UNDERSTAND?"

I said, "I've got it. Did something happen?"

"No. But I had a bad feeling from the moment that I dropped you off. I called a friend who knows about hotel security. I had him do the break-in and bring your things here. They're in the trunk."

Minerva shook her head and said ironically, "Thoughtful."

His answer had no irony, "I thought so."

⌗

We arrived at the airport after a maddeningly slow progress through Beirut rush hour traffic. At the international terminal Mahmud removed our luggage from the trunks. I paid him to maintain the fiction that he was just another cabbie. I threw in a very generous tip.

He squinted at me in disapproval. "Don't let anyone see you tipping like that."

I just said under my breath, "Ingrate."

Sally said, "I'll bet I've got some of your undies in my bag."

Minerva said in absolute deadpan, "Don't flatter yourself, dearie."

I helped them into the terminal, and we got in line at the American Airlines ticket desk. When we reached the end of the queue, I explained that business called us away from our vacation. We were in a hurry. What was the earliest flight out?

The ticket agent looked at her computer screen and said, "Well, you could just make a flight to Madrid. You'd then have to wait a couple of hours and catch a red-eye to Dulles. It would be tight though.

"The next flight would be to London. The first class seats are all full on the connecting flight to Dulles, but you could go economy."

No one was excited about that. So, she went on, "The next flight with first class available would be in 18 hours. You'd have to stay over, and you'd have to pick up your bags and re-check them before the next flight."

Both the ladies nodded enthusiastically at that possibility. Minerva took my arm and said, "We could stay over at the Cauldron." I agreed, so we took that flight.

We had just over an hour till flight time. We went through security and found a little pub where we had a drink and ordered some take-away to eat on the flight.

When we reached our gate, they had already called first class. We entered with almost the last boarding group. Our seats were again as they had been flying into Beirut.

We were all exhausted by the day and just wanted to sit quietly and read or stare out the window during the flight. After we were up in the air, one of the hostesses came over to us to ask what we preferred to eat. We'd forgotten that we would have a meal. She chatted us up gaily. How had we enjoyed our stay in Beirut? Beautiful wasn't it? Had we visited the Corniche?

Finally she asked, "It is a little surprising to see a young couple traveling with one of the mothers. Is it a special holiday?"

Minerva reached for her handbag. I took her arm. The stewardess went on gaily, "Are you newlyweds?" All three of us raised our left hands and displayed two wedding rings and Sally's ringless finger.

The stewardess looked from one to the other of us and rushed off to get our meals.

Minera asked, "Why did you stop me? I was just going to turn her into a rat."

I said, "When you say things like that, you say, 'Just Kidding.' Don't make bad jokes. I'm too tired for it."

"I wasn't joking."

Sally said, "I don't think the 'stew' will be bothering us with idle chatter anyway."

The rest of the flight was quiet.

□□ □□
□□ □□

We arrived at Heathrow shortly before midnight. Our next flight was at 5 PM the next day. Everyone was tired and cranky. Sally was for just spending the night at a hotel on or near Heathrow like the Radisson Blue. Minerva, of course, just said that we ought to just disapparate to the Cauldron.

For once, I agreed with her. Sally stared at me as though I were a traitor to the cause of Muggle transportation. She gave in. We found a hallway going back to some loos. We walked in until we were out of sight – mostly. Minerva just grabbed our hands without warning, and we found ourselves outside the Cauldron feeling like we had a class A hangover. Even Minerva was looking kind of woozy, but no one pressed the point about the superiority of Muggle transportation.

She continued to hold our hands. I opened the door, and we

struggled into the Cauldron. Inside, we found that there was only one old wizard at the bar, firmly placed in his cups.

I took the initiative. "Tom, we'd like two rooms for the night. We don't want to be disturbed before lunch."

He nodded wisely and said, "I've got two adjoining rooms." He pulled two keys from behind the bar and said, "Don't worry about rates. We'll settle up at lunch."

I nodded gratefully, and we headed upstairs. Somehow we got into the room and into bed without our clothes on.

I didn't sleep until lunch but it wasn't much shy of 11 AM that I woke. I reached over for Minerva but found that her side of the bed was empty. I guessed that she was showering.

Indeed as I was still rubbing the sleep out of my eyes, she entered the room wearing a robe with her hair bound up in a towel. She came over to the bed and sat on the edge of it. She unwrapped her hair and began to towel it dry. Some water landed on my face. "Hey, watch how you dry that lovely hair. I won't need to go to the bath to shower."

She smiled and said, "I'll bet I know a way that you can get wet and you won't complain." She demonstrated. I then went to the bath and showered. Even with my patented 5 minute shower, we were lucky to get down to the dining hall by noon. There was a large crowd, but apparently, Sally had reserved a table for us. She was sitting at it, drinking coffee.

She commented, "I've been waiting here for ages. And I bet you two weren't even asleep for the last two hours."

There was nothing that we could say. However, once lunch started the two ladies did have a lot to say. They wanted to go to Madame Malkins to shop for clothes.

I couldn't resist the temptation to kid them a bit. "You ladies are never satisfied. You just bought a whole new wardrobe appropriate for the coming months of summer and still you want to shop."

Minerva said, "Considering the loving-kindness that I've been showing you lately, you should be overjoyed to allow us a little fun together."

I couldn't really argue with that so I said, "When you're right, you're right. You're welcome to shop. As a matter of fact, I should really go into Gringgotts to check in. I'll catch up with you at Madame Malkins."

Then an afterthought occurred to me, "I understand why Minerva wants to shop there. But why do you, Sally."

She rolled her eyes. "Let me count the reason. #1, I work in a Wizard school. I should be dressed appropriately. #2, I have a wizard boy-friend. I want to please him. #3, I work for a stylish witch. I don't want to be out-dressed by her. Do you need more?"

"No, no. Enjoy yourselves. Just get me into Diagon Alley, and I'll be happy."

They did. I went directly to Gringotts. They went farther in toward Madame Malkins. I entered the Gringotts lobby and was practically run down by a goblin whom I'd never met. He squeeked, "Oh, Mr. Wendt. You are Mr. Wendt, aren't you?"

I reluctantly admitted to the fact. It seemed like being greeted this way was not a propitious happening, but I stood my ground. "Yes, I am."

"We've been trying to find you for weeks." He certainly seemed earnest.

I admitted that I'd been hard to find for a couple of weeks. He rushed on, "Oh, would you please, please come to speak with the president of the bank?"

I asked what the problem was. The goblin shuffled his feet and admitted that he didn't know. "They don't trust me with such things. It's way above my pay grade."

I then asked him what his name was.

"It's Grobonski, sir."

"Very well, Grobonski, I'm willing to see the bank president, but I have to leave by 2:30 PM."

The idea seemed to shock him. His squeak became even more high-pitched and he asked, "When will you be back?"

I shrugged, "I don't' know."

I don't know what his response was. His voice had reached the ultrasound range. If I had a dog around, he might have been able to tell me, but sadly, there were none about.

Grobowski composed himself enough that his voice re-entered my hearing range. "Please, have a seat here. Let me consult with the higher-ups." He started to run off and then turned back, "Would you like something to drink or eat. Water. Butter Beer. We can have a fruit tray sent out. Maybe biscuits?"

"No, I'm fine."

"Are you sure?"

"Yes, go. Go."

I sat in the waiting area for about ten minutes. At the end of that, Grobowski returned and took my arm in his excitement. "Come, come. The Bank President has a half an hour he can give you, but it has to be right now."

I acquiesced, and Grobowski led me back into the interior of the bank. I'd been there a number of times, but never at a run before. We rounded a couple of corners in the corridors and arrived at the impressive entrance to the Board Room. I went in and the receptionist didn't waste time. "You may go in immediately." I recognized the President, Glazblatt, immediately as well.

"It's good to see Glazblatt. I hear that you're somewhat anxious to see me."

"Anxious. I wish that it were only anxiety. We have a major problem that affects the entire bank. I want to consult with you about it."

"OK. But I'll have to charge my customary rates for consulting."

Glazblatt nodded, "I thought so. You've never gotten over being ousted from the Board of Directors when Riddle was in power."

"Oh, I don't hold grudges. I know that you had to do it when Riddle was in power, and I've been too busy to really be an effective Director."

Glazblatt slyly asked, "Well, at least you're back as a Director now. That report you gave at the last Board meeting was very helpful"

I was dismayed, "I may decide to resign! I wasn't a Director for long that first time, but I now know the kind of workload you put on the Directors. I don't have time for it – especially now."

"We'll pay you handsomely." Of course, a Goblin's idea of handsome pay was not necessarily mine.

"You just want my ideas on the cheap."

Glazblatt frowned, "All right. We'll pay you a reasonable amount for your ideas, and if you really don't want to continue as Director, you don't have to be a Director."

I nodded. "I won't work for free."

Glazblatt was not happy but he wasn't disconsolate. "Of course, of course. What is it, 2% of the gross profits from any idea that we implement."

I smiled. Even in disaster the Goblins are penny-pinchers. "I think it was more like 2.7%."

He smiled. "Yes, yes. Your standard fee. Highway robbery."

I could tell that he was getting back into spirits. If he were really desperate, he'd never argue over fee. But I knew he enjoyed this repartee, so I said, "It's a bargain. If you don't make money, I don't get paid a thin knut, and if you make money from the idea, why do you care if I get a decent return on my efforts."

"Yes, yes. Let me explain. The last quarter we've noticed that our vault rental revenue has been going down. It's fallen disastrously this quarter. We're in desperate straits."

81

I listened and asked, "Why is the revenue going down?"

"Well, it started when people downsized their vaults. Not a lot at first, but as time went on, more and more were doing it. Then people started completely closing out their vaults. They took their gold and went elsewhere!"

I understood his consternation, but only calm analysis would help. So I asked the obvious question, "Did you ask anyone why they closed their vaults?"

Glazblatt wailed, "Of course, we did! And do you know what they said!"

"No, what did they say?"

Glazblatt's look of desperation relaxed some. "Well, they all said something that was a variation on one idea. The Muggle banks offer what they call 'interest' as an inducement to use their vaults. We did research. Interest is a payment that the Muggle banks pay to the owner of the vault to leave their money with them! That's the opposite of our business model. We collect a fee each month to store people's valuables. Muggle banks PAY a fee to store people's valuables! How can we ever compete with that?"

"I have a question. Do Muggle banks accept galleons these days?"

Glazblatt wailed, "That's the worst part. They use our services to convert their galleons into pounds and then put them in Muggle banks!"

I had some trouble keeping the laughter back,but I managed it, "OK. There's two key points.

"First, the Muggle banks have a business model that is the same as yours for part of their business. They rent what they call 'safety deposit boxes'. These are just the same as your 'vaults.' And you actually have an advantage in that business. Your vaults are much larger than safety deposit boxes.

"Second, the thing that Muggle banks have that you don't – interest bearing accounts—is strictly for money. Muggle banks borrow money from their customers and pay for the right to use that money. Their trick is being sure to pay less interest than the amount that they make from using their customers' money.

"Now, I know that Gringotts invests in money-making projects. So, you know how to make money with money. But you only use the bank's money."

Glazblatt nodded. He was beginning to see the point. As a matter of fact, he saw it very well. "So, we can make even more money by using our customer's money and paying them interest."

"Sure. And you have an advantage there over Muggle banks too."

Glazblatt was puzzled and was about to ask the obvious question, but I anticipated him. "Your advantage is that most of your customers would still want to keep their non-money valuables in your vaults. So, would you want to do business with two different banks?"

Glazblatt shook his head, "Of course, not. Unless one bank paid interest, and the other didn't." Then his eyes lit up, and he repeated, "And the other didn't."

"Exactly."

Glazblatt smiled broadly and beamed, "You'll get your usual commission, of course."

I nodded meaningfully, "Of course."

Glazblatt had an afterthought. "Is there anything we can do for you?" The last words were said hesitantly, as though he were afraid that there might just be some favor he could do for me.

I started to say "no" and then had a second thought. "Maybe. I'm looking for someone who recently cashed quite a lot of US Treasury bills. Do you know what I'm talking about?"

Glazblatt waived his hand negligently, "Of course, I know T-bills. As a matter of fact . . ." He stopped, and his face took on that too, too casual appearance that alerts people familiar with Goblins that they should be alert for traps. He went on, "As a matter of fact, we cashed a rather large number of high denomination T-bills very recently."

He went on oh so carefully, "Of course, I really couldn't discuss the transaction with someone off the street."

I rolled my eyes, "Off the street! You know me and have done business with me. You know very well that I can be trusted with confidential matters. Off the street, indeed!"

He nodded sympathetically, "Oh, I really would like to help you, but what would the investors think if we shared that sort of information with anyone who wasn't a bank employee or better still . . . " Here he paused for emphasis. "A bank director?"

I had to admire him. He wanted me to promise to stay on as a director, and he'd found a way to bribe me. "All I promise is a single term, and it's already started."

Glazblatt nodded enthusiastically. I guess I didn't drive as hard a bargain as I could have. Oh, well, it could have been worse. He reached his hand across the desk, almost leaping over it. We shook. I'd never really attended more than a single meeting the last time I'd been on the board. I guess I owed them to complete that term.

But now, I would get my part of the bargain. "OK, Glazblatt, who's been redeeming T-bills in large quantities lately."

Glazblatt didn't seem to signal in any way, but the receptionist entered. Glazblatt told her to send for Rakastava. A few minutes later, the Goblin entered.

She, for it was a female, had a briefcase. Glazblatt asked her to sit and he asked the question, "There have been some transactions involving T-bills lately. Who initiated them?"

She looked from one to the other of us. She seemed disturbed and stated the cause, "Sir, I didn't think we shared bank business with *Outsiders*." She was staring straight at me.

Glazblatt wasn't disturbed. He simply said, "There aren't any outsiders here. Allow me to introduce the latest member of the Board of Directors."

Her stare was no less direct, but she seemed to relax after a moment. "Then, you must be Professor Wendt of Hogwarts?"

I admitted it.

She nodded and said, "Congratulations. You are the only non-Goblin member of the board. Perhaps you won't be too disturbing to work with."

Glazblatt got up and said, "I've got a lunch appointment that I can't break. I'm sure that Rakastava can fulfill all your needs."

I extended my hand and we shook. She held my hand a bit longer than necessary. "Perhaps, we should have dinner sometime."

I glanced at my watch and was reminded how little time I had left. "Sometime, but not today. I have appointments that won't wait."

Was I mistaken that she sighed. It was brief, and it was followed immediately by a very business-like recitation of the list of transactions. There was only one that I was interested in – the first.

The list was headed by the Sept XC Suisse. They had transacted 100 of the bearer bonds for far more than nearly ten million pounds. I whistled. "Do you usually carry ten million pounds that you can afford to let go of at short notice?"

She smiled coyly, "Do you find such abandon with funds stimulating?"

"I find it astounding for a conservative establishment like Gringotts."

She stretched her arms and hugged herself. "To put Sept XC in our debt by that little gesture is a very worthwhile investment." She paused and added, "Like putting you in our debt by giving you this information."

I nodded. I was beginning to wonder if I'd made such a good deal after all, but I was stuck with it. "Well, thanks for the information. I'm sure I've made myself very indebted to you."

She walked around the desk and sat on its edge, "You really should make time for dinner with me. You will not regret it." As she said that, she leaned forward and touched my arm negligently.

I rose quickly, thinking, "Is she hitting on me!" I backed toward the door and repeated, "I really have an appointment that I can't miss."

She walked with me to the door. "I'll see you out. The passages here can be confusing."

"I've been here quite a lot. I don't worry about finding my way out."

She came closer, put her hand on my arm again, and said, "It's no trouble. I'll enjoy the walk – with you."

I stepped as briskly as I could but Rakastava easily kept pace and slightly increased the pressure on my arm. "We have quite a nice food service here. We could stop at my office and order something. . ." She trailed off.

I made the last turn that took me into the corridor that went to the Main Lobby. I was doing an Olympic grade walk at that point. When I had just about reached the door, her hand's grasp tightened on my arm, and she pulled me around to face her. Her long mane flowed around her shoulder. She looked up to me and said, "You must really let me properly express my appreciation of you before you go."

I just grimaced and said, "No, I don't." I turned, opened the door and strode out into the open air of the lobby. When I did, I saw the face that I know best. She was half-way across the lobby, but her smile was no more heart-felt than mine. I strode quickly to her, and we both said by way of greeting, "Let's get out of here!"

Outside, she said that we needed to get over to Malkin's in a hurry. We did, and we found Sally finishing a purchase. She said, "You two are always keeping me waiting. How could you have found someplace to . . . uh . . . well, you know."

I shook my head, "We have to get to Heathrow. Let's get out where we can catch the Tube."

Minerva frowned at me. I answered the frown, "Don't frown at me. There's no reason not to take the Tube." She still frowned. "OK. OK. We'll go by disapparation."

Sally laughed and said, "It's not that bad – really!"

"Yes, easy for you to say. You don't have to do it every day of your life and twice on holidays."

She just kept laughing.

We did leave Diagon Alley and even the Cauldron. Of course, Tom was unhappy that we'd not had lunch at his establishment. We couldn't help it. We had a plane to catch.

As we stood outside the Cauldron, Minerva took each of our hands and we ended up in a deserted hallway at Heathrow. Check-in and security were not awful, and we found we had a little time for a meal.

Minerva had complained about airport fast food so many times that we had developed acronyms so that she could complain quickly about whatever was bothering her at the moment. As we sat outside a Chili's restaurant, she said, "F.F."

Sally stared at her and said, "Thanks!"

Minerva was confused and asked, "What was that for?"

"You told me we were BFF didn't you?"

Minerva shook her head, "No. I said FF, and that was for Wendt."

Sally turned a little red-faced and said, "OH." Followed by "What is FF?"

I answered, "That's Minerva's acronym for Fast Food. She has a whole lot of them. That way she can complain without bothering anyone but me."

Sally nodded, but Minerva wasn't through with it, "What does this Buff mean? No, wait! I don't think I want to know."

Sally laughed and said, "It isn't bad. Quite the opposite. B. F. F." she made a point of pronouncing clearly and separately, "means Best Female Friend or sometimes Best Friend Forever."

Minerva smiled and seemed to contemplate it a moment. "Good. Yes, we should be BFF. . . " She hesitated again as she took a bite of taco and then said, "There was a time when I was afraid that you were Wendt's BFF."

Sally nodded, "There was a time when I kind of wanted to be his BFF."

I had had enough of this conversation. "Look, you two. We've got to postpone the mutual admiration society – they're about to call our flight."

We arrived at the terminal in time to board with our fellow first class passengers. It was late afternoon. The three of us were all seated in the same row. Minerva and I were on the right side of the plane and Sally on the left. Sally had broken tradition and insisted on the window seat on her side. That meant that she and Minerva couldn't talk freely, there being a seat and the aisle between them.

Minerva commented to me, "Why in the world would Sally want that beastly window seat – especially when she could talk with me across the aisle?"

I answered, "Just wait until we get into the air and you'll see."

Minerva continued to grumble. "Bloody overcast drizzly day. I don't see what there is to see out that little window."

"Just wait."

My case was not helped by the long wait in the queue to get to the takeoff runway. We finally arrived and took off. The drizzle had been beading on the outside window, slowly rolling down the window and out of sight. Now, as we accelerated, the drops streamed horizontally across the window and then disappeared completely.

It took us a couple of minutes to climb through the clouds, and then we broke through and could see the cloud-tops through the window. I took Minerva's chin in my right hand and slowly turned it. She mis-interpreted my intentions and planted a joyous kiss on my lips and moved on to my tongue.

When we broke, I said, "That wasn't quite what I had in mind, but it will do nicely. I wanted you to see this." I turned to the window and leaned back into my seat as much as I could so that she could see it. She gasped. She has never admitted it, but it was a real gasp of amazed rapture.

It was a sight to gasp at. The late, late afternoon sunlight filled with lots of red, illuminated the cloud-tops turning them to blood. The backs of the clouds were a dark contrast to the golden light everywhere. She actually asked to trade places. I did happily. One does not withhold a glimpse of heaven from those who have never seen it.

After we changed places, I said, "This is what the artists call the golden hour – the last hour before sunset. It's filled with an amazing golden sunlight that you'll never forget. It's the hour that painters and photographers love more than any other."

She didn't say a word. Who would? With such beauty, constantly changing as our plane rushed through the sky we were struck dumb with awe.

After quite a while, when the sun had set completel,y and the sky was mostly dark, the moon rose behind our plane and flooded the cloud-filled night with silver light that had it's own incomparable beauty.

The pilot's announcement that we were approaching Washington National airport was greeted by Minerva with a sigh of regret. "That was never an hour. We barely got in the air and now we're having to land."

I smiled and looked up from my Scientific American. "I'm afraid you're right. That was almost five hours."

She sniffed and said, "No way that was five hours."

I shrugged and pointed at my watch. She just sniffed again.

I amplified, "Well, it shows you the paradoxes of travel. The Golden Hour was stretched out quite a bit by the fact that we were traveling west nearly as fast as the sun. Then the Silver Hour, when the light of the moon is most wonderful, got stretched out as well."

Washington in the Spring

We landed, and Minerva was properly impressed by downtown Washington, DC at night. She commented, "I'm ready for bed. It's got to be past midnight.

Sally just shook her head. "No. It's not even midnight in London. Here, it's just a little past 7 PM."

"That doesn't matter. My body says it's time for bed, and I'm going to bed!"

Silently, I echoed her determination. We picked up our bags and went through customs. I actually recognized the customs agent that I had had before. He glanced at my passport and said, "Yes, Mr. Wendt. I thought I recognized you.

"Let's see, you've been to Lebanon. Business or pleasure?"

"Strictly pleasure. We thought to bring back some gold, but we couldn't find anything that we really liked."

He smiled, "You mean nothing the wife had a fancy for?"

I smiled too, "If the wife ain't happy . . . "

"Ain't nobody happy." He finished the aphorism for me. He glanced at the visas on my passport. "You stayed overnight in England I see."

I nodded, "Yes, there's a nice little inn there in downtown London that we both like a lot. We could have gone straight on to Washington, but we decided to have a fun last evening of the trip."

He stamped the passport, and I went on out of the secured area with my wife and Sally. Before we reached the outside of the airport, a man carrying a placard with the word, "WENDT" printed boldly approached us.

He reached us and said, "Come with me."

Minerva grumbled in my ear. "I wanted to disapparate us directly to the hotel, but NO. I was being lazy."

There was a Hummer waiting in the pickup lane. Before our escort said anything, I knew it was for us. So, I picked up the pace and Minerva, who is always game for a brisk walk, did so too.

Our escort started to call out to us to wait, but when he saw where we were going, he stopped the shout mid-word.

He arrived simultaneously with us and opened the door for us. When we were all inside, I asked, "Where are we going?" I expected the Pentagon or maybe the FBI headquarters.

Instead, he said, "We're headed for Andrews."

Minerva asked, "I suppose that isn't a charming Bar-B-Que restaurant?"

He replied, "You suppose rightly. It's a US Air Force base."

He refused to make any other statement despite our most clever attempts to wheedle it out of him. At least it wasn't a long ride. We drove directly onto the tarmac. We found ourselves parked beside a hangar. Outside it was a C-130 transport.

I said to the occupants of the back seat, "I've got a bad feeling about this. I think we landed in First Class only to turn around and board another plane in No Class."

It turned out that I wasn't right. That is, that I wasn't wholly right. Ballard and Harris were waiting for us. Harris shook hands with us and promptly said, "Sorry, but you're turning around directly to get on this plane and head for the Middle East."

Minerva was on the point of whining, but I interrupted her to say, "Don't you want to hear what we found out, before we go traipsing around the world?"

Ballard said, "I suppose I ought to. Can you tell me in five minutes or less?"

"Yes. We found out what happened with the gold that Minns stole."

"OK. You've got 4 minutes. What happened with it? We were pretty sure that Baghdadi bought it. Do you know anything else?"

I smiled. I had a boatload of useful information. "Yes, Baghdadi bought it. He also tried to shortchange Minns."

Ballard interrupted, "So, it was Minns."

"Yes, it was Minns who actually transacted the deal, but we're not sure if he was acting alone or had any of the other four or, indeed, others involved.

"For my money, I think that he was strictly working alone."

Harris objected. "But, it looks like there was a regular battle that took place at ISIS's hiding place."

I laughed. "Believe me; what we found out from Baghdadi convinces me that he could have pulled it off by himself. He even delivered it by himself."

Sally added, "And when Baghdadi tried stiffing him, Minns single-handed forced them to stand by the original deal."

Ballard smiled. "Good work. Is that all?"

"No. Minns got Treasury notes for the gold."

Harris was about to curse, but he caught himself. "In a way, they're harder to trace than currency. Some banks are happy to sit on them and give unrecorded currency in exchange. Bad luck."

Ballard noticed my smile, "You look like the Cheshire cat. What more do you know?"

No one else knew what I was about to say, so my companions were definitely surprised when I said, "I know what bank got the T-bills."

Harris was getting impatient, "Who, then?"

"The Sept XC Suisse."

I was disappointed at Harris's lack of reaction. "Well, it's something. We'll go to work on them and see if we can find anything out."

That set Ballard to thinking. "Well, let's see. What are we going to do?"

After a minute, he said, "I guess we're going to have to break you apart. Wendts you get to go where we originally intended. Harker, you get to work with Harris and Pearson on the Swiss bank."

Sally's jaw dropped and she asked, "Did you say, Pearson?"

Harris's face went through several expressions that included surprise, suspicion, and even amusement. "Do you know a Pearson?"

Sally asked, "Is his name Phil?"

Harris's face went back to suspicion, "Yes? Do you know Phil Pearson?"

Her smile had been growing and now turned radiant, "If he's the Pearson that I know, yes! Where did you get him?"

Harris frowned, "We didn't 'get' him. He was dropped on us by an obscure organization that seems to be an NGO that I've never heard of. Somehow they found out about this operation, and we have to accept their help."

Sally was laughing now, "I'll bet that organization is the Aurors."

Harris's face now turned to further consternation, "I suppose I have to admit that it is the Aurors – whatever they are."

Minerva returned to practicalities and asked, "I'll trade you. Tell me what an NGO is and I'll tell you what the Aurors are. Also, where

91

did you originally intend us to go?"

He waved the questions away with a hand gesture. "You're going with me. No time to waste. Come on."

Minerva looked at me as though I should know what he was talking about. I just shrugged back. We both had to trot to keep up with him as he ran to the C-130 that was parked near the hangar.

The tail section was open and a ramp led up into the plane. There were a lot of packing crates tied down and a narrow walkway up toward the front of the plane. He ran up the walkway and we followed. When we got to the front of the plane, we found several jump seats along the inner bulkhead of the plane. He pointed at them and said, "Strap yourselves in. We'll be in the air in a couple of minutes and I'll be back to let you know where we're going."

Minerva sneered and simply said, "M.T." I knew that was short for Muggle Transportation.

I said, "Well, I can answer the question about NGO's, anyway. That is an acronym for Non-Governmental Organization. Examples would be Doctors Without Borders—a volunteer organization. They have doctors who treat people who don't have access to medical care, especially in war-torn areas."

Minerva nodded and said, "We have something like that—Healers who volunteer to treat poor witches and wizards."

The tail of the plane was closed up rapidly, and we taxied out to a runway. We were apparently cleared for takeoff because the plane wheeled around when it reached the end of the runway. The pilot simply powered up the engines and we were racing down the runway. We were quickly in the air.

Minerva frowned at me and asked, "I didn't catch where we were going."

I shrugged, "I don't know anything more than you do."

We appeared to reach cruising altitude, and shortly after that, Ballard came back into the cargo hold. He sat and buckled himself in. Over the drone of the motors, he explained what we were doing.

"We found the bomb-maker. He's in North-west Iraq. Or, I should say that he was there. We kidnapped him, and we'll be seeing him shortly. You'll get another opportunity to exercise your interrogation skills."

He then asked for details on our interrogation of Baghdadi. Minerva gave a moving account of what had happened.

Ballard frowned and said, "You really think that he did the robbery by himself? Just loading a truck with half a billion dollars worth of gold would be a job for a crew with a fork-lift. Had he already killed the guards or had he forced them to help him in some way?"

Minerva's voice shuddered a little as she said, "I think it was a one man job."

Ballard leaned back and closed his eyes for a moment. "One half billion dollars of gold would weigh a minimum of twenty tons – probably more. Are you telling me that he loaded it by himself?"

Minerva didn't say anything. Ballard went on. "What about how he crossed more than 300 miles of battleground in that truck! How many checkpoints did he have to go through?"

This she had an answer for. "How many guards did Minns evade when he escaped from the VA?"

Ballard was thinking about that when Minerva raised another point. "When did he learn to speak idiomatic Arabic?"

Ballard was drawn out from his reverie, "What do you mean?"

"I mean, did he study languages while he was at the VA hospital or in the army?"

Ballard concentrated for a couple of minutes, "No. I'm sure he didn't study languages there. I can't quite remember from his file if he had any languages before he went into the hospital." He thought some more.

I suggested, "He served a couple of tours of duty in Afghanistan and Iraq. Is it possible that he picked up good Arabic that way?"

He thought some more. "I think that most service people pick up some of the native language but usually nothing more than, say, pidgin Arabic."

Minerva repeated, "Baghdadi said that he spoke fluent Arabic. I got the impression that it wasn't pure school Arabic either. It was idiomatic Arabic."

Ballard said, "Just one more inscrutable feature of Minns. Still, it's hard to believe that he discovered where the gold was, waltzed into the camp, and waltzed out with it all by his lonesome."

I brought them back to the here and now, "By the way, just where are we going?"

Ballard responded, "Yemen. We have friendly relations with them. That's where we frequently take people to be interrogated,"

□

It was a long flight. We re-fueled in flight. That rather gave Minerva a start when the plane showed up just off our wing. I was napping but she wasn't. She pulled urgently on my sleeve and exclaimed, "Isn't that

93

plane too close to us!"

I looked over and agreed. I was about to ask Ballard about it when I noticed that there was a hose being reeled out from the tail of the airplane. I answered her, "That's an airplane that's going to re-fuel this one while we're still in the air."

She stared at me a minute then said, "You're kidding of course."

I shook my head.

"But isn't that dangerous?"

"I shrugged. Yes. But they do that fairly frequently."

"None of the airplanes I've ridden on have done that."

I smiled, "They were not military."

She contemplated a moment. "Uncomfortable, dangerous, boring."

I laughed, "Yes. All the best features of Wizard travel."

She snorted, and we both tried to catch some sleep. At that point we'd been flying for a dozen hours with that little break in Washington.

I was awakened by a bump and for a moment was not sure where I was. Minerva mumbled something like, "This is the lumpiest chair I've ever sat in." Then we were both awake.

Ballard said, "OK. We just landed in Yemen. Rise and shine. It's noonish but no lunch until we reach our destination."

I grumbled, "I thought Yemen was our destination."

We got up, dragged our bags with us, and found a helicopter waiting for us, rotors spinning. We boarded. There was a soldier in the back with us who helped us with seatbelts and headphones. He announced through the headphones, "Welcome to Air Yemen. We know that you don't have to spend your transportation dollars with us so we want to make the flight as quick as we can.

"Make sure your seatbelts are securely fastened. Please look around you and notice the two emergency exits to your right and left." He made an exaggerated motion, pointing at the doors next to us. "We've conveniently left these doors open in case it's necessary to rapidly exit from the cabin such as in the fairly likely possibility that we strike a foreign object such as a surface to air missile. If you're sitting next to one of these emergency exits, and you don't want to jump out in case of emergency, please trade places with someone who does.

"Our flight time today will be approximately 45 minutes to our undisclosed destination where the weather is a balmy 93, and the skies are always clear.

"On behalf of our captain, Major Steinbrecher, let me wish you a pleasant flight."

Shortly before the speech ended we took off. Minerva took my arm and dug her fingernails into it. I gently removed them from my forearm and patted her hand. "This won't last forever."

We flew close to ground level, and I judged over a hundred miles per hour. We crossed mountain ridges and some desert before reaching our destination. It was a camp with several permanent buildings and some large tents. There was a short airstrip and a hangar. We touched down near the hangar.

Our host bid us farewell. "We hope you all will fly with us again soon."

Minerva commented, "It can't be soon enough for me."

The air was very dry, heat waves shimmered in the distance and a Hummer drove up to us. An officer got out and welcomed us. We all got into the Hummer, and we drove off down the dirt track that ran alongside the buildings.

"I'm Colonel Jacobsen. I'm in charge of this facility. It's a detention center for high-value prisoners who we figure have information that's worth the time and effort to extract.' He then named us, showing that he knew us already.

"They tell me that we have common interests."

Ballard answered, "Yes, we need information too. I understand that you captured the bomb-maker."

The Colonel smiled like the crocodile who has just seen some fresh meat. 'Yes. He's a tough sonofabitch." It was all said as a single word. I reflected that he seemed like a tough sonofabitch himself. "So far, he's not had much to say about his wartime occupation.

"Let me be honest with you. The only reason you're here is that somebody pretty far up thinks that you guys are wizards at interrogation. I hope you are."

No one said anything. That was just as well because we had just pulled up at a building that was unlabeled, but somehow I knew was where the interrogation went on.

The Colonel led us inside and introduced us to a lieutenant and a corporal. The corporal was the translator, and the lieutenant was the brains of the operation. The lieutenant was named Soames, and the corporal was Capella.

The Colonel introduced us and told the lieutenant that he was responsible for our comfort and that we were responsible for interrogation.

Soames acknowledged the assignment and led us to an office. There were several computers and a couple of other soldiers who were never introduced to us. Soames did all the speaking, "Let's get off on the right foot. I'm in charge of interrogation of this prisoner, and all

95

your questions get approved by me first. Capella does the translating, but he doesn't translate for you until I say so. All interrogation techniques have to be approved by me before being used. We've heard of the Geneva conventions here, but our hearing isn't perfect."

His manner softened somewhat, and he asked if we'd eaten recently.

Minerva was blunt, "Not in the last 12 hours."

Soames actually smiled and said, "Well, we can do something about that anyway."

He led us to the mess area. There was a kitchen, some tables and chairs, a TV mounted high up on a wall, and not much else. Soames said, "I'm pretty sure that there's some leftovers in the refer." He led us into the kitchen. A cook was watching a pot boil. The cook said, "You're welcome to anything you can find in the refer. Are you going to introduce me to our guests?"

Soames simply said, "No."

The cook just nodded.

We scrounged and found some rice and chicken casserole, a bowl of fruit salad and ingredients. There was an ice machine in the corner and a stack of water bottle cases in a different corner.

We managed to put together a decent meal – certainly not up to Hogwarts standard but not bad. As Minerva, Ballard, and I ate, Soames went on about the rules of engagement with the prisoner. "We'll not tell you his name. You have to sign an NDA about the techniques we use here. Is that clear?"

Minerva asked, "NDA?"

Soames shook his head and asked, "You guys are for real? You've done interrogations before?"

I said, "We have unorthodox techniques, but they are effective."

Minerva repeated, "NDA?" with more insistence.

Ballard said, "Non-Disclosure Agreement. You agree not to tell anyone what happened."

She said, "Why would I want to admit to anyone that I was involved with this?"

Soames went back to the question of techniques, "What technique do you want to use with the prisoner?"

I answered, "We need to know more about the prisoner before we decide."

Soames asked, "Like?"

Minerva asked, "Does he understand English?"

Soames looked over at Capella and asked, "What would you say?"

Capella was tall, thin, almost wiry. He had wavy short hair and had not said anything so far. Now, he scratched his right ear and said, "I don't think he has any English. I tested him with a poor translation of something he had said. He didn't blink an eye."

Minerva looked at me and said, "Let's take a pleasant little walk."

Soames said, "I'm not sure that I want you wandering around here unescorted. It's pretty dangerous."

I said, "That's the price of playing. We have to be allowed to do these little consultations in private from time to time."

Soames thought a minute and said, "Well, don't go out of sight of this building."

We walked outside, and I immediately regretted my suggestion. It was hot, the sun was a palpable force, seeming to attack us. So, I was in a hurry to get back in the shade, "What is it?"

"I don't think I can use the Imperious Curse if he can't understand my commands to him."

"But don't you have control without words?"

"I have control, but I can only get him to do something if he can understand my commands."

I thought on a few seconds and said, "The Veritas Serum?"

She nodded.

"Then, let's get back in."

The little group was as we left them.

Ballard asked, "That was fast. What's the result?"

Minerva said, "We need to get a small dose of a drug that I brought along into him. It can be mixed with water. It's tasteless, odorless, and has no color. Can we manage that?"

Soames smiled. "Not legal."

Ballard asked, "But can we do it?"

Soames answered, "Of course."

I asked, "When can we start?"

Soames thought a minute. Then he said, "I think we need to give him the rest of the day to recover." With that he rose and left the room. He turned at the door and said, "Corporal, see that the Wendt's have a room. I'll be back for more discussion over evening mess." With that he exited.

Capella nodded, "Yes, he needs to recover from the latest enhanced interrogation session. I hope your techniques are more effective than ours."

With that encouraging note, he turned to the question of our billeting. He took us to a barracks and showed us a room that had a dresser, a bed, a chair, and a desk. There was an overhead light fixture and a reading lamp on the table. We set our luggage down, and

Minerva immediately got most of her clothes and laid them out on the bed.

I asked, "Do you think we'll be here long enough to justify unpacking."

She didn't look up as she re-folded and put clothes away in the dresser. "I hope not." We then napped until dinner. And when I say "napped", I don't mean that we made love. I think that neither of us wanted to make this place seem any more normal and tolerable than it already did.

Dinner was better but not up to the standards of anywhere we'd been since this ordeal started. There was discussion of the plan for the next day. We'd get up for breakfast and prepare for the interrogation that would start at ten.

Minerva asked how we'd get the victim to drink our concoction just before interrogation. As she spoke she noticed the pile of cases of bottled water and she asked, 'Do you have a small syringe?"

Soames smiled. "Sure. That's the most sensible way. Just give him an injection."

Minerva shook her head violently, "No. No. That just won't do. It won't work unless he drinks it."

Soames was becoming short-tempered and asked, "Why in Hell does it matter?"

Minerva was not one to be intimidated, "Because you can inject him until Hell freezes over, but our potion will not work unless it goes through the stomach." She could see that he was about to object and immediately added, "I don't know why it needs to be digested, it just does. I won't have you wasting any of my precious potion by injecting it in him!"

That pretty much closed off conversation for the rest of the meal. There was some discussion of the Cub's chances for the pennant this year, but that talk pretty much ended when Minerva asked what cub we were talking about.

□□

The next day after a rousing breakfast of burned eggs and cold oatmeal, we were about to leave for the interrogation building. Minerva insisted on having the syringe. Soames opened his brief case, drew it out, and placed it on a napkin on the table.

Minerva took the syringe and asked for several bottles of water. Capella got up, went into the kitchen and brought back a 6-pack of plastic water bottles. Minerva smiled approvingly and said, "Pay special attention to which one of these I inject with my potion."

She opened her purse and pulled out a small vial. Then she opened it and used the syringe to withdraw a small amount. Then she injected it through the base of the bottle. She then handed it to Capella and said, "We won't come into the Interrogation Room until our man is there. Wendt here will be carrying the water. As he comes in, he'll toss a bottle to everyone in the room. He'll take great care that our victim gets the one that I've just injected, won't you dear?" She patted my arm as she said that.

"You'd better believe it." I said.

She went on, "Everyone will open and start drinking immediately. Any questions?"

Ballard asked, "What if he doesn't drink?"

Soames said, "It's hot here. People get de-hydrated quickly. He'll drink before the mornings out. We'll just do normal interrogation until he does."

So that was the plan. At 9:45, Ballard, Minerva, an escort, and I arrived at the interrogation building. They had apparently started the process already, because we were ushered immediately in, and the subject was standing on one foot in a corner while Soames was asking questions, and Capella was translating.

I started breaking off bottles and tossing them to people as they became aware of us. The prisoner watched the whole time. He was not the first or last to whom I tossed a water bottle. Everyone opened and took a drink – except the prisoner. He held it, apparently afraid to put it down. Maybe he thought that it was another subtle torture – forcing him to hold a bottle of water while he was thirsty.

The questions went on, and the answers that weren't answers kept on as well. Eventually, he looked around and asked a question himself. The translation was, "May I drink?"

Soames took a couple of minutes in elaborate thought. Then he said, "Yes."

The prisoner opened the bottle and took a small sip. He washed it around in his mouth and spit it out. I began to wonder if we would have to force him to drink it. The questioning resumed and then he took a small sip.

Soames continued the questioning, "Where did you assemble bombs?"

The translator said, "I work everywhere."

The questions continued for a few minutes. They were mostly ones that we had heard before. Then, something strange happened. The prisoner opened the bottle and took a long drink as though he were thirsty. A few minutes later, he stopped standing on one foot.

Soames started to say something, but Minerva snapped, "This is it. Shut up. Tell him to come to the table and sit."

Capella translated, and someone got a chair to put at the table where we were sitting. The prisoner walked almost indolently over to the empty chair and sat down. He said nothing.

Minerva asked, "You made the bombs with shrapnel?"

The translated answer was, "Yes."

"Where did you work?"

He named several towns that I didn't recognize but Soames smiled as they were named. He asked, "Did you work in Sinjar?"

The answer was a flat, "No."

Minerva asked an important question, "Do you understand English?"

He answered, "I know numbers and few words."

She nodded and asked her next question, "Where did the shrapnel that you used in most of your bombs come from?"

The answer was, "Iraq." Even I understood that.

"Where in Iraq?"

"I don't know how to tell you."

I looked over at Soames, "Do we have maps?"

The prisoner volunteered, "I know where gravel is on map."

Soames said, "I can do better than that." He got up and left the room. In a few minutes, he returned with a laptop. He said, "Have the prisoner look at the screen." There was a webpage with a Google map on it. He asked the prisoner, "Touch the place on the map where the gravel is."

The prisoner stared a minute and then put his finger on a spot on the map called Zakho.

Soames said, "Shit. Almost in Turkey." Then he zoomed into the map near Zakho and asked, "Point again?"

The prisoner just shook his head. Soames pulled out his service pistol but I said, "Wait. He's doing his best. I know." Then I turned to him and said, "Describe the place where the gravel is."

Then there was a lengthy discussion between the translator and the prisoner. There were questions and answers both ways. Finally, the translator said, "He says that the place is like a shallow bowl. The gravel is scattered all around and even outside the bowl, but there's less outside."

I was excited now, "Ask him how wide the bowl is."

"He says maybe 50 meters, maybe 100."

I hurried on, "How tall is the rim of the bowl."

Quite a bit of discussion followed and then the answer, "Maybe the height of a man."

Soames changed Google to show satellite views and drilled in much closer and asked, "Do you see anything on the screen like the bowl?"

The prisoner said something that I realized without translation was "no."

Soames scrolled the image and asked again. This process continued several times, and then the prisoner put his finger on the screen, covering what looked like a small crater.

Soames was about to stop when Ballard interrupted him. "Let's keep looking. That might not be the only spot that looks like the 'bowl'."

So, Soames and the prisoner kept going.

We passed noon and kept going. When we finally finished, we had identified seven crater-like areas that might be the objective. Soames asked which he thought it was.

The answer was, "Don't know."

Soames looked at Minerva searchingly. "Are you sure that he's telling the truth?"

She nodded.

⬚
⬚⬚

We were having a late lunch. Soames was reviewing where we stood. "So, what's our next step?"

There were shrugs around the table. However, I had an idea, "We know that what we're looking for looks like gravel, right?"

Someone said, "Sure. So?"

"Well, we can't tell from Google which ones have gravel and which don't. How about a closer view? Can we get a Predator to fly over those areas?"

Soames reflected, "It depends on how much pull you fellows have got. I'll get on the horn after lunch and see."

I told Ballard, "You'd better get on the horn too."

We didn't hear anything for a couple of hours, but Soames was all smiles at supper. "We've got a Predator for tomorrow afternoon. They'll fly over all seven areas. But I sure hope you guys find what you're looking for. They expect a lot from this."

Just after supper, a helicopter landed. What appeared to be another

101

prisoner disembarked and was led away to the cell block where they were kept. Soames commented as we watched the excitement, "He's a high-value prisoner."

Minerva asked, "What makes him a high value-prisoner?"

Soames just smiled, "I can't tell you, and you didn't hear that from me."

The next morning, we watched them set up for the Predator flight. It was coming from a base in Saudi Arabia. There was a laptop and a second screen – a very large monitor. Apparently, the predator wasn't operating because that screen was black. The laptop was working though. It had a window that showed a map and another window that showed something odd – a chair at a table. No one was sitting there.

Soames gave us a quick overview. "When it's flying, we'll get a view from the camera in the Predator on the big screen. The small screen has a view of the position of the Predator on the map and a view of the operator. We'll all have headsets so that we can talk to the operator while he's working – give him directions and so forth.

"We'll link in with the predator when control is ready to run our part of the operation. Right now they're predicting after 1PM local."

And that was it. Nothing was going to happen for a couple of hours, so we just sat around and drank hot tea. The chef had found us some tea bags and hot water was no problem. We tried to discuss what we'd do but frankly there was nothing much that we'd do except look for signs of gravel in the crater-like structures that we'd identified.

The time passed slowly until lunch except for one brief incident that shows just how boring life at this base was most of the time. A little before lunch, we heard a helicopter landing. Everyone jumped up to see who was on-board. It turned out to be a couple of guards and someone who might have been the head of ISIS or a local postman for all we knew.

However, Soames had better intel than we did. He told us, "That's a member of a guard unit that works directly for the inner circle. He's a high value prisoner. He might even be able to tell us where the members of the inner circle are right now. That would be big!"

And that was it until we had lunch – the second most exciting thing of the day so far.

After lunch we wandered up to the control computer that we'd seen in the morning. Everyone got headsets. After about 15 minutes when I'd given up hope that anything would happen, the headphones went live, the big monitor showed a scene that took us a minute or two to adjust to. When we had, it was easy to see that we had a birds-eye view of someplace in the wilderness. The map on the other screen showed a red arrow when the Predator was.

A voice came over the headphones, "Predator C control to Control Y. We're ready to go. Mark on the map where we're going."

Soames marked the first location with a stylus on a tablet that was next to the laptop.

The voice on the headphones acknowledged the location, and we could see the Predator symbol on the electronic map change course to head for it. The view of the ground moved faster.

Minerva clucked her tongue on the roof of her mouth and exclaimed, "I've got to hand it to you Muggles. When you're good, you're good!"

Soames asked, "Did you say 'buggles'?"

She just stared at him as though he'd just said something strange.

By this time the Predator had the first target in sight. The voice in the headphones said, "OK. I don't see anything in particular. What are we looking for?"

Ballard answered, "Gravel."

The voice in our headphones said, "No Sheeeit."

I agreed, "No shit."

The voice asked, "What special kind of gravel is that?"

Soames just said in a low voice, "That's above my pay grade and yours too."

The voice said, "Yes, sir." He circled the site for about a minute and said, "This is a dry hole."

Everyone agreed. Soames said, "Here's our next target." He drew a small circle on the screen.

The voice said, "On my way. By the way, what's everyone's name? I'm Corporal Brandeis."

We all gave our names and ranks where appropriate.

Brandeis asked, "Three civilians. Interesting."

Soames snapped, "Not of interest to you. As far as you know they're military."

By this time, we'd reached the next target. He immediately descended to a low level and we orbited the crater. Everyone agreed there was nothing.

On to the next target. It was a "dry hole" too. I was beginning to get worried but I didn't say anything. Nobody else did either.

The next one turned out to have some scattered deposits of what very well might be gravel. We all decided to mark it a positive and moved on.

The fifth and the six were duds and we all began to think that we might have it nailed. But we were wrong. The last site was strange. It appeared to have some gravel scattered around but not lots. There was a fair amount of discussion about whether it should be included as a positive. Brandeis cast the deciding vote. He was the closest thing we had to a photo analyst because he flew Predators nearly every day and stared through its camera for hours on end. He was a definite positive, so finally we went with his judgment.

Soames discontinued the session with Brandeis and told him that we'd probably not be using his services again. He slammed the laptop lid closed, and the secondary monitor went blank. He then said, "Well, what's the next step?"

I asked, "What do you recommend?"

He scratched the beginnings of stubble on his cheek. Then, he said, "Well, you could go looking at both sites. As far as we know, either or both could have real gravel. The Predator view just isn't good enough to tell. But, if it were me, I'd not go to any more locations than I absolutely had to. That's deep in ISIS territory. I wouldn't want to go to even one spot. Don't you people have any other way of picking between the two of those sites?"

We were all staring down at the floor. Not even Ballard had anything to say. Then an idea occurred to me, "Can we get a satellite view of those two locations?"

Soames said, "Well, it's theoretically possible, but you'd have to have pretty good pull to get them to re-target a surveillance satellite for you. I could ask."

Ballard said, "You do that and try to get them to give us the best view theoretically possible."

Soames agreed.

The rest of the day beat the morning for boredom. The next day looked to beat the previous until late afternoon when Soames came into the cafeteria where we'd taken to hanging around. He sat down with us.

Minerva asked, "Would you care for some cards? We could teach you Back-Alley Bridge."

He laughed. I think it was the first time I'd heard him do that. He shook his head and said, "No, I've got a diversion for you.

"My boss thinks that you could earn your keep by helping us interrogate the new prisoner. The brass are hot to get him to tell us where his former bosses are. What do you think?"

Minerva frowned, "We don't have an unlimited supply of the

serum. Is this really important?"

Soames liked understatement. He just smiled and nodded. Minerva looked to me. I looked to Ballard, and he said, "Yes."

Soames asked, "Can we start now?"

Ballard looked to Minerva and asked, "What do you need?"

She thought a moment and said, "Does he speak English?"

Soames went to check.

He returned and said, "Very broken. You'd spend all night exchanging names if you had to do it in English."

She just mumbled something like, "Bloody . . ." Then she said, "We'll work it the same way as before. I'll inject a bottle with serum and we get him to drink some and we're off."

It seemed like it would be easy but things went off the track from the beginning.

We worked it exactly as before. I entered the room after the prisoner. I tossed water bottles around. We all drank up, but he didn't. That was OK. We just started the interrogation as before, fairly confident that he'd eventually start drinking. We went on for two hours. Our water bottles were empty. His was unopened.

We took a break. Outside we had a conference. Minerva asked, "It was soooo easy with the bomb-maker. What's going on with this guy?"

Soames said, "The bomb-maker was just a technician. They didn't train him about interrogation. His time is too valuable making bombs. This guy is an elite soldier. He's trained about interrogation."

Capella asked, "Can we just force it down his throat? It wouldn't be as bad as water-boarding."

Soames just shrugged.

Minerva asked, "What is water-boarding?"

Soames said, "Oh, it's simulated drowning. Scary but if you know what you're doing it's not bad."

Capella asked, "Permission to speak frankly?"

Soames shrugged again.

"Water-boarding is not simulated drowning. It's the real thing. If you don't know what you're doing, a lot of times it ends with somebody going out in a body bag."

Minerva's eyes widened and her mouth opened, but she didn't say anything.

Soames said, "Let's do it. Capella, send in one of the guards, we'll brief him."

Minerva found her voice, "But you don't have to have him drink it all. If he just drinks a little, in a few minutes, the rest is easy."

Soames nodded. A PFC came out of the room and inquired, "Sir?"

"The prisoner needs to drink a little of his water. Just follow my lead. You'll know when to act."

Minerva asked why we hadn't just talked in the room with the prisoner. "After all, he doesn't really understand English, does he?"

Soames said, "The good soldiers are decent at reading body language. I'm not giving anything away."

The PFC saluted and went back in the room. A minute later, we returned. We all resumed our chairs. Soames picked up a new water bottle and lifted it as though it were a glass of champagne. "Let's have a toast – a toast to the Prophet."

The prisoner seemed to recognize the word, "Prophet". He just gazed warily at Soames as Capella translated.

The translated response was, "I don't drink with infidels."

Soames said, "You don't honor the Prophet?"

Capella had hardly translated when the prisoner spit back a response. Capella didn't translate. He just said, "A commonplace comment about your mother, Major."

Soames said, "I think we have to teach this son of ISIS a little Wisconsin hospitality. . . Now!" With that the three guards moved suddenly from behind. Two seized his arms and pinned them behind him. The third, grabbed the water bottle, efficiently opened it,forced the prisoner's mouth open, and stuck the bottle in.

The prisoner tried to cough it out, but some had gotten down his throat. After that he suddenly relaxed and most of the rest of the bottle went down easily. The prisoner's head lolled forward.

Then Minerva said, "Go ahead. Ask your questions."

Soames said, "OK. Everyone go. You don't need to know this."

Minerva shook her head. Ballard said, "We're staying. You don't know what we need to know."

Soames looked ready to issue an order when Minerva smiled and said, "If you ever hope to have our help again, I'd let us stay."

He looked around at the people in the room. Only the prisoner seemed not to be paying attention. Then he nodded assent.

From then on, we were in on everything.

The first question that Soames asked was, "Why did you surrender to us?"

A: "I was afraid to stay with ISIS."

Q: "Why?"

A: "I was assigned to guard one of our hoards of gold."

Q: "Why did that scare you?"

The answer was lengthy. He spoke rapidly and Capella finally had to tell him to stop. Capella then said, "He's telling a long story. I think it's best if we hear it all without interruptions and then ask questions."

Soames agreed.

Capella began telling the story.

I was a captain of the [untranslatable word] guard. My duty was transporting gold from one of our hiding places to whenever we needed to buy something – weapons from a weapons dealer, local currency, Euro's.

One day I was sent to our main hoard to get fifty million dollars worth of gold. We drove across country to the remote cave. When we arrived, we were challenged as normal. The guards checked our written orders, and verified that I was who I claimed to be.

The commander came out and we talked. He asked, "Have you come to clean us out?"

I laughed, "No. No. Just a small withdrawal. I only want 50 million dollars."

With that the commander looked troubled. His lips pursed and said, "Come along then." We went to the tent that he used as an office. Inside, with us alone, he told me what had happened the day before.

"Listen, Abdul. Something terrible has happened."

"What could have happened?" I gazed at his face that was becoming progressively paler and paler. I was beginning to fear something truly awful.

He quickly glanced around as though he were afraid that someone might be listening. Then he said, "Yesterday, a truck came down the path that you just took. It had a single man inside. He was wearing a robe with a hood, and I didn't get a look at his face, but it didn't seem important at the time.

"He came with orders as complete and valid as yours. The signature was identical to the one on your documents – the very same!"

He seized my arm and said imploringly, "No one questioned the orders or the stranger – not even I. I don't understand. You must help me."

I was mute throughout. I couldn't imagine how that could have happened.

He then led me into the cave. He turned on the lights, which revealed the large area that had been tunneled out. There were the normal crates containing the gold and the stores of arms and food. He led me to one of the crates. He opened it, and we found that there was

107

some gold left but only a very little.

We loaded it all into the truck that I'd brought. We weighed it and discovered that there were fewer than 30 million dollars worth left. I took the wheel of the truck rather than the driver, and we drove off.

After we got out of sight, I stopped the truck, ordered everyone out – all ten of us – and I had them sit on the shaded side of the truck. They were all heavily armed. I had been thinking the whole time that we had been loading the truck and driving. I made my decision, speaking coolly, calmly, and deliberately.

"Did any of you notice anything unusual at the bank?" That was what we jokingly called the gold hordes.

No one answered for a while. I urged them, "This is important. It is worth our lives."

Then Hassan spoke hesitantly, fearing to name the cobra in the tent, "There didn't seem to be enough gold loaded in the truck."

I nodded, "You are right. We took all the gold there was and it was very much less than there should have been."

Someone else asked, "How could that be! All seemed to be well."

Here was the critical point. I had to tell my idea just right so that they would go along with me, "I think that the guards have stolen the gold. There is no other possibility. I do not know why they didn't immediately flee, but however it happened, we are all in terrible danger. Our leader will not believe that anyone connected to the 'bank' is innocent – including us!"

Someone else exclaimed, "You are right! We are lost! We will be burned alive!"

There were murmurs of agreement.

I nodded and said one word. "Unless." I said it softly, almost too softly to be heard.

Someone asked what I'd said.

I repeated it louder.

The cries of "Unless what." were rising when I told them my plan.

"The dirty swine have stolen the gold, and we must avenge our leader! We will execute them ourselves – all of them. We will fall on them unawares and we will kill them all as though they died defending the 'bank'. Then we will return with the gold we have and say that robbers raided the 'bank', killing everyone. They were in a hurry and didn't take everything. We recovered what was left."

I hesitated and let them think about it. Eventually all nodded and agreed to the plan. We then prepared to return. All made sure their weapons were loaded with safeties off and magazines full and ready to replace. We wore body armor. Everyone checked his neighbor. Then we got back in the truck and turned around.

We drove back to the camp. I would tell the guards that we had forgotten to get the paperwork signed. Once we were inside the camp, all jumped from the truck, picked targets, and began firing. It was a fierce battle and would have been brief, but there were three who had taken refuge in the cave. We had to go in and root them out one at a time. We had no casualties but several wounded. I explained their wounds as due to a small raid on our truck on the way back.

We were believed. The leader sent another group in to check. Everything was as I said. Every one of us was questioned closely. Everyone stuck to the story.

A few days later, I was called into the ISIS accountant's office. I and my unit were being assigned to guard a new gold repository to replace the one that had been robbed. It was an "honor."

I am a man who can make quick decisions. I decided to leave ISIS and surrender to the only group that I would be safe with – the Americans. I stole a truck – the one that I had used to collect the gold. I took with me a couple of trusted friends whom I ran into on the way. We got past the first couple of checkpoints with forged papers saying we were going to make a payment to an arms dealer.

After that we ran into one more checkpoint. We had to run through it, hoping to luck.

We were lucky.

My friends swore they wouldn't surrender to the Americans, so we parted and I was eventually caught by Iraqi forces. I told them who I was and tried to convince them that I had valuable information for the Americans. So, I ended up here.

At this point, Ballard couldn't resist laughing. Of course, Soames wasn't happy about that. He called a halt and dragged us out of the room.

"What the hell are you laughing about?"

Ballard was now laughing so hard that he couldn't talk, so I answered. "We knew that the gold repository had been robbed. We knew that dozens of men had been killed. It is funny. It wasn't who we thought at all."

Soames looked at me very hard – as though he could read my thoughts. "You knew that dozens of men had been killed? I didn't."

Minerva said, "You didn't need to know."

Soames looked from one to the other of us, maybe trying to figure us out. "OK. Let's go back in, but if any of you laughs again, I swear, I'll . . ." He didn't finish his sentence.

Back in the Interrogation Room, Soames asked, "Where are the top leaders of ISIS."

The answer was that he didn't know.

Soames took out a cigarette and lit it. It was the first time that I'd seen him smoke. He asked, "All right. Then where was the last place that you know they were and when were they there?"

The prisoner answered quietly, systematically, thoroughly. He listed a half-dozen names and locations and when they had been there to his knowledge. He didn't have recent information about two of the leaders. For the other four the information was two to four days old.

There were lots of other questions, but after we got the information about the leaders, Soames sent the list out with us to be delivered to the duty officer in the situation room.

We dropped off the papers, and Ballard took us back to the cafeteria. He wanted to talk alone about OUR situation. We all got bottles of water and he started, "Amazing. Minns walked in by himself and drove off with nearly half a billion dollars in gold."

He shook his head and went on, "AND, he didn't kill anyone or even have to injury anyone. I suppose he was speaking idiomatic Arabic."

Minerva said, "He wasn't the cold-blooded killer that we thought either."

Ballard shook his head but added, "Don't forget how he treated Baghdadi."

We talked about our next steps – what we would do when we decided which site or sites were our best bets.

Eventually, Soames and Capella arrived for dinner. "Well, you folks did just fine. I think Central Command may have some work now that they have locations for some of those vipers."

The next day would have been completely boring except that toward the end of the day Soames showed up at our make-shift office in the cafeteria and told us that the satellite had been repositioned and that they'd take photos in the morning when the light was good for our sites.

The next day about 11 AM. Soames caught up with us. He was carrying a manilla folder with some oversized paper overlapping its edges. He said, "Come up to my office."

We followed him and reached his office, which was a small room with an old World War II desk and a couple of chairs. There was a laptop and a file cabinet. We all sat around the table, and he laid photographs out on the desktop. They were black and white and seemed to be immensely detailed.

I recognized the top one immediately. It was site #4. Ballard looked at it and said, "No. That can't be it. The land is roughly bowl-shaped but I don't think it can possibly be the crater of a meteor. What looked like gravel is actually rippled sand."

I wasn't so sure, but after I looked at it for a while, I finally agreed with him. What's more Soames agreed almost from the get-go.

Ballard pulled that photo off and revealed a couple of images of the site from a different angle. There it was really obvious from the shadows that it was rippled sand.

After pulling them off the top of the pile, the next photo showed site #7. That was our most unlikely, but in the top photo I was not so sure. In the next couple of photos at different sun angles, I was sure as was everyone else. That one had deposits of gravel spread around. The highly eroded bowl of the land looked more like a crater too.

Then we were faced with the next decision. What would we do? Soames had no doubt. "You have to go in there and take samples out."

Minerva sniffed, "Easy for you to say. What do we do? Ride in on camels disguised as Bedouins?"

Soames sniffed in his turn, "Not at all. We have Delta forces in Iraq still. They do the odd job like this occasionally. They usually fly in at night and capture a high value-target like our bomb-maker. But I suppose they wouldn't be above snatching some gravel."

So it was decided. Soames got in touch with Central Command and before the day was over, we knew that we'd move operations to Iraq.

Huey at Five Dark Zero

We arrived at the make-shift heliport the next morning near dawn. I'd not had enough sleep, and I'd had dreams of crashing in the ocean and swimming to Arabia where ISIS soldiers were waiting for us to make us walk the plank. It was a confused dream, and I was actually kind of happy to wake and be able to leave the dream behind.

The "cabin attendant" from our last flight was present. He had his usual banter as he made sure we were strapped in and had our headphones on and connected, "We're happy that you've chosen to travel again with Air Yemen. Please observe all the safety precautions outlined in the overhead labels. Keep your head down when exiting the aircraft. We hate to have a beheading on our watch.

"Your captain will be taking off in. . ." At that point, the helicopter lurched into the sky and the narrator switched tense, ". . . has just taken off."

I asked, "We haven't heard our destination."

The answer from the pilot was, "That's right. Don't expect to. Although I can say that the country that we're heading to is the only country to own an English Soccer team."

Ballard mumbled, "Saudi Arabia."

He'd stolen my thunder, I knew that answer.

We'd taken off in the dark, and as the sky slowly lightened, we discovered that we were over a sea and with no shore in sight.

Minerva mumbled something like, "Over the sea in a helicopter."

I couldn't blame her. I wasn't all that happy about it either. However, shortly we turned back toward the rising sun and shortly crossed the shoreline. We then crossed over limitless sand, then limitless mountains, and then over sand and rock and nothing much beside. It reminded me of flying over the western mountains of the US during a drought.

We eventually reached a base. It had a real airstrip and real buildings. We discovered that they even had air-conditioning, which was a blessing beyond measure even in the spring.

After landing, we went to the base commander's office and learned that their orders were to help us retrieve something from a location that we would share with them. He had very little interest in knowing what we were after or why.

He took us down a corridor to an office. It was inhabited by several men who were wearing sergeant's stripes. He introduced us to a Staff Sergeant Baker who was to be our guide here. The commander bid us good luck, and I had the impression that he would just as soon not see us again.

Staff Sergeant Baker on the other hand was friendly. He took us to the officers' quarters where we were assigned a couple of rooms.

As soon as we had dropped our things, Baker took us to the "caf" as they called it. He gave us the lay of the land in a couple of minutes. "OK. You're here to get something off a field somewhere in Northern Iraq in unfriendly territory.

"My job is to get you there and back, alive and, if possible, with what you want. Sound right?"

Ballard nodded. "That's close enough."

Baker nodded too. "That's good. Now, here's the problem. My boss wants you off this base as quickly as possible. But his boss—a couple of levels up the line—wants you to stay until you've got what you want, so you see where our mutual interest lies?"

Ballard said, "Sure. We want to get out of here with our objective as quickly as possible. You want us out of here as quickly as possible."

"Right. Now, it would help me a lot if I knew what you were looking for."

Here's where I anticipated troubles. Ballard said, "We're here to collect some gravel."

Ballard didn't crack a smile but took us outside and pointed north. "There's a few square miles of gravel about five miles north of here. Are we done?"

I stepped in, "No, sir. We want special gravel that you find in only one place. We've got map co-ordinates."

Baker nodded, "You all do. I guess I should see them."

We went back inside, and he looked at our maps and satellite imagery. He leaned back, "Well, it's not the hardest place to get into or out of. But it has its problems.

"It's near the edge of the range of our helicopters. I'd put this party together with a couple of Hueys and an Apache. But the Apache doesn't have the range to get there and back from here. So, we'd have to borrow an Apache from Iraq. That means a rendezvous. That's tricky over hostile territory.

"Do you get the idea? I'm not excited about this mission. Is there any way that we can do this anywhere else?"

Ballard shook his head.

Baker went on, "And then there's the lady. Does she have to come?"

I nodded enthusiastically. "Believe me, she's worth her weight in, well, let's say gold."

Baker shook his head mistrustfully. "Right."

He leaned back and gazed off into the upper atmosphere for a few minutes. "OK. If that's the way it's got to be, I'll put together a team to get you in and out. They'll be Delta force – our top people. You'll fly in on two Hueys. We'll rendezvous with an Apache to give us air cover."

He looked at all three of us carefully, "We're out at the far end of our range. You'll have maybe a half-hour to find what you're looking for and leave. If you're not ready to go at the end of that half-hour, we'll leave – with or without you. Understood?"

We all nodded.

"OK. Then take it easy. We'll do a practice run locally with all the equipment and people. It should be easy. You're just looking for gravel. It's a remote area. We're lucky and nobody notices us. Quick in and quick out. No muss no fuss."

"Tomorrow night would be the quickest we could put a practice together but don't hold your breath waiting."

He walked us to the cafeteria. "This is probably the best place for you to hang out while I put things together."

But then we kept going. We reached what turned out to be a supply depot. When we got there, he spoke to the quartermaster. "We need gear for these folks. For a night mission. Helmets with night vision. Camo. Body armor. No weapons. Got it?"

The quartermaster had it. It wasn't that hard getting equipment that fit us all as I'd feared. Apparently, they had women in the unit, and they had gear that fit Minerva pretty well. She had a little trouble getting her bun compact enough to fit under the helmet, but it worked out OK in the end.

□

The next couple of days were boring. Baker suggested that we go for hikes each day with full gear on. He had us start with short jaunts of a mile or so, and we were up to three or four miles at the end of the days. Everyone was sore all over, but we hung in.

On the second day, there was a meeting with the team that Baker had put together. It happened in what they called the "ready room". There were three seats in the front row reserved for us.

Baker led the meeting. "Alright, lady and gentlemen, you'll find under your seats the mission profile for this mission. I'll give you the fifty thousand foot level. We can have a few questions. After you've studied the profile, we can go into greater depth.

"Here's the story. The three guests are mission specialists. They are civilians. Their names are Professor Wendt," Here he indicated Minerva. "Professor Wendt and Mr. Ballard."

"Don't be confused. Mr. Ballard has a PhD in physical chemistry. He just prefers not to use the title." At this point, someone dropped a pencil in the back. "Have you got anything you'd like to say back there?"

There wasn't a sound. Baker continued. "We have to have mission specialists because this is an unusual mission. It is a geology mission." Somebody in the back coughed.

Baker said, "Mr. McGloughlin, would you like to comment on geology?"

McGloughlin just shook his head and said, "No, sir."

Baker went on, "Good. As you'll see from the map in your mission profile, we're going deep into ISIS territory. There are definitely limitations imposed by the geometry of this mission and the fuel limitations of our aircraft. You will fly in, rendezvous with an Apache escort, land, and deploy the mission specialists who will collect samples of gravel."

At that point someone gagged in the room. Baker was clearly looking for someone to discipline, but he wasn't sure who was responsible, so we just went on, "The mission specialists will have thirty minutes at most on the site to complete their mission and return to base. They are aware that when the thirty are up or when the team lead calls time, they must be gone."

He looked around the room. Then he said, "Are the implications of that clear to everyone?"

There was a general chorus of "Yes, sir"s, and Baker gave the order, "Dismisssed."

Everyone got up and began filing out, including us. However, one of the team, a woman, came up to us and addressed Minerva, "Ma'am. May I have a word?"

Minerva agreed.

The team member said, "My name's Cecilia Kong. Could we have a little girl to girl talk?" She looked over at Ballard and me.

Minerva said, "I'm Minerva. Of course, where do you want to go?"

Kong sort of suppressed a giggle and said, "Let's go to the Ladies'."

Minerva agreed. Ballard said that I would go with him to the cafeteria. We did.

□□

Ballard had left the "caf", but I stayed nursing a glass of ice tea. After a while two female non-coms entered the "caf". They seemed to be heading toward my table, so I rose. I discovered right away that the one in the front was Kong.

I started to say something when I noticed that the one following was Minerva. Besides the desert camouflage fatigues that she had been wearing before, she was wearing a camo cap. The thing that had really camouflaged her was the fact that she was wearing her hair completely differently than she ever had. Her hair was in a very tight bun at the nape of her neck – apparently the standard military rig for women.

I smiled and said, "Well, what do we have here? It's the perfect little girl soldier!"

She smiled too and said, "Pretty good camouflage?"

"Good camo or not, I like it."

They both joined me at my table. Minerva said, "Cecilia was kind enough to help me style my hair so that it would be out of harm's way and wouldn't interfere with hat or helmet.'

I nodded, "Thanks very much. You've added substantially to Minerva's toolbox of feminine wiles."

Cecilia just nodded imperceptibly and said, "In exchange, I have a couple of questions."

I shrugged, "I'll answer what I can and lie about what I can't."

That brought a smile to her lips. "Well, how about this? What are you really doing? You guys aren't geologists. At least, Minerva's not a geologist."

I opened my mouth and started to say, "Well, we're more being

116

astrophysicists." I was interrupted by Minerva kicking my shin. I gulped in the midst of "astrophysicist" but finished the word. Then I looked at Minerva and said, "We can talk about that. Everything isn't confidential."

Minerva frowned, "Just keep going, and we'll see."

So, I would have, but Kong asked, "Oh, come on. That's even more preposterous than Geology. At least, there are rocks out there. I don't see any stars – at least none that you can't see here."

I soldiered on, 'Well, it's not stars that we're looking for – exactly. A very small sample of a rock that was far older than any other rock found on Earth before turned up in a facility in San Antonio. We traced it back to that crater out there. It's bad luck that it's so hard to get to."

Kong pressed the point, "In the mission profiles there are high resolution satellite images. The NAS doesn't re-purpose those satellites for fun. Why?"

I had an easy answer, "We did a favor or two for them. I think they were happy to do that little favor for us."

She wouldn't give up. She leaned in and drilled me with her eyes, "The Army is not doing this mission for astrophysics. They're not doing it for old gravel. They expect to get something out of it other than pi in the sky."

"You're probably right. I don't know what they want, and I don't particularly want to know. I just want someone to get us there and get us out in one piece with some of that gravel."

She said, "That's where I come in. I'm one of the pilots." She hesitated and then said, "I suppose we have to leave that where it is, but, I've got another question."

"Shoot."

"What is it with the two of you? Are you really married?"

"Sure. So?"

She looked exasperated, "Well, isn't it a little strange. I mean. You two are sort of February – September."

I laughed, "Well, I'd consider it more like March – July, but I won't quibble. Say February – September, so long as it's late February, very early September."

She turned to Minerva, "What kind of witchcraft is this."

I laughed and asked Minerva, "Yeh, what kind of witchcraft is it?"

Minerva kicked me in the shins again and said, "No witchcraft."

I agreed. "Yep. It's just. Oh, I don't know. Maybe I've got a predilection for, intelligent, beautiful, mature women." That, at least, didn't win me a kick in the shins.

Minerva agreed. "The hardest thing with him." She realized what she had just said and corrected, 'The most difficult thing about him was trying to discourage him."

I smiled. "I wore her down. It only took me a dozen years."

She frowned, "It wasn't that long."

Kong just shook her head. "Well, if you ever are willing to share, what your secret is or . . . ."

Minerva's smile broadened. "I'll never share – anything."

Kong got up and left.

Minerva turned back to me. "Why did you tell her about astrophysics?"

I smiled, "In the first place, I was right. It isn't a secret, for one thing."

She said, "And the other?"

"Well, the best way to lie is to . . . "

She finished it, "Tell the truth or at least as much of it as you possibly can."

"Right. She has enough of the answer to satisfy. It's wholly true although it's not the whole truth. As two professors and an NSF staffer, we would reasonably have no other reason for our interest in that gravel.

She laughed, "And here I thought you were flirting with her."

I didn't even dignify that with a reply.

Then she asked me, "Once you told me about an English Literature instructor that you had at Ohio State. Did she remind you of that instructor?"

"Oh, I suppose vaguely. They are both smart, attractive, wear their hair roughly the same way. They're about the same height and weight."

She asked, "Nothing more?"

I shrugged, "No.

□
□□

The third day there we got the word that we would go on a training mission. I have to hand it to Baker. It was an impressive group. We boarded the helicopter with 6 others. They were all in full battle gear and I thought that they must be carrying two times what we were at least. There was another helicopter, and it had even more troops than we had.

We got into the air shortly after sunset. We flew around for about a half-hour while it got good and dark. We'd not tried our night vision goggles yet. We landed and discovered that there was even a helicopter overhead orbiting our position.

Once we were out of the helicopter, we practiced putting on the goggles, turning them on and blundering around for a half hour. We had brought along some pails and we even ended by collecting a little gravel.

It was a stretch to say that the goggles gave you night vision. Oh, you could see things in a kind of sickly green light. Sometimes you could even tell what they were. I almost picked up a scorpion thinking it was a rock. It probably wouldn't have mattered. We all wore flexible tough gloves that I don't think a rattlesnake could bite through.

Baker finally called quits. We all got back in the helicopters and took off. Again, we flew for a good while. Then Baker surprised us. "Gentlemen and Lady, we're going to try a real drill. You have 30 minutes. Collect your samples and get back to the helicopter. Understood."

We understood. This time, the helicopter rotors didn't stop whirling. We stumbled out, got our goggles working and started looking for gravel. There wasn't any close to the helicopters. We divided up and went out looking. Ballard found some and Minerva did as well. I was still looking when Baker called, "Five minute warning. Back to the Hueys NOW!"

I swore and turned back toward where the helicopters were and started trudging. Then there were explosions all around us. "What the HELL!" I screamed into my mike.

Baker swore and shouted, "Two minutes. We're off in two minutes."

I ran as best I could. I heard someone shout, and someone else said, "Man down."

I kept running. The helicopters had already started hovering. I was the last one back. Hands grabbed me and pulled me in. We lurched and rolled. I was lucky to be able to stay in the helicopter let alone find a seat and belt in.

Then suddenly, we were level and flying smoothly. I found a seat, buckled in with some help, and shivered all the way back to the base.

When we landed, Baker had us all gather in a hangar and sit down around him. "Well, lady and gentlemen, that was a live-fire exercise."

Minerva nudged me, "What in the world does that mean?"

I whispered, "It means they were firing real . . ." I was interrupted. Baker looked at me and said, "Perhaps, Mr. Know-It-All would like to explain a live-fire exercise."

I stood, looked around for a friendly face and didn't really find one. "Well, it means that somebody is firing live bullets."

Minerva raised her hands, waving them. Baker said, "Yes, Ms. Minerva. Do you want to ask Mr. Know-Iit-All a question?"

She nodded and asked, "Does that mean that we could have been killed?"

I asked hopefully, "In theory, yes. I hope the chances were very small, right Staff Sergeant?"

Baker said, "Right you are, Mr. Wendt. The next exercise will be real and you stand a chance of dying."

There were a few more questions for the professionals in the group. Baker was not very happy with them. After he dismissed us, he pulled us aside and took us to the "caf."

Baker surprised us. "You did fairly well. You kept your heads and got back in time. You even got some of your precious gravel. I think we will move on the day after next. Get a good night's sleep."

It was long after midnight when we got to bed. Minerva and I just dropped into bed, snuggled and kissed for a couple of minutes and were asleep almost in mid-kiss.

The next day was a rest day. We did a couple of short hikes and had more fun in bed.

The next day, Baker joined us for breakfast. He asked us, "Nobody asked for a piece?"

Minerva asked, "A piece of what?"

I wasn't going to make myself a laughing stock by guessing at an answer. Baker replied, "I mean a weapon."

No one had an answer why. Of course, I was carrying my weapon in my purse. Minerva was carrying a very potent weapon somewhere on her person. I don't know about Ballard, and he did not offer a reason.

Baker shrugged and said, "Whatever your reason, it's good. You leave the weapons to us, and we'll leave your rock collecting to you."

That afternoon Baker gathered the entire team and gave us the final pre-flight briefing. "We're going tonight. You've all studied the maps. The pilots will try to put us down on top of a gravel deposit. There will be an Apache flying cover over us. There's not much moon tonight." He hesitated and then went on, "That's the good news.

"The bad news is that we only have one Huey tonight. All the others are in a big hurry-up operation. I haven't heard anything about it until now. That means that half of the team isn't going tonight. Huey B team, you have to sit this one out."

No one was happy about that, but apparently we were stuck. We would assemble just after dinner, suit up, and wait on the flight line until the moon set. We had a little over two hours to fly before we reached our site # 7.

The single helicopter taking off seemed very lonely. We had flown for about one and one half hours when we rendezvoused with the Apache. At that point, Minerva took my hand and squeezed it. We couldn't speak without sharing with everyone, so we stayed quiet.

At five minutes away, the pilot announced the time. We could feel the helicopter descend. The ground was absolutely dark. We put on goggles and turned on night vision. The interior of the helicopter seemed as bright as day. I looked out the open doorway and could see the ground rising to us.

We hit the ground hard, and Baker's voice was whispering in the most intense whisper I'd ever heard, "Go! GO! GO!"

We got out, and I immediately started looking for gravel. There was none to be seen. Baker told us to spread out. The professionals found some rocks and set up behind them. The helicopter rotors kept spinning slowly, the muffled engine barely audible. As we spread out, I saw some gravel. I tried running toward it, but it was more of a fast shuffle. I reached the edge of it, dropped to my knees and pulled out a sample bag. I opened the zip lock and started shoveling some in.

At that moment, I heard gunfire. Baker shouted, "Apache. Locate that fire and shut it down." I heard the wind of the Apache fly over my head while I sealed my sample bag. Then the chain gun of the Apache opened up. It was like a chainsaw ripping through some tough wood.

I started to get up and then realized that I'd better stay close to the ground. I felt the whistle of bullets going over my head and then stop. I was half-way back to the Huey when I heard a terrible crash behind me. I looked around and saw the Apache slew at a crazy angle. The pilot seemed to get control of it, and then it fell in a sort of controlled roll. It managed to land mostly sitting up. I saw the pilot's door open, and he came out. So did the co-pilot.

Meanwhile there was firing everywhere. I was sure that our team was returning fire, but there seemed to be fire coming from everywhere.

When I got close to our Huey, I saw Minerva appear from nowhere. She shouted, "I don't think there's enough room for everyone in our helicopter." The pilot and co-pilot of the Apache had reached the helicopter and the rest of the team was close.

Baker shouted at two men, "You two stay behind."

Minerva screamed, "No!"

I thought I knew what she had in mind. I said calmly to her, "You'll have to pull rank. Use *Imperio* on Baker." I was pulling off my gloves and Minerva already had hers off. She took a minute to find Baker. He was helping one of the pilots who was wounded toward the helicopter. She took off at a run toward him. I caught up with her just before she reached him. She shouted, "Leave him with us!"

He didn't hesitate but knocked her over and kept going. He didn't even answer her.

She pulled her wand, so I knew that she'd said the spell. He stopped. She was up again and to him. I heard her say, "Get the rest in the helicopter. Leave Wendt and the pilot. Where's the best place to take this wounded pilot?"

Baker didn't hesitate, "Riyadh air base, Saudi Arabia."

Minerva just said, "Go!" He ran to the helicopter, gave the most explicit orders that I'd ever heard that boiled down to "Take off now. If you argue you'll be spending more time in the stockade than you knew existed." They did.

Minerva took the pilot's hand and mine, and suddenly we were in a hospital emergency room. All of a sudden there was a nurse beside us asking where we came from.

I said, "He's an army pilot who's going to bleed out on your floor if you don't gct moving."

Her training kicked in, and she ran to her desk to call "Code Blue." Meanwhile a couple of armed MP's came over to us with sidearms drawn. One of them said, "Stand slowly and put your hands over your heads."

I didn't have to say anything because I felt the gut-wrenching experience of disapparating. We re-appeared in the dark. A short distance away there was a fence and sodium vapor lamps.

I started to ask where we were, but Minerva supplied the answer before I could ask. "We're outside the base we started off the evening at."

We stood up and started to follow the line of the fence, looking for an entrance. We hadn't gone far before somebody inside the fence called something out to us in Arabic.

I shouted back, "We're the Wendt's. We flew out of here earlier tonight."

An answer came back, "Whoever you are, down to your knees with your hands on your heads facing toward the fence."

I whispered, "Wait here or disapparate into the base commander's office?"

She whispered back, "I think enough Muggles have seen us disapparate today."

So we waited. We waited a good long time. Finally a vehicle's headlights appeared approaching us outside the fence. It pulled to a halt a good hundred yards from us. Someone got out and shouted at us.

"Stay where you are. Take off your clothes. Then stand and walk slowly toward me."

Minerva shouted back, "I'm a woman."

"I don't care if you're King Kong. Follow instructions or you'll get shot."

Minerva whispered, "I think he's serious."

I answered, "You think?"

We followed instructions. Off came the helmet, the body armor, the camouflage, the boots. Oh yes, the boots came off too. I had the rest of my gear off and started to stand, and I was told in no uncertain terms that EVERYTHING came off. So we went on taking things off – boots, underwear, pack – everything.

Minerva hadn't gone more than a couple of steps before a woman's voice said, "Lady. Let your hair down out of that bun. NOW."

Minerva did. Her hair went down almost to her hips. She brushed it in front of her, and I couldn't help thinking of Venus on the half-shell. That made me think of something that was very irrelevant to our situation but when you're in danger, the strangest things come to mind.

We were told to get into the back of the truck with a couple of MP's. They had drawn sidearms, and one of them recognized us. He asked, "Aren't you the civilian contractors?"

Minerva answered, "We're two of them."

"You flew off earlier this evening. How did you get back?"

I said, "We can only tell your commanding officer."

The other said, "Well, shit, what are we supposed to do with them?"

The first thought for a moment. "We'll throw them in the stockade, get them some fatigues, and wait for the CO to deal with them."

By this time we'd reached the main gate and drove through. That night was long. I was happy that they'd let us share a cell. The borrowed fatigues were roughly the right fit but a bit tight on Minerva. She was worried about how she looked in them.

I agreed, "I wish they'd not given you any fatigues. You look much better in your all together."

She just said, "Shut up."

The next morning, we were awakened shortly after sunrise. We found ourselves led to the base commander's office. Ballard was already there—in civilian clothes. We were still wearing the borrowed fatigues.

The base commander was rifling through some papers as we sat in his office. Eventually, he said, "According to these reports, you two somehow talked Staff Sergeant Baker into leaving you behind with an Apache pilot who'd been seriously injured.

"Then you showed up outside our perimeter fence without the pilot. You arrived over an hour before our Huey arrived with the rest of the unit that you'd left with early that evening.

"There are at least three flat-out impossibilities in those reports—not the least of which is talking your Staff Sergeant into leaving people behind. I want an explanation right now."

We should have agreed on an explanation—even a crazy one—while we were in the stockade, but we were far too tired to think straight even if we'd had the idea.

I had an inspiration and started before Minerva could, "Sir, you don't have a need to know. What you do need to know is that we got back safely, that the pilot is in the Riyadh Air Base hospital, and we haven't done anything to jeopardize the lives or mission of our unit, this base, or the US mission."

He took that in for a moment and leaned forward, "Yes, your mission. Just what is that mission?"

Minerva answered, "You don't have the need to know that."

He responded, "Well, something that you need to know is that I can keep you in the stockade until I find out what that mission is."

Ballard, who had been silent up to that point, said, "I'm afraid you can't. Check with your commander. We . . . uh . . . our mission has priority over your prerogatives."

That clearly angered the commander, but he must have had a discussion about the priority of the mission before we arrived. He just straightened the papers on his desk and said, "Get out!"

I started to ask about our personal things that had been left outside the base, but Ballard hurried us out of the office. Outside he said, "Your things are back in your room at the barracks."

Minerva asked if we'd got our samples.

Ballard said that he didn't know about the samples that we'd gotten but he had a sample bag full of the gravel. He went on, "Get yourselves packed, and let's get out of here before we have any more problems come up. I've reserved a Huey to get us to the Riyadh Air Base."

B1B

We reached the landing pad for helicopters, and there was indeed a Huey waiting for us. It turned out to be the same one that we'd flown out on the previous night. It had the same crew too. This time, though, there were only the pilot and a crew chief back in the passenger section of the helicopter.

He knew we knew our way around the Huey so he didn't help us get belted in or our headphones on. As soon as we did, he gave the OK, and the pilot took off.

After we were out of sight of the base, the pilot, Cecilia Kong, asked, "Just how did you two get back to base before we did? I was sure that you were going to end up in an ISIS recruiting video showing Americans getting beheaded."

Minerva smirked, "Not me. I'd be on the video showing Brits getting beheaded."

"Seriously. How did you pull that off? You were alone, weaponless, surrounded by ISIS fuckers. I couldn't believe that Baker left you behind."

I said, "You tell me. How do you think we did it?"

The crew chief said, "I know! They sent you in an Osprey. It can do vertical landings and takeoffs. It's a lot faster than we are."

The pilot came back, "I don't know. The Osprey would have to have come in almost as soon as we left and would arrive not long before we arrived. I just don't think that would do it."

We road in silence for a few minutes—that is, if you call riding in a helicopter silent. Then the pilot spoke again. "Maybe a Harrier. There are two seater versions. They can do over a thousand clicks. If they sent three or four as soon as we sent our distress call, they could have been up there in a half-hour or so. With one pilot and one empty seat they could have beat us back to the base by a good margin. The third Harrier goes directly to Riyadh airbase with the wounded pilot."

I could tell the crew chief wasn't buying it entirely. He was making a face of concentration. Then he said, "Do you think they," indicating us, "could last out there for half an hour without some sort of cover fire?"

I interrupted them, "I have a question for the two of you. Can you think of any other way we could do it?"

That question had them thinking in silence for a while. Finally, the pilot said, "I can't think of any other way."

The crew chief shook his head and just said, "Nope. Me neither."

I went on, "Well, there's your Sherlock Holmes answer."

The pilot asked, "Sherlock Holmes?"

"Sure. He once said that if you've eliminated everything that's impossible, whatever is left, regardless how crazy, must be true."

The pilot said, "Well, you're right about one thing. We'll never know. We don't have a need to know, but I like the Harrier idea. Almost everything works fine except why in the world did they land outside our base?"

The crew chief wasn't satisfied but he only said, "Sure, you'd like the Harrier idea; it was yours."

The rest of the flight (and there wasn't much left) passed in the quiet of rotors spinning. We landed, and there was a welcome party waiting for us.

There was a hummer, a driver, and an officer. He introduced himself and said, "Somebody's in a real hurry for you to get back stateside. They've got a plane waiting for you."

Minerva just slumped a bit and said, "Of course. What else should we expect but another plane waiting for us?"

The hummer took us into a large hangar that held a large sleek airplane that looked like something out of science fiction. There was a man standing beside it in some sort of flight suit. He strode forward and said, "I'm Major Rawlings. I know who you are already. We've got flight suits for you in the ready room. We're going to get off schedule unless you hurry up and get changed into them."

Inside the Ready Room, there were three suits. Rawlings helped us suit up. After the previous night, none of us were too touchy about undressing in public.

Minerva did object when Rawlings said, "You'll have to let your luggage catch up with you. We've only got room for a few personal belongings."

She opened her mouth to object vocally but nothing came out, and she shrugged. "What indignity is left to us?"

She took her purse with wand. I took mine with Glock. I also took my dopp kit with razor and a few other things. Ballard just shrugged and said, "Let's go."

Rawlings was cheerful as he escorted us back to the plane. "Well, this baby is just large enough for us. I think the two gentlemen should take the offensive and defensive weapons officer seats, and the lady should take the co-pilot seat up front.

Minerva was charmed, "Why thank you sir. Do I get a view from that seat?"

"The best in the plane. Your friends get a view of instruments."

Well, there were indignities left untried. I had no interest in being separated from Minerva, but I was stuck in the back with Ballard.

We mounted ladders into the plane. We had help strapping into the unfamiliar seats, but the hatches closed a lot sooner than I hoped for. Rawlings fired up the engines, and we taxied out to the runway. We seemed to have priority because we hardly slowed as we turned onto the runway, and the acceleration hit us. And I do mean "hit". Of course, I could only see what was happening on a video monitor.

Once we were in the air, Minerva observed that the ground seemed to be flying away under us.

The pilot said, "Yes, ma'am, this is a B1B bomber. We're cruising faster than the speed of sound."

The flight was one of the most boring that I'd ever had. Ballard wouldn't talk about anything to do with our recent experiences. Minerva was enjoying the view and light banter with the pilot.

At one point she noted that the sun didn't seem to be moving much in the sky.

"Right you are ma'am. We are flying fast enough that the sun seems to stand still at this latitude when we're flying west."

Most of the time we were over sea – either the Mediterranean or the Atlantic. At one point Minerva exclaimed, "Oooh. Why are we slowing down?"

Rawlings started to explain about in-flight refueling, but Minerva noticed the tanker before he'd finished. She surprised him by interrupting him with the exclamation, "That's a tanker, isn't it?"

"Yes, ma'am, you're right. You're right knowledgeable about military airplanes, aren't you?" He said it with just the right amount of admiration in his voice to make me wish again that Ballard were in the co-pilot's seat and Minerva back here.

However, all things eventually end. We saw the Atlantic seaboard approaching, and I knew that we couldn't have more than an hour left to wherever we were going. I asked the pilot, "Where are we going? Andrews?"

The pilot said, "I don't know where WE are going. I'm flying this plane to Dayton."

Ballard asked, "Why in the world Dayton?"

"Because that's where this plane and I are based. I have no idea where you're going from there."

So there was to be another destination for us. Minerva seemed to be having such fun talking with the pilot about instruments and navigation and so on that I didn't have the heart to point out that we probably weren't done with traveling yet today.

I watched the ground flow past below us on a video screen. Suddenly I realized that we were approaching a large town. It was Pittsburg. It was easy to recognize because of the three rivers joining in the center of town. I started paying attention then. We flew over or near I-70 from then on. Consequently, I wasn't surprised when Columbus appeared ahead. We skirted around it to the south. I had a pang of homesickness when I caught a glimpse of the Ohio State campus and its signature horseshoe-shaped stadium.

We had been slowly descending, probably since Pittsburg. We were clearly lining up for a landing. We left I-70 to the south of us as we went in a long arc that ended with our gliding south.

We landed, and the ground crew helped us out of the bomber. Minerva was giving the pilot an enthusiastic thank you for the exciting flight, but her happiness was short-lived. There was a Hummer parked nearby. Another officer greeted us, and we got into the Hummer. He was quick and to the point.

"We're going to the ready room. We've got some fatigues that shouldn't fit too badly. You can change there, and we'll take you to. . ."

Ballard interrupted, "I don't want to know just yet where we're going, if that's all right with you."

As we changed in men's and ladies loo's, Ballard got out his cell phone and turned it on. I'd completely forgotten about mine. I opened it up and found that its battery had run down. Ballard's had had the same fate.

The officer was hurrying us along. "Quickly, we've got to get on the road."

We got in the Hummer, and we were quickly on a freeway. I considered where we might be going – either south-bound toward Cincinnati or north to the airport. It was north. I didn't want to disappoint Minerva before I had to, so I didn't say anything.

Apparently, the officer didn't want to talk about it either. When Minerva asked where we were going, all he would say was, "We're going to Vandalia. It's quite close. We'll be there in a minute."

She didn't pressure him and indeed despite the short drive, she'd fallen asleep and was leaning on my shoulder. She woke when we skidded to a stop in front of the terminal. I helped her out.

She gazed around a minute as the officer hurried us along and then it struck her, "This is an airport, isn't it?"

I shrugged agreement. She just stared at me as if to ask, "When will this endless day up in the air end?"

The officer got us into the first class line where you whisk through rapidly with little fuss or muss. He pressed boarding passes into our hands, and we were too occupied with getting out passports to pay attention to the passes themselves. After we were through security, I looked at the pass and found the gate that we were using. We only had about twenty minutes to get to the gate. At the gate, they were doing the last call for our flight. We were the last passengers in the jetway to the plane. The stewardess helped us find our seats and stow our couple of small carry-ons into the overhead racks. I helped Minerva get belted in.

We'd barely done that when the plane started backing away from the terminal. A stewardess came on the intercom to welcome us all to the flight and announce that with the good weather and favorable winds, we'd probably land in Dallas twenty minutes early.

Minerva shook her head as if to waken from a light sleep, "I could have sworn she said 'Dallas'."

I replied, "I'm afraid you're right. Ballard, do you have any idea why we're going there?"

He shook his head, "None. My cell phone battery is dead or I'd try calling to find out why."

The stewardess just then reminded us to turn off our cell phones and other electronics.

It was a measure of how tired we all were that Minerva slumped against me before we'd even taxied to the runway. I pulled down the shade of my window and decided to see if I could get some sleep although I rarely get much when I'm flying.

We took off.

During the flight, I waved off the stewardess when she came by to offer us a meal. I was hungry, but I'd rather let Minerva sleep than get something to eat myself. I tried to get interested in the airline magazine in the seat back but it only had articles about golfing in the Rockies and learning the Texas Two Step in Fort Worth. I finally found the cross-word puzzle and tried working it. Ballard seemed to be able to nap some, but I just couldn't.

We did arrive ahead of schedule, but we were taxi-ing around the DFW airport for a half-hour before a slot opened for us at the terminal. We could have called someone if we had working cell phone batteries.

Minerva had just mumbled something and drifted back to sleep when we arrived at a terminal. Eventually we had to get out. All three of us dragged ourselves up the jetway to the terminal. Then we dragged ourselves to the baggage claim for our flight even though none of us had baggage.

In the terminal itself, every now and then some total stranger thanked us for our service. I wondered what they would have said if they'd known what our service had been.

I started to ask Ballard what he suggested we do after we stepped out into the Texas air. The discussion was unnecessary. When we walked through the security revolving door we found a familiar face waiting for us. Harris was standing next to a baggage carousel.

He shook his head when he saw us. "I've never seen a more dispirited bunch of soldiers in my life."

Despite the thank you's, I'd forgotten that we were wearing fatigues. Ballard just said, "Get us to a hotel and let us sleep for about a year."

Harris said he was sorry, but I don't think any of us believed him. He then explained why he was sorry, "We've been holding up on this raid for you three to show up. We need you." He corrected himself, "Well, really, we only need Minerva, but I figure you both want to be along."

By this time we were in a black Escalade. Harris was going into details. "We've got this lead. We're going to a local apartment to interview someone who appears to be an accomplice of Minns."

That perked us all up. It appeared that the lead was not more than a half-hour drive from the airport. On the way, Harris filled us in.

"OK. We've not got a lot of time before we get there. Just listen and get ready mentally for this meeting.

"Our target is a small business owner, Lewis Morse, who owns a management company called 'Inheritance LLC.' Strange name but that's what it is. He's leasing a warehouse in Wichita, Kansas. We've traced Hadley to it."

Ballard practically leapt out of his seat, "How did you find that out? Did all that stuff come out of the blue?"

Harris smiled, "We've not been sitting on our hands while people have been globe-trotting. Actually it's mostly the Boring Guy that's responsible."

We all stared at him and he relented, "You know the BG. That's what it stands for, right, Boring Guy?"

I didn't dignify that with a reply.

Harris went on. "He lives in a small apartment in a suburb called Euless, We've got a unit there keeping surveillance on him. He's at his home from which he operates the business. We want to question him. That's why you need to be here Ms. Wendt. My contacts in the DOD tell me that you did an amazing job interrogating some pretty hard types the last week or so."

I had to agree, but Harris was going on. He leaned toward us as though he were afraid someone would hear us. He even softened his voice, "We're not going in heavy. We're going to make it as friendly as we can."

Minerva interrupted, "Heavy?"

"Sure. No guns. But we do have support. The unit that's been doing surveillance is ready to come in heavy if we need them."

Minerva mumbled under her breath, "Great."

By this time we were off the freeway and driving down a major street. Harris said, "We're just a couple of blocks away. If you've got important questions, now's the time."

I searched my memory for anything that I should know before we went in. Then I said, "Minerva goes in last."

Minerva kicked my shin. Even in the confined space of the car, it hurt. I said, "Minerva objects to that, but it's doesn't make any difference. She's the most valuable member of this team. She goes last."

Another kick to the shin didn't dissuade me. Ballard agreed. By this time we were pulling into a parking lot of a small apartment building. It turned out that this was not Morse's apartment building. The surveillance team was using an empty apartment there. We went up to the 3rd floor where the apartment was. There were half a dozen men. They all had their suit jackets off and several were wearing holsters under the jackets. There was a video camera with a strong telephoto lens that was aimed at the second story landing of a stairway that had a glass wall.

Harris asked, "He still in there?"

Somebody agreed.

Harris said, "OK. We're going in – just me, the Wendts. I want a couple of you stationed in the hall just in case we need backup." Seemingly by telepathy, two men put on their suit jackets and just like that we were off. We crossed the street, and entered the apartment building. Somehow one of our 'friends' had a key that opened the security door and we all went up to the second floor. Our two ghosts stationed themselves at opposite ends of the hall at the entrance to the stairwells.

We three walked on to apartment 2E. Harris knocked on the door.

A voice drifted out, "Just a sec. I'm on my way."

The door opened, and we found ourselves staring at a man who was probably in his thirties. He was wearing shorts and a short-sleeve dress shirt. He was in fair physical shape but had begun balding at the temples. Harris spoke for us, "I'm Phillip Harris, a special agent of the FBI." At that point he opened a small fold that had an ID in the window.

The man stared at it and reached his hand to take it. Harris snapped it shut and said, "Agency policy forbids us to surrender our ID to anyone. If you want a closer look, you may, but not to touch it."

Morse said, "I suppose you're for real. What can I do for you?"

Harris asked, "Are you Lewis Morse, owner of Inheritance LLC?"

"Yes. That's me"

I'd like to ask you a few questions. Would you mind if we came in to sit?

He shrugged and asked, "Who are the military types?"

I introduced Minerva and me, emphasizing that we weren't military but not making it at all clear what we were. He didn't seem to be bothered by the ambiguity.

He invited us to sit and asked if we wanted instant coffee or anything.

We all declined with thanks.

He sat on a wheeled office chair. His living room appeared to be his home office as well. He had a desktop computer, printer, and a small file cabinet. He rolled the chair close to the sofa where we sat. The sofa was not elegant, but it was new and clean. The whole room, except for the office desk, seemed orderly. He asked, "What can I do for you?"

Harris asked, "You are employed by Phillip Minns, aren't you?"

He leaned back in the chair and said, "Not to the best of my knowledge."

Harris continued, "But you did lease a warehouse in Wichita, Kansas, didn't you?"

He nodded, "Sure, but there's no Minns who's using it. It's somebody whose initials are P. H."

Harris asked, "Then Hadley. Did he hire you to lease the warehouse?"

Morse shook his head, "Not to the best of my knowledge. It was part of my business model to lease it for Hadley, whoever that is."

Harris was beginning to be exasperated. Morse would probably never have noticed, but I saw him glance down at his wristwatch. He only did that when he felt frustrated. Harris went on, "OK. Why did you lease that property for Hadley?"

Morse nodded and leaned back in his chair almost to the point where he fell over. He sighed, "I suppose that I knew it was too good to be true."

Harris's glanced at his watch again. "You'd better tell us everything from the beginning and it had better fit together tight."

Morse leaned forward and nodded agreement. "Yes."

□

I started out to my job a little late that morning three weeks ago. If I hadn't, I might never have gone along with the deal that came in a Fedex box that morning. I was skating on the thin edge if you know what I mean.

Anyway, I thought I might be fired this time, and the box was from Switzerland of all places. My curiosity couldn't stand waiting for the evening.

I ripped open the box and found inside, a number of pages of paper. They were stapled together into four groups. The smallest was a two page letter. It was from a Swiss bank officer. I scanned copies of all the contents of the box.

The letter basically said that I'd been selected to run a business for the owner of a certain Swiss bank account. There was a cashier's check for me to prove the earnestness of the offer. It was for $17,000. It was for me whether I agreed to start the business or not.

The sequence of tasks for me to do was laid out in great detail in the largest bundle of sheets. It involved filing paperwork to form an LLC. The paperwork was already completely filled out, including my name. All it needed was my signature. There was paperwork to open a business account. As soon as that was done, I was to send the account number by email to the bank officer. As soon as he had it, he would wire transfer money to the account to let me begin operations. There were detailed instructions about the operations that I would run.

The letter assured me that nothing that the instructions detailed would break US, Swiss, or international law.

I was so shocked by the contents of the box that I didn't go to work at all. Instead, I called my sister and invited myself to dinner with her and her husband who was a corporate lawyer. Until the evening, I read through all the papers—several times.

It all seemed so random. Why did somebody with a Swiss bank account want to bankroll me? I'd never shown any interest in having my own business. I didn't believe that anyone could possibly know enough about me to justify trusting me with seventeen thousand let alone the much larger sums that would be transferred to the business account if I opened one.

That evening, I took the box to dinner. My brother-in-law, Ed, had never been happy about having me for a brother-in-law. Dinner was uncomfortable. When we reached desert, he became truly unpleasant.

As he sipped his coffee after dinner, Ed said, "I saw that you have a FEDEX box that you brought with you. It's got a business proposition, doesn't it?"

I shrugged, "Well, . . ."

He didn't wait for an answer, "It's something that you found on the internet and sent away for. Probably cost you a couple of hundred dollars. You can make hundreds of thousands in weeks, right?"

My sis tried to intervene, "Now, Ed, you really don't need to be insulting. Even if he does have some money-making idea, you should at least listen."

Ed said, "You probably want me to help you finance it. All you need is a couple of thousand dollars, right." He hesitated a second and said, "Right!"

Sis started to object, but I spoke up, "No. Ed's right. The box does have a money-making business idea."

Ed stood and said, "I'm not buying. You might as well leave right now."

Sis's mouth dropped open. I guess she'd never heard him speak like that before.

But I stood up too. "That's not exactly the way it is. I was hoping to get your advice about whether to accept the proposal in that box. I don't need your money—just your brains. I have to admit they're good about business when you want to use them."

Ed didn't know quite how to respond to that. I pressed my temporary advantage. I walked over to the piano bench where I had laid the FEDEX box, retrieved it, and handed it to Ed. "Would you have a look at everything in this box and tell me if it's legal?" I didn't have a lot of savings, but I said, "I'd pay your normal hourly to consult with me about the legality of the proposal."

Ed's attitude changed a little, "Well, I'd be happy to spend an hour or two looking at it. And, I'd do it *pro bono*."

Sis walked around the table to him and put her arm on his shoulder, "Ed will take as much time as it takes and won't charge you a dime, right, Eddie?"

Ed doesn't like her to use that pet name in public, but he was rather stuck and embarrassed and said, "Yes. I'll give it a good look." He picked up the box and took a minute looking it over—as though he were afraid to open it. He commented, "Switzerland. You ordered something from Switzerland?"

"I didn't order anything. A FEDEX guy showed up at my door this morning and handed it to me. Oh, yeh, he had me sign for it too."

Ed opened the box and took out the letter. He scanned it quickly and said, "Oh, Lewis, this is an old scam. They send you a 'cashier's check'. You cash it, and then you send them some money—less than the cashier's check. Then you find out that the 'cashier's check' was a fake."

I smiled a little private smile. "Read on."

He did. He scratched his head. He stood up and walked around the table while reading the letter. Finally, he sat down again and looked at the sheaf of instructions. He set them down and said, "This is interesting. I'd even say amazing. I want to look at it a lot more carefully.

"But one thing that I can say right now is that the cashier's check—if it's good—is yours. I don't see how you can get into trouble cashing it. I'd suggest that you cash it tomorrow. Let it sit in your account for a few days. That should be enough to find out if it's good or not. If it's a forgery, it's quite a good one."

Sis's eyes popped. She was surprised that I could provide something that would stump her husband—even if only for a few days.

He went on, "I'll take a very careful look at the rest of these documents. I don't see where this account owner is headed with this. I don't like that. Also, I don't like that you don't know who he is or even what nationality.

"On the other hand, there's nothing obvious about it that's phony or illegal. Give me the rest of the week." He added, "And maybe the weekend to look this over. In the mean time we should find out whether the check is good or not. If nothing else, it could provide you a nice little nest egg, and it will provide me with some light entertainment." He laughed at his own joke and actually shook my hand as I left for home.

The next day at the bank was interesting. They know me at the bank fairly well. I've never held a job that had direct deposit, so I always bring my check in to deposit. I could use the night depository, but I like the feel of depositing my paycheck in a public way. The bank teller looked at the check and whistled. That all by itself made it worth depositing it in the bank lobby.

He asked me to wait while he called over a bank officer. I sat down in the waiting area. It took about twenty minutes because the bank was busy that morning. The teller and the bank manager talked briefly, and then the manager came over to where I was. The manager was holding the check. He invited me into his office.

"Mr. Morse, we don't get cashiers checks from foreign banks very often. When we do, especially if it's for a large amount of money, we have to report it because it is possibly part of a money laundering scheme. I wanted you to know that before we deposit the check." He looked serious—serious as only a bank manager can. He went on, "Are you sure you want us to deposit this check."

"Yes, sir."

The manager nodded and went on, "Then, we'll put most of the amount on hold until we've verified that the check is good. I strongly advise you not to send any money to anyone until we've done that."

I nodded, "No sir. I don't intend to. I have a lawyer friend," I guess I could call him a friend, "whom I've consulted."

The manager seemed skeptical, "All right. That's good."

He sat a moment, thinking, and then asked, "Is this part of some money-making scheme?"

I smiled at that, "I am considering using the money to start a business. As a matter of fact, if I go ahead, I'll be opening a business account here."

It surprised me that that didn't encourage the manager. However, he didn't say anything more, but he completed the deposit himself, and we parted.

A few days later, I received a call from the bank. The check had cleared, and I had the money. With that, I started carefully examining the business plan that came with the check. I was actually quite anxious to start on it.

Finally, the weekend came. Sis had invited me over for dinner on Sunday. When I arrived, my brother-in-law was as serious as I've ever seen him. However, he has a rule that he will not discuss business over dinner. It was the longest dinner that I'd ever struggled through. Ed was in no hurry though. I didn't know whether that was good or bad.

He finally finished desert and leaned back with his cup of coffee. "Well, I've looked over those documents very very thoroughly. I've gone to my law library a couple of times, and I have to admit that I can't find anything wrong with them."

He hesitated for a sip of coffee. "I have to say that it seems OK. They seem to give you every sort of release of liability that there is. That doesn't mean that you are immune from being sued if something bad happens as a result of what they do on the leased properties. I'd recommend that you have a heart to heart with them to find out exactly what they're up to. Also, I'd check on them periodically to be sure that they stick to the business plan for the property that you lease for them."

I almost couldn't believe what I was hearing. It actually sounded like Ed was saying that it was OK to go ahead with this business opportunity. So I asked him that.

"Yes, it seems like they are being generous with you without being too generous—if you know what I mean."

I nodded enthusiastically.

"So, if you feel up for this, I'd say go for it. I'll help you if you get into any legal problem, but that may not be much more than finding a good attorney for the sort of problem that actually arises."

Sis was beginning to be a little nervous about my actually doing this thing. She was behind me 100% when it was theoretical, and it was a question of whether I was sensible and wouldn't waste her husband's time. Now that I might actually start this business, it was an entirely different matter. She actually argued against my doing it.

Her arguments boiled down to three. I'd never met whoever was hiring me;. I couldn't keep him from doing something really bad with the property that I leased for him: finally, there was an awful lot of money involved. What happened if some of it got "lost". Maybe it was actually a money-laundering scheme.

All week I'd been getting more and more excited with the prospect of starting this business, and the prospect of some danger involved actually stimulated me.

So, the evening ended with my determination to go through with the proposal. Sis was worried to death about me, and Ed seemed to have a respect for me that I'd never had from him before.

The next day, I followed the detailed instructions about how to go online and sign out an LLC, file for an EIN from the IRS, and set up online access to the state tax office.

I walked into my bank the next morning. Now there was a question. How did my "angel" know with what bank I did my banking?

When I walked into the branch manager's office with all my paperwork filled out, including EIN #, he did a double take. "You're back already!" was all that he could say. After looking over the application for a business account, he just shook his head and commented that everything looked fine. I walked out of the bank a full-fledged businessperson.

The next day, I followed the script for leasing a warehouse in Kansas—Witchita to be precise. The script included questions that the leasing office would probably ask and corresponding answers. The conversation went as expected. They were skeptical that a new business would have the financial backing to lease their warehouse, but I followed the script and offered to transfer to their account the first three months rent plus the last month's rent.

That took some courage on my part. I'd just sent my account information to Switzerland by Fedex overnight, but how quickly could they get money into my account. The amount of my initial payment was almost $100,000!

However, the next day I received an email. There was a deposit in my business account. I logged on to the account and found that it was well over a $300,000. It was enough to cover a year's lease.

The day after that, I got a call from the company I'd been dealing with. They made a counter offer. If I put up 6 months rent immediately—that day—I could have the warehouse. I nonchalantly replied that if they'd give me their bank information, I'd wire it to them today. There was a gulp at the other end of the line. I think they weren't expecting that, but they were trapped. They gave me the account number and routing number. I went to the bank and arranged the transfer.

Two days later, I flew to Kansas City and rented a car that I drove to Lenexa, Kansas where the leasing office was. We signed the papers. They gave me the keys to the front gate and the various doors in the building.

They gave me a tour of the building, which had obviously stood unused for years. I began to wonder if my invisible partner knew what he was doing. It took me the next couple of days to assume responsibility for utilities and the phone line.

A couple of weeks before that process would all have been daunting to me. Now, with a stuffed bank account, it all seemed as easy as a walk in the park.

Of course, I had only one problem. Who was going to accept the keys from me? I went back to Dallas and sat wondering how I'd find out to whom I'd turn the keys over.

⊞

The next Sunday, Ed called me himself to invite me to dinner. The feeling at dinner was electric. I could tell that Ed was dying to know what had happened with the business, but he still wouldn't break his rule of no business discussed over dinner, but I was going to teach him a lesson about unreasonable rules.

When the coffee came out, he let go of his excitement. "What in the world happened!"

I drew the revelations out with Ed hanging on every word. When I'd finished, he was not satisfied. "Well, who is going to use the warehouse, and what are they going to do?"

Here, of course, I was stuck. I had no idea.

Ed wasn't satisfied. "So, you still have the keys. Your mysterious sponsor has not stepped forward or appointed anyone to act as his agent?"

I had to shake my head, "No."

Ed stood up and started pacing. He seemed about to say something a time or two but eventually, he sat down. Seeming to answer an internal question, he said, "No." softly and then looked up at me. "What's your plan?"

I so much expected a suggestion that it took me back. I thought a moment and said, "Well, I'm going to give my 'sponsor' a couple of days, maybe the rest of the week. Yes, the rest of the week. Next week at this time, if I've not heard from him, I guess I have to start spending time up in Wichita to keep an eye on the property."

Ed thought about that for a long time and finally said, "I guess that's the best idea. Keep in touch. And I mean more frequently than weekly. I want to know what happens." He said that with real determination.

I could only agree. We called it an evening. Sis was more than a little worried. When we hugged as I left, she whispered to me, "Make that every day!"

Ed needn't have worried. It was only a couple of days, on Wednesday, when I received a Fedex letter box. I ripped it open and found a single typed page addressed to me.

The letter instructed me to go to the Starbucks at Beltline and the LBJ freeway near the DFW airport at 9 AM the next day. I was to bring keys and anything else required to use the warehouse. There was no further information—no names, no descriptions of who would meet me, and no explanation of the purpose that he or they had. I resolved then that I would find that out before I surrendered any keys.

The next day, I was at the Starbucks very early. I didn't mind waiting a couple of hours if it added any to my safety. I arrived, bought a copy of the *New York Times*, a cup of coffee (Trente), and a blueberry scone. I took a lone seat away from the corners and tried to be inconspicuous.

It was a long vigil. The *Times* had some interesting articles but I had no idea how long two hours would be in a coffee shop. After 45 minutes, I began the crossword in desperation. The Wednesday *Times* crossword is not awful. I began to get interested in it. When nine AM arrived, I was engrossed in getting the last few clues.

When he showed up, I didn't even notice him. The first thing I did when I realized that I was being watched from a range of about two feet was to glance at my watch. It was 9:01. I then looked up.

He was short, had hair that was a light brown and had begun to grow over his ears. He was clean-shaven and was wearing a short sleeve dress shirt—light blue. He wouldn't have stood out in a crowd any more than I wanted to.

The first thing he said was, "You have something for me." It wasn't a question. It was a positive statement that would brook no disagreement.

I was determined to prove that he was the right man before I handed anything over. I asked, "Who sent you?"

His answer--instinctive, instant, innocuous—was, "No one sent me."

I corrected my question, "Who are you working for then?"

"No one."

"Then how did you know that I would be here?"

His answer was so matter-of-fact that I was stuck for a moment. He said, "I knew."

He didn't sit. He didn't ask to sit. He just stood there waiting for me to hand the envelope of keys that I had over to him.

I was not going to be put off that easily, "I'm not going to hand anything over until I know more. What's your name?"

He was still unmoving. "You don't need to know it."

He actually had me there. Did I really need to know his name? I wanted to, but somehow I couldn't think of a reason that I needed to know it. But I wasn't through. I asked, "What are you going to do with the warehouse. I HAVE to know that before I give you anything."

He smiled at that, "I suppose that I should tell you that. As a matter of fact, I need more help from you, so I do have to tell you.

"I'm researching diseases," was the deadpan answer.

That was a surprise. That answer suggested a lot of questions. I started with the most obvious, "Well, Dr. . . ." I suppose that I was hoping to catch him off-guard. I hoped he'd complete the name.

He only said, "I'm not a doctor – either PhD or MD."

I asked, "What drug company?"

"I don't work for anyone."

I was getting frustrated. "Well, somebody's putting a lot of money up for you to do your research. You don't mean to tell me that you don't know who they are?"

"I don't."

I was stymied for a moment. It irritated me that he was standing all this time, and I had to look up to see his face. "Well, dog gone it, sit down so that we can talk properly—face to face."

For once he did as I asked. He pulled a chair up beside the little table that stood between us. He sat, and we were very nearly looking levelly at each other.

I decided that I might get some information by following the hint he'd given earlier. "You said you needed some more help from me. What is it you need?"

He had been holding a small portfolio the whole time that we'd been talking. He pulled it from under his left arm and opened it. It contained a few sheets of paper stapled together. He pulled those sheets out and handed them to me as he said, "I need some equipment delivered to the warehouse. These sheets are order sheets for a couple of supply houses. Please see that they are executed as quickly as possible. I will move into the warehouse and hope to begin work next week."

I accepted them and looked them over. There was quite a lot of equipment – centrifuges, chemical equipment, chemicals. I'd never taken more than high school chemistry, but I recognized some names. There were organic solvents and some chemicals that I could not pronounce let alone know their uses.

This was the critical point. If the prices quoted on the purchase orders were accurate, I had enough money in the account to cover these purchases. Should I?

At this point, I glanced up and found that the serene visage of the other was no longer serene. He asked, "Is there something wrong on the order?"

I opened my mouth to speak and thought hard about my next words. "There was nothing in my instructions about ordering or paying for equipment."

The line of his lips hardened and compressed, "I don't think your employer will object to anything I've asked for."

He started to rise, and a sense of real threat filled me. Would he attack me here in a Starbucks? What was he capable of? What was he not capable of? That came from a small voice inside my head.

I decided not to test him. I rationalized my decision. There was nothing dangerous on his shopping list (as far as I knew). This was not so surprising? Why else was I drawing a large salary?

I made a quick placating gesture with my hands, "That's OK. I just want to make sure that I'm not doing anything against my sponsor's interest."

The tension immediately left the room. He relaxed and sat again. "Good. Please get to work on that."

I nodded and pulled the small envelope with keys and a few pages of instructions on using the electronic security system that the warehouse had. I handed it to him.

He opened the envelope, poured the keys out into his hand, glanced at them for a moment, and poured them back into the envelope.

"Don't you want to know what each key is for?"

He simply shook his head.

He then pulled the few printed sheets out of the envelope. His glance was even more perfunctory than it had been for the keys. He slid the pages back into the envelope.

I was getting exasperated by this nonchalance. "Come on. Don't you even want any description of how the security system works?"

"Why? I'll have no trouble with it."

"Whom should I have this equipment sent to?" I asked.

He had stood and was mostly turned to leave before I finished the sentence. From the other side of his back he answered, "Just use the initials, P. H."

I asked him what his cell phone # was. Now he was turned completely away, and he walked on but said over his shoulder, "I don't have one."

That was the only time that I've seen him. I don't know how he got to the Starbucks or where he'd come from. I was stunned for a moment by the suddenness of his departure. By the time that I got up and started to follow him to see how he left, he was out of sight.

I went home. I wasted no time in writing checks drawn on the business account and getting the purchase orders in the mail – FEDEX next day. Then I called Sis and invited myself over to dinner. She accepted immediately.

That evening, after dinner was over, I told them a story about what had happened that day. Everything I said was true, but I added details made up out of whole cloth.

The meeting was detailed in a letter from my "sponsor". It had names, addresses, etc. It named the person who was to use the warehouse. His name was Patrick Harmon. He was a chemist who was doing research on a cancer cure. He'd tried to explain what the theory of the cure was, but I had to admit that I just didn't "get" it.

I had ordered some research equipment that was to be delivered to the warehouse.

Why wasn't he doing his research at a drug company? Well, his company (which he wouldn't name) was worried about industrial espionage, and they were doing everything they could think of to keep it a secret. And now that I'd told my closest relatives about it, I had to ask them to respect that secrecy.

Ed was uncomfortable. After we'd talked, and I was about to leave, he walked out on his porch with me. He expressed his doubts, "Look, I'm a lawyer, and I take depositions and cross-exam people in court. It's my business to know when people aren't tell the 'truth, the whole truth, and nothing but the truth'.

"I know that story is NOT any of those three things. I can't identify what's truth and what's not. Now, do you want to tell me what the truth is? You don't have to tell your sister, and I won't tell her if you don't want me to, but at least tell me." The request almost sounded like a desperate plea. He continued, "Give me a dollar."

The preposterousness of that request made me laugh. "Are you panhandling now?" I immediately regretted what I'd said. I said so. It was a stupid jibe. Ed had been straight with me so far. He deserved better. It was just such an unexpected request that it caught me by surprise, and I laughed.

Ed was quite decent about it. He said that he'd have said something similar in my place. He then turned really serious, "Give me a dollar as a retainer. Then I'm officially your lawyer and our conversation is privileged—I can't be forced to reveal it in a court of law."

I thought about it. He was probably being straight with me. I reached in my wallet, which rarely had a bill in it much larger than a single. Now, it had tens, twenties, and by gosh, I'd forgotten that it had a fifty at the moment. I didn't have a single. I handed him a fiver. "OK. I'm sorry, I don't have a single."

He nodded and accepted it. He then said, "You're my client now. Do you have anything to tell me in the strictest confidence?"

I nodded and then said, "In the first place, almost everything I told you was true. Or if it wasn't true, it was a reasonable deduction from what I know. The whole truth is contained in it. I've just exaggerated what I know some."

He looked down at his shoes, took a deep breath, and said, "How about nothing but the truth?"

I grimaced. "OK. I'll make it simple. Leave off the full name. I just have his initials. I don't know who's sponsoring him—whether it's Pharma or a government or . . ."

Ed grimaced too, "Or a drug dealer."

The answer that came to my head was instantaneous, and I knew, true, "No. It's not that. He's not working for profit."

"How can you possibly know that?"

How did I know that? I thought about my conversation with him. I started speaking, and I wasn't sure just where the answer came from, but I knew it was true. "You had to see him and hear him. He just is not motivated by greed. His motivation is . . ." Here I stopped because the word that came to mind was too strange. I barely knew it, let alone used it, but it was there and the right word.

Ed asked, "Yes?"

"Ethereal."

Ed stared at me and then nodded his head. Somehow I'd communicated to him the sense that I had of the "rightness" of the mysterious intent of P. H.

Wichita

When he'd finished his story, we had questions. Harris wanted most of all to get a copy of the purchase orders or at least an accurate list of the things that were on them.

Morse nodded, "I was careful." He reached into a desk drawer and pulled out a manila folder. Inside it was a sheath of papers. "I made copies of all the purchase orders. Here's the first." He handed several sheets to Ballard. He went on, "The rest are in here when you want them."

Ballard greedily pored over them. After a quick but thorough examination he said, "Just as you say. I don't recognize all the chemicals, but you could be doing almost anything with the rest from making aspirin to refining heroin."

He handed them to me and asked me to see what I could make of them.

I asked, "How did he communicate with you for the rest of the purchase orders?"

"By mail. He didn't even use FEDEX."

Harris asked, "When was the last time that you heard from him?"

He pulled out the last purchase order and looked at the date. "Six days ago. Has he done something since then?"

We all looked at each other, and Harris said, "We're not sure."

Morse chuckled, "When people say, 'I'm not sure', they almost always mean, 'I don't know.'"

No one commented.

Harris spoke for all of us. "We're out of questions for the moment, but we'd like for you to stay available here in the Dallas area for at least a couple of weeks."

"No problem. At the moment, all I have to do is sit here, wait for instructions and collect my salary. I suppose after a couple of weeks, I should go up to inspect the warehouse if I don't hear from—what did you call him—Harley?"

Harris said, "No, Hadley."

□

We left the apartment and went back down to the cars. We stood outside them while we had a consult—more accurately while Harris and Ballard had a consult. The upshot was that we were all going up to Wichita to take a look around at the warehouse. Ballard rode in the back seat with Minerva and me. He told us how they'd found Hadley and how Brahms and his wife were involved.

Minerva leaned back against my shoulder and mumbled, "Wake me when we get to Hogwarts."

Harris switched to the jump seat so that he could face us. "This is how Brahms found Hadley. He's been analyzing all the video that he could get his hands on. And, by the way, I should say, complaining steadily about the slow bandwidth and the lack of remote computing power.

"Anyway, he got a positive match on Hadley at the Kansas City airport. He was checking in at a Southwest counter there. The flight was going to Miami. It took us a while to find out where he went next from Miami.

"He'd already left the country by the time that Brahms turned him at Kansas City. In Miami he changed airlines and flew on to Manaus, Brazil."

Minerva, who apparently was half-way listening, exclaimed, "You mean to tell me that you don't check international flights for these people?"

Harris grimaced, "Well we do, but they don't always travel on their own ID's."

That quieted her down. However, it got me thinking. "Did you find out what ID he was traveling under?"

Harris hung his head, "Well, that's the thing. He had a second ID that was really under his own name."

My jaw dropped at that, "How can that be possible! Under his own name?"

Harris said, "Oh, it's not so strange. There are lots of people in the US that have the same name as others – even an unusual name like Minns. When we have an international no fly list, we use the passport

146

control number not the name. He had a second passport with the same name."

Minerva stared at him. "How is that possible?"

"He was really clever. I guess that's no surprise. He used his birth certificate to obtain a second Social Security #. Then he used his birth certificate and the second Social Security # to get a driver's license in a different state. Then he used his new Social Security #, new driver's license, and original birth certificate to obtain a second passport."

She pressed, "Surely that's illegal!"

"Well, the only step that's really illegal is getting the second Social Security #. But no one pays a lot of attention to that. And I'm not sure that it's technically illegal at that. Maybe claiming benefits under more than one Social Security # is. It must be. I think."

I said, "I hope you're being more careful with the others. Like using names to catch them when they fly rather than passport control #'s."

"Yes, we've learned our lesson. The trouble is that we've only learned it very recently. We don't know where any of the Four are right now."

Minerva stared at him again. He answered the unasked question, "Oh, we know where Hadley was 4 days ago. We don't know where he is now. He's probably not moved to another country but we can't be sure. He might have moved again before we figured out how he was getting around."

On the drive up, Minerva and I got a review of what had been happening stateside. The FBI had set up a command post on the other side of Wichita from the warehouse. They had an observation post a block away in a small rented office on the third floor. They had established contact with the local police and the State Highway patrol. Both were co-operating, which was to say that they were staying out of our way.

Minerva asked, "What about Pearson and Harker? What have they been doing?"

Ballard replied, "We'll let them tell you for themselves. They're at the command post right now."

We arrived at the command post and discovered that it was a double-wide mobile home converted to an electronic hub where we could have contact with all the people working on this case throughout the world. They had installed cameras that observed all sides of the warehouse. They had infrared and optical sensors so we had 24 x 7 coverage of the building and the surroundings.

When we arrived, we found that Sally and Pearson were waiting for us. They were even more anxious to hear what we had been doing than we were to hear their adventures. At least, they knew we had been in the Middle East. We didn't have any idea what they'd been doing.

There wasn't a quiet corner of the command post, so we decided that we'd stay in their motel room with them at least for this night and get an idea of what had been happening with them.

Sally had a rental car. She drove us to their motel. Fortunately, there was a restaurant next door. We had a late night dinner and told them our story of the Middle East and the interview of Morse who was managing Hadley's affairs.

By the time we'd finished those stories, it was getting truly late, so we moved the venue to our room. It was a "suite" with a bedroom and a living area with a fold-out sofa bed. There was a little argument about who would get the sofa bed. We all wanted it, but we played a wizard game for it. You put two objects, like coffee cups on a table. Each wizard transfigures one of the objects into one of three things: a bat, a rat, or a cat. Cat beats rat. Rat beats bat. Bat beats cat. Of course, ties retry. It took Pearson four tries before he beat Minerva with bat beats cat. I think Minerva let him win. Anyway, they got the sofa.

We got ready for bed, but I insisted on hearing what Sally and Pearson had been doing. They didn't resist. They admitted that they had to leave the country the next day to pursue Hadley, and they might not have time then to tell us their story if they didn't now.

There was a small fireplace in the suite. I suggested that we light a fire and have a campfire story.

Minerva had never heard the term. I explained. "In the US, lots of people go camping. Most kids have been on at least one camping trip—if not with family, then with the boy scouts or the girl scouts or some group. One of the standard features is a campfire. People make 'smores and take turns telling scary stories."

Of course, Minerva wanted to know about 'smores. So, I took her out to the food vending machine and found Hersheys chocolate and marshmallows (much to my surprise) and even graham crackers.

Pearson, of course, got a roaring blaze going in the fireplace before we had even returned. The kitchenette had some forks. I demonstrated roasting a marshmallow, putting it on one piece of graham cracker, putting a piece of chocolate on top, and eating it while still hot.

Pearson, though an American, had never seen a 'smore made. He knew about a brand of cookie by that name, but he declared that it didn't hold a candle to the real thing. So, we each made a couple of 'smores and Sally started the story. She insisted that she tell it because she knew me well enough to anticipate the many irritating interrupting inquiries that I would ask and could forestall them.

⊏⊐

Your revelation about the Swiss bank Sept XC Suisse caused Harris to go there to get the Swiss to reveal details of transactions that Minns executed with the account.

He insisted that Phil and I come along in case they needed some persuasion to reveal account details. Of course, Harris was right. The Swiss are notorious for protecting the privacy of account holders.

We arrived early in the morning, but Harris insisted that we get a good day's rest before taking them on. Also, the State Department had requested the Swiss to turn over account detail information, and we wanted to give them an opportunity to comply. So, we checked into our hotel, got as much sleep as we could, and then in the late afternoon took a tour of Bern.

The next day, we went to the bank for a 9 AM appointment. Harris had made the appointment for us. We were kept waiting only a few minutes and were taken into the office of someone who was described as Personal Assistant to the Chief Compliance Officer, Denise Chevalier. She wore a grey tailored business suit. Her shoulder length blonde hair spread over both shoulders and toward her breasts. She was standing when we entered.

As soon as we were well into the large office, she motioned us to seats with an economy of movement that I actually admired. She spoke good English but not without an accent. The accent was closer to French than German. Before she was seated, she asked "Wish you a beverage?" It was an unusual way to phrase the question, but I wasn't too surprised. Harris asked for a cup of coffee. She picked up the phone and spoke rapidly. I couldn't make out the language.

She then sat and said, "Please tell me which of you is Mr. Harris?"

She didn't need any more information to identify us all. The coffee arrived. Her secretary brought in two—one for Harris and one for Ms. Chevalier.

Then she came directly to the point, "Mr. Harris, you are American FBI. But who are your associates?"

Harris smiled involuntarily. He'd apparently practiced this introduction, "Mr. Pearson and Ms. Harker are private contractors that the FBI has hired to help with the current case."

Chevalier leaned back and drew out an "ahhhh." She went on, "Zen, you two are private investigators?"

149

Pearson smiled too, "Let's just say that I am with the security arm of an NGO."

Chevalier nodded, "Yes. NGO. Non-Governmental Organization. Which organization?"

Pearson was cool. "You'll never have heard of it. It's the Auror Agency."

Chevalier moved forward on her chair, "Aurora? Yes, I've heard of Aurora."

"No, I didn't say Aurora. Let's not spar. My agency values its privacy as much as many of your clients."

Chevalier turned to me, "And you, Ms. Harker?"

I was glad that she'd asked Phil for details first. I tried to be as cool as he was, "I work for an English school. I'm afraid that you'll not have heard of it either. It's Hogwarts. I'm the Personal Assistant to the Head of the School."

Chevalier asked, "Why are you on Harris's team?"

Harris interrupted, "I'm only going to say that she's a resourceful young woman who has proved her meddle in some very difficult situations." He added, "She was on the team that defeated the 'Souls'."

Chevalier was impressed, "Oh, my dear, I see why Mr. Harris might want your help.

"Now, let me tell you that we can't be of assistance to you. The bylaws of our bank don't permit it."

Harris objected, "You've received the letter from the State . . ."

Chevalier interrupted, "Of course, we have. You want the transaction history of one of our clients. That is against our obligation to our clients, and although we sometimes stretch a principle in important cases, I see nothing in ze letter that is particularly urgent."

She had paused, probably to formulate a difficult sentence. Harris began to object, but Chevalier went on, "No! Hear me out.

"If there were proof that this client of ours were an arms dealer or drug dealer or were laundering money for a criminal cartel, of course, it would be a different case. However, you have not shown any such thing." With that she placed both her open hands palm down on her desk with a gesture of finality that it was hard to argue with.

Phil set his jaw and said, "This man is a US Army deserter, and he's obtained his money by thievery in the country where he was serving."

Chevalier actually laughed. "Yes, we know that his money came from an act of theft from the ISIS organization. I don't know about deserting, but nothing in your State Department letter mentions deserting or anything like it."

Harris spoke then, "Well, Mr. Pearson is not technically right. Minns is guilty, at this point, only of being Absent Without Leave. That is a minor infraction, but we believe that he is in the process of planning something much more serious—some act of terrorism or an even more serious crime."

Chevalier laughed again, "Well, when you have evidence of that please come back, and we'll have another pleasant conversation. But for now, I think our business is *finis*."

Harris looked at me appealingly. I asked, "Wait. We'd like to speak to the Chief Compliance Officer, please."

She only smiled as she said a very definite, "No."

Phil looked at me and said, "*Imperious*?" softly.

I nodded. With that, he pulled out his wand and said, "*Imperio*." Chevalier stared at the wand for a moment and said, "Oui?"

I ordered, "Speak English."

She repeated in a flat accent-less voice, "Yes?"

Harris asked, "Can you print the list of transactions we want?"

With no apparent emotion she just said, "No."

Phil asked, "Why not?"

The answer was simple, "I don't have the authority?"

Harris asked, "Does your boss have the authority?"

She simply said, "I don't know."

"Would he know who does have the authority?"

It was the only hesitation that we'd encountered. She finally said, "Maybe."

Phil commanded, "Get him in here right now."

She picked up the handset of her phone and dialed a number. After a moment she said, "Yes, Clarisse, this is very important, I don't care if he's with an important client."

Another minute passed, and then she said, "Mr. Mayer, I'm sorry to interrupt but this is important. Please come down to my office immediately. . . No. this should only take a few minutes. . . .. I'm speaking English because the people in my office only speak English."

She hung up the receiver and said, "He will be here momentarily."

She was right. The door opened, and a thin ascetic man entered. He wore a dark gray suit and looked like he might have been athletic—his build was what some people call wiry. He took in the whole room as he entered it, and strode directly to Chevalier. "What is this about? Are these the Americans who want us to surrender client information?"

Chevalier nodded.

With that I said to Phil, "*Imperio*."

Mayer didn't even notice. The spell struck him, and he stopped speaking immediately. Phil said, "Sit."

Harris said, "You received a letter from the US State Department about giving us transaction information about an account."

Mayer didn't say anything.

Exasperated, Harris went on, "Turn it over to us immediately."

The flat monotone voice responded, "I can't."

Harris asked, "Why not?"

Mayer answered briefly and to the point, "I don't have authority. Only the banker handling his account can request that."

Harris swore almost inaudibly and then said, "Bring that person here immediately."

Mayer said, "He is on vacation and won't be back until next week."

I asked, "Isn't there anyone who can access that account here?"

Mayer seemed to think a minute. "I think Information Technology can."

Harris was long past losing his temper, "Well get someone from IT up here who can do that."

Mayer picked up the phone and dialed a number. He spoke in German, but none of us thought it necessary to get a translation. At the end, he said, "They have someone coming."

The IT guy entered the room next. "*Was passiert?*"

The room that had seemed so large was now beginning to seem crowded. I commented, "It's as bad as King's Cross on the first day of school." Pearson just grunted in response.

Harris tiredly said, "English, *bitte*."

The IT guy said, "My English not so good is."

"That's OK. Ms. Chevalier is going to give you an account number and you're going to print off all transactions against it."

The IT guy immediately looked up to Mayer. Mayer looked at Phil, who nodded, then Mayer said, "Yes, please."

The IT guy said, "Your authority?"

Mayer said, "*Yah, yah.*"

The IT guy still seemed to hesitate. It was at that point that Phil pointed his wand and said, "*Imperio.*"

The IT guy walked around the big desk and sat at Chevalier's chair. Everyone except Chevalier and Mayer followed him and watched as he restarted the computer. He logged in and got to a very different screen than Chevalier had used. The IT guy asked, "Account number?"

Chevalier picked up the letter and read off the number slowly and precisely.

The IT guy did quite a lot of keying and even a little swearing; finally he had a screen with columns of business names, amounts in Euros, dates, and balances.

Harris nodded, "Great. Print that off for us."

The IT guy said, "I can't do that."

Harris couldn't believe it. He'd forgotten that under the Imperious curse, you can't lie, "Why not?"

"Security."

Harris said, "Shit!"

Then an idea occurred to me. "I'll take photos of the pages with my phone."

Harris slapped his forehead, "Of course. Do it and let's get out of here."

By this time it was near 1 PM. A woman opened the door and said, "Ms. Chevalier, you have an appointment."

Phil didn't even ask. He just turned, pointed his wand and said, "Ms. Chevalier is ill, don't let anyone in."

The secretary immediately turned and closed the door behind her.

Meanwhile, I'd asked the IT guy to keep scrolling the screen and I kept taking pictures. When he'd finished, I checked my photos and was satisfied, "That's it. Let's get out of here."

Harris agreed, but Phil said, "Wait. I've got to do a memory modification spell." He walked around the room, one by one, pointing his wand and saying *"Obliviate* three hours." When he'd finished, we left the office and found the secretary whom he'd *imperioused* and *oblivated* her memory for the last half hour.

We left and went directly to our hotel, checked out, and went to the airport. We changed our return flight by a day and waited for our flight.

⊡

Sally finished her story and said, "Now, we're going to be on our way to our next assignment, Brazil."Minerva and I were surprised. I assumed that she meant Rio or San Paulo, but it turned out she meant Manaus.

Minerva asked the question on my lips, "What in the world is in Manaus?"

"Hadley for one. Or at least he was there a few days ago."

I asked, "How did you find out that Hadley was there?" Then I remembered what Harris had said, "OK. I know how you found out that he was going there, but what in the world is in Manaus, Brazil?"

153

Phil answered, "Brahms eventually traced him on security video in the Manaus airport and got a couple of glimpses of him in video on the waterfront in Manaus."

Minerva asked, "The ocean?"

Sally responded, "No silly, Manaus is landlocked except for the . . ."

We all supplied, "Amazon River."

I asked, "So you figure what he's doing has something to do with the River?"

Phil said, "We don't know. That's why Sally and I are going there."

Minerva asked, "Who's going with you?"

The two of them looked at each other and said, "Nobody?"

I asked, "Do either of you speak Portuguese?"

Phil asked, "Does Hadley?"

I was disgusted with this failure to understand our opponents, "He does by now. He probably picked it up on the flight there."

Sally rescued the situation. "The State Department is supporting us. They'll help us find a translator. Besides, I took college Spanish. It's pretty close to Portuguese."

Minerva muttered, "College Spanish."

I asked, "Why isn't Harris or at least Ballard going along?"

Sally said, "The transaction log that we got opened a treasure trove. It found you Morse. We know where Connover is—exactly. And we expect to know where Reynaldo is shortly.

"Ballard is going to take you two along to find Connover. Harris is running the show here. He thinks this warehouse is going to be their future base of operations."

I still wasn't happy. "Just what are you going to do when you find him—if you find him?"

They looked at each other and Phil shrugged, "I'll use the *Petrificus Totalis* curse on him, and then we'll be in the driver's seat."

I shook my head in disbelief at his *naiveté*. "You two had better come up with a backup plan. I don't think that will be as easy as you think."

It was now well after midnight, and I was ready for bed. We got into the queen-size bed, and Minerva snuggled close.

I asked, "How long has it been since we slept last?"

"You mean real sleep—not dozing in an airplane seat?"

"Yup."

Minerva yawned and said, "I've no idea."

Then she asked, "What is our backup plan?" emphasizing the "our".

The light was out, but she knew that I had just shrugged. Then I had a thought. I reached under the bed for my purse.

Minerva said in bored tones, "Oh, that gun. You think it's the solution for everything."

I laughed, "Isn't it?"

In answer to that, she ran her hand along my side that was not resting on the bed, and as it slipped down over my stomach she said, "It's not a solution for this." She knows my vulnerabilities perfectly. Her hand hadn't reached it before it stood straight up and I had her inside my arms and I was inside her.

My last coherent question was, "No foreplay for you?"

Her answer was, "What makes you think there won't be?"

The next day I was still aching from the workout she'd put me through the night before. Neither of us was totally awake before the phone in our room rang. I picked it up. It was Ballard, "Come on. We've got a raid on, and I want both our witch and wizard on the scene. Just dress. Forget about breakfast."

We were up and dressed quickly. Sally complained about how late we were up the previous night making a racket.

Ballard showed up at our room shortly after that. We drove to the command center.

There was a large black truck there and a number of FBI people who reminded me a lot of the military we'd been with lately when we were getting ready for the operation in Northern Iraq. The only difference was that they had FBI stenciled in big bold letters all over their uniforms. One of them signaled us to join him near the truck. When we arrived, they tossed each of us a helmet and a flack jacket with FBI stenciled on it. His only comment was, "Get suited up. We're going to have a last minute briefing in five."

He was surprised at how quickly Minerva got suited up. He asked her, "Have you been in combat recently?"

She smiled charmingly and asked, "Do you need to know?"

He admitted that he didn't, and just then Harris gathered us around him. There were a dozen agents, the four of us, and Ballard and Harris. Harris, was efficient, "Our guests here are contractors who know a lot about interrogation and are battle-tested." I thought that was a bit of an exaggeration. "They come in at the end when things are clear.

"We don't know what we'll meet. We might conceivably run into

155

Minns himself. If not, any or all of the others may be there. Our number one priority is. . ."

This must be a standard question because it got an immediate unison answer, "Safety first."

Harris went on, "We are pretty sure that there's a lot of chemical equipment and chemical reagents. We don't think there will be problems with dangerous gases but . . . "

There was the chorused answer, "Safety first."

"We want to take all of the four persons of interest ALIVE! Our contractors can't interrogate a corpse."

Minerva whispered in my ear, "That's not strictly true."

I hissed, "Shut up!"

"So, the SWAT team goes in first. The contractors hard behind them as soon as the scene is clear. The scientists last."

"Half of you will watch the three sides of the warehouse. The rest will go in the main entrance. Are we ready for forcible entry?"

One of the SWAT teams affirmed that they were.

Harris finished, "OK. Saddle up. Let's go."

The SWAT team got into the black truck. The rest of us were in two black Escalades. We caravaned out. It was a short drive, but it seemed a lot shorter trip than I wanted. When we got a block away, the caravan stopped. There were a half dozen who got out of it and ran ahead of us.

Minerva asked what they were doing.

Harris answered, "Setting up the perimeter so that no one can escape other than through the front entrance."

After several minutes, we drove on to the main gate. We stopped. Two men got out. One was carrying the largest bolt cutter that I'd ever seen in my life. They approached the gate, shrugged, and simply slid the fence open.

Sally commented, "Trusting, aren't they?"

Harris said, "Yeh, OR they have a big surprise for any intruders."

Sally herself shrugged.

We drove in and parked in front of the high main entrance to the warehouse. Out came the man with the bolt cutter. There was a shrug and he slid the door open slowly. We were parked so that we didn't have a line of sight into the warehouse. The truck was parked across the entrance. Harris commented, "Here's where we get out."

The other Escalade wasn't disgorging anyone. Minerva asked, "What about them?" pointing at the other car.

Harris said, "They're the scientists."

Sally mumbled, "I wish I were a scientist."

Harris was wearing a radio. I hadn't noticed it before because it was designed to be inconspicuous. He began giving us a play by play as the team entered the warehouse.

"No one visible. . . Found the lights." That was obvious. The interior was suddenly much brighter. "There are crates that are labeled with chemical names. . . Building is pretty much empty. . . Large back room. . . Not locked. . . Entered. . . "

There was a long pause. Then Harris continued. "Two double-wide trailers. . . Entered one. . . Power and water is connected. . . Set up for habitation. . . practically nothing personal."

There was a hesitation. Then Harris threw open the door next to him and said, "Get moving. We've got a situation."

I asked, "What happened?"

The only answer I got was, "You'll see."

Harris led the way in. We went through the essentially empty warehouse. There was what I guessed was a firewall with a large sliding steel door that was most of the way open. I could only see wall as we approached the door.

When we arrived in the door, I could see the two double-wide trailers parked near one of the walls. The nearer looked like an ordinary trailer with nothing unique. On the other side of the trailer was another trailer that we had only a very poor view of until we rounded the nearer trailer. When we did, what we saw stopped us in our tracks.

The leader of the SWAT team came up and explained. The trailer was completely enclosed except for what appeared to be an improvised airlock. The enclosing wrapper looked like a very heavy plastic like shrink wrap—except much thicker. It was possible to see the trailer itself through the shrink wrap and what we saw looked pretty normal.

The team leader said, "On the other side of the trailer there's some sort of filter arrangement and there's some sort of system maintaining positive air pressure inside the shrink wrap."

Harris looked at the rest of us who had come along—Ballard, Sally, Phil, Minerva, and I. "What do you think this is?"

Ballard didn't hesitate. "It's a clean room."

I agreed. Minerva asked, "That's a lot of trouble to keep from having to do housekeeping."

Phil looked at me, "Is she always like this?"

I just shrugged. The team leader explained further. "We don't want to go in without being sure that we'll not let something dangerous out or without having someone in a hazmat suit."

Ballard immediately looked at me and said, "If we get a couple of hazmat suits here, can the two of you get in there without breaking any seals?"

I looked to Minerva. She asked, "You mean without opening that fancy door?"

Ballard nodded.

She concentrated a moment, seeming to look inward and then asked something strange, "Can I go in the other trailer?"

Everyone except Phil stared at her. Harris looked a question at the team leader. He said, "Sure. It's safe as far as we know. There's still a couple of guys in there looking for evidence."

Minerva walked around the trailer, and we heard the door open. Then, after a moment she returned. "Sure, if we have to, I can get Wendt and me in there."

At that Sally spoke up, "No, sir, boss. You don't go in there. Phil and I will."

Both Minerva and I said simultaneously, "I'm pulling rank on you. You won last night. We get the fun today."

Minerva stared at me and asked, "Since when are you her boss?"

Sally spoke up again, "You both are."

Harris had called for two hazmat suits, so we had to wait. While we were waiting I asked Minerva, "Why did you go into the other trailer?"

"Let's go in there, and I'll explain."

Harris said, "As soon as they arrive, I'll bring the suits in to you."

As we entered, Minerva said, "He understands."

"What does 'he' understand?"

"That I have to be able to visualize the interior of the other trailer to disapparate. We'll do it from here."

While we were waiting, the SWAT team had finished whatever they were doing. After they left Minerva grabbed my arms, pulled me to her and kissed me with an intensity that had less to do with love-making and far more to do with another emotion. When she released me, she said, "Just in case we don't get another chance to do that."

Then we waited.

□□
□□ □

It was a while before the suits arrived. When they did, Harris came in with the technicians who suited us up. These were not ordinary hazmat suits. Rather than filters, they had their own oxygen supply.

Minerva laughed when they'd finished with me, "You look like a ruddy astronaut."

All I said was, "You next."

After we were suited up the tech said, "It's pretty near automatic. If you come back alive, we'll unsuit you."

Harris said, "You've got a camera on your head with light in case it's dark in there. Look around. You don't need to interpret anything. That's what the scientists out there in the other car are for."

There was a radio in the helmet. I heard his voice coming from two sources. Harris was going on, "DON'T come back through here. Apparate outside the main entrance. You can do that, right?"

Minerva just nodded but that didn't satisfy Harris, "Say that out loud."

Minerva just said, "Right." The tone of voice she used told me that she was getting impatient.

I suddenly had a worry, "Can you disapparate me through this suit."

"That's why we kissed. It helps me keep contact with you. Let's not burn any more sunlight as you sometimes say."

I nodded, held out my hand, and felt the universe spinning around me. And then it was clear that I was someplace else completely different. The double-wide had been pretty much gutted. There was just one large room with lots of chemical equipment. I saw what I thought must be the centrifuge that Morse had ordered.

Minerva smiled—at least that was what her voice sounded like, "It looks pretty safe here."

"I reserve judgment."

We walked around looking at all the equipment. We heard comments from Harris, Ballard, and unidentified people whom I guessed were 'scientists'."

"No equipment is powered on."

Someone else said, "Look at those boxes."

We walked over to the pile of boxes. I asked, "Do you want us to open them?"

There was a heated debate about that. Some wanted to leave everything as it had been so that they wouldn't know we had been in the trailer. Others were afraid of booby traps. Others wanted to see if the labels matched the content and wanted us to open them. The final decision was, "Just show us the shipping labels and we'll try to inventory against the orders that we have from Morse."

So, we walked around the room, looking at shipping labels. There was another argument as to whether we should remove the bills of lading from the plastic sleeves they were in. The final decision was that we do that and then return them as much like they were as we could manage.

At times, the FBI gave us precise directions on how to replace boxes when we'd had to move one to get to another. They had the recordings of the video that we'd just sent, and I suppose they were using it to make it look like we'd not touched anything.

Finally we finished, and they gave Minerva the last instructions, "Apparate to five feet from the building and about 10 feet from our truck. We'll wash you down, check for dangerous substances and get you out of those monkey suits."

By this time we were hot, bored, and tired. I took Minerva's hand and we spun the world around and arrived about where they'd wanted us. As soon as we stopped spinning, we were bathed in some kind of foamy spray and then in what I supposed was clear water. All of the liquids were trapped in a child's inflatable swimming pool.

They had us step out, lifting a leg, having it sprayed, and then stepping on dry pavement. Then the other leg followed. They wrapped up the pool in a big plastic bag, which went into a truck that had not been there before. Then they disrobed us.

We then had a meeting. Conspicuous by their absence were Sally and Phil. When asked where they were, Ballard said, "They had to make their flight. They left shortly after you went into the 'clean room'."

Both Minerva and I were disappointed not to have said goodbye and good luck to them.

Harris said, "You can talk to them as soon as they touch down in Manaus."

That just didn't seem the same.

⊞

We had a meeting in the FBI Control Room. They had a room with a meeting room table that would seat about eight or ten. It was Ballard, Harris, a scientist named Korngold, Minerva, and I.

Harris was in charge of the agenda. He asked Korngold what we knew.

Korngold looked around the table. "A great deal and—really—not very much." He seemed to like paradox. Long ago, I'd learned to just go with the flow with those types.

Korngold went on, "Here's what we know." He ticked points off

160

on his fingers.

"The inventory of the clean room matches the Purchase Orders that Morse gave us with a couple of very minor discrepancies. There was a box of sample bags and hand wipes missing. I assume that Hadley took them with him."

"The chemicals could be used in the refining of various schedule 1 drugs, but there was nothing that could be synthesized into schedule 1 drugs.

"It's theoretically possible to make explosives using some of the chemicals but why? If he were going to do that, there are far better chemicals that he could have bought.

"None of the equipment has been used – not even to test it. That is very strange, but what isn't about this business?

"There is an exception to that. He's maintaining positive air pressure in the clean room. He has a battery of filters in place to keep particles down to 1000 angstroms out.

"He's upgraded the wiring and circuit breakers in the trailer to carry much higher currents than the original design.

"And that's it. It's set up and ready to go for whatever purpose that he's got in mind. God knows what it is."

Harris asked me, "What did you two observe in there. I know that we saw almost everything you did, but there's a difference between watching remote video and being there.

I thought about it. Gazing up at the ceiling a thought came to me, "I don't think he cared whether we found this. We didn't find anything that made it difficult for us to get in. There were no locks. There was the air lock, but I bet we could have just worked it if we'd wanted to.

"Think about it. He didn't try to hide anything. The warehouse is as immaculate as – well, probably more immaculate than it ever has been. I bet he removed lots of junk that had just been lying about when he arrived.

"It's like he was expecting guests and cleaned house for them.

I looked around at the faces at the table. Only Korngold had a comment, "He's faking. This is just a decoy. The real lab is somewhere else."

I shrugged, "Could be."

Harris came in. "We know where all the half billion is. It's either in the Sept XC Suisse or it's here or it's with Connover. If there's another spot, how's he bankrolling it?"

I asked, "What about Reynaldo? Doesn't he need money?"

Harris answered, "Apparently, his starting funds were enough for whatever he is doing. He's got no money from Minns."

161

Apparently somebody had ordered out and just then a couple of agents came in with tubs of carry-out Chinese food.

After dinner, we all went to the hotel where we were staying. Ballard went with us to our room on the way to his. He encouraged us by revealing that the next day we – Minerva, Ballard, and I – were going to Sweden.

Minerva called after him as he walked down the hall, "Why?"

Ballard just waved his hand at us without fully turning.

Minerva muttered, "Bloody Bastard."

"Yeh."

Sodermanlands

Our airline tickets said Stockholm. Ballard had just handed them to us as we reached the Kansas City Airport.

Minerva pressed, "Isn't it about time to tell us why we're going to Sweden?"

He lazily asked, "What good would it do you to know?"

I couldn't resist saying, "He's got you there."

She kicked my shins and whispered in my ear, "I'll have *you* tonight."

On the way from our arrival gate to customs Ballard finally loosened up. "We are here to catch up with Connover. He's been doing business with a certain boutique metallurgy firm in Sodermanlands. That is a district west of here."

I just said, "Go ahead."

"You probably wonder how we know that Connover is here."

I just smiled, "I probably know you're going to tell me whether I want to know it or not."

Ballard just smiled and went on. "There was a very large payment—75 million dollars made to that firm from the Swiss account."

Minerva finished, "And who do we know who is an expert on metallurgy?"

Ballard just nodded.

We went to a Stockholm hotel and rested as best we could for the rest of the day—and night.

We got a call in the late hours of the night—locally. My body was too confused about the time to really know. It was from Sally. She and Phil had arrived in Manaus.

163

"Is this an OK time to call? It's pretty late in Sweden."

We were using the conference call function of the cell phone. Minerva jumped in, "Oh, I'm in never-never land right now. I have no sense for the time. Why not?"

Sally went on, 'We've got a State Department translator for now, but I think he's going to bail out as soon as we can get somebody ourselves."

Ballard wanted to know what they'd done.

"Well, we checked in to our hotel and we went out to try to pick up Hadley's trail. We found a hack who picked him up at the airport. He took him to the waterfront."

Phil came on, "We're having dinner. Our theory is that he didn't come here for Manaus itself but to get into the rain forest. Who knows why, but I've got a hunch that he found someone to guide him into the interior. With some luck, we'll find somebody whom he's talked to."

Ballard agreed, "That's good. I'd think that an American looking for a boat for hire or a guide would be possible to track down."

"We'll get in touch tomorrow and let you know our progress."

"Good. Finish your dinner."

□

The next morning, we hired a cabbie for the day who spoke decent English. He drove us out of Stockholm to the address that we provided.

As we drove, we discussed the plan for the day. Ballard said, "I've decided not to warn this firm that we're coming before we arrive."

I asked, "You mean we're making a . . . a . . ."

Ballard supplied the word which I couldn't quite call to mind— cold call. "Yes, we're making a cold call. I don't want to take any chance of Connover being scared off."

It was already early May, but there were still little mounds of partially melted snow here and there in the shade of stands of trees. We approached a small town that had a few industrial establishments on its outskirts.

We pulled into one. On the outside it looked like a typical rust-belt small foundry. The brick walls showed decades of wear, and the windows were mostly sooty. However, the office building part of the structure looked much newer. The windows glistened in the late morning sunlight. There was a small parking lot that had been recently paved. We parked, and the cabbie accompanied us to the main entrance. There was a small reception desk in the center of an overlarge atrium.

The attendant greeted us in Swedish, and the cabbie interpreted. He asked something that caused the attendant to nod and say, "Yah. Yah.

"I have some English. But more comfortable am in Swedish. What can I do for you?"

Ballard explained that he was a department head in the US National Science Foundation. We'd come to discuss metallurgy with the company CEO.

The attendant got lost during the introduction and shook her head, "Please. I lost am. Swedish, please."

The cabbie translated what Ballard had said, at times haltingly, to her. But she nodded vigorously.

She then launched into a vigorous, rapid discussion with the cabbie. When they finished, he translated. "Miss Bergstrom is sorry, but she did not receive your request for an interview, and Mr. Engdahl has a full. . how do you say it? Schedule?"

Ballard agreed, "Yes, schedule is right. Please give our apologies for not requesting an interview earlier. We just have a little break in our travels and thought we might be able to speak with Mr. Engdahl for a few minutes."

After translation, Bergstrom made a phone call, spoke at some length—apparently about getting us an ad-hoc appointment. Her down-turned lips showed that we were out of luck. She turned to Ballard and explained that in Swedish followed by the cabbie's translation.

Ballard wasn't disturbed. He countered, "We are really here to discuss the fifty million dollar project that he is running."

Even before translation, Bergstrom perked up when she heard "fifty million dollar". I don't know if it was only because of the size of the amount or possibly she deduced that we knew that the company had such a contract.

As soon as the translation was complete, she whirled without comment, dialed a number, and began a rapid conversation that maybe even our translator didn't catch.

Bergstrom hung up, turned to us and said in English, "You go up to room 229 now. Mr. Engdahl see you. He has the good English. You don't need translator."

I thought to myself, "It's nice to catch a break once in a while."

We apparently were expected to take ourselves up, which was fine with me. We found the room quickly and were somewhat surprised to find upon opening the door that it opened directly onto the spacious office of the company President.

He was standing and strode over to meet us. "Welcome. Welcome. I hope you had a good trip so far."

We admitted that we had. He opened the conversation, "How do you know about our latest project?"

Ballard must have decided to maximize the surprise factor because his reply was, "Do you mean the one for James Connover?"

Engdahl gulped visibly, "How do you know about Mr. Connover?"

Ballard said, "That doesn't really matter, does it? I can assure you that no one in your company revealed that name to us—even indirectly. We know that he's doing some amazing things, and when we heard that he was working with your company, we wanted to learn more."

Engdahl was suspicious but invited us to sit around his desk. We did. Then he picked up his phone and spoke briefly with someone. It turned out to be Ms. Bergstrom. She entered the office carrying a tray with several bottles of water and glasses. In very good English she asked, "If anyone wishes coffee or tea, I would be happy to get it for you."

Everyone was satisfied with water. Engdahl began, "Are you here because Mr. Connover has done anything illegal?"

Ballard looked to me to answer that question. I nodded ruefully and improvised, "Mr. Ballard is with the American National Science Foundation. I and my wife are professors at an English school." I didn't want to give any more information than the absolute minimum to be honest. "To the best of our knowledge and belief, Mr. Connover has not done anything illegal, and we are not here to arrest him. We have no such authority and don't wish it.

"We are here to learn about the amazing things he's been doing."

Engdahl relaxed somewhat and was no longer sitting on the edge of his chair, but he pursued the point. "Why don't you ask him himself?"

I still seemed to be the spokesman. "Mr. Connover is something of a recluse. Frankly, he seems to be reluctant to discuss his . . . uh . . . ."

Engdahl eagerly supplied a word, "Inventions. Yes, he is very secretive about them." Something I'd said seemed to open Engdahl up. He went on happily, "Those inventions are amazing. I can talk about them freely because I don't understand them in the least."

As a matter of fact, he seemed anxious to talk about them now that he thought that we weren't a threat to Connover or their deal.

He got up and signaled that we should stay seated, "I want to show you something amazing."

He walked over to a credenza and opened the lower drawer. It seemed to be mostly empty, but he brought out several objects and walked back to the desk. He cleared a spot on his crowded desk and placed them in line before us. There was a flash drive, something that looked vaguely like a flash drive, but I was pretty sure wasn't, and two oddly-shaped pieces of some intensely black material. The flash-drive-like object was cylindrical about an inch in diameter and maybe six or so inches long. The two really unusual objects looked as though they had been part of a very large ring. The cross-section was elliptical, and the ends of each piece were flat as though the original ring had been sliced into many pieces by a very sharp knife.

Engdahl laughed as we stared at them and asked, "Well! What do you think?"

None of us had any thoughts. The objects were that unusual.

Engdahl finally picked up the two odd-shaped objects and tossed one to Ballard and one to me. "Well, they're not going to bite you. Examine them!"

The one tossed to me took a different trajectory than I'd expected from its appearance. It looked extremely solid and dense. When I tried to catch it where I thought it should go, I was surprised and almost missed it. It didn't travel as far as it should have gone.

When I had it in my hand, I could tell why. It was extremely light. As a matter of fact, it was so light that I thought it must be made of Styrofoam. I asked, "This is the strangest Styrofoam that I've ever seen. What is it?"

Engdahl almost cackled, "Bizarre isn't it. I can tell you what it's made of—iron tungsten, titanium, but no plastic."

Ballard stared at the thing in his hand and just said, "Impossible."

Engdahl took the object that Ballard was holding and said, "Watch this." With that, he dropped it in his glass of water. Not only did it float but it seemed not to penetrate the liquid at all.

I commented on that.

Engdahl cackled again, "Yes, the surface tension of the water is enough to completely eject it from the water." He then took it out of the water, dried it with a napkin, and handed it to Minerva. "Touch your part to the other along the matching edges, Ms. Wendt."

She did. I was holding the other, and I felt a distinct click as the two touched. He then said, "Now try to separate them."

The two of us tried to do that. Finally, I took both ends of the new combined part, but I couldn't get it to budge. Ballard asked, "Those are vacuum welded, aren't they?"

Engdahl smiled, "Something like that, though I'm not at all sure that it's vacuum welding, as you'll see in a minute. And, of course, there's no vacuum in this room."

I handed the welded part to Ballard to examine. He turned it over in his hand, seeming to weigh it. He gave a half-hearted try to separate the parts and then handed it to Engdahl. But Engdahl wasn't done with it. His eyes twinkled as he asked, "Don't you want to know what the other object is?"

I was beginning to think of Engdahl as a sort of dwarf—a real craftsman in his field and delightful to talk with—IF you can keep him from being overwhelmed by his favorite subject. We all nodded.

He tossed the object to Minerva and told her, "Take that—Connover calls it a depolarizer, although I don't understand why. Then run either tip around the welded object along the weld."

Minerva began to object that she couldn't tell where the weld was. Engdahl shook his head and said, "You don't have to be precise."

She did so. As she passed the wand (I couldn't help but think of it as a wand because in Minerva's hand it just reminded me of one) over the part, nothing seemed to happen until she had completed the circuit. At that point, the two parts simply fell apart.

Minerva must have had a hint of what would happen, but she was startled none-the-less by the suddenness and thoroughness of the dissolution of the union of the two parts. She opened her mouth involuntarily and said, "It's just like . . . "She didn't finish the statement.

Engdahl spoke it for her, "Magic." His smile seemed to split his face in two.

Ballard stared in disbelief. I would probably have as well, but I'd seen so many bizarre things happen at the hands of that woman that I'd pretty much maxed out.

Ballard leaned back in his chair and stared at the ceiling. When he came back to earth, he said, "Tell us everything you know about him."

□□

I was sitting in this office, having lunch. I was reviewing some 3D designs and enjoying the break from real work—being a salesman, trying to convince a bicycle manufacturer to try a titanium alloy bicycle. While I was looking at the model from above, Mr. James Connover walked into the room.

I run a casual shop. He came through the door wearing a tailored suit. He was polite, spoke colloquial Swedish, and somehow seemed casual—all at the same time. I thought that the accent was from one of the northern cities. He had an appointment at one o'clock and had simply walked in five minutes early.

Connover said, "Do you mind if I look over your shoulder?"

I was feeling in a generous mood. I shrugged and agreed.

He looked at it a moment, took my space mouse and rotated the model. Then he said, "You know, you could make it thinner here . . . " He rotated the model a bit more, "And here. It would be as strong and you could knock 10 maybe 15 percent off the weight."

I started to object, but he interrupted, "The point of greatest stress, is here. The rest doesn't have to be nearly as strong."

I stared at the model and said, "I'll run a simulation and see.

"Now, I assume that you're my one o'clock?"

Connover just nodded.

"Very well, from your letter, I gather that you want to make some models with a new alloy that you want to test. We'd be happy to help you with that."

Connover nodded again, "That's true, but that would only be the beginning of what I need. I've brought along complete 3D models of all the parts that I need." He reached into his slim briefcase and brought out a flash drive. He handed it over to me.

I put it in a USB port of my computer and was shocked, "That's thousands of parts!"

Connover nodded, unperturbed, "Yes, three thousand seven hundred twenty-three to be precise."

"When in *Gott's* name do you need these parts?" I began to think through the schedule for orders that we currently had.

"Three weeks . . from tomorrow."

I usually don't use profanity with potential clients but this went beyond the pale, "You're flipping insane. There's no way that we could do that. We have orders ahead of you. We . . . We . . . "

He asked, "What is your choke point?"

I looked more careful at one of the files, opening it in my cad-cam software. I mumbled to my self, "Fucking idiot." The tolerances were incredibly tight. What I said was, "Well, the real choke point is our laser machine tools. The process we'd use is 3D printing to make a blank for the mold, lost wax molding, followed by laser machining. We're good with the 3D printers, and we could run the molding process with two shift,s but we don't have half enough laser machine tools."

He was utterly unfazed. "We can help you with that. I've already placed an order for ten laser machine tools. They won't arrive here for a few days, and there'll be time to set up and calibrate."

It was then that I became really scared. He seemed to be serious. I actually believed that he had them ordered and shipped. He came in here absolutely convinced that I would work with him. I asked, "And I suppose that they aren't leased. That I'll own them when we're finished."

He shrugged, "Of course."

I thought about where we'd put them. I had a "future line" laid out with power, venting, etc. It was a dream that I'd someday have a second production line. It looked like it might just come true.

I had a different question for him, "Just how did you choose me for this job? There are larger firms that could fulfill your order without the necessity to buy laser milling machines."

He started in listing the considerations as though he were in a board meeting of his company, "There are several factors that went into our decision. Certainly the capability to do the work was important but not the most important factor. There was integrity. We didn't want to be distracted by extraneous issues like arguments over the detail terms of the agreement. As a matter of fact, we wanted a gentleman's agreement, sealed by a handshake with no written agreement. We wanted someone who was flexible. We wanted someone who would be excited as we were by the project."

This cold fish didn't seem to me like he would be excited by anything, but he had the right man in me. I still couldn't believe that he didn't want a written contract, "Now, laddie, I think that a man who doesn't put things on paper is a man who is asking to lose a lot of paper, if you know what I mean."

He smiled at that, "Oh, I don't mean that we don't need documents. For one thing, I want a written estimate with details of how you came up with the estimate. We'll write detailed procedures for the production and testing of these parts. If you involve lawyers, though, you have given up your soul to an alien."

I had to laugh at that. "OK. Yes, I'll get you a decent estimate— accurate to say 5 or 10% by tomorrow. I'll have to reschedule some of the work I've got right now, but I think I can swing it. I'd like to have 25% in advance of the work, and we'll have a schedule of payments until the end of the project."

He surprised me again. That would be something that would happen again and again on a daily basis. But this time, he surprised me by saying, "No schedule of payments. I'll pay you in full before we start."

That caused my jaw to drop open. I couldn't help exclaiming, "Are you mad, man!"

He looked me straight in the eye, and I felt like he was searching my soul from top to bottom. "I told you that our most important criterion was integrity. I trust you and expect you to trust me completely." With that he held out his hand. That was to be it, the binding contract. Even before I'd given him an estimate, he was ready to bind himself and me.

Not for the first time or the last time, he'd scared me to death. I knew by intuition that if I let him down, I would regret it dearly. It took me at least a minute to decide, but he continued to hold his hand out as though it had taken only a few seconds. Finally, I extended my hand, and we shook.

He then started to explain the "hard" parts of the job. He had a special alloy that he wanted to use. It would be the same alloy that he used for every part. The flash drive that he had given me contained a specification for the alloy. That alloy had to be formulated extremely precisely and mixed completely. It had to "cook" and cool slowly but stay molten until used. It couldn't be poured into ingots to be melted and cast later.

He left after our meeting had gone on for three hours. I immediately got on the phone to all my customers to explain that I couldn't make the delivery date that they'd requested. Some had been long standing customers who knew that I wouldn't put them off without a good reason. Others, of course, were new and requested that I refund them their deposits—even if we'd done substantial work on their order. I didn't mind that, and I happily added those losses to the estimate for Connover.

I stayed in the office until after midnight with my chief engineer and the shop steward. We worked the estimate for Connover and examined it upside down, right side up, and inside out. We agreed on the estimate, and I printed it. It had ten pages – mostly appendices with details of calculations.

The next morning at 8 AM, Connover came into the office. I had my receptionist send him up immediately. He came in today in jeans, a sweater, and steel-toed shoes. That morning, he stole my soul. This was a practical man who knew metallurgy and came to work on the shop floor.

We started in my office. I handed him the ten page estimate. He gave a cursory glance to the front page. Then he turned to the rest of the pages and scanned them quickly.

He looked up from the document and said, "Your estimate of forty-three million dollars and small change seems good to me. I've already arranged to have forty-five million deposited in your main corporate account. I think you may have missed a few minor details but even if that is not enough, we'll deal with it when you need more money."

At that moment, my receptionist came in, "Sir, I think you should look at this notification that we just got in the email. There's a deposit from a company that I don't recognize. I don't know how much it is, but . . ."

I dismissed her and said, "I'll have a look right away."

I logged onto our account and saw that there had been a deposit of forty-five million. I didn't recognize the company either. It certainly wasn't the one on the letter-head of the letter of introduction that I'd received for Connover."

I looked up at Connover, "Do you know a company by the name of Relia?"

He didn't seem surprised, but he admitted that he didn't know that name.

"Well, they seem to have put up forty-five million US dollars for you. You ought to know them." That brought up a question that had been kicking around in my head since the day before. "Just who do you work for anyway? I assume that Connover Enterprises is your own company, but I don't believe that this job is for your benefit. Who are you acting as an agent for?"

This was another scary moment. He just said, "I'm not working for or as an agent of or on anyone else's behalf. I've never heard of this Relia company before."

I was becoming exasperated, "Well, man, you're not doing this for your own entertainment; there must be a purpose to it! What is the purpose?"

He smiled a shy smile, one that I'd not seen yet. "There isn't any purpose."

I stood and walked around the desk and sat down beside him in a guest chair, "You cannot NOT have a purpose. Come now, I'm committed to you. What is your reason for this?"

He simply answered, "I don't have a reason."

We walked down to the shop floor. What more can you do in a situation like this. When we arrived, a man I didn't recognize walked up with my shop foreman. My shop foreman said, "This guy is trying to deliver twenty tons of high purity iron that we didn't order. He claims . . ."

The trucker held out an electronic tablet. It had an invoice on it. It showed there was no balance due. He simply said, "Just sign for it. It's yours free and clear. Then I can unload it and get on my way."

I looked up at Connover. He gave the most cursory glance at it and said, "Sure, that's ours."

In a moment of exasperation that would be repeated many times, I asked him why he didn't mention that there was a shipment of iron on the way.

He shrugged and said, "I didn't know it until now."

I so much wanted to smack that indolent grin off his face. Of course, we needed twenty tons of high purity iron. No, nobody should be surprised when it shows up because why? Because we need it. Who pays for it? Who orders it? Who even knows that we need it? The answer, of course, is nobody that we know.

That was the way the whole project has been going. We need something, and it just shows up. Nobody has to pay for it. Nobody cares who it came from.

But that wasn't the most surprising thing that was to happen.

⊡

A few days later, we had our first batch of the wonder metal going. That was what I had begun calling it in my head. We'd made a couple of molds as a test. They were simple—just cubes. I thought that we were ready to pour. But, NO. As we were getting ready to pour, Connover said, 'I've got one last preparation to make."

By this time, I'd stopped being surprised by things, so I just shrugged and asked, "What do we need?"

"I've got it out in my van. I'll just be a few minutes."

He ran out of the shop. About five minutes later, he returned with a dolly. On the dolly was something that looked like a cross between a small rack server and an industrial electromagnet. It had thick cables extending from the server thing and connecting to two metal plates.

Each of the plates were thick, and I'd have guessed quite heavy, but Connover moved it as though it were made of cardboard. He placed the plates on either side of the mold.

I asked if it needed power.

In a sort of distracted way, Connover just said, "No. It's self-contained."

Of course, it had self-contained power. Why would you design one of those things without self-contained power? He pushed a toggle switch and nothing much happened besides a couple of lights on the simple console turned from black to amber to green.

Then Connover said, "OK. Start pouring. Very, very slowly."

I nodded, "Do as he says." I had an intuition. My shop steward frowned, but he began the pouring process—very, very slowly.

173

What happened surprised everyone there except Connover. The mold filled almost immediately. We'd poured hardly any of the metal in. The shop steward swore profusely, something like this, "God-damn, Bloody, Jesus fucking Christ, there's a bubble in the mold."

Connover shook his head. "No that's just about right. I think it'll be all right."

The steward turned rapidly and walked off.

The next crazy thing that happened was that Connover walked over to the mold and felt it. I screamed and almost ran after him, but somehow, the mold was cool. Connover said, "Break the mold, and let's see how it came out."

I couldn't keep myself from swearing a little at that point, but I told one of the workers to break the mold off. I warned everyone to be careful of liquid metal splashing.

When he did begin breaking the mold, it was clear that the metal had solidified. Connover walked over and felt the metal. It wasn't even hot!

I shouldn't have been surprised by the next thing that happened, but of course, I was. Connover picked up the one foot cube with his hands. It should have weighed over 150 kilograms but he tossed it to me, and fool that I am, I caught it. It couldn't have weighed much over a kilo.

I should have known to suspect that. We had poured so little metal in there that it couldn't have weighed much. I thought I knew what had happened. There was a bubble in the mold, and the cube was hollow. Later, we sliced into the cube to prove that. It was solid metal.

But that was later. Now, we were working on the next test mold. It was another cube. It came out cold and perfect—as far as I could see. There was something wrong, though. Connover felt the surface carefully. He ran the palm of his hand over one surface slowly. He just shook his head. "No, this isn't right. We need to do another one."

I stared at him and declared that he was crazy.

He just shrugged and said, "OK. Let's run them both through the laser milling machine and test them."

I agreed and wondered what his test would be.

The milling machine worked slowly on them. I had begun to wonder if it were not functioning properly, but Connover was satisfied.

When they were finished, he placed the two of them on a table and slowly pushed them together. They seemed to me to fit together perfectly. Connover just shook his head and said, "Pull them apart."

I shrugged and did so. They stuck a little because the surfaces were so smooth and perfectly matched, but there still was air adsorbed on the surfaces and that lubricated them so that they slid across each other.

Connover just shook his head again. Then he picked one up and tossed it into the recycling bin. It was the one that he'd declared bad earlier. "Make another mold, and we'll try again."

It was already late in the day, but I had started the second shift with some temporary workers. It took a while to print another model and make the mold. We'd brought in a dinner, and by the time we were done with it, the mold was ready to pour.

The original crew had insisted in staying on and pouring this one. Everything went the same as far as I could tell, but Connover was happy with this casting. We went to the same table with the new model, and I slid the two together. Before they met, there was a snap, and the two bonded together. Connover nodded, completely satisfied.

I tried to separate them. This time I had absolutely no luck. The crews were excited by this bizarre behavior. Someone suggested trying to use two electromagnets to separate them. It took a while, but we rigged up a fixed electromagnet to rest on the floor, and the other was on a crane. We powered up the electromagnets, and they both clamped onto the bonded parts. We applied force, and nothing happened. We were applying tons of force, but they wouldn't budge. I examined them with a magnifying lens. I couldn't see the slightest hint of a seam.

That was it for that day.

The next day, we began working in earnest, but the first thing we did before proceeding was to do one more test on the original cubes. Connover had a small wand-like device. He grasped it and rubbed it along the place where the seam would have been had there been a seam. Nothing much happened until he had completely rounded the bond. Then he picked up one of the two cubes and carried it away.

He said, "That's the final test. Every part bonds to at least one other part. We'll do them in sequence. The final test has two parts—do they bond automatically, and can I release them with the de-polarizer."

After we finished and tested each part, they were individually packed into heavy plastic bags and placed into crates for shipping. We didn't know where we were going to ship them, but I'd begun to believe that like everything else, when we needed that information, we'd have it.

The days went along. We worked 6 days a week, two shifts a day. After a week, workers volunteered to work twelve hour shifts so that we had two 12 hour shifts. We were working around the clock. With about a week left to our deadline, I'd begun to think that we might just make it.

Then, something completely unexpected happened. The union sent someone to our office. He came along with two burly "assistants." They walked into my office like everyone else. The conversation began and was not too bad.

The union officer introduced himself and came straight to the point, "I understand that you have our members working 12 hours a day, 6 days a week. But they're only getting regular wages."

He was right. Everything had happened so quickly that we really didn't have time to get the overtime pay set right. I admitted as much, "You're right. It started with workers being anxious to finish the project on time. They volunteered to work extra hours, and we sort of fell into the 12 by 6 routine without completely thinking it out. But I'll set that straight. Everyone will get double overtime."

Strangely that didn't seem to satisfy the union official. "Yes, after the fact. I think that we need to access a little penalty for the many union rules that you've broken."

I was anxious to be reasonable, so I said, "Really, anything that's reasonable, I'll be happy to go along with. Just name it."

A sly smile came over the union man's face. "I was thinking that we don't want to end up in court—either you or I. I think that we might arrange something quietly. No publicity. You just pay a penalty to the union pension fund, and you don't even have to pay overtime."

I smelled a rat in Kronigsberg, but I just listened as he went on.

"I think that a reasonable payment might be two million dollars, don't you?"

I gagged at that and stood to say something when the two "assistants" rose quickly and towered over me.

The union man went on, "Let's go out in the shop, and let me show you something."

I followed them out. When we reached the shop floor, the union man said, "I think you can see how fragile this operation is from up on the catwalk."

With his two henchmen behind me, I was jostled up the stairs to the catwalk. At least their leader went before me.

When we were up, he said, "It would be really too bad if something fell into the cauldron of melt over there, wouldn't it?" We all moved closer to it.

He went on, "Now, I think that you might just want to rethink your position, eh?"

176

I hadn't noticed it happen, but Connover had been on the shop floor, and he'd followed us up on the catwalk. Just at that point, he cleared his voice and said, "Well, Mr. Larsson, I think you'll find that only one thing might fall off this catwalk."

The union man noticed Connover for the first time. He seemed about to say something, but before he could, as his mouth was opening, he took a step forward on the catwalk. Then he took another. He then put a foot up on the lower railing. What came out of his mouth was, "No! Stop! Get him, Lagman."

Lagman reached into his pocket for something, but his hand came out empty and grasped the railing. He stared wildly down at the hand that seemed to have a will of its own. The other "assistant" looked at the both of them and took a deep gulp before doing nothing.

Meanwhile Larrson had grasped the hand rail and appeared to be preparing for a leap over the railing. He screamed, "Stop it." His other foot lifted onto the lower railing and lifted him higher into the air. "No! I give up. Don't make me jump!" The left foot rested on the top railing and was beginning to lift him up so that he was standing on the top railing like a diver on the high board before a "cannonball" leap.

Connover looked directly at him and asked, "Are you absolutely sure that you're not ever going to bother Mr. Engdahl or anyone else who works for this company. Or allow anyone else to?"

There was no answer. His legs tensed, and one leg went out over empty space as though it expected to find solid footing under it. His body began to lean forward, moving his center of gravity out past the railing. I was convinced that nothing could prevent the fall that was just beginning. Then he screamed, "Ya! Ya! NEVER." And instantly his fall seemed to stop in mid-air, and then he fell backwards onto the catwalk. His two assistants relaxed slightly and moved forward past me. They helped Larsson up and carried him back the catwalk toward the stairs. That brought them past Connover. They cringed away from him as they passed him. Larsson looked up as they passed and asked, "What are you?"

Connover mumbled something in English that sounded like, "Yeh, I wonder."

That was the last that we heard of any of the three. We started shipping parts the next day. We finished a day ahead of schedule.

Engdahl finished his story. I asked him, "What was the address that you shipped to?" However, I immediately interrupted him and asked, "Wait, let me guess. It's in Wichita, Kansas, USA. I don't remember the street number but if you tell me, I'm sure I'll recognize it. The ship-to name is P. H.."

Engdahl looked to be on the verge of swearing. What he said was, "Sure! Of course, everyone knows everything about my business!" He then asked, "How in the world did you know? Yes, it is a Wichita, Kansas address. It's a warehouse. And the addressee is P. H.."

Ballard said, "Yes, we were there a couple of days ago. Its tenant is out of the country at the moment, but we're trying to find him."

Engdahl observed, "You're not National Science Foundation, are you?"

I answered, "Yes, he is. My wife and I are professors in an English school, but you might say that we're all on loan to the FBI."

Engdahl nodded.

Minerva asked, "Have you shipped the last of the parts?"

Engdahl shook his head. "No, we're finishing packing and expect to have them off tomorrow."

She went on, "Do you expect to see Connover again."

"Yes, as a matter of fact, he was supposed to meet me today. He should be here by now. He was going to oversee the last of the shipments going out. I suppose that you want to meet him."

Ballard nodded and then added, "I've got a feeling that you're not going to see him again."

Engdahl agreed, "I'm afraid not. I really would like to have, though. He's an amazing man. I really want to know how he came up with that metal formulation . . . and the polarizer . . . and the de-polarizer."

Ballard said, "I don't think he'd have answered your questions. Maybe he couldn't, any more than he could answer your question of what the purpose of these parts are."

Engdahl asked the group in general, "What do you think the parts are for?"

We all just shrugged. I asked him, "Do you have any idea?"

Engdahl just shook his head.

Minerva asked the really important question, "Can we have a copy of the data on that flesh drive?"

I corrected her automatically, "She means flash drive."

"Oh, yes. Of course. I'll make a copy of it for you. He never asked me to keep it secret."

He made the copy and asked us if we would stay for lunch.

We declined with thanks and went down to find the cabbie. He was in the cafeteria having a cup of coffee and reading a newspaper. We collected him and got on our way back to the hotel.

Once on our way, I made a request of Ballard, "Let's do a layover in London on the way back."

"Why?"

"I want to give a copy of that flash drive to the Boy G."

Ballard thought it over for a while and agreed. "Yeh. In for a penny, in for a pound. I guess it would be stupid not to have all the good minds that we can find in on figuring it out."

Minerva brought up a point, "Don't we want to prevent those shipments from arriving if we can?"

Ballard looked from one to the other of us and asked, "What do you think? What would they do if we intercept those shipments?"

I thought a few minutes and said, "I suppose they'll just find someone else to produce them and be more careful—about everything: about where they make their parts, about where they put their assembly building, about where they get their money."

Minerva cursed, "Drat it all. We might never find them again."

Ballard nodded, "That's what I think. Let's just keep tracking the parts, tracking the money, and most of all tracking the people."

Tokyo

The flight to London was quick compared to most of our travel recently. As soon as we landed at Heathrow and got through customs, we were on our way to Hogwarts.

There was a little dispute about how to make that trip. Minerva wanted to disapparate to the Leaky Cauldron and then take the Floo network to Hogwarts.

When he heard that proposal, Ballard said, "Why take two leaps of those accursed wizard ways of travel, when you can do it with one?"

I had a tremendous amount of sympathy for him, but Minerva didn't (as usual), "Look. If we disapparate directly there, we'll have to walk from the outskirts of the village. We might as well take two jumps and land in Hogwarts, which we can do via floo."

Ballard looked at me in exasperation. "I know you don't like it any more than I do. Vote with me. We've got the majority."

"Oh, man, Ballard, it's easy to see that you're not married. Haven't you ever heard the adage, 'If momma ain't happy, nobody ain't happy'? I'm completely out of it. You're the only one with a dog in this fight."

He frowned, realizing that he'd just lost. Since Minerva was the only one who could disapparate, we were stuck with Minerva's plan. We arrived at the Cauldron, and it was strictly a pass-through. She led us directly to the hearth. I detoured past the bar and told Tom, "Sorry. We're on a mission." I plunked down a couple of galleons and added, "Have one on us!"

Tom smiled and wished me a good evening.

We arrived in Minerva's office. As soon as we had stopped spinning, she threw her arms up and sighed. "You know, I now know what Potter meant when he said that this was the only place he was really happy."

It was close to midnight. I accompanied Ballard down to my office and had him take my bedroom. Of course, I'd not spent any time in it in a long time. I bid him good night and added, "See you in the morning for the breakfast of your life."

Ballard just grunted something, and I was on my way back to my bed.

The next morning, we met for breakfast in the Great Hall. Ballard had beaten Minerva and me down. I sat with him at the head table. Mornings are informal at Hogwarts. There was no one else near us. He was enjoying crepes and begnoits. He asked me, "Do you ever get to the point that you think these Hogwarts breakfasts aren't a slice of Heaven?"

I broke off eating the buttermilk buckwheat pancakes to comment, "Let me answer that question with a question of my own. Do you ever stop thinking that March Madness is a little slice of Heaven?"

He actually laughed and said, "I take your point."

Minerva just chuckled and repeated in a tone of ultimate dismissal, "March Madness – M. M."

After breakfast, we went to the Shrieking Shack. We discovered that neither Brahms nor Sinistra were there. With nothing else to do, we just found chairs in the Control Room. Ballard checked emails on his phone. Minerva had brought along a stack of mail that had collected while we were gone.

I asked about that. "Why didn't the owls find us when we were traveling?"

She frowned at me and said, "Now, really, you should know the answer to that as well as I do."

When I didn't throw my waving hand up like Hermione, she said, "Really! The post owls were following us as best they could, but you can't expect an owl to match one of you jet planes. They finally caught up with us here."

I tried to think of an objection to that, but there didn't seem to be one. Meanwhile, Minerva almost left to go back to her office to finish answering the letters when Brahms and Sinistra entered the room.

Minerva demanded, "Where in the world have you been?

Sinistra shot back equally, "What? Do you expect us to be in the office 24 x 7. Don't we have the right to have a night off?"

I broke up the nascent fight by saying, "Brahms, we brought a little present for you."

He immediately perked up and demanded what it was.

I reached into my jacket pocket and pulled out the flash drive.

Brahms eyes widened till they were like dishes. "Just what do you have there?"

I smiled, "You know very well what I have here." I began to hand over the flash drive. As I did, Ballard's phone rang. He answered it.

He said, "It's Ms. Harker and Mr. Pearson." He then was obviously speaking to them. "We're here at Hogwarts with the Wendts and the Brahms's." After a pause, this was followed by, "Sure, we can do a conference call. Hang on and give us a minute to set up."

The B. G.'s face fell but he manned up and said, "OK. Let's go. The Conference Room is better set up for this." He led the way down, and when we arrived, told Ballard, "We've got a blue-tooth enabled sound system here. Set up your phone for it, and we can listen in comfort. The code is, of course, 0 0 0."

The B. G. turned on the speaker system, and after dealing with feedback, we were ready to go. Sally said, "It's lucky we caught you all. We're about to head off into the wilderness where there won't be any contact for a while."

Minerva smiled, "You've had luck then?"

"We sure did." Then she told us their story.

□

We started, in the morning, working the outfitters. Our process was that we went into an outfitter with the expressed intent of preparing for a trip into the rain forest. The outfitters would typically give us a standard list of things that we needed—larded on with every conceivable thing that you might need. We'd look over the list.

We'd haggle over it and then we'd ask, "We have a friend who came recently to outfit for a trip. He's an old pro. Maybe you could tell us what he bought."

The clerk would ask, "Well, who is this friend of yours?"

We'd give him Hadley's name, not sure whether he'd use it or not, and showed him Hadley's army photo, retouched to make it appear he was wearing civilian clothes. The clerk would hem and haw and say something like, "Well, I'm not sure. This looks a little like someone I've seen here."

At that point, I'd get out my purse and pull a couple of fifty dollar bills out of it. The clerk's memory would suddenly clear up miraculously—almost magically. The first couple of times, the clear memory reveled that Hadley hadn't been there.

But on the third try, we hit pay dirt. The clerk's cleared-up memory revealed that Hadley had been there. I asked what equipment he'd bought. The answer to that question required more clarifying. He had a list that was drastically pared down from the standard over-the-counter list. Basically, it consisted of a one-man tent, a rugged back pack, a few tools including a military grade hunting knife, one pot, water purification tablets and a month's supply of surplus MRE's.

Phil had never heard of those. I explained that it meant "Meals Ready to Eat". They're compact, nutritious, don't require cooking, and are sealed against accidents like falling in a river.

We next asked about Hadley's skill at Portuguese. The clerk said, "Oh, I knew right away that he was American. He'd probably taken a couple of years of Portuguese in college, but he'd never lived in a country where they spoke Portuguese."

We asked if there were anything else that he could tell us about Hadley. The clerk was cagey about that. He clearly wanted more money—lots more money.

Phil was getting tired of feeding him money, so he pulled out his wand. Then we got the information. I can tell you. I can see why he was holding out for more money. He had a treasure trove.

ꠏꠏ

Hadley asked for recommendations of guides to take him up the Amazon. The clerk was obviously intending to get his palm greased for the information. Hadley had separated the bills that he wanted to use for this bribe, and when the inevitable "ask" had come, he reached in his pocket and pulled out the folded bill with only the denomination showing.

The clerk smiled for an instant—an instant that Hadley didn't miss. The clerk had turned the smile into a grimace—as though he couldn't countenance taking money for information.

Hadley performed the required dance, "Information has value. There's no reason that you should give away something of value that you possess."

The clerk looked relieved at the honesty of Hadley's position. He started the standard spiel, "There are several reputable companies that will provide excursion assistance—either small groups or individuals."

Hadley gave information away for free, "I would require a guide to take me alone up the Amazon and up tributaries of my choosing."

The clerk made a face, "Well, most of the ones that I'm aware of will require you to take one of their packaged tours. Although for an individual client, some will modify an existing package for the individual's tastes."

Hadley smiled and shook his head, "I need someone who would be willing to take me where I would go without pre-determined destinations."

The smile came back to the clerk's face and this time it didn't leave. "Well, that's rather special. There aren't a lot of guides who would be willing to do that."

Hadley added, "I have an additional requirement. It would be necessary for the guide to have passing familiarity with the local tribal languages."

The clerk's smile was wide indeed now. "There are few indeed who can offer that. Finding such people without . . . uh . . . help would be very time-consuming."

Hadley had been prepared for that possibility. "Do you believe that you can help me find such people?"

The clerk tried to judge Hadley. How much would this neophyte who speaks decent Portuguese but is far from an expert be willing to pay? The stranger was completely impassive. No tremor moved over his face. The clerk thought that the only error would be to ask too little. He opened his mouth to speak.

Hadley had reached into his pocket and pulled another folded bill forth. It had a denomination revealed. It was not the number the clerk had in mind. He opened his mouth to speak again.

Hadley spoke first, "You have to accept this or not. If not. I leave immediately with my purchases."

The clerk made a snap judgment, "That is not necessary. I have three guides in mind. They all know the river. They all know some native languages. They are all willing to do, what is the phrase," Here the clerk switched to English, "Anything for a buck."

Hadley nodded approvingly, "That is the phrase."

The clerk wrote down on a piece of paper three names and addresses. He wrote in Portuguese.

Hadley laid the folded bill on the counter.

Neither spoke again.

⌷
⌷⌷

"The clerk that we spoke to gave us the names in the same way—written on a piece of paper." We left to find these men.

We found the first tending his boat at his dock. He was tuning the engine. He acknowledged that Hadley had been there. We hadn't even

184

had to show him the photo.

We asked through the interpreter, "Did someone ask you about taking him up the Amazon recently."

The man said, "A short American, lived in Lisboa for many years, speaks Portuguese like a University professor?"

We admitted as much.

"Sure. He wanted to go up the river with no plan. Just travel until things 'smell' right.

"I told him that he was crazy and wasting his money. He could waste his time and money as he liked. I had more important things to do with my time."

Phil asked, "And you have no idea where he wanted to go—other than up the river?"

"The fool, of course not. Not a bad recipe for getting yourself killed."

I asked, "I suppose that you think that anyone who tried to follow him was a fool as well?"

"No. Anyone trying to follow him is an even bigger fool."

Phil came back, "And you'd not consider doing it for quite a lot of money?"

The guide just shook his head in disgust.

We went on to the next address. It was another dock. The boat owner was scraping his boat, apparently preparing to paint. He looked us up and down and said, "You're looking for that crazy professor, aren't you?"

Our translator said that we were.

The boatman nodded and said, "Well you missed him, and I've no idea where he went. Maybe he found a crazy man to take him up the river."

I asked "You called him a professor. What made you think he was a professor?"

He stared at me and asked, "Do you know him at all?"

I wondered. I supposed that we really didn't know him at all.

"He talked like one. He used big words. He was probably from the South. Maybe Rio."

"Did he tell you what he was doing?"

"Oh, he said something about collecting rare plants and flowers. That's another thing. Who else wants to do that other than Biology professors?"

We admitted the justice of that and asked him if he would be willing to try to follow Hadley.

He just laughed and turned his back on us.

We wished him a good day.

The third boatman was not at his boat. We asked around and eventually found someone who knew him. He suggested that we go to a local cantina where he was probably celebrating something—maybe the invention of beer.

We found him. There were only a couple of people in the bar. We had to loosen his tongue with a shot of vodka. When we'd done that we asked him about Hadley.

"Hadley? That was his name?"

"Yes." I got out our photo. The boatman glanced at it for only a second. "Yes, that's him.

"He wanted me to take him up the river and let him be the guide. 'Why did he need me?' I asked. What do you suppose he said?"

I guessed, "He needed someone to speak the local languages."

While the translator was starting to give my answer, he already had answered his own question, "He needed somebody to translate for him."

"He wasn't like you. He was from the South. Yes, Sao Paolo. It had to be. He couldn't have been Rio."

Phil said, "Then you turned him down. Why?"

The answer came swift and hard, "He wanted to be the captain! The captain of my boat!"

That left us with nowhere to look. The translator asked, "Did you suggest anyone to him who would let him be the Captain?"

He turned wily with that question. "Just how much do you want the answer to that question?"

Phil mumbled, "This much." He pulled his wand and didn't even bother to do *Imperio* silently."

We got a name and a dock number. Phil wanted to *disapparate* us there, but I talked him out of it. We took a cab. When we got there, of course, the dock was empty. We found a neighbor who told us that he had hired himself to a Brazilian who wanted to go up the Amazon.

I asked how he knew that he was a Brazilian. The man said, "Oh, he knew the neighborhood. They joked about the silly foreigners who'd come here for The Cup games."

That made us huddle up for a conference about what to do next. Over dinner, we discussed options. They boiled down to the following:
- Go home and hope that Brahms would turn him again.
- Wait here at the airport, hoping that he'd show up here again.
- Try to follow him.

The last option seemed crazy at first but became more and more reasonable the longer we thought about it. We already knew good guides to take us. We would stop in every village along the way to see if anyone had seen the two of them. We had already got equipment for the expedition.

By the end of the meal that was our plan. This morning we were up early. Neither of us could sleep well. We are just now calling you. After this call, we'll go out and try the three guides we talked to yesterday to see if we can find one to take us.

Minerva and I had mixed feelings about this expedition. We didn't try to talk them out of it, but we certainly didn't encourage them. Brahms argued for waiting until he returned to fly back to the US.

It was all pointless. So, we moved on. Brahms had an announcement of his own, "We've found Reynaldo. I picked him up at Port Columbus, after boarding a flight for Neruda, Japan. We were lucky. By the time he arrived, I was able to start finding and using video cameras on the street. I think that we'll be able to find where he is at the moment."

Ballard nodded and said, "I'll get on the way there as soon as we get back into the US."

Minerva added, "I suppose that we'll join you."

Ballard seemed deep in thought and spoke slowly, "I don't think so. I want somebody magical in Wichita all the time from now on. They seem to be closing in on their objective—whatever t is. I want every resource we can manage there when they start acting."

You could hear the doubt in Minerva's voice as she asked, "And you think that you can handle one of them in Japan by yourself?"

We had come to a turning point. Up till now, every time we'd gone pursuing one of these people in this group that even now we hadn't given a name, there had always been a wizard along. This broke the mold.

Ballard's lips formed a hard line. "No, I'm going, and you two are staying in Wichita—at least until Pearson and Harker are back."

Sally objected, "But we have no idea how long we'll take tracking Hadley down. AND, we will be out of cell phone range until we get back to Manaus."

Phil reminded her gently that they could disapparate back to Manaus daily to use the cell tower system. You could hear her slap her forehead in frustration.

Sally recovered quickly and asked, "What about Connover? What

187

did you learn about him?"

Brahms leaped in before Ballard could speak. "Wait! Wait! They brought me a toy. I want to see what I can deduce quickly from it before they tell you."

He had brought along a laptop. He opened it and slipped the flash drive in. He glanced at the screen for half a minute and then said, "OK. You've got Cad files in here . . . wow . . . a scad of cad files. There are thousands.

"So, this group is building something—or a bunch of somethings. They went to a custom metallurgy shop, so they're probably using a special alloy and maybe they need high precision parts. That all fits in with their profile. That's about it. What else did you learn?"

Ballard looked a little disappointed. "Well, we didn't learn a lot more than that actually. There's a file in there that gives the precise alloy that they used and from the owner of the business we learned that Connover spoke Swedish like a native. I guess that's like the Portuguese-speaking Hadley, eh?"

Sally agreed.

Ballard went on, "We learned some important details—like how they're being shipped to Wichita—by container ships."

Sinistra who'd been pretty quiet up till now asked, "What about the alloy? What are its properties?"

Ballard reached in his pocket and pulled out a small sample of the metal that Engdahl had given us as a souvenir. He tossed it to Sinistra and said, "This is a failed part."

She caught it and hefted it in her hand, "Wow, this thing could float away on a breeze. What about strength, melting point, conductivity, other physical properties?"

Ballard's smile disappeared. "Uh. . . we didn't get any of those yet. As soon as I get back to Washington, I'll turn this over to an NSF lab and we'll find out about those things."

She mused on that, "This wouldn't be bad for making aircraft—except it might be too light."

A big smile came over Brahms's face. He actually said, "LIGHT BULB!"

Aurora asked, "You've got something don't you?"

Brahms laughed. When something strikes him as really funny, his laugh quickly turns to something more like a wheeze. I don't think I've ever heard anyone laugh like that. This was one of those occasions. "Sure I do. It just occurred to me that these thousands of things are all parts of one or more objects."

Aurora sniffed, which was a little like Minerva's, and said, "Well, we already pretty much figured that."

He went on, "I can figure out how they fit together and give you a picture of what the thing looks like!"

I said, "I can provide you a little help on that. The parts weld themselves together when you join two parts that have surfaces that match exactly."

His eyes widened at that. "Super. That makes the problem much easier. These parts form a graph."

Minerva frowned, "Come on. A graph has got little bars or maybe lines on a grid on a piece of paper. Don't graphs have to do with showing numbers? How can those things make a graph?"

I could see from the look in Brahms's eyes that we were in for a lecture. I hoped he'd keep it short and sweet.

"That is one kind of graph, but another kind of graph is like a network. You have points on the graph or network connected to other points.

"I've got an idea that the graph of these parts make one device when all the parts are interconnected."

Ballard asked, "How long for you to do this analysis?"

Brahms leaned back and closed his eyes. "I haven't done much work with graph theory, but I'm sure there are programs to automate that. I don't know. I'm going to make it my highest priority."

Brahms thought that was a statement. Ballard seemed to take it as a question. "Yes, I think that's a good use of your time for now."

Sally tied things together. "Let's agree to do a conference call at this time each day. It'll be around noon at Hogwarts, around 7 AM here, and I think early evening in Japan."

That was agreed, and we parted company. Sally and Phil were on their way to find a boatman. Ballard, Minerva, and I were on our way to Heathrow to catch a plane for Washington D.C. The Brahms's were on their way to the Control Room of the Shrieking Shack.

We arrived in Washington at about dinner time. We changed planes and continued on to Kansas City. Ballard was going to drop off the metal sample and then move on to Japan.

We arrived in Kansas City and decided to stay overnight there. The next morning, we stayed in the hotel. We picked up some food in the lobby and went back to our room. I called the Boy Genius. He was in his Control Room along with Aurora.

He informed us that we were the first to call in. About ten minutes later Sally and Phil joined us. They were in a Starbucks. Sally commented, "You can't imagine how wonderful it is to be in air-conditioning."

Minerva said, "Are you kidding, we were in the Saudi desert for days. Even with air-conditioning that's got to be worse than a Starbucks in Manaus."

We waited another fifteen minutes for Ballard. We then agreed that he might still be in the air. So, we started.

Brahms reported first, "I've found some graph-solving software and I've got it installed. Before I can start using it, I've got to convert the CAD files into something that can be used by the graph software."

I asked, "OK. How long?"

Brahms hummed for a minute. "Oh, say a day or two to get a data format settled. Then a day or two to translate the files. Maybe a week until we're rolling."

I decided that I was running the meeting in the absence of Ballard, so I nominated Sally and Phil next. "What's going on in the Amazon?"

Sally answered, "We convinced the second guide that we interviewed yesterday to take the job. He needs a day to get ready. We're finishing buying supplies. We think we'll start tomorrow early."

Aurora asked, "How did you ever talk him into taking you? Wasn't he the one who declared you even crazier than Hadley?"

Phil answered, "We gave him a price he couldn't refuse. We bought him a new boat that he would use to take us up-river."

Minerva said, "Congratulations! That sounds great!"

Internally, I had to agree, but that didn't mean that I was happy, "OK. Do your best. We'll be hoping for a report from the road tomorrow."

I turned to us, "We're in Kansas City. We dropped Ballard off in Washington. We plan on going to Wichita later this morning and check in with Harris."

As I was speaking, someone was calling in. Brahms was controlling the conference call. When he had him connected, he announced, "Mr. Harris has just joined us."

Harris said, "It's just me on this end. Ballard wanted me to report for him this morning. He dropped off the metal sample at the main NSF laboratory, and we expect a report by tomorrow or the day after.

"Brahms, have you got an idea where Reynaldo is yet?"

Brahms hemmed—a sign that he'd let that slip to a secondary priority. "I'm still working on it. I've got an automated search going on with all the cameras that we can find in Japan."

Harris apparently didn't catch the embarrassment on the part of the B. G. "Good, keep up the good work." I could imagine the shade that Brahm's face was turning, but I didn't say anything.

Harris went on, "There are deliveries starting to happen at the warehouse. A container truck pulled up and parked at a receiving dock. They didn't try to find someone to provide a bill of lading or sign for the delivery. They left the container and drove off in a cab.

"What do you think we should do?"

Brahms perked up, "Parts. God, what I wouldn't give to see the inside of that container."

Harris said, "You and me both. But there are a couple of problems with us just waltzing up and breaking in.

"For one thing, we really pushed the envelope getting a warrant to examine the warehouse the first time. We came up empty and any judge is going to laugh in our faces if we come to the well a second time.

"The second thing is that we actually know what's supposed to be in that container. We have the bill of lading from Sweden, and I can't believe that anyone has tampered with it.

"Finally, if we break in there, we're just giving these guys one more reason to pull up stakes and go to work someplace else— someplace harder for us to find. I'm beginning to think that we want to let them keep going. Let them get far enough along that we can figure out what they're doing. At this point, I've not got the foggiest notion. Do any of you?"

Minerva shrugged, shook her head, and then realized no one could hear any of those. She said, "Bloody Hell if I know."

I agreed. Sally said, "They're building something fairly big out of metal in the middle of a continent nowhere near an ocean or even a lake. What would that be?"

Pearson didn't say a word.

The Boy Genius picked up on what Sally was saying. "An airplane? But why? They could buy a fleet of them. It's hard to judge, but from the design of those parts, I don't see how they could be building a skyscraper, and who would want to build one in Wichita Falls, Kansas?"

I corrected him, "Wichita, Kansas."

"OK. OK. The only thing I can see is a space ship."

That had come out of the blue. I asked him, "Let's assume you're right. Just how are they going to propel that? They haven't been collecting anything to make fuel with."

I could imagine the B. G. shaking his head. "OK. Drop spaceship.

A fair-sized radio telescope then." I could hear in his voice the excitement that had seized him, "No! No! I've got it, a transmitter and maybe receiver."

I thought a minute, then another. No one else said anything. "Could be. The thing that bothers me about that is just what are they going to transmit?"

Harris added, "I'm more concerned about who they would transmit to." That was a thought that had us all silent for a bit.

Then the B.G. hmmmed for a while and re-iterated, "And to whom?"

No one else had any ideas. So, we adjourned the meeting until tomorrow. Next time, we hoped that Ballard would join us.

⊞ ⊞⊞

We rented a car and drove down to Wichita. We stopped on the way and bought some supplies that we sort of needed. Minerva wanted cosmetics. I wanted dental floss. Harris had a hotel room reserved for us. We checked in after lunch and went to his Control Room.

It was deadly dull there. All we had to do was watch TV monitors that surrounded the warehouse and hear hourly reports of nothing. That went on for several days. That isn't to say that there wasn't progress on some fronts.

Sally and Phil were sailing up the Amazon. They stopped frequently to check if Hadley had come past. Often, they found that someone remembered him. Fishermen on the River pay attention to whomever plies the River. After several days, they had progressed more than 400 miles.

Sally commented that she didn't know whether she was more fascinated by the variety of animal and plant life along the way or more depressed by the humidity and temperature. The only saving grace, of course, was getting to return to Manaus for an hour for breakfast and air conditioning while we had our daily conference call.

Brahms had begun to get the occasional video hit on Reynaldo, but seemingly never at a destination. Always on the streets—which were relatively easy to monitor. He also thought that he was close to completing a model of the object that the parts formed.

Ballard had been doing his own research. He'd hired a detective agency and had them looking for Reynaldo. No luck there. The trail that they could follow led from the airport via shuttle and then went absolutely cold.

The next day's reports provided some surprises. Sally reported on their progress. "We finally reached a point where the trail went cold. The trace was lost just after we passed a major tributary. We decided that they must have followed the tributary. That paid off. We didn't find another trace of them for more than thirty miles. But then, at a small village, we found someone who recognized Hadley's photo. He was a native who didn't speak Portuguese. Our guide could speak his language.

"Hadley and his guide had taken a small tributary a short distance up that river. Hadley had taken almost a full day at that village. Apparently, he was learning the native's language. They talked at length about herbs and plants. The native claims that Hadley hadn't known a word of the language when he arrived, but when he left, he could speak as well as the guide could."

Phil said, "We stopped there, even though it was early afternoon. We talked at length with everyone who knew anything about Hadley. He seemed to be searching for rare plants, but he couldn't describe what he was looking for."

It was a day for breakthroughs. Brahms showed us a rendering of what the parts assembled into. Brahms prefaced his unveiling with a comment, "It's not what I thought he was building."

Minerva asked, "Well, what is it?"

Brahms just shook his head. "You tell me." He then transmitted an image that we projected onto the large screen in our Control Room. It looked like a donut. Brahms waited for comments and gave up after a couple of minutes. "You see, it looks roughly like a donut. It has a hollow interior." With that, the donut opened up to show a strange cross-section. It had several chambers and seemingly three levels.

I stared at the image from half-way across the earth. An idea occurred to me, "It kind of looks like a tokamak."

Brahms agreed, "That thought occurred to me. But it isn't."

Minerva asked, "I thought a tomahawk was an American Indian weapon. You know, sort of like an ax."

Sally said, "You're right about what a tomahawk is. I don't know what a tokamak is though."

Brahms answered her, "It's a magnetic containment device for keeping very hot plasmas confined. There was a while when people thought it might be used to build a nuclear fusion reactor."

Ballard said, "That's got to be it. It makes sense. These guys figured out how to make it work! It explains the secrecy, the obscure materials, and the mountains of money they used."

Brahms frowned. It was visible even on the small screen we were

193

watching the video conference on. "Afraid not. Don't be disappointed that you didn't figure that out. You'd have to see the entire interior to know." With that he made the exterior of the model mostly transparent. He only said, "See."

Nobody did.

He tried again, "Don't you see? The interior is divided into many chambers."

Everyone was still silent.

"None of them goes completely around the ring." He stared at the screen. "Does anyone get it?" After a moment, "Anyone?"

Then Aurora cleared things up. "Tokamaks have a single chamber that goes all around the ring. The plasma flows around the thing like a particle accelerator. Right?"

The B.G just said, "Trust me. It's not a tokamak."

Ballard asked how the search for Reynaldo was going.

Brahms who was looking harried said, "Oh, come on. We just had a big break-through. How much do you want?"

That ended the meeting.

⊡⊡ ⊡
⊡⊡ ⊡⊡

We were still bored to tears for the next day or two. Connover still hadn't shown up, but another container shipment did. It was just as boring as the previous one.

But then a real break-through happened. It was Brahms again. He was so excited that he insisted on starting the reporting. "I've got him."

Ballard was becoming bored at sitting in Tokyo with nothing to do but sight-see. "Who have you got?"

"I've got Reynaldo."

That woke everyone up.

"Where is he?"

"I don't know where he's staying, but he has been going to an electronics firm. It's not one of the big ones, and I don't know how to pronounce the name, but I've checked the security video camera recordings for a week. He's shown up there every day. I'll email everyone the name and address."

Ballard was definitely awake. "Get those to me right away. I'm going to pay him a little visit tomorrow."

There ensued a debate about whether he should wait for backup and what sort of backup that he should wait for. Ballard argued that we wanted to minimize the chances of scaring away Reynaldo. It was clear

194

that we couldn't prevent him from going ahead without backup short of not giving him the address and company name.

Sally in particular didn't want Ballard to go in alone. She said, "These people have walked right past ISIS, taken on professional thugs, and serious criminals. You would be a piece of cake for them. Please don't take the risk. You had a witch along with you in Sweden. Connover didn't take you because she was there."

He answered, "That's the point. I'll never have a chance of seeing him with a wizard along. Look, I'm not going to threaten Reynaldo. I just want to talk with him and find out what they're doing."

He then pointed out, "You're going after Hadley."

She shot back, "But I've got a serious wizard with me. That's different."

We ended that conference call without anyone being happy about it. Brahms sent the company name and address by email to all of us. After the conference call ended, Minerva, Harris, and I talked about it further.

I asked Harris, "What do you think? Is Ballard taking an unnecessary risk?"

He gave me a searching look and said, "You still don't know Ballard that well. I met him almost at the beginning of this. He is about as determined as they come.

"When we first met, he'd already convinced the head of the NSF that Minns and company represented a serious threat. I thought I was being given a dead-end assignment at the Bureau. I would seriously have considered resigning if I didn't love working for the Bureau so much.

"He was determined, patient, unrelenting. He eventually won me over. You're never going to convince someone like him once he's made up his mind. And believe me; he's made up his mind on this.

"If I thought we could delay him for just one day, I'd hop on a plane right now to be there when he goes in. I might just do it anyway.

"To answer your question, I think he is taking an unnecessary risk, but there's no delaying him. We just have to hope it comes out all right."

Minerva said, "I know someone like that." She looked meaningfully at me. "It took him a little longer to convince me to marry him, but he is that—determined, patient, never-relenting."

We had the usual call-in the next morning. As usual, not everyone joined at the same time. And as usual, we proceeded when at least three of the groups had joined.

Pearson started off, "We reached the end of the tributary that we were working on. Off course, from online maps, we knew we were close. There's a small village near the source of that tributary. We found Hadley's boat there."

With those words, a thrill went through all our hearts. Was this going to be the big "reveal?"

He proceeded, "They had been there only two days before. Our guide was not fluent in this tribe's language, but we got the main ideas.

"There had been an argument between Hadley and his guide. Hadley wanted to go on by himself. The guide thought he was crazy and needed someone along in case tragedy struck—if for no other reason.

"Hadley had apparently picked up the local languages quickly. He pointed out that the only reason that he needed his guide along was for translation, and that wasn't necessary any longer.

"After consulting with the tribe about local plants, Hadley was ready to proceed. The guide declared that he was going along. Hadley let him.

"So, we're gearing up to follow him into the rain forest. We're pretty close to the border with Venezuela. We might cross over in his pursuit. At least we can disapparate back to Manaus when we need to. I don't know how he's getting back other than by boat. So why did he want to send his only means of travel away?"

That question was met by silence.

The Brahms's had nothing in particular to report. The B. G. was looking for Connover and Minns without any success. When we'd talked that to death (a matter of two or three minutes), the elephant that was not in the room made an appearance.

The B. G. never is afraid to mention the elephant, so he did, "We haven't heard from Ballard yet."

Minerva suggested giving him a call. The B. G. agreed and made the call. The phone rang and rang. Finally, voice-mail picked up and said, "Ballard. Leave a message."

Somebody blurted something about calling us, and the B. G. hung up.

I said, "I think we'd better consider him missing in action.

Brahms, why don't you devote some computer time to searching for him—you know, just in case. We'll get in touch with his hotel and the detective agency that he employed."

And that was the end of the meeting.

Minerva and I spent a lot of time on the phone with Japan. We couldn't find anyone who had seen him after 4 PM local time in Tokyo.

We continued having our usual conference calls. Everyone had only negative things to report.

Sally and Pearson and their guide had gone deep into the jungle. On their final report from the rain forest, the GPS showed that they were on the border of Venezuela. They'd not found Hadley or his guide. They gave up. No one could blame them. They would be technically guilty of an illegal border crossing if they went further. They would take their guide back to his boat after the call was over and then return to Manaus where they'd catch the earliest plane that they could back to the States.

Brahms had not found any sign of Connover, Minns, or Ballard. He was looking pretty haggard these days.

Harris admitted that he considered seriously going to Japan to try to track Ballard down. As he was speaking, an agent approached us signaling wildly. Harris said, "Hang on a minute. Somebody here has something urgent. At least, it'd better be urgent."

It turned out to be urgent indeed. The agent simply said, "We've found Ballard."

Everyone stared at him. Harris practically jumped out of his seat. "Where is he?"

The agent looked somewhat flustered, "Well, maybe 'found' was too strong a word. He's here in the United States somewhere."

Harris just echoed, "Somewhere?"

"Yes, sir. He caught a flight from Neruda the same day he disappeared. He landed in . . . " He looked down at a paper he was holding. "Tacoma, Washington. He seems to have disappeared then. . . Oh, one other thing. He went to a bank branch in Tacoma and cleared out his checking account. He walked away with about $8,500."

Harris asked, "What about his credit cards, his phone, friends? Has he made contact with none of them?"

"Sir, you know perfectly well that we've been monitoring his phone for incoming and outgoing calls or text messages. None. There have been no emails out from any of his known accounts. He's not used any credit card since he bought a ticket to Tacoma." He hesitated and then added, "Oh, yes. He went through customs in Tacoma using

197

his passport."

Brahms added, "I just searched the Tacoma video recordings. He took a cab there. I've got the license. We've got a trail."

I muttered, "Sure. And it will go cold as soon as he left the cab and paid for it in cash." Then I asked more loudly, "How long will $8500 in cash last you if you're trying to stay hidden?"

Harris muttered, "A damn long time if you go to ground in some hole in the wall in the West and just eat, sleep, and wash your clothes.

"Damn, I wish I had twice as many men as I do just to hunt Connover and Minns. Now, I've got Ballard as well."

I said, "I know we don't have any jurisdiction in Japan, but let's go find Reynaldo, Minerva."

Brahms cleared his throat.

I had a bad feeling about this. "Speak up, Brahms."

"Well, I forgot to mention that Reynaldo didn't show up at the electronics company yesterday."

All that I could think of to say was, "Great."

We were stuck. We didn't know where anyone was. We could only sit in Wichita, hoping that somebody would show up.

Wichita

We didn't have a long time to wait after all. Two days later, Connover showed up. It was at noon. Minerva and I were sitting in the Control Room, having lunch. I didn't notice it happen, but one of the FBI agents said, "Look at the front entrance. A cab just pulled up."

It had. A tall black man emerged with a small duffle bag. He reached into the cab, apparently to pay the cabbie. Then he walked up to the main gate of the warehouse and pulled it open as though he'd done that a thousand times before. He walked briskly to a side door and entered.

The agent shouted, "That's Connover, five'll get you fifty."

We all looked at each other. We'd had discussions about what to do when one of them arrived. I picked up my phone and called Harris who had gone out to lunch at a Braum's restaurant. We'd kidded our Brahms's more than once about opening an American chain of ice cream and fast food parlors.

Harris answered, "Can't this wait until I get back from lunch."

I said one word, "Connover."

He answered with two words, "Be there."

I don't know whether they used the siren any on the way here, but Harris showed up in record time. He sat at the console and looked over the various views of the warehouse, "Any action?"

"None."

We all sat, silent with our thoughts. Finally, Harris looked to me, "What do we do?"

I asked, "Can we arrest Connover for anything?"

Harris thoughtfully said, "I've been asking myself that for some time. I don't see that we can." There was more thoughtful silence followed by, "Maybe we could do something with the passport but. . ."

He gazed up into the air and then said, "No. I wouldn't want to go that route."

I went on, "How about surveillance? Can't we do anything with infrared or something?"

He shook his head. "We've done everything we can. The building is just not good for IR or other technologies."

Then he looked up. "We can probably pick up sound from inside. If he talks with anyone, we might get that."

Minerva laughed, "Talks with anyone? Who would he talk with?"

Harris said, "Maybe on the . . . phone . . . Oh, yeh. They never make phone calls." He thought a moment. "I'll get a tech to set up something to monitor sounds inside the building.

They had it set up in a couple of hours. When we started monitoring the sound we discovered that Connover liked to listen to Miles Davis.

For a while we listened to Miles Davis and the sound of crates being opened and the "cling" of parts snapping together.

Sally and Pearson took the wise measure of stopping for a little R & R on the way to Wichita. They flew into Miami and spent a day on the beach. They arrived in Wichita in time to catch a few Miles Davis sets.

While we were all sitting in the Control Room being bored to tears, we got a call from Brahms. He was excited, "He's on the way."

Harris, instantly alert, asked, "Who?" He was leaning forward on his chair toward the monitors.

"It's Hadley. He's just arrived at Kansas City airport. He must be coming toward you."

"Good work! I'll get in touch with the KC office and have somebody tracing him in minutes."

We sat in suspense as Harris got in touch with the KC office of the FBI and got them moving. Meanwhile, we were on a heightened alert. There were extra agents on the streets around the warehouse. Every camera was being monitored. Of course, nothing happened.

After a couple of hours a phone call came in. It was a KC office agent reporting, "We had no trouble finding people who'd seen Hadley. He took a cab to downtown. He didn't go to a hotel or a car rental agency. For a while we had no idea where he went."

One of the agents behind us was saying, "Buses, buses," under his breath.

The agent went on, "Then someone realized that where he was dropped off was around the corner from the Greyhound terminal. Again, we found that one of the ticket agents recognized him. He even remembered where he'd bought a ticket for. . ."

The agent behind me said, "Wichita, you . . ."

But he was interrupted by the continuing narrative, "Oklahoma City."

Harris interrupted them both, "He's going to get off at the Wichita stop. He may have already. Get somebody down to the Wichita Greyhound stop." The agent behind us ran out the door.

About ten minutes later Harris got a phone call. He answered, "OK, He didn't catch a cab. He'd be here if he had by now."

There was a pause while he listened and then he said, "Yes, check the city bus schedule."

Harris said to the room in general. "I want Hadley stopped before he gets to the warehouse. I want to talk to him on the street."

Minerva wrinkled her brow, then asked, "Why don't you just walk up to the warehouse, knock on the door, and ask them questions when they arrive?"

Harris actually looked like he'd been stung by that question. He started to answer, "In the first place, they can just refuse to answer questions or even refuse to invite us in."

Minerva muttered, "Like vampires, are you?"

Harris snorted, "I heard that."

"You were meant to."

He went on, "But, doggone it, the real thing is that I'm afraid that Connover might actually let me in. I don't want whatever happened to Ballard to happen to me!"

She asked, "And you think you're safer from that on the streets?"

His face turned a luminous shade of red, "Well, yes." He didn't make eye contact. We never found out what Minerva would have said next because we were interrupted.

Someone monitoring a couple of screens said, "He's on his way. I think he just got off a city bus. He'll be at the warehouse in a couple of minutes."

Harris picked up a walkie-talkie, keyed the mike, and said, "I want him detained. Don't do anything illegal, just surround him if you have to. I'll be there in a minute."

We watched Hadley walk down the street, apparently unaware that he was the subject of a dozen pairs of eyes at least. We could see several agents walking briskly toward him. He'd just reached the chain-link fence surrounding the warehouse. It was at least ten feet tall and was topped with razor wire.

When the closest agent was about fifteen meters away from him, he stepped back from the fence about a couple of meters. What happened next Hadley had absolutely no hesitation about. We've watched the video again and again but even in slow motion, it's hard to believe what we saw.

He ran at the fence, seemed to take two steps that carried him up the fence, used the fence to push off with both hands, and flipped over the fence backwards. Even in the replay, we can't tell if the backpack he was wearing brushed the razor-wire or not. He landed smoothly and walked toward a side entrance to the warehouse.

Everyone was caught completely by surprise. The agents on the street who were preparing for some sort of runaway break were standing flat-footed. In the Control Room we just stared in disbelief. We had all stood unconsciously and looked around the room surprised to find everyone gaping.

Harris flopped down into his chair. He just shook his head slowly and looked up at me, "How can we . . . "

He was interrupted by someone who had kept his wits about him, "Mr. Harris, the mailman just visited the warehouse."

He answered phlegmatically, "Yeah and . . ."

The other was almost cocky in his reply, "And he picked up something."

Harris jumped up and said to Minerva and me, "Come on. This may be a break." He turned to someone and said, "Get them to detain that postman until we arrive."

We three ran out of the double-wide and onto the street. It was just a couple of minutes drive to the warehouse. The scene we encountered as we got close was comical. Two agents were walking briskly alongside the postman, gesticulating and apparently not having things go their way.

We quickly joined the group and had to join in the brisk walk that was being led by the postman. Harris said, "I'm special agent Harris of the FBI. I want to talk with you."

The postman, who was black, in his late thirties, and in pretty good shape, simply said, "Who's stopping you?"

Harris said, "You just picked up something at that warehouse back there."

The postman said nothing.

Harris asked, "Well?"

The postman shrugged—which is no mean feat if you're walking briskly, have a postal pouch over your shoulder, and have your head turned to talk with someone walking beside you.

Harris said, "I want to see it."

The postman said, "I believe you. Do you have a court order?"

Harris's mouth dropped open for the second time in fifteen minutes. He almost fell behind, but he got back into stride and said, "Of course not. We just saw you pick up something at that warehouse."

The postman actually chuckled, "Then you've got no business looking at anything that I might or might not have picked up at that place of business. I'm a US Postal Service employee in the pursuit of my duty—which in this case is protecting the confidentiality of the United States Mail."

Harris's mouth closed in a tight line. "But I'm FBI."

The postman just said, "And I'm United States Postal Service. Go find yourself a Postal Inspector if you don't like my . . . "

Harris interrupted him, "Couldn't you at least tell me who the letter or package or whatever it is is addressed to?"

The postman said, "No, sir. Could you tell me what case you're investigating?"

Harris recognized when he was defeated, "No. Have a good day."

The postman speeded up slightly and said over his shoulder, "You too, sir."

Minerva complained, "What did you need us for? You handled that just fine all by yourself."

He didn't say anything. Minerva can be as persistent as anyone. This time she really seemed like she was dealing with a recalcitrant student who just didn't want to work. "I asked you a question. You came and got us. You wanted us because we could get people to give you straight answers. So why didn't you use us? This seemed like a prime opportunity."

Harris's face turned red. I'd never seen that before. He looked like he was going to hold it in, but then he spoke. "This is the United States!" He hesitated as if that were the whole answer.

Minerva was relentless, "So. This is the United States. You didn't have any trouble using us other places."

Harris was almost plaintive, "But I'm an officer of the United States government. I can't do anything illegal."

She shot back, "You didn't have any trouble sitting by while Pearson used the Imperious to get the Swiss ice maiden to talk!"

Harris compressed his lips and this was squeezed out, "That was Switzerland. We can do things overseas that we can't in the US."

Minerva asked, "Who says?"

"The Attorney General."

Minerva became really scathing as only she can, "Oh, so the high and mighty Inquisitor General says it's OK any place but the High and Mighty US. I suppose it's just fine in England!"

Harris just said, "Oh, can it." He then slowed his pace even more and headed back to the command post.

□

Two days later when we came into the command post Harris was pacing again. When asked what had happened, he looked around the room, seemingly desperately looking for something, then pulled his pen out of his breast pocket, and threw it to the desk, "Damn. Reynaldo drove into the warehouse sometime late last night in a rental truck. There was someone else in it with him. He helped unload it. Then he drove the truck off."

I suggested, "That sounds like it could be a good lead."

Harris just nodded. "Yes, we've got him in the next room interrogating him. Let's see what they've got."

We entered the room and made it truly crowded by our presence. Harris introduced us and asked for a quick review of what the interrogators had learned. The man himself, Jason Nee, gave it.

"There's not much to tell. I live in Portland, Oregon. I got a phone call from this Reynaldo person. I'm a handy-man. Reynaldo wanted me to rent a truck for him and drive it here to Wichita.

"I'd never done anything like that before, but he offered to pay all expenses—both anticipated and unanticipated as he said. He would pay for the one-way truck rental. He bought me a one-way fully refundable airplane ticket back to Portland so it didn't matter when I left. We would both drive and arrive here in about 24 hours. He'd pay me for a minimum of 40 hours.

"I had to use my credit card for the rental and my driver's license but he paid me the whole amount in cash in advance.

"I agreed. I picked up the truck and drove it to the dock where a freighter had landed. I gather that he'd taken passage on the freighter as well as shipping the two crates that he had. They loaded them into the truck with a fork lift, but when we arrived here, he had two friends in the warehouse who helped us unload the crates. They broke the crates down and it all happened so quickly that I didn't even need to help him unload them."

All of us really woke up when he said that he'd seen the crates unloaded. Harris was cool. He asked as casually as he could, "So, what was in the crates after all?"

Nee shrugged. "Oh, there was what looked like a bunch of rock-star amplifiers. Each one was shrink-wrapped in plastic. It was hard to make much out other than a bunch of slider controls like a sound board. I think that some of them had keyboards and computer displays but like I said it was hard to tell."

He thought a minute. "It was pretty dark in there. They hardly had any lights on in the warehouse. I don't know how they managed to unpack all that equipment without good lighting.

"Anyway, Reynaldo gave me a nice bonus when we finished and wished me good luck. I drove off to return the truck, but you people stopped me before I could do that."

Harris nodded throughout the narrative. "OK. You've never seen or heard of Reynaldo before this job?"

"Right-O." He seemed to be the most laid-back character I'd seen in this little adventure. Of course, he'd already been paid well and what could we do with him. He'd not broken any laws. He seemed not to know anything. He was actually leaning back in his chair while Harris thought.

Eventually Harris said, "OK. Mr. Nee. I'm satisfied. We'll want you to hang around and sign a statement that will be typed up from the recording of your interrogation. You're free to go then."

He was still relaxed, "Can I return the truck?"

Harris sighed, "No. It's evidence. I'll send somebody with you to the rental agency. They'll take over the rental. We'll make sure that you have a release from the rental company that relieves you of responsibility for the truck."

He smiled at that. "Sounds premium, Mr. Harris. It's been good dealing with you." With that he shook hands with Harris. We felt like WE'D been dismissed.

As a matter of fact, there was no reason to stay. One of the agents who'd been interrogating him came out with us. Harris asked, "What do you think?"

"He's good. I think we've gotten all that we can from him. We'll give him the standard spiel about getting in touch if he remembers anything more, but I don't think we'll hear from him."

Harris nodded.

Ballard Redux

The next day, I suddenly realized that it was Memorial Day weekend. I pointed that out to Harris.

He shrugged, "What do you want to do? Have a picnic?"

I was trying to think of some snappy reply when I remembered something, "Is the Memorial Day race on right now?"

One of the agents said, "Sure. Do you want to watch it?"

I nodded. He shrugged, "I'll bring it up on this screen." He indicated one in front of him. The race was on its seventy-third lap. I walked over behind him and watched over his shoulder. Minerva followed me—probably more from boredom than anything else.

When she had watched the race for about ten minutes she asked, "What in the world do you find interesting about this? It's just cars going round and round in a circle, no?"

The agent said, "Yes, just like a horse race."

Minerva retorted, "It's nothing at all like a horse race. A horse race lasts maybe two minutes—tops. A horse race doesn't involve noise produced by dozens of automobiles being driven twice as fast as their engines will stand.

"Horse races are gentle things attended by men in Ascots and women screening themselves from the sun with parasols. You can almost hear the individual clops of horse-shoes as they complete a single circuit of the course."

She was just beginning to wax eloquent when she was interrupted by Harris whose phone had just rung. He had picked up and shouted, "Quiet in here. I can't hear a damn thing."

He then appeared to turn his attention to whoever was on the other side of the phone connection. "I can hardly hear you. Where are you?"

His jaw dropped and he exclaimed, "What in the devil are you doing in the infield. . ." That was followed by, "Who did you say you were again?"

Minerva looked at me and asked with her lips, "Infield?"

I put my mouth next to her ear and said, "It's either baseball." At that her face fell. "Or a car race." We both then said together, "Indianapolis!"

He grabbed a piece of paper and a pen and began scribbling madly. "Listen, Ballard, can you get yourself to the airport?"

He paused and then said, "I don't care how much money you have. I'll have a ticket waiting for you at the American Airlines desk. Do you hear?"

He was apparently satisfied because he said, "Don't waste any time talking to me with all that racket in the background. You just get to the airport, and we'll be waiting for you when you arrive."

That ended their conversation. Harris ended the call, and we all pummeled him with questions. "Who was that?" "Where is he?" "What happened to him?" and the like.

Harris just said, " It's Ballard. We can de-brief him when he arrives here. Talbot, get him a ticket for the earliest flight to KCK on American Airlines from Indianapolis and have the ticket waiting for him at their counter. Let me know when he's to arrive." There were additional mumblings about Indianapolis.

He turned to Minerva and me. "Let's get to the airport. I don't want him to wait a minute."

Minerva smiled, "There's no big hurry. As soon as we find out what flight he's on, we can arrange to get to the airport quickly." She winked. "If you know what I mean."

Harris mumbled, "I was hoping to drive there."

It turned out that we were better off not driving. The next flight was an hour and a half off. He could just make the flight, and it would arrive at KC in about 3 hours. We could just make it there in three hours by car, but why kill ourselves getting there when we could disapparate at our leisure and get back much faster?

We went behind the trailer to disapparate about an hour before the scheduled arrival time after assuring ourselves that Ballard was on the flight. We decided to do things by the book. We arrived outside the secured terminal area, and Harris pulled rank with the TSA to get us inside.

The officer on duty insisted that he had to get in touch with his boss to let us in this way.

Harris just stared him down and said, "You can take that chance if you like. But if you make us wait, I assure you that your next assignment will be Anchorage, Alaska."

Once inside the secured area, we went to the terminal where he was to arrive and waited.

There had been some bumpy weather in the area and the arrivals were backed up. As it was we ended up waiting almost two hours at the terminal. Harris groused that we could have driven just fine. Minerva was not buying it. At least it kept them busy as we waited.

When Ballard stepped off the jetway, we almost didn't recognize him. He was wearing a light windbreaker, a black tee-shirt with no design, jeans, and sneakers. Oh, yes. He was wearing a pair of sunglasses as well. He was well-tanned and seemed to have been getting a lot of exercise.

He strode up to us and asked, "What the hell has been going on?"

Harris smirked, "Exactly the question I want you to answer."

I said, "Let's get back to the command post, and we can deal with both questions better than here."

Ballard looked puzzled and then said, "Oh, we're going to travel the wizard way."

We found a quiet hallway, made sure no one was visible, and there were no security cameras. Then we all joined a hand as though we were in a football huddle preparing for the next play.

Harris said, "On three, FBI." He counted off the three. All three of us Muggles chanted "FBI" on the third count. Of course, Minerva just stared at us puzzled, and then we went into the eighth dimension or wherever you go when you disapparate.

She took us to the same spot that we'd left originally, and we were quickly in the Interrogation Room of the command post. Everyone in the command post greeted Ballard as though he'd returned from the dead. In a way, he had. For all we knew, his body had been lying at the bottom of a ditch somewhere in Idaho.

When we were all seated in the Interrogation Room and the video recorder was going, we decided that Ballard should go first.

He frowned in concentration. We waited as patiently as we could. Finally, he said, "I'm sorry. This is going to be disappointing for you. I've tried to remember every detail that I possibly could. It's pretty thin."

Harris's lips closed and tightened, "Give us what you've got."

□

I was in Japan, of course. When you discovered where Reynaldo was, I went to the business office to learn what I could about him before confronting him.

I completely struck out there. They would admit that he was a client of theirs but they wouldn't give me any more details. When pressed they admitted that they were a custom electronics manufacturer.

I ended up in the public relations office of the company. The man who met me introduced himself as "Fred". He said that his name would be too hard for me to pronounce correctly. "When most who speak only Western languages pronounce my name, it comes out sounding like a word that means 'ass' in Japanese. You don't mind just using my Western nickname, Fred?"

"No, sir. It makes things easier for me too."

He waited—patient, impassive—for me to begin the conversation in earnest. I said, "You realize that I am an employee of the National Science Foundation but am currently on loan to the United States Federal Bureau of Investigation?" He nodded so curtly and almost imperceptibly that I almost didn't proceed.

"Do you further know that I am here in that official capacity to learn what it is that a US national is doing in Japan?" Again there was the almost imperceptible nod. I proceeded, "Well, then, would you assist me?"

He slowly shook his head, "Mr. Ballard, you should stand in front of a mirror and practice your speeches—paying particular attention to how you sound when you state your case. You, an employee of the US NSF, have come to this company to learn secret details of a Japanese company's dealings with an electronics inventor."

I was about to speak but he interrupted me, "No, not just an inventor, an electronics genius. Does this not sound like industrial espionage?"

I tried to remain as impassive as "Fred" was. "Are you aware that Mr. Reynaldo is more than an electronics genius? Are you aware that he is part of a small group that has attacked an ISIS stronghold and plundered it of a tremendous amount of gold without suffering casualties?"

Fred smiled for the first time. He asked, "Perhaps Japan should award him the Red Ribbon? Are you accusing him of performing a meritorious service to the world of free peoples?"

209

I had my moment of maximum dynamic stress at that point. I could have said quite a lot of things. I finally did say, "I am saying that I can not name the act of generosity or horror that he is not capable of."

Fred simply said, "I would be breaking my company's code of ethics if I were to reveal to you what you wish to know."

I thought a moment. As I was thinking and studying "Fred's" face I had the idea that he might actually like to help me. The smile had not entirely left his face. We both sat motionless, quiet with our hands folded on our laps. Finally, after a timeless interval, I asked, "Is it within the bounds of your company's ethics to tell me whether anyone in the company knows the purpose of what you are making for him?"

The smile ticked up a fraction. "You are, of course, aware that our company manufactures custom electronic circuits of the most delicate and fine dimensions."

I nodded slightly as encouragement.

"Even a child might surmise that we are making integrated circuits and circuit boards for him of unique design."

I nodded again by the barest amount that I could manage; not wanting to break whatever spell allowed him to yield this knowledge.

"I feel that I can ethically tell you that we have no idea what the purpose of these circuits is."

It didn't surprise me that they didn't understand the purpose of what they were doing. It did surprise me that they would agree to make something without knowing its purpose. The surprise must have shown on my face, for he went on, "It is not only I who wishes that we knew what these circuits are for."

I took a chance. "I believe that you have given Reynaldo some work space here at your company. Might I see him sometime? Would you arrange that?"

Fred frowned, "I'm afraid this delightful conversation must come to an end now." With that, he rose and walked out of his own office by its rear door.

I had no choice but to leave by the office's main entrance. His personal assistant was waiting for me. She escorted me out of the building all the while regaling me with the tourist highlights that were nearby.

When we reached the door, I commented, "I can't express how helpful you've been."

Her smile turned crooked for an instant and she said, "And they say that Westerners can not be subtle."

That afternoon, I decided to wait outside the offices of "Fred's" company at a Starbucks across the street, determined to encounter

Reynaldo when he left. That day, he must have left by some other exit because I didn't see him.

The next morning I took up my post again. It was a chill day but I wore. . . Well I wore the windbreaker that I'm wearing now. I was the only customer who sat outside. I sat outside all through the day. I ordered sushi for lunch. I was afraid that I would have to order something for dinner. I had been working through a copy of the *New York Times* throughout the day, barely taking my eyes off the main entrance to the building.

I was rewarded that evening for my patience. Not only did I see Reynaldo exit the building, he actually walked up to me and introduced himself.

"Mr. Ballard. I don't think we've met since San Antonio, but I'm glad that we have now. What can I do for you?"

I invited him to sit so that we could discuss a couple of questions that I had.

"Oh, Mr. Ballard, you are too shy. Allow me to invite you to my apartment and show you what I've been working on."

That presented me with a question that I had been dreading. Should I beard the Lion in his den? I flipped a mental coin but before it landed I decided. "Yes, of course. Can we order something to eat? Carryout perhaps?"

"Oh, don't temporize. Wouldn't you really rather learn the answers to all the questions that you've been asking?"

I agreed. He hailed a cab. His command of Japanese seemed to be phenomenal. He gave the cabbie instructions with complete confidence. He then turned to me, "The apartment that I have is not particularly easy to find. I frequently have to talk the cabbies through the route carefully."

The cabbie seems to have taken the instructions well. He sped off and didn't hesitate at any turning. We arrived at Reynaldo's apartment building. I didn't see a single sign in English in the last couple of blocks of our approach. He exchanged a few words effortlessly with the people whom we met in the building—apparently also tenants. We reached his apartment. He simply turned the doorknob and we entered.

He asked, "Wondering that I trust my possessions with the neighbors?"

I grunted.

"That is why I chose this neighborhood. It's quiet, peaceful, populated with people who respect themselves. No locks are needed."

We stepped into the room and I was not surprised by the spare interior. There was a futon, a large table that seemed to be used as a workbench, and a boom box. When we entered, Reynaldo picked up a remote control and started the boom box. What played made me think of Bach. It was a piano solo work. Maybe it was a prelude. He neither asked permission nor forgiveness for the music.

There was another room that I took to be a bathroom. Its door was closed. There was a room that was little more than an alcove that served as kitchen. There was a small refrigerator, a stove, several cabinets. There was not even a microwave.

I walked to the workbench/table and asked, "Something you're working on?"

He came back and said, "Yes, a small prototype for experimental purposes. Would you like to see it?"

He didn't require an answer. The model consisted of a rough wire framework containing a ring. There was what looked like an elaborate mouse pad with something that roughly resembled a mouse. He raised it off the pad and twisted it in a complex manner. The wire frame thing immediately lifted off the table and soared into the air with no apparent support. It wasn't spectacular but it appeared as though it had been put together haphazardly with little thought. As Reynaldo made minor gestures with the mouse, the object soared about the room.

Reynaldo replaced the mouse on the pad, and the object returned to the table. He sighed. "I wish I knew what that is for. I sometimes am worried about it."

I tried to approach the subject obliquely, "What concerns you?"

"Oh, just that these things come into my head. They're amazing, even astounding things like that flying carpet or the shield. I know. I mean, I JUST KNOW how to build them. I know how to use the primitive technology that we have to produce them. Then I build them. But what are they for? WHAT ARE THEY FOR? It frightens me sometimes that I don't know that."

I weighed my next words carefully. I didn't want to scare him off, but I had to see if he could help us prevent these things from being built for this project that these people had running. I turned away from the object on the table, "You know that I could help. I could help you to not make these things. It . . ."

Those were the last things I remember until today at the Indianapolis 500. I was in the infield, and I suddenly realized that I had to get back to our team.

I didn't have my cell phone. I had lots of cash in my wallet. I looked for a public phone. Of course, there wasn't one. I started walking around asking people if I could use their cell phone for a quick call. To a few I held out a twenty dollar bill to pay for the use of their phone. I guess that scared them off. Then I just asked, and the first person said, "Sure. Just don't call outside the country. Take your time." So, I called.

□□

I was the first to ask the question, "Where were you from the time that you were in Reynaldo's apartment until today?"

He looked into his hands on the tabletop before him as though the answer were hidden there, "I don't know. I just don't know."

We never gave up on that question for a long time. One of us would spring it on him at random. We phrased it in different, subtle ways. We asked what the weather was like recently. We asked him about sports. I suppose we hoped that we would surprise it out of him. We never did.

He then had lots of questions for us, "Where is everyone?"

Of course, he didn't mean "Where were all the people in our group." He meant THEIR group.

We slowly and carefully explained the histories (as far as we knew them) of each person in their group. Everyone was here—everyone except their leader. Where was Minns? No one knew.

When we became tired of the mysteries of their group, we tried to puzzle out what had happened to Ballard. Of course, we knew a certain amount for sure. They were things of which he himself had no idea. We reviewed them and hoped against hope they might trigger one of his own memories. They never did.

We knew that he'd not checked out of his hotel. We knew that he'd packed no more than enough for a carry-on. We knew that he'd bought a first class ticket to Seattle. We knew that he'd boarded it and de-planed in Seattle. He went through customs.

After going through customs, he went to a branch of his bank and withdrew all but the bare minimum required to keep his account active for 6 months.

After that point, it becomes sketchy. FBI investigators revealed that someone who matched Ballard's description bought a bus ticket from Trailways for Provo, Idaho. However, no one could prove whether he'd actually boarded the bus or where he got off, assuming that he had boarded it. We know that he had at least the eight thousand plus dollars that he withdrew from his account.

His photo, description, and ID information had been distributed to every law enforcement agency in the US. He was listed as a missing person. No one ever reported seeing him.

We sent investigators to Indianapolis to try to trace backward his movements. No one at the local bus stations within a thirty mile radius of Indianapolis recognized him. The person whose cell phone he'd borrowed was tracked down. He hadn't seen Ballard before that incident. None of his friends at the race had either.

One day he found a receipt from a restaurant in Wyoming in his windbreaker. That led us nowhere.

However, while that investigation was going on, something else happened that was much more significant.

Lenexa

We were in the command post staring at the TV monitors. It was a normal boring day when a panel truck pulled up the street where the main entrance to the warehouse grounds was located. We were notified immediately. Ballard was the first to give the order, "Stop that truck."

Our people on the site had already begun that process before the order was given. We all were on our feet racing down the street to the stopped truck. The side of the truck read, "McMinn Grocers."

When we reached the driver's side, the driver was already out of the truck surrendering his driver's license. He was saying, ". . . All I'm doing is delivering an order of food."

The agent who was doing the questioning asked, "May we see the invoice?"

The bored driver shrugged, "Sure."

We all crowded around the man with the invoice. Sure enough, there were enough foodstuffs to feed a small army for a month. Almost all of it was non-perishable. Harris demanded to examine the contents.

The driver protested, "Look, I've got other customers, I can't be sitting here all day."

Harris promised we'd be quick. He kept his promise. A half-dozen agents took the invoice and checked off every item. Nothing omitted. Nothing added.

Meanwhile, Harris asked how the order had been made. The warehouse didn't use the phone. There was no internet service. How had the order arrived at the grocers?

The driver was matter of fact about it, "We got a letter in the mail. It had the precise items and quantities. They'd even filled in and toted up the prices. But for such a large order, we decided to give them a 2% discount."

"And they paid with . . . what?"

"They had the total already. There was the exact amount in cash in the envelope with the order."

Harris asked, "And they trusted you?"

The driver, for the first time, was incensed, "We're an honest business. Never shorted anyone. Never overcharged. Even give discounts for good customers."

The crew quickly finished the inventory and assured us that there was nothing contraband that might be delivered to the warehouse. Harris sent the driver on his way.

We walked away dejected. Harris said it best, "Is that what we've devolved to—delivery inspectors?"

Ballard shook his head, "Police procedure?"

Harris snorted, "Yeh, slow, plodding, boring, in the end ineffective."

It didn't help any that later that day Harris took a call. We only heard his half of the beginning.

"Yes, sir. . . Yes, sir. . . No, sir. . ." There was a long pause and then he said, "Can we do this as a team conference call?" There was a little hope in his voice that was soon dashed. "No, sir. Let me just move to the Conference Room where it will only be me on the line."

He entered the Conference/Interrogation Room and shut the door behind him. He was there for what seemed like an hour. Maybe it was less. Anyway, when he came out, he called the inner circle together. "Come on in to the Conference Room. We need to have a talk." Again the Conference Room door closed—this time behind us.

Harris sat at the head of the table, "OK. This is the gist of the little talk I had with the Director. We've been burning money like there was no tomorrow, and there's precious little to show for it. He's given us a week to get a substantial lead showing that there's something illegal or very dangerous going on here. If we don't, he's shutting us down.

"So, we're going to have a little brainstorming session here. You know the way this works. Everyone shouts out any ideas that hit you— the crazier, the better. Then we analyze them and take the best to act on. Come on, what have you got?"

Sally volunteered to—indeed was actually anxious—to be the scribe. The ideas that came out at first were obvious with obvious holes in them that you could drive a MAC truck through.

A few of the ones that weren't utterly impractical were: Sneak a camera in via food shipment. Hire a salesman to go in and try to sell them business insurance. He could video the interior while he was there with his cell phone. Set the building on fire.

That last one was Minerva's suggestion. It might seem crazy, but we started fleshing it out to see how we could make it work. Sally suggested crashing a light plane into the building and having the gas tank catch on fire. Someone else suggested that the firefighters could be a military crew that would carry in video equipment to be placed permanently.

Harris was bemused, "You know I really like that idea. It's daring, unexpected, there would be lots of diversion created." Then he shook his head. "Of course, the one problem is that it's strictly illegal on so many counts. Wanton destruction of property. Unauthorized search—and seizure. Reckless Endangerment. Ah, well."

Most of us fought for the idea but we could see that Harris wasn't buying it. He just said, "Maybe as a last resort."

The next couple of days we poured over the other ideas hoping that something would come up. But it didn't.

□

Then something did come up.

It was a phone call from the Boy Genius. As he frequently does when he has made a discovery, he talked faster than his tongue could keep pace.

"Oh, everyone in Conference Room. Big. Hurry. Not minute lost."

We herded together everyone. We closed the Conference Room door and locked it—who knew what crazy thing he had in mind.

I asked him to take a drink of water and count to five. He chugged a bottle of water and spit a lot of it out counting, but when he finished he shocked us all.

"I've got HIM."

Ballard was catching the spirit of the BG or maybe the malady, "Who HIM?"

"Minns. I know where he is!"

That got us into action. Harris beat Ballard to the punch, "OK. Where exactly?"

"Do you know Lenexa?"

We all looked around at each other. No one knew it.

"It's a suburb of Kansas City on the Kansas side. The address I'm going to give you is a Lenexa address. 1055 Mockingbird Ave. It's an apartment building."

Ballard actually laughed. "Do you know what apartment he lives in?"

217

There was a dead silence for several minutes, then the BG said, "I didn't say that he lived there. It's where he is—right now. The apartment is on the third floor but I don't know what the number is."

Harris jumped up and walked out of the Conference Room. He boomed out, "Listen up! We've go Minns at an apartment building in Lenexa, Kansas. 1055 Mockingbird Ave. How fast can we get the local office to get there?"

Somebody said, "A half-hour if we're lucky. An hour otherwise."

Harris's mouth formed a tight line. "Get them going. I need the two best athletes in the Conference Room right now." Everyone looked at each other and then there was a consensus formed silently. One man and a woman stood and trotted into the Conference Room.

Harris frowned when he saw who they were. "OK. Listen. You get this once and you're off. You're under the command of these two civilians for this exercise. You do what they say. I don't care how crazy it sounds. You're going to Lenexa with them."

The woman asked, "Which of us drives?"

Harris replied quickly, "Listen. Neither. They do transportation. What they'll do will seem crazy before and after it happens, but just suck it up.

"We know where Minns is RIGHT NOW. You're going there with the Wendts. Don't ask questions. Take her hand and shut up."

I give this to them. They could follow orders. They both took Minerva's right hand. I took her left. Sally stuck her tongue out at us. I knew that she wanted to go, but there was no arguing with Harris when he was in this fell mood.

We hit the ground. Minerva and I were expecting to be turned inside out, and though we came down off balance, we didn't fall. They had no idea what was going to happen, but they hit the ground and rolled. They were up, guns drawn, and roughly back to back in two seconds flat.

He just said, "Where the Hell are we?"

I responded, "1055 Mockingbird Ave, Lenexa, Kansas."

She just said, "No, shit!"

Minerva said, "None at all."

We took a quick look around us. I asked the agents, "What are your names?"

The man answered, "Roberts. This is Cagney – no relation to the actor."

Minerva looked at me and said, "Stay here."

She disapparated and returned in about twenty seconds. "There are four exits: Main front door, rear door to parking lot, fire escapes at the ends of the building."

Cagney said, "I wish we had a couple of more men. We could cover all the exits and do a room by room search."

I said, "We can still do that." I explained that Minerva could disapparate around the building like she just had and make two or three circuits of the building every minute. No one could exit and get very far before she was back. Then the three of us could do the room by room search. I suggested that the two of them go room by room and that I would watch the hall to make sure no one left while they might be in a room.

I suggested that we start on the 3rd floor because that was where Minns had been seen. Cagney did a mock salute and said, "Yo's in charge, boss."

I couldn't help laughing, "And they told me the FBI doesn't have a sense of humor."

Roberts, Cagney, and I entered the apartment building. Minerva disappeared from the front of the building. We walked up the stairwell to the third floor. I positioned myself at the middle of the hallway and reached into my pocket for my purse. I opened it and worked the Glock out without taking it out of my pocket. I then worked out the loaded clip that I'd been carrying around with me since the beginning. I had to pull the gun and clip out to load it. I turned away from Roberts and Cagney while I did that.

It was slow work. I heard the unvarying routine dozens of times that day.

"Hello, ma'am (sir), I'm agent Cagney. This is agent Roberts. We're with the FBI." At this point credentials would be held up but not surrendered to the person who answered the door.

The person at the door then either expressed an interest in helping or not. Regardless, the response was, "This is a purely routine inquiry. Have you seen this man today?" At that point, they brought out the photo.

There were only three doors where there wasn't an answer. Roberts was ready to move on to the next floor. I wanted to bring Minerva up to disapparate into those apartments to look around. Cagney objected that that would leave the exterior unguarded. We kept going.

We worked our way through the rest of the floors. Support arrived from the Kansas City office of the FBI, and they helped us finish. By the time we were done, all the floors were covered, and a watch was left on the apartment building in case Minns returned.

We disapparated back to the command post and debriefed. I pointed out that we hadn't learned why Minns was there.

Cagney reminded us that we hadn't found anyone who had seen Minns, so how could we find out why he was there?

I requested that we get the Boy Genius on the line for the discussion. He was in his Control Room working the video feeds.

I asked him, "You said that you couldn't tell in which apartment Minns was located. Are you sure that you can't get us at least a hint?"

He nodded, "That's been worrying me since I gave you the location. I've been trying to use subtle clues in the video to decide which apartment he was standing outside of. I think it was 323 or 325. It was definitely in the middle of the hallway. It was on the odd number side."

"Thanks."

Then he surprised us, "Oh, yes. One more thing. It was strange. The door was open but he didn't go in. It was sort of like he was a salesman who was trying to talk whoever was talking with him to let him in, but he never got in. He left about five minutes after you guys went ballistic after him."

Minerva asked, "Are you sure about his talking to someone? He wasn't just standing at the door knocking?"

"No, the door was definitely open. But from the security camera angle I couldn't see in."

She went on, "Then how in the world did you two not talk to someone who'd seen him?"

Roberts shrugged. Cagney said, "I can't see it." She referred to her notes. "We definitely talked to people in those two apartments. How they didn't know about it, I can't imagine."

Ballard said, "I think we should pay another visit to #323 and #325 tonight."

There was an argument about who would go this time. It was Pearson and Sally who won. They pointed out that being fresh faces might make a difference. Harris had Chinese take-out, and we talked about the approach for later that night.

When they got back, we debriefed. Sally talked us through it.

Phil and I took Ballard to the exterior of the apartment building, and we checked in with the stakeout that was going on there. Ballard asked if we could borrow an agent. Agent Cooper came with us. Then, we went in.

We started at apartment 323. The door was answered by a middle-aged woman who seemed to be in her early forties. Agent Cooper introduced himself, "I'm FBI field agent Cooper." He had his credentials out. The lady barely glanced at them. But she didn't invite us in.

"What do you want?"

"We're doing a routine investigation. A man, Phillip Minns, was seen entering this apartment building yesterday, and we're trying to find someone who might have seen him."

She yawned, "Sure. Some other agents were here earlier. I told them everything I knew—which is nothing. I can't help you." She started to close the door.

Cooper quickly said, "Wait. Is it possible that there was someone in the apartment besides you at about that time who might have seen Minns?"

"Are you kidding? No. There hasn't been someone else in this apartment since the '90's."

"Thank you ma'am. Here's my card. If you should happen to think of anything—no matter how minor—that might be of interest to us, please call the number on that card any time of the day or night."

She gazed at him contemplatively and said, "Any time? Maybe I will."

She shut the door, and I observed, "Agent Cooper, I think you have an admirer."

Phil chimed in. "Yeh, I wouldn't be surprised if you got a call next Saturday round about 11 PM from a witness who just remembered something important."

Cooper just said, "Can it. Safety before levity."

The #325 was a different story. The door was answered by a man. He took a very careful look at Cooper's ID. He asked about us. Ballard showed his NSF ID and explained that he and Phil and I were private consultants for the agency in this case.

The man finally identified himself as Robert Stokes. He asked what we were investigating. Cooper said, "I'm sorry. The Bureau doesn't comment on ongoing investigations except where necessary as part of the investigation."

Stokes set his jaw, and I thought that he might just declare that Cooper would have to comment as part of the investigation, but he didn't. He just looked determined. He did tell us, "OK. What can I do for you?"

Cooper explained about earlier and asked if he might have seen Minns.

Stokes said, "I wasn't here at the time. My wife was. I'll call her."

The wife's name was Brenda. She explained that another agent had spoken to her, and she had not seen Minns.

Cooper pressed onward, "Is it possible that there was someone else here who might have seen Minns?"

The Stokes immediately looked at each other. Cooper didn't miss that. "There was someone else here wasn't there?"

Stokes's jaw set again, "Well, there wasn't anyone who could have seen him."

A little steel came into the voice of Cooper which had been all sweetness up to now. "You do realize that it is a felony offense to lie to a Federal officer and also to impede an investigation of the Bureau?"

Stokes's eyes widened, but he stood firm in his silence. Mrs. Stokes said, "It's just that our daughter couldn't possibly have seen or spoken to this Minns."

Cooper went back to silk, "Why is that ma'am?"

I thought I heard her voice catch for an instant, "Our daughter is deaf. She was in her room studying. She didn't hear when the other agents knocked at our door. I don't see how she could have seen this Minns."

Cooper persisted, "Ma'am, would you mind very much if we spoke to your daughter for a few minutes."

She nodded and then explained, "Please come in. She's nine years old. She isn't good at all at reading lips, but she's great at sign language. I'll sign your questions. Then, I'll translate her answers."

It sounded awkward but we agreed. Mr. Stokes left the front room to get the daughter. He came back with a bright, happy nine-year old girl. She had her hair pulled back in a pony tail. Her mother led her to the sofa where she sat between her father and her mother. Mrs. Stokes signed something and Mr. Stokes said, "Jenny, these people are policemen who want to talk with you about something that happened today." She pointed at Cooper and said, "This is agent Cooper, Miss Harker, Mr. Pearson, and Mr. Ballard." It took a long time to sign our names.

Jenny smiled a big smile and signed, "I've never met a policeman before. Can I see your badge?"

Cooper said, "Of course, but you're not allowed to touch it. I'll hold it where you can see it easily." He knelt in front of her and held up his credentials for her to see.

She signed rapidly and Mrs Cooper signed rapidly as well. Her dad gave up trying to translate. Then Mrs. Cooper said, "Jenny is surprised that you're FBI. She wants to know if you've ever caught any terrorists."

222

I gulped. That question came way too close for comfor,. but Cooper wasn't fazed. He just said, "I'm afraid I've only chased bank robbers and forgers."

Jenny signed, "That's probably exciting too."

Ballard asked, "Jenny, did you see someone at the front door. It would have been in the late afternoon?"

Jenny nodded, and everyone except Ballard jumped at that.

Ballard went on, "Could you tell me which of these pictures he is?" He pulled out the four photos that we'd all been carrying with us for a long time. He showed Connover first.

Jenny just said, "He wasn't black."

Then came Hadley. She shook her head.

Then was Minns. Jenny's eyes widened, and she nodded enthusiastically. We didn't need Mrs. Stokes translation to know that she'd seen him.

Mr. Stokes signed and said, "Jenny, how did you know that he was at the door?"

There ensued a lengthy spate of sign language between the three of them. When the maelstrom of flying fingers and eyes flashing back and forth trying not to miss anything that was said finally ended, Mrs. Stokes said, "Jenny insists that she 'heard' this Mr. Minns and that she came to the door to answer his call. Neither my husband or I can see how this is possible."

He added, "It's true that Jenny senses things that neither my wife or I do, but I don't see how this is possible."

Ballard asked, "Jenny, what did Mr.. Minns say to you?"

There was another flash of hands between Mrs. Stokes and Jenny. Her husband kept up roughly, "First, he didn't say that he was Mr. Minns. He is the . . ." Here Mr. Stokes stopped and said, "I didn't get that."

I had a spooky idea that I knew what she'd said. Finally, the speeding conversation ended and Mrs. Stokes reported. "Jenny didn't know the Sign Language symbol for what Minns said he was." She stopped, choked up by something, and then went on, "She spelled it phonetically." She stopped, apparently trying to hold back tears.

Mr. Stokes seemed affected as well but he could talk, "Most deaf people can't spell things phonetically because they don't know what a word sounds like."

I thought it might be "the Lieutenant". I said as much. Both the Stokeses were shocked that I knew that.

He swallowed hard. "She also said that he talked to her about heaven."

Cooper had questions, "What did he say about heaven?"

This time Mr. Stokes signed. His wife seemed too affected still. The answer was, "Jenny says that the Lieutenant says that Heaven is where the deaf hear."

Cooper followed on quickly, "Did the Lieutenant touch you, Jenny?"

The answer was, "Oh, yes."

Cooper reacted—a real rarity. He squinted and his lips formed a tight line, "Where did he touch you?"

The answer was, "He touched my heart. I felt like he was a good man."

Cooper followed up again, "Did he say that he'd be back again?" She nodded.

We questioned her more but there didn't seem to be anything more that she knew. We left. Cooper left one of his business cards as he always did with the usual request to get in touch immediately at any time if anything more occurred to any of them.

We left and walked down to the street level. When we reached there, Cooper said, "I think we've got a pedophile here."

Ballard asked, "But he didn't 'DO' anything."

Cooper nodded, "The usual pedophile profile is to work slowly, gain the trust, and even the love of the victim and then 'DO' something."

We left Cooper at the stake-out. We went into an alley and disapparated. We arrived outside the trailer and when we went in found Harris waiting for us. He was on the phone.

It turned out to be Cooper who'd called Harris immediately after we left and was reporting in full. It took a while, but after it was over, Harris collected everyone and took us to the Conference Room.

⬜
⬜⬜

Harris had pulled Minerva and me from our post watching some of the video cameras—a truly boring job. We went into the Conference Room and Harris spoke.

"I've just been on the phone with field agent Cooper who went with Ms. Harker, Mr. Pearson and Mr. Ballard to try to find whomever Minns had been speaking with yesterday. They succeeded. I want to call the Director to report what they found, which should be enough to keep the investigation going. I want you all here to either be available to testify and/or hear what happens. We may not get through

224

immediately, but I have a feeling that he'll want to talk with us from my conversation with him. Anyone have comments?"

Minerva said, "I hope you don't expect Wendt and me to comment, since we weren't present."

"Only if you can shed light on anything that's been said. I won't call on you. If you speak, it will only be because you volunteer or the Director asks you a question."

With that understanding, he made contact with the Director's Office. After a little wheedling, he convinced his personal assistant to contact the Director. The Director would speak to us but not immediately. Harris elected to stay on the line.

The half hour of Muzak was almost more than I could stand, but after you've listened to an evening of Celestine Warbeck at the Weasleys, there's not much in the way of music that you can't endure. The personal assistant announced the Director. She announced all the people who were on the conference call and then dropped off the line.

The Director was to the point, "You interrupted my bridge night with my wife and another couple. This had better be damn important. You've had a development in Wichita?"

Harris was direct with the Director. "Yes. We found the leader of the group, Minns. We discovered that he'd visited with a deaf nine-year old in Lenexa, Kansas without the knowledge or permission of her parents."

The Director was silent for a moment. "Do you think this could be a case of pedophilia?"

Harris looked over at Ballard, who nodded, then said, "Yes, I think so."

"Do you have sufficient evidence to indict?"

Harris took a deep breath, "No, sir. We don't. But I think that we have enough to bring him in for questioning."

The Director was silent for quite some time. "Pedophilia is bad, very bad. But have we been spending all this money to track down one pedophile? And one that we don't have enough evidence to indict yet?"

Harris had begun sweating, "That's about the size of it."

Ballard asked, "Mr. Director, this is Adam Ballard."

"Ah, yes. You started all of this, didn't you?"

"Yes, sir, I did. May I say that we're missing the larger context here? It isn't one possible pedophile." Harris had winced at the word "possible". "It's a group that is pursuing a goal that we don't understand in the least. They are building an object that we have the plans for but don't have the least understanding about. They are using materials which are completely beyond the material sciences that we have. They are using electronics that the manufacturer doesn't understand any more than we do."

His voice kept rising imperceptibly as he spoke. The force of will behind that voice was palpable. He went on, "These people have done everything that they've done completely in the open, and yet we don't have the least understanding of them. There is almost literally no imaginable goal that I would say was impossible to them. I think it's desperately important that we understand what they are doing."

The Director hesitated but little and replied, "Well, then. Bring this Minns in. Question him. Use any legal measures to keep him off the street. Try to force his associates to open up to you."

His voice as well rose as he spoke. "Do it now!"

It was apparent that this was the end of the interview, and that we had the permission to continue at least for a while. The Director hung up.

Harris said, "Just bring him in, right? Does anyone have any ideas how we do that?"

Pearson said, "Let's get Brahms on the line."

It was evidence how disturbed we were that we'd forgotten the time difference to Scotland. Harris called Brahms who answered immediately and announced that Aurora wasn't there, but we went on anyway. Brahms said, "She's grading final exams, but I'll bring her up-to-date. Go ahead."

I asked why he was still up.

"With Aurora up, I decided to keep checking search results. Don't you ever work late?" He sounded testy, which is really a departure from his normal positive attitude.

Ballard took the point, "We need to find Minns—not just where he is at this moment but where he's actually living."

Brahms harrumphed and said, "You don't think that I've not been pounding the video streams from Kansas City?"

Harris took a deep breath and said, "Concentrate all your efforts in Lenexa, Kansas. We'll put all the men on the ground in Lenexa that I can muster."

Brahms hummed, "Ahhhh! If he's in Lenexa, I'll get you some results soon. That is, unless he's living under a bridge."

I said, "I hope your idea of soon is a day or two."

I could see the determination in his face even though we were not doing video when he replied, "No more than that."

I went on, "That's as much as we can hope for. Let's go."

We'd been spending a lot of time in the command post, and we only went to our hotels to shower, catch a little sleep, and change clothes. We were out of the command post when Brahms and Aurora called.

We arrived and were met by Harris who told us that we'd just missed Brahms's call. "He's got Minns! He's in an apartment building close to downtown Lenexa. He has video of Minns leaving the apartment itself this morning. Brahms was able to follow him for a while via video but he lost him when he got on a bus.

"We're having a meeting at 11 AM to plan how we'll arrest him."

Minerva commented afterward that she suddenly wasn't so sure that she actually wanted to meet him.

11 o'clock arrived, and we all trooped into the one Conference Room that we had. All the ladies in the group sat. There were still several ladies standing, including Minerva. She stood beside me. The Conference Room was packed beyond standing room. There were a couple of people standing in the door-frame of the room.

Harris started the meeting. "Ballard and I have been brainstorming this plan. We think it's good, but if anyone has suggestions, we want them. I'll present the plan, and Ballard will give a pep talk."

I tried to imagine what a "pep talk" could possibly be in this situation. But Harris was going on with the tactical plan. The plan seemed rather plain vanilla. No one who was hearing it seemed surprised or awed although I was a bit surprised at some of the measures. It was to happen tomorrow after Ballard left the apartment and as he returned to it.

There were several units that would make the arrest. Harris started his presentation at the outside of the apartment building and worked his way closer and in to it.

At the extreme perimeter were to be two military hum-V's borrowed from an army base nearby. They were to each hold five men. They were to stay on adjacent side streets until the operation began, but as soon as it began, they were to position themselves at the ends of the street on which the apartment building was. They were to block the streets and not let anyone onto or off of the street. They were also to be surveillance and backup in case something went badly wrong.

On the rooftops of adjacent apartment buildings across the street from and behind the apartment building would be two sniper teams of two each. They were mainly for surveillance, but on direct verbal orders and only on direct verbal orders from Harris, they would take

227

down Minns if he got away from everyone else. Until the operation actually began, they were to remain hidden, invisible from the street or the lower levels of the apartment building of interest.

So, who handled surveillance until the operation proper began? Brahms (who was in on the conference remotely). His team would watch all security cameras in the area. When he saw Minns enter the apartment building, the operation would begin.

Inside the building, there would be two teams of five inside the two fire escapes. None of their doors were ever locked. They would check out everyone entering and leaving the building through those entrances. They would turn away anyone attempting to enter the building through the doors after the operation began.

When Minns left the elevator on his floor, the elevator would be turned off from the Fire Control Room by two agents stationed there.

The building management was being approached and would provide a key to Minns room. A team of six would enter his room an hour after he left in the morning. That team would be led by Ballard. It was their duty to detain Minns and deliver him to the Kansas City FBI office for questioning. One of the HumVee teams would take him there. The other HumVee team would go along as escort.

Brahms asked the question that was burning on at least four other tongues. "What about the Wendts and Pearson and Sally? What will they be doing?"

Harris said, "They're our roving defensive backs. They are to stay at the command post monitoring the video of what's going on. If a wheel or rather to say, several wheels come off the operation, they are to disapparate wherever they can be of use and do . . . well, do whatever they can."

Harris then turned over the meeting to Ballard who was to give the "pep talk".

Ballard was every bit as business-like as Harris. "I've been asked to be brief. Brief I will be. Lieutenant Minns, . ." It was the first time in a long time that I'd heard him referred to by his military title, ". . . is probably the most dangerous man you will ever meet in your lives. He has so far not killed anyone—as far as we know. But he is perfectly capable of killing on a second's notice and without using any weapons. Everyone who has stood in the way of any of the people in this group has been eliminated. So far, the elimination has not been lethal. There's no reason that it couldn't be though. I was taken out for over three weeks.

"We very much want to take this man alive and unharmed, but he may not give you a choice in the matter. I advise you to decide how you will act in advance. Then don't rethink. Carry out your decision without hesitation of any sort.

"Good luck to us all."

After we left the conference, Minerva commented, "With a pep talk like that, how can we go wrong?"

Engagement

The next morning, we were up at 4 AM, preparing with everyone else. Everyone, including Sally and Minerva were suited up in black with FBI emblazoned on all surfaces. We were all wearing Kevlar. I had commented that Kevlar was the new black.

Sally said, "What do you mean 'the new black'? It looks to me like it's the old black."

Minerva asked, "Do you really think we need to be wearing this medieval armor?"

I looked at her hard, and she recanted, "OK. OK. It just reminds me how dangerous this could be."

Pearson commented, "That's what it's supposed to do."

It did seem silly sitting in the command post watching a sampling of the video cameras in and around the apartment building in air-conditioned discomfort.

The teams deployed at 6 AM. The Humvees were in place on side streets. The rest of the team was in several Tahoes a couple of blocks further off.

At 8:30 AM, Minns walked out of the apartment building. The video streams were coming via England and had a second or so delay. All of the video that showed Minns had his image surrounded by a yellow circle.

He turned left at the street and walked off about a block. When he reached the end of it, he crossed the street and proceeded on the cross-street to the right. He disappeared on one camera and came up on another. He stopped at a bus stop and got on when the next bus arrived.

Brahms had been on the conference phone since we'd started. He commented, "I'm going to try to find out where he goes today."

I just wished him good luck.

We were able to follow him, too, on the cameras that Brahms was using. The bus went straight along the street, and the view was passed from one traffic camera to another smoothly. I wondered why Brahms hadn't been able to do this before.

About twenty minutes later, the bus stopped at a residential bus stop, and the yellow circle popped onto the screen. I gasped, "Brahms, did you see him get off?"

"Of course, you twit. Do you think I'm a twit?"

There happened to be a traffic cam pointed down the street on which Minns was walking. Minns stopped about a third of the way down the block in front of what appeared to be a two story brick house. Brahms exclaimed, "What are you doing, Lieutenant?" Then on one of the video screens a Google Maps screen popped up. "OK. Let's have a look at Street View.

Sure enough, there was a street view showing the house straight on along with its house number, 229. Of course, it had been taken at least months before. Brahms was running a private commentary out loud, "OK. Lieutenant, who are you visiting? A little balloon popped up beside the house that said, "Johnny Subaru, Alice Subaru, John Subaru."

There was a pause. Minns seemed to be just standing there staring at the house. Brahms asked, "So, Lieutenant, are you going to go knock on the door or not? Are we fishing or just cutting bait?"

Minns stood there for what must have been a half an hour. At one point, Brahms asked if we should alert the posse that we had Minns cornered. I shook my head and then realized that Brahms couldn't see it. Sally beat me to the punch, "No. We stay on the plan."

After a while, a very spooky thing happened. Minns turned back so that he was facing the way that he'd come down the street, and then he looked up almost directly at the camera. Brahms exclaimed, "SHIT! He can't know we're watching."

I said, "I wouldn't be so sure of that."

Then the spell was broken. Minns turned about face, walked down the street and turned the corner onto a cross street. Apparently there wasn't a camera there. He just disappeared off the screen.

□

We turned back to the video of the apartment street and settled in for a long wait. Somebody ordered lunch. We had pizza and soda.

Then about 2 PM, things started to happen. Brahms was on the line, "He just got off the bus at your stop. He should be turning the corner shortly."

He did. He showed up on our screens. We watched him walk down the street. When he'd almost reached the apartment building, he paused and looked around. Brahms exclaimed, "Shit. He's made us." But then he kept walking. Brahms added, "Maybe not."

We switched to another camera in the lobby of the building and watched him walk to the elevator. There was even a camera in the elevator. We watched him ride up to the fifth floor—his. He got out, and the hall video camera picked him up. He walked to his room, turned the doorknob, and walked in.

I exclaimed, "Didn't they lock the door when they set up camp?"

Brahms replied, "He doesn't lock his door."

There was no camera in his apartment—an oversight on our part. The view in the hall was unchanged for several minutes. Then Minns walked out. Brahms was on it instantly. "Minns left the room by himself. He's going to the elevator. Everyone ready. Can anyone get hold of the team in the apartment?"

No one could.

Meanwhile to our amazement, the elevator was working. Brahms called out, "Teams in the stair wells, Minns is going down the elevator."

Harris broke in, "Divide in two. Keep half your team in the stairwell, the rest go to the elevator and intercept Minns."

We got acknowledgments from them.

Brahms switched to the camera in the lobby. The elevator door opened, Minns stepped out, but there was no one there from the stairwell teams. Brahms said, "Harris, we lost the elevator teams. You're up."

Harris replied, "HumVees, we're up. Drive down the street and intercept Minns. My Humvee takes the front. The other takes the parking lot at the back."

Minns went out the back entrance. The sniper on the roof behind the apartment building reported, "Minns just walked out the back. I've got him in my sights."

We switched our view to the security camera at the back of the building. We saw him walking placidly toward the back fence of the complex. I noticed that no Humvee had shown up. So, I said, "Humvee's not in the back."

Harris said, "Sniper B. Take him down. Don't kill him if you can avoid it."

There was no answer. Brahms reported, "He just went over the

232

wall. He took it like an Olympic high jumper."

Harris said, "Wendts, you're up. Disapparate onto the street he's on. Stop him."

I looked over at Minerva and said, "As soon as we land, spot him and stun him. If you can't. . ." I was getting my Glock out and loading it. ". . . I'll try to."

She frowned but nodded. She took my hand, and we were tumbling through space. I tried to roll with it and get up. I was facing Minerva and couldn't see Minns. Apparently, she could because she raised her wand but suddenly covered her eyes as though shielding them from a blinding light. I rolled around and brought my Glock up. I thought, "Hit his legs if possible," but suddenly there was a blinding light. I didn't think but just fired three rounds. Later, when I tried to reconstruct what had happened, I remembered that I hadn't seen anyone on the street. Maybe that was why I fired. The blinding light ended a minute later.

Minerva had recovered too and had come to my side. At the same time, a black Humvee pulled up. Somebody opened a door in the back and said, "Get in." We did.

Harris said, "Did you see which way he went?"

We both shook our heads.

Harris said, "Let's assume for the bus line. Go."

We must have reached 80 before we reached the intersection. Somebody had put a flashing light on the roof and had the siren going. We took the curve and turned left.

I said, "Look for the closest city bus." There were two on the street each going in opposite directions.

Harris said, "Take the closer one." It happened to be going the same direction as we were.

We pulled up by the bus. There must have been an external intercom on the Humvee. Somebody used it to say, "City bus, pull over and stop."

They did. We all got out except the driver. Everyone was brandishing a gun except for Minerva. The bus driver had gotten out and went straight to her. I guess he figured that she was in charge because she didn't have a firearm. He asked, "What can I do to help?"

She said, "Unload the bus. Everyone. All with hands up."

Apparently, Harris was satisfied with the instructions. He didn't say a word. Everyone slowly filed out. No one even remotely resembled Minns. We searched in the bus, under the bus, and even on top of the bus. Minns wasn't anywhere.

Harris called Brahms and asked if he had seen anything.

233

Brahms just said, "I lost him completely when he went over the wall."

The only other team that we heard from was the "A" sniper. He reported that the other Humvee had stopped while rounding the corner of the building.

Harris got us back in the Humvee and said, "Let's see how many dead we took."

As it turned out, we hadn't taken any dead. It took anywhere from a half hour to four hours for people to escape the paralysis they suffered.

We had a post-mortem that night. It wasn't pretty. Harris had to admit that no one was at fault. His team was the only one that wasn't hit but he had to admit that it was luck, pure dumb luck.

In the midst of the gloom, the Boy Genius pointed out one bright spot. "Don't forget that something very strange happened this morning with Minns. That's a lead that we can follow up on."

No one really thought it was much of a bright spot, but everyone was happy that there was something to look forward to the next day other than licking our wounds.

□□

The next day we had a brief conference and decided that Ballard, Harris, Minerva, and I should go to interview the Subaru family. There was a brief argument over whether to drive or disapparate. Minerva won that argument.

We appeared in an alley next to the street at about 9 AM, Saturday morning. Ballard thought that it was likely that we'd find everyone at home.

Harris led the way, as usual, because he had The Credentials. He knocked on the door. It was answered by a woman who seemed to be in her thirties, but there was a worn appearance around her eyes that made me wonder. She was polite. How could she help?

Harris produced his credentials and explained that we were with the FBI, and we were doing a routine investigation. Could we come in?

Of course. What were we investigating?

Harris explain, "We'd really like to talk with everyone who was in the house yesterday morning if possible."

Certainly, she'd get her husband.

John Subaru was a tall thin man. He was dressed in jeans and a green work shirt. Perhaps he'd been planning to do some work around the house.

More introductions and then Harris popped the question. "Yesterday, did you notice anyone hanging around outside your house?"

The two looked at each other in puzzlement. He answered, "No, why?"

Ballard answered the question, "We have reason to believe that a person of interest to us spent quite a lot of time outside your house on the public sidewalk. It was almost half an hour. And you didn't notice at all?

Mrs. Subaru said, "NO," more emphatically than I liked. She amplified, "I was distracted about that time and didn't have any spare attention for the street. John was at work. This person didn't knock on the door or," and here she gave a little gasp ". . . look inside a window did he?"

Harris was definite, "No ma'am. We're quite sure that he only stood outside your house on the sidewalk gazing at it."

Minerva asked, "Alice, was there anyone else in the house at this time who might have noticed?" I immediately thought of a lover. Perhaps she was very distracted indeed.

She said, "No. No one else could possibly have noticed anything." Then she flicked a glance over to her husband. I had to think for a moment to recall of what that flicked glance reminded me. Harris had begun his interview closing ritual: thanks, business card, if you remember anything.

But then I remembered, and I interrupted him. "Ma'am, you don't happen to have a child who might have been in the house at that time?"

She gasped, "How did you know?"

Her husband quickly interposed. "It's impossible that he could have seen anyone."

Harris glanced at me. We'd heard that before. He asked gently, "Could you tell us why he couldn't have seen anything?"

Alice's eyes went to the floor, and her husband said, "Come with me." He then led us back into a short hall that led to a bedroom. In the bedroom was a boy. It was hard to tell how old he was, but I'd have guessed ten. His head lolled to one side and he showed only a flicker of recognition that anyone had entered the room. Still, his mother came to him and hugged him, patting him on the back, and saying in a slight sing-song, "Johnny has guests this morning."

His father said, "His is a case of severe Downs syndrome."

Alice said with a sob, "The distraction that I had was Johnny. For about a half hour yesterday, maybe while your 'person of interest' was outside, Johnny was very disturbed—as disturbed as I've ever seen him."

Then she whirled on us, "Was that man out there because of Johnny."

The idea surprised us all. We were all thinking that, but how she could have guessed was beyond me. Fortunately, Harris answered. He retained his composure and simply said, "Let's go back into your living room to discuss this a bit more."

Once we arrived there, he said, "Mr. and Mrs. Subaru, I can't comment on ongoing investigations, but I can tell you that we will be posting a twenty-four hour watch on your home."

That seemed to disturb Mr. Subaru more than I expected. He stood and paced, "You mean that you think there is danger to Johnny?"

Ballard said, "Our interest is in this man. We very much want to take him into custody to interrogate him. Let me assure you that we have no intention of allowing him anywhere near your home. We'll be discreet. No one else need know."

That statement didn't satisfy anyone, but, really, it was the most that we or anyone could say.

We left the home and got in the Black Tahoe. Harris phoned the command post. His instructions were simple. He wanted twenty-four hour surveillance on this home. We weren't leaving until the first team arrived.

When we got back to the command post we had an impromptu team conference call with Brahms. The eight of us were present across two continents. Harris reviewed what had happened. Then he stated the situation eloquently, "Everything we've tried has failed. It broke my heart to leave that couple with the Downs syndrome kid thinking that we could protect them or him. It's time for brainstorming crazy ideas."

Brahms asked, "What do we know about what's going on in the warehouse?"

Ballard answered, "Well, they've been building their machine—whatever it is. The sounds of parts snapping together has ended. Whatever they're building, they seem to have it finished. Which means, I suppose, that they will be moving on to the next phase of the project—whatever it is."

Brahms came back with a thought, "Then isn't it time to strike now—while they're in transition?"

Harris nodded, "Fine. Just how do we do that?"

Brahms seemed on a roll, "You asked for crazy ideas. How about demolishing the warehouse?"

Harris exclaimed, "What?"

"Yes, just use eminent domain or whatever you call it to seize the warehouse. Force them to move whatever it is."

No one dignified that with further comments. Then an idea hit me, "What about having a surprise safety inspection? Bring in the county or state or city building inspector." No one said anything. This time it was because everyone was thinking carefully about it.

While everyone was deep in thought, an alarm went off. It was on the phone from the Shrieking Shack. Brahms said, "May not be necessary. One of the automated searches just found Minns. It seems to be another house in a different part of Lenexa."

Harris said, "Give us the exact address. Sally, Pearson, Ballard, go. Pearson, when you get there, drop him immediately. Stun him or whatever. No questions. Don't give him a chance to escape.

"Brahms, is he outside or inside the house?"

"Inside now. I couldn't tell who let him in."

Harris turned back to Pearson, "What are you waiting for. GO!"

They took hands and disappeared from the room leaving a small whirlwind where they had been. Harris tried to keep the brainstorming going, but we'd lost three from our meeting, and we were all too interested in what was happening on the street to really be effective.

Eventually, we just watched the video from the traffic cam where Ballard had gone. We didn't see them disapparate onto the street, but we did see them walk onto the street and casually down the street toward the house in question.

Nothing happened for about ten minutes. Then, Ballard called us. Harris put him on the conference phone. "We've decided to go into the house. Any objections?"

We all looked at each other and Harris said, "No, go ahead."

They started walking toward the house. Then they stopped and apparently had an animated discussion. Finally, Pearson disappeared. The others ran to the house. As they got close, the door opened and Pearson stuck his head out. He motioned with his hands for them to come. They broke into a real run and entered the house.

We started to discuss sending a second team in to investigate when the three re-appeared in the Conference Room.

We all started to talk at once, but Pearson quickly took over because he was answering the questions that we all had. He started the explanation after he got everyone's attention.

We arrived and waited as long as we thought we could afford to. We had no idea what was going on in the house, and we all wanted to know what was happening.

There was a heated argument over what we should do. The Muggles wanted us to all rush the house and try to overwhelm Minns at once. I thought that going into the house stealthily by disapparating and making myself invisible using the *disillusionment* spell was the best way. In the end, I had to use the ultimate argument. I just did it.

I landed in the second floor and immediately used the disillusionment spell. I then used the *muffliato* spell to make sure that no one could hear me.

None-the-less, I found that it was nerve-wracking walking down the stairs trying to avoid squeaking boards. When I got to the main floor, I began to investigate. I went through a dining room and on to the kitchen. I found that a boy, who couldn't be older than eight was sitting at the table eating a sandwich.

As I approached him, he turned and asked, "Did you come back, Lieutenant?"

A glance at his eyes showed that he was blind. I answered, "No. I'm Phil Pearson. We were concerned about you being here alone with the Lieutenant. How did you know that I was here?"

He laughed, "Well, you weren't as loud as an elephant, but I could hear you step on the squeaky floor-board at the door to the dining room."

All I could say was, "I see." And then I regretted it, but the lad didn't seem to be disturbed by my reference to my vision.

I asked, "How is it you're here by yourself?"

"Oh, Mom had to go to the store for something. She'll be back shortly. I'm not a baby after all. I can take care of myself for a half hour or so."

I caught myself before I said, "I see."--again. What I did say was, "I'm with the FBI and I have a couple of friends outside. May I ask them in?"

He gave a broad, elongated, "Sure."

When they were all in, we asked him a couple of questions, "This Lieutenant that you talked with—what did he talk to you about?"

"Oh, you know, where was my mom, what grade was I in, did I like peanut butter and jelly samichs. I said YES to the samich. He made me one. I'm eating it now.

"He asked me what I thought Heaven was like."

I was afraid to ask what he said to that question, but Sally did. He said, "I'll get to see Daddy and Mommy's hands in Heaven."

Sally gasped. I couldn't say anything.

Just then, we heard someone open the back door. I pulled my wand. It was his Mom. He apparently recognized her step because he called out, "Hi, Mom! Guess who's here."

She was carrying a shopping bag. When she saw us, she dropped her bag and ran to him, "Oh, Tommy, who are these people?"

He proudly said, "They're FBI."

She looked at us suspiciously, "Let's see ID."

I took out my FBI Contractor credentials and my Auror card and said, "Actually we're all contractors for the FBI. You can look at the FBI ID, but they don't let people touch it. But you can examine my Auror ID. The Aurors are a private security organization."

Both Sally and Ballard had their contractor ID's out, and Ballard had his NSF ID as well.

She looked at them for a while. When she fingered my ID, she asked, "That's an unusual symbol on your badge. What does it mean?"

I glanced at the circle circumscribing a triangle with a vertical line within. "I only know that it's an ancient philosophical symbol. It is something like the Mason's symbol."

Then she asked, "What are you here for?"

Ballard said, "Maybe it would be good if we talked in private."

His mom said to us, "Yes." She turned to Tommy and said, "Would you please go practice the piano. These people might enjoy hearing you play."

He went into another room, and we heard him playing softly.

Ballard said, "We are here because there is a person of interest whom we are trying to find. He was here at your house a short while ago."

She gave a small gasp and said, "You mean in the neighborhood?"

Ballard shook his head no.

"Outside our house?"

Again, no.

The sinews of her neck stretched as she said, "In our house?"

Ballard nodded.

She buried her face in her hands. When she lifted her face, her eyes were bright.

I said, "We'll have a twenty-four hour watch on your house. We want very much to apprehend him."

I finished with our usual routine: business cards, don't leave your son alone, if you remember something, get in touch—any time, day or night.

◫

I watched Harris as Pearson related what had happened. When Pearson had finished, he stood suddenly. "God Damn it, we've got to stop this thing. Ideas!"

We had forgotten that Brahms was still on the line. He said softly, almost diffidently, "What about military help?"

We all stared at the conference phone. Harris banged the table. "The military is supposed to stay out of domestic actions, but this is too much to be borne. I'll get hold of the Director and see if he'll go along with it."

Fort Riley

The next morning, we were driving up to Fort Riley, Kansas. Harris was with us along with Ballard. Sally was driving. It took two solid hours to get there. Minerva was mad that we hadn't *disapparated*, but Harris had pointed out that no matter how we arrived—whether walking after having *diapparated* outside the camp fence or inside the fence—it didn't matter. It would not look good.

So we drove up to the main gate and found that we were expected. A corporal was waiting to guide us to the base commander's office. He got in the Expedition that Sally was driving. He gave her directions. It was a large base, and it took us nearly fifteen minutes to get to the main office building.

We were given photo ID badges at the reception desk. Then the corporal led us up to the second floor. We were led into the outer office and asked to wait there. It was a lengthy wait.

We were finally invited to enter the commander's office. We did introductions. The base commander was Brigidier General J. T. Eventreur. He requested that we just refer to him at JT. It was easier than his last name.

He launched into a little speech as soon as we were seated, "Do you know why I had to make you wait?"

Harris answered the superfluous question, "No, sir."

"Well, I've just been on a conference call for the last hour with no lesser luminaries than the Secretary of the Army and the Director of the FBI. They gave me a little lecture on how I am no longer the commander of this base. Do you know who the commander is?"

We just shook our heads.

"Well, I'll tell you who is. He's sitting in this room. He's

Mister. . ." He put special emphasis on that word, ". . . Ballard sitting here. And do you know who the second in command is?"

Again, no one dared speak, "Well, it's Mister Harris, here. So, I'm at your disposal. What are we doing?"

Then he added a little request, "I hope I haven't overstepped my authority by inviting two of the regiment commanders to this meeting."

Ballard just shook his head.

General JT got up, walked to the door, and made an exaggerated show of opening the door and inviting the two regiment commanders in. He introduced them as they entered, "This is Major Griggs who commands the Air Cavalry unit stationed here. And this is Major Penrose. He is the commander of the Mechanized Cavalry unit stationed here" He turned to them and said, "Gentlemen, I've summoned you here to be introduced to the new base commanders— Mr. Ballard and his adjutant, Mr. Harris. Since they are the base commanders now, I'll defer to them in explaining what is going to happen. As my last official act as base commander, I've just put the base on DefCon III."

Both of the Majors showed little signs of surprise, but didn't speak. However, Minerva did speak, "If I may speak, what is DefCon III."

I said, "It's the highest alert level that the US military has."

General JT nodded approvingly and said, "Perhaps you'd like to elucidate further?"

I smiled, "No thanks."

Major Griggs, looking directly at General JT said, "Permission to speak, Sir."

JT just nodded.

"DefCon III requires the base be locked down. No one can leave the base OR enter it without the base commander's permission. The base perimeter is guarded with deadly force. All units are to be ready to act on a moment's notice. Tanks are fueled and have live ammunition at all times. I suppose it's the same with Air Cavalry."

Major Griggs just nodded.

Minerva nodded and said, "If I may ask, why are we on DefCon III? Is there an active terrorist threat?"

JT simply said, "I defer to the base commander to explain."

Ballard wasn't happy, but he said, "The best person to explain is the consultant, Mr. Wendt."

All eyes turned to me. I got up and thought a moment. More as temporization than anything else, I asked Gen. JT, "Do you have an overhead projector that I can use?"

He simply pointed upwards. He opened the laptop at his desk. He said, "It's ready to go."

I asked Ballard, "May I use your phone?"

He nodded and handed it over.

I pulled the USB cable for my phone from my purse, hoping no one would pay attention to it, and connected the phone to the laptop. The projector was warming up while I searched the photos on his phone. I found the pictures that I wanted and then opened them. I found the photos of the four.

I opened, downloaded, and distributed them around the desktop of the laptop and thus on the blank wall where the projector was pointed. Everyone seemed fascinated—even General JT. I then began to speak:

"The four men you see are undoubtedly the four most dangerous men on Earth. They are all geniuses who are off the Stanford Binet Scale. They each have a specialty of their own."

Griggs asked, "They are in uniform. Are they in the Army?"

"They used to be. It's been months since they went AWOL." I asked General JT, "Do you have a pointer?"

He simply pointed at the desk, and I saw the laser pointer. I used it for the rest of the talk.

"This is Sergeant Connover. His specialty is Materials Science. He's made a general construction material that is like carbon nanotubes on steroids."

Penrose asked, "Nanotubs?"

I frowned at him and puzzled for a minute. "I can't explain it. That's the point. Nobody can explain this material."

"This is Corporal Reynaldo. His expertise is physics, electronics, control systems, and God knows what else.

"This is PFC Hadley. His field is Biochemistry, Genetics, and Retroviruses, whatever they are.

"And then we have the master—Lieutenant Minns. His subjects are Finance, Psychology, Intelligence." At that, there was a small uproar. I spoke over it, "Oh, yes. Intelligence—in every sense of that word. The rest of the crew only follow orders. I have a feeling Minns is giving them."

Griggs asked, "So, what are they doing that's got everyone riled up?"

I puzzled over that too and said, "God, I wish we did know. They're building something in a warehouse in Wichita. We have the plans for it. We haven't got the least idea what it's for."

Penrose leaned back, "You're scared."

"Shit, yes, I'm scared. Look, we've tried time and again to detain these people. We can't lay a finger on them. A few days ago, we mounted a real effort to capture Minns. We knew where he was living. We had two FBI SWAT teams deployed. We had snipers on buildings adjacent to his apartment building. We had half a dozen agents in his room waiting for him. We had teams in the two fire escapes.

"He walked into that trap unarmed. He walked out of it, and nobody laid a finger on him."

Griggs said, "No one could touch him?"

I frowned, "Well, I did get three shots off. It was desperation, and none of them came within a county mile of him."

Penrose laughed.

General JT asked his first question, "So, what do you want us to do?"

I took a deep breath. "Stay on high alert. Be prepared to move on a second's notice. Minns is located somewhere in Eastern Kansas. When we find him—and we will—be prepared to go after him. We think he'll try to rejoin with the rest of his group in Wichita."

Griggs asked, "We're more mobile and have at least as much fire power as Major Penrose. Why does he have to be on high alert?"

Penrose snorted.

I was disgusted, "Have you not been listening to anything I've said? We will need every resource we can bring to bear and even that may not be enough."

Penrose asked, "Why not a preemptive strike. We could mount a blitzkrieg on them and take that warehouse. Where would Minns be then?"

I just shook my head. "You don't get it. Don't you think Minns could assemble another group? Then where would WE be? Hummmm?

"We've got to take him if we take anyone. I guess I've not been clear enough. Let me tell you a true story.

"A couple of months ago Minns single-handedly took on the main treasury of ISIS."

General JT asked, "You mean in Iraq?"

"Yes, I mean in Iraq.

"He looted one half billion dollars in gold from them. Yes, that's Billion with a Big B. He didn't kill anyone or even injure them."

Penrose whistled.

□

Three days later, we were trying to get a line on where Minns had disappeared, but it seemed hopeless.

244

Brahms was concentrating all the computing power that he could beg, borrow, or steal on scanning video feeds.

On the third day, one of the surveillance groups—the one at Tommy's house saw a champagne Dodge Grand Caravan with deeply tinted windows approaching Tommy's house. The FBI field agent, Rowcliffe, would have dismissed it, but the front window was illegally tinted so that you couldn't see anything in the interior. He pointed it out to his partner.

His partner said, "I've got a bad feeling about this."

Rowcliffe said, "Yeh, why don't you get out. I'll start the car."

The partner drew his service automatic. The car had stopped by now. Then the door flew open at the house, and Tommy ran out the door and ran completely confidently up to the now-open sliding door of the minivan.

Rowcliffe's partner had his gun up, but he didn't want to take a chance of hitting the boy. He got back in the Tahoe.

In the mean time, the van had pulled out and accelerated. As it drove past, the Tahoe's engine sputtered and died.

Rowcliffe swore and started the engine. His partner was on the radio to the command post. "This is Bartlett at Tommy Frederick's house. Somebody in a champagne Dodge Grand Caravan—late model— just picked up Tommy. I didn't get the license."

Rowcliffe said, "Kansas THX-1123."

Harris was on duty at the command post. "Where are they now?"

Bartlett said, "They lost us. Our engine stalled just as they passed."

Harris said something like, "The Hell!"

At the command post, Harris said to the room, "Find out whose van that is."

It was only a couple of minutes and someone said, "It's a commercial rental. A local place. I'm getting them on the phone now."

In less than a minute, the entire room could hear, "This is Rent-R-Us, the cheapest rent in the Kansas City area. What can I do for you?"

Harris said, "You're on speaker phone. This is FBI special Agent Harris. You rented a champagne Grand Caravan, license THX-1123 to a man. Who is it?"

The voice said, "That's confidential business information. How do I know who you are?"

Harris said, "That van was just used in a kidnapping of a nine year old blind boy. Would you like to go for accessory after the fact?"

The voice changed completely, "No, sir. It was rented to a Lieutenant Phillip Minns."

Somebody asked, "How did we not get that from the credit card company?"

The voice said, "Because he used cash?"

Harris asked, "You don't require a credit card?"

"No, sir."

Harris said, "OK. Just stay available if we have other questions, Mr.. . ."

There was silence, and then he said, "Oh, you mean me. I'm Ned Flanders."

Harris said, "Notify the other surveillance groups."

Somebody said, "Already done."

It was long after the fact that we discovered it, but Jenny had disappeared from her apartment without her parents realizing it.

Harris said, "Get hold of the Subaru's surveillance. Minns is coming for them.

Someone said, "Done." Then he added, "The Subaru's are on an outing to a local Mall. The surveillance group is with them but . . ."

Harris's voice was taut, "But what?"

The answer took a minute. "A champagne Dodge Grand Caravan just pulled up as the Subaru's were leaving the mall. A man — we think it's Minns—jumped out, grabbed the boy as his father was transferring him from his wheelchair to the van, and drove off."

□□

Minns had just driven off with the last of the kids from Lenexa. He'd lost himself in the traffic around the Oak Park mall. Back at our command post, Harris made the decision to have the surveillance driver park and asked, "What now?"

Ballard took a deep breath, held it for what seemed like a minute with eyes closed and then said, "We know where they're headed. Harris, can you get a highway patrol helicopter here to pick us up. We'll start an air search and send out an Amber alert."

Harris got on the phone to the Kansas Emergency Response Center.

Ballard then looked at us. "I think it's time to call out the cavalry. You two head for Fort Riley and get them moving—both air and mechanized. I've a feeling this is the big one. Get everything out. Have the tanks head south toward Witchita on US 77. You two take to the air and run the show from the sky. We'll try to locate them here."

I nodded, and Minerva just said, "Shit."

Harris had stepped away from us because his conversation was becoming louder and louder. Finally, he said to the room in general, "I'm putting this on the speaker. Don't leave yet, Wendt. You should hear this conversation."

Harris switched to the speaker phone and introduced the watch commander at the KERC. "This is Lieutenant Carlisle of the KHP. He wants to try to detain Minns with KHP officers."

Ballard rolled his eyes. I'm glad that Carlisle couldn't see that. He then started to say something that I knew that he would regret later—he was that mad. I intervened.

"Lieutenant Carlisle, we really need your help. It would be extremely helpful if your troopers could keep traffic off of I-35 between Lenexa and Witchita. Also, clearing US-77 between Fort Riley and Witchita could be critical to our apprehending Minns. You see, we're gong to use air and mechanized cavalry from Fort Riley to stop Minns."

Carlisle's voice was drawn as tight as a bowstring. He was obviously trying to control his voice. "Sir, whoever you are, apprehending people on the highways is our specialty. We do it all the time and with minimum injuries and casualties. You really should leave this to the experts and not involve the military. We should have no trouble stopping a single vehicle."

Minerva was on the verge of apoplexy. She broke in and there was no doubt of the tension in her voice, "Mr. Carlisle, you should confine yourself to speaking about things that you understand. If you had been dealing with Minns as long as we have, you would never make such uninformed statements." I had never heard a 6th year put in his place more effectively. "Minns has escaped. . . no, that word gives us too much credit. He waltzed out of our best efforts to arrest him—including two FBI SWAT teams and a . . . a . . . wi." At that point, I interrupted her. There was no point in drawing too much on his credulity. "Let us, who know him, run this, and you support us as best you can." She ended with such finality that even he could say nothing. "I'm leaving now. Do as I say."

At that she hopped out of her chair, I followed as quickly as I could, and Minerva just took my hand without warning. It had happened enough that way that I wasn't surprised. We left Wichita under clear skies. When we landed outside the headquarters building of Fort Riley the skies were overcast and looking like rain later.

Minerva smiled and said, "Let's go to the top." I knew that I was looking at another *disapparation*—this time just outside the base commander's office. I just tried to grin and bear it.

This time, I was so disoriented that I staggered for a moment trying to get my balance and orientation. Minerva, of course, was striding to the commander's office. I caught up just as she opened the door to the outer office. The assistant there gasped, but miraculously, recognized us. She forgot herself for a moment and exclaimed, "How the Hell did you get in here?"

Then she relaxed and said, "Of course, they said that you might drop in anytime without warning." She picked up the phone receiver and hit a button. After a second she said, "It's them. I'll let them in now."

She did. Inside, there was the base commander and another officer. The officer was just saying, "We'll take this up later." He promptly left without giving us a second look.

JT just got up and said, "This is it, isn't it?"

We didn't have to say anything because he immediately added, "It's got to be time-critical. Just head down to the helicopter hangar. I'll call ahead and get the unit commanders there for orders."

Minerva took my hand and the last I saw of the base commander was him starting to cover his eyes. We landed. Nobody was there other than a couple of maintenance men working on one of the Apache's. They didn't even look up when we arrived. I started to walk over toward them when a jeep pulled up behind us.

The battalion commander jumped out followed by his 2nd in command. "OK. What's the mission?"

"A champagne Dodge Grand Caravan is heading for Wichita. It's got Minns and half a dozen children in it. Our objective is to stop the vehicle and apprehend Minns. We want to avoid harming the kids, of course, but we've got to stop Minns."

He looked down and spit, "Damn! Where are they?"

"We'll know soon, but we think they're someplace on I-35 near Kansas City."

He rolled his eyes. "With our luck, this side, I guess."

Minerva nodded.

"Shit. Well we've got to get in the air. Who's directing this?"

I glanced over at Minerva, "We are."

"From my Apache, I suppose?"

I nodded. By this time, the rest of his crews were arriving, and I thought I recognized a jeep carrying the tank battalion commander. I was right.

Meanwhile, Major Griggs was asking the maintenance crew what helicopters were ready. One of them answered, "They all are except the one that we're working on. The heads-up display has gone bonkers. The rest are fueled, armed with 30 mil and missiles."

"OK." He looked over at another officer who was nearby waiting for instructions. "Sapinski, sorry. You're out of it. Your Apache's not flight-ready."

By this time the rest of the helicopter crews had assembled and several of the tank commanders. Griggs went on, "OK. Gentlemen, here's the story." With that, he turned to me expectantly.

Just then my phone rang. It was Ballard. They had a rough location. I told him that we were about to take off. I then turned to the assembled troops.

"OK. Here's the situation. Our objective, Minns, is driving a champagne Grand Caravan, Kansas license THK-1138. He's just passed Ottawa, Kansas on I-35. We've got a Kansas highway patrol helicopter following him and keeping us up to date.

"Our goal is to stop the car and apprehend Minns. He's got 6 kids with him. We don't want to harm them. My idea is to land in front of them and cut them off. We probably want someone to land behind to both prevent following traffic from getting involved and prevent them from reversing and going backwards.

"Minerva and I will be in control from the air in Griggs's Apache."

The tank battalion commander, Penrose, had worked his way to the front. "What are we doing?"

"You'll be the fallback if we don't get him. Go down US 77 as fast as you can and be prepared to block I-35 and stop them. If we have to use you, it will be close to Witchita, so get into that area as quick as you can."

"We'll be there in just over an hour."

I was stunned, "Really?"

"Sure, we can hit 80 if we need to."

Minerva smiled, "Do it." She used the tone of certain command that I'd heard a few times at Hogwarts. People, generally followed directions from her when she used that tone.

Griggs looked around, "Questions?"

No one said anything for about 5 seconds. He gave the word, "Mount up!"

Griggs helped us into his Apache and put the headphones on our heads. Meanwhile, Griggs started the engine and we heard his voice in our headphones. "When you want to broadcast so everyone in our command can hear you, let me know and we'll go on the air. Got it?"

I answered, "Right."

Then he said, "Hold on tight."

We did. The acceleration into the sky was breath-taking. We climbed to what I thought must be about three hundred feet, and the ground spun away below us

Minerva still didn't quite get the idea of headphones and microphones. She leant over so that her lips were close to my ear and shouted, "And you say that Wizards like to get sick when they travel."

Griggs laughed and said, "I heard that."

She came back instantly, "You were meant to."

I asked, "Where are we making for?"

The co-pilot answered, "If what you say is true, I think we can intercept them around Emporia. I think we'll get there in about 15 minutes."

In about 10 minutes, Griggs went on the air with instructions, "In about 5 minutes we'll arrive at I-35. The first one to spot the car wins a beer on me when we get back. When we've made it, Sparks and Scott will cut off traffic from behind. Wilbur set down about ½ mile in front of the car and blockade it. Everyone else stays in the air as backup."

Someone asked, "What if they try to ram us?"

Griggs said, "That's above my pay grade. What about it Professor?"

I said, "Lift off if you can. The next helicopter sets up ¼ mile down the road and abandons ship. God, I hope that doesn't happen."

We had about two minutes to I-35. Griggs went down lower. It seemed like tree-top level. There weren't many trees, but it scared me anyway. Minerva grasped my arm but didn't say anything.

Griggs said, "I'm flying toward KC along I-35. Sparks you go the opposite way. Everyone else stays high."

The view that Minerva and I had scared me shitless. We were barely above ground level and flying down the median strip of I-35. But shortly the helicopter slewed around so fast that our stomachs were in our mouths. Meanwhile we heard Griggs shout, "Ya Hoo! Got em. Sparks, Wilbur get in place. They'll be on you in a minute."

We had leveled off and were flying parallel to the highway and starting to climb. With altitude, we could see the Dodge ahead of us and what I guessed must be Wilbur further ahead. He was descending and hovering slightly above the ground. We had nearly caught up with the Dodge and were slowing. The Dodge seemed to be going as fast as ever, and I thought that we'd see a collision if Wilbur couldn't ascend fast enough.

Our co-pilot spoke, "I make it a collision in 15. . . 10 . . . " Then two surprising things happened. Wilbur's helicopter seemed to be accelerating toward the Dodge, and the Dodge glided onto the median strip.

Griggs shouted, "Are you playing chicken?"

I've crossed median strips once or twice in my life. At low speeds, it's not pleasant. At the speed the Dodge was going, I expected it to flip. But, it didn't. It seemed to glide above the ground level and over to the other side.

Of course, that was as bad. The traffic coming the other way was light, but even closing the distance at maybe 150 miles per hour, somehow there was no collision.

The Dodge swerved back across the median and was driving stably—as though nothing unusual had happened. Meanwhile Wilbur was in the air again and circling back to follow the Dodge.

Griggs was on top of things. "Wilbur, set down behind the Dodge and try to block traffic. Sparks, Scott, set down ahead of him – Scott take South-bound. Sparks take North-bound. Richards, take the median."

Griggs apparently had pulled back on the stick sharply, because we swooped up suddenly. Belatedly, he commented through the headphones, "Sorry. I forgot for a minute you were here. We're going up to get a better view of the action."

With that, he went into a long shallow bank so that he was orbiting the spot on the highway where Richards was settling into a landing. Minerva and I had a good, if ever shifting, view. Griggs transmitted, "Sparks, Scott, Wilbur, be prepared to take off immediately. Keep your rotors going in case Minns is crazy."

The scene was almost surreal. There was a lone Dodge minivan driving directly at the line of three Apache helicopters. It seemed unhurried, but I was sure that it was proceeding near the speed limit.

Griggs whistled and said, "I guess he is."

But Minns wasn't crazy. Just as the helicopter blocking the south-bound lanes revved its rotors and started to take off, Minns left the road, entered the median strip, crossed the North-bound lanes and went off the side. There was a gap between the last helicopter and the highway fence just large enough for his van to scoot through. Shortly, he'd crossed the north-bound lanes, the median, and the left south-bound lane and was cruising south.

Griggs swore, ending with, "God-damn it. Get in the air and after that son-of-a-bitch. The next time we won't leave him a hole that a mouse could crawl through."

Minerva interrupted. "I don't think this is going to work."

I thought a moment while Griggs was directing his helicopters and then I broke in, "Griggs. Just keep pace with Minns. I've got another idea. Put me on the channel to the tanks."

251

The tank battalion commander had gotten his tank commanders together and said, "OK. Everyone saddle up. We're going to go down Henry Drive to I-70. Merge on and proceed to US77 interchange. Take it south-bound. As soon as we get on it, I want you all redlining it. We make 80 if we can. I'll get the civilians on the Highway Patrol to clear it as much as they can. Questions?" He didn't hesitate but immediately said, "None. Good. Saddle up. I lead."

When they'd got started, his driver asked the question on everyone's mind, "Are we going to use any of these hyperbaric rounds that we're packing? Stateside?"

They called the commander "Z" (but not to his face) for reasons that were obvious to everyone who'd served with him. For one thing, the name Z (if it was a name) was painted on the cannon barrel of his tank. It stretched all around the barrel. One had to look carefully to perceive that it was a Z since you couldn't see all of it at one time.

There was endless speculation in his command as to what the Z meant. As a matter of fact, there was a lottery going that by now was approaching $3000 concerning the meaning of the Z. Originally it had been voluntary, but as time passed, and people came and left the command, it had come to be a sort of initiation.

By now there were strict rules. Everyone who was rotated into the unit had to enter the lottery. There was a sliding scale for the contribution to the lottery. PFC's had to ante up a twenty. Corporals contributed a fifty. Sergeants had to throw in a cool hundred. Lieutenants were required to post two hundred. There was active debate about what a major would have to serve up. The popular figures were four hundred and five hundred. But there was a small minority that insisted that one thousand should be the price of admission.

If the unit ever discovered what the Z meant, the pot would be split equally among the people who had entered with the correct name. When the pot had gotten above one thousand dollars, it had been invested in certificates of deposit registered to an LLC that had been formed to manage the pot. The name of the LLC was, of course, Z LLC.

There were a variety of entries for the meaning. The most popular was "Z is for Zombie". It was understandable given the character of the commander. But there were a variety of others. Another popular entry was Z is for Zed, meaning zero. However, there were a plethora of others, such as Z is for Z-bar, Z is for Zod, referring to Superman's nemesis from the planet Krypton. Z is for Zen. That last was a reference to the cold calm that the commander exhibited at all times. There was a single entry for Z is for Zagreb. No one knew if his family were from Yugoslavia but it seemed feasible to the PFC who had submitted it.

Sanders, who'd been in Penrose's command for a long time had actually made two entries. The first was just after he rotated into the unit. It was not original. He was one of the Z is for Zombie partisans. But after a while he put a second entry into the lottery.

His second entry was Z is for Zamboni. When asked to justify that strange entry, Sanders's reply was, "Do you know what Penrose's favorite sport is?"

People considered, and several came up with the right answer, "Ice Hockey."

Sanders continued, "The Zamboni machine is a feature of every single Hockey game.

"For another thing, Penrose has a cold character—cool under fire and seemingly emotionless. Finally, Zamboni machines operate on ice and grind it under them—just like Penrose grinds his opposition under him."

The Z would simply not comment on those speculations.

He had his head out of the turret, and he scanned the horizon. Once they'd gotten onto US77, there were a few sparse stands of trees along the road and then nothing. It was a lonely stretch of road. That was good. He didn't want to get into an argument with a tractor poking along at 25 mph.

On I-70, they'd had to hold below the speed limit because of the traffic. He took the exit to US77 pretty fast and had knocked down a sign or two on the off-ramp. The traffic pretty much left the highway as though the column of tanks were fire trucks running the siren hard. But once they'd gone under the I-70 underpass, the traffic dropped off quickly, and their speed had increased to near 80.

He'd called that FBI contact, Harris. Harris had been ahead of him. Supposedly, the Highway Patrol was already ahead of him on 77 clearing the route of casual traffic. So far, he'd not seen any. So far, it had been an easy drive—a walk in the park.

Then, he heard the siren. He didn't think much of it—probably just another highway patrol car passing them to keep the way clear. However, the siren whine was decreasing in frequency too much—as though it were slowing. He looked over, and at the same time his driver's voice said in his headphones. "Lookee here. A County Cop Car!"

It certainly was. It was traveling the wrong way on the north-bound lane and had pulled even with the lead tank. The County Sheriff had apparently turned on his external speaker because the crew of the tank could hear clearly, "Now, boy, just pull over raaat now."

Z was not much impressed. He activated his exterior speaker and said, "Pull over yourself. We've got orders."

The answer was, "As the duly authorized Sheriff of Dickinson County, I require you to pull to the side of the road. NOW!"

The driver of the tank smiled, but, of course, Z couldn't see the smile. Z just drawled out his reply, "No, sir. We've got our orders."

The driver of the tank ventured to ask, "What do you suppose he'll do now?"

Z just said, "I don't much care."

At that moment, the County Cop revved his engine and pulled ahead of the convoy, disappearing into the distance.

About ten minutes later the convoy passed a pair of law enforcement vehicles. They were in the north-bound lane. One was a Highway Patrol cruiser pointed north. The other was a Dickinson County Sheriff's cruiser pointed south. A highway patrolman was standing beside the Sheriff's car with a citation book in his hand.

⊟⊟

Sheriff Custer of Dickinson County was fit to be tied. He had been about to pull across US77 to block the tank convoy that was breaking nearly every traffic rule in the book when a State Highway Patrol vehicle, its siren going, had approached from the south. It had pulled up to his car and blocked his way forward. Now, this Highway Patrolman was trying to pull rank on him and give HIM a citation.

"Sheriff Custer, what did you think you were doing, trying to block this US military convoy on orders to make it to Witchita ASAP?"

"But they don't have any right to flout the laws of the State of Kansas and the County of Dickinson regardless what they are doing."

The patrolman shook his head slowly, "Haven't you been monitoring the emergency channel? The Governor has declared a state of emergency, and martial law is in effect."

Custer's mouth was opening and closing without effect. Finally, words came out, "I don't care if the President of the New-nited States of America has declared martial law. I have to enforce the laws of Dickinson County.

"Now, move your cruiser out of the way so that I can do my sworn duty!"

The patrolman's partner got out of the cruiser carrying his sawed-off shotgun. The sheriff's mouth quivered just a little as he said, "Now what are you boys fixin' to do?"

The partner walked over to the front fender beside the left wheel and said, "I think that we're authorized to take any reasonable action to insure that that convoy isn't stopped." With that, he pumped the shotgun, pointed it at the tire, and pulled the trigger. The tire promptly began to deflate. The partner walked around the county cruiser slowly, almost majestically, pumping the shotgun once when he reached a wheel, aimed and fired the shotgun. He deflated all four tires.

The sheriff's face fell, and just then the lead tank of the convoy sped past.

Z commented as they passed the sheriff. "I don't think we're going to be bothered by that gentleman again."

They had proceeded about another ten miles down the road when Z heard the radio silence break. "This is Wendt to Major Penrose, over."

Z replied, "Penrose to Wendt. Go ahead. Over."

"OK. We've run into some problems stopping Minns. We'll need you to intercept Minns just beyond Cassody, KS. Divide into two columns. One will block the entire interstate highway from fence to fence behind Minns. The other will block it fence to fence about two miles down the road. We'll have a helicopter hovering over each spot so you'll know where to make for. Do you have that? Over."

"HUA. Two columns. Each makes for one of the two Apaches hovering over I-35 near Cassody, Kansas, right? Over"

"You've got it. Make sure there isn't the slightest hole. Minns is as slippery as a scalded cat and can get through a gap as small as a mouse hole. Over."

"HUA. Over."

Z was silent for a while and then went on the intertank channel. "All right. We're splitting into two columns. Sanders leads one column east toward Cassody. He'll rendezvous with an Apache hovering over his target. He'll lead his column across I-35 and completely block it from fence to fence. No gaps whatsoever. You're the rear guard. You see that Minns doesn't double back and escape. Got it?"

"Yes, sir. Sounds easy."

"Yeah, sounds."

Z went on, "The rest join my column. We're going to make for the other Apache further south. We'll block his path to Wichita. Understood?"

There was a chorus of "HUA's."

He went back on the air as they approached Florence, KS. "OK. We split after we pass US 50 and reach open country. Sanders heads immediately across country. We continue along US 77 a bit further before we break away across country."

He turned off the radio and told his driver, "Make sure that you make for the Apache further down the road."

The driver nodded invisibly and said, "It's a good day to die."

Z said nothing.

After about fifteen minutes, they saw a bend in the road ahead where 77 headed further toward the south. The Z said, "At that gentle bend leave the road and head due south-east."

As they headed cross-country, there was no sign of I-35 for about ten minutes. Then, the driver spotted the two Apache's ahead. He started to point them out to Z, but he'd spotted them too. He said, "I make them. Head for the further one."

The driver commented, "Nice spring day. Blue skies. I've got a bad feeling about this."

Z said, "Just keep driving."

About a mile from I-35, they encountered a creek with brush and a few scraggly trees growing around it. The driver asked, "Take it at speed?"

"Slow down."

The driver slowed to about 25, and they plowed through the trees, across the shallow creek and up the short bank on the other side. Then they were back to speed. And there was the Apache that they'd lost sight of for a few minutes. It seemed much closer than it had on the other side of the creek.

The helicopter pilot, Griggs, was back on the radio. "Minns just passed the first column. You've got to get on your high horse and move. You've not got more than two minutes to block the road."

The Z just smiled and then said to his command, "You heard our spotter. We've got to move. We'll break through the fence just about now." His words were punctuated by the "zing" of tensioned wire snapping. "I'm taking the center of the south-bound lanes. I'm lining up at 45 to the roadway. Everyone else park parallel to me. Don't leave any gaps! Let's go! Let's go! Let's go."

The rest of the tanks in the column lined up as he wanted them to.

He asked his driver, "How long till they hit?"

"Can't quite see them yet, but can't be more than 90 seconds." He added after a couple of seconds, "Do you think they will hit us?"

He almost didn't have to ask, because the answer he expected drawled out of his boss. "I don't really care."

He continued, "Everyone needs to be ready. If they stop, be prepared to go in pursuit on foot. If they somehow break through the fence, and their vehicle keeps moving, we follow and overtake. They can't go across open country as fast as we can.

"If everyone abandons the car, I want you. . . " All knew he was talking to the gunner, "to put a round in that car. I don't want it going anywhere."

"Do you see the car yet?"

The driver answered, "Yes, the laser makes it just over a klick. It seems to be slowing down some, too."

Z nodded. This chase was going to end right here and now.

The driver said, "It's ¾ klick away. . . Now half a klick. . . 400 meters. . . "

Then something no one expected happened. The tank started to shake. As a matter of fact, all the tanks started to shake. Z shouted, "What the hell's going on?"

The driver said, "The tank's backing."

"Do you have the cleats set?"

"Yes, sir."

As they spoke the tank started vibrating as it scrapped across the highway. Z shouted, "Get moving back in place."

"Sorry sir, the tracks are moving, but the tank's still backing. We're chewing up the road something awful." He added, "Target 100 meters."

By this time the road was almost completely clear of tanks. The car sped past at 60.

Z cursed again, ending, "What the fucking Hell? Get us turned around. We're going to run it down."

The tanks backed and got rotated so they were pointed toward the fast disappearing car. Z asked, "Can we catch it?"

The driver did some quick calculations. "Maybe. We'll be on the outskirts of Wichita if we do."

Griggs was on the radio again, "We're following Minns. But I'm pretty sure he's headed for that warehouse."

Z—definitely not cool at the moment—said, "We'll stop him before he gets there if we have to push him off the road."

Z heard the voice of that civilian woman. "I don't think so. I've got a feeling that he's just been playing with us." He growled and swore that he'd prove her wrong.

The driver commented, "Just passed El Dorado, Kansas. Outskirts of Wichita 12 klicks."

Z shut off the radios and asked the driver, "Can we catch them before they get into Wichita?"

The driver shook his head, "We're about ¾ klick behind them, and we're only making 4 klicks better than they are. They'll beat us to the first exits."

Just then one of the tank commanders behind them came on the radio. "Penrose, I'm behind you and can make better time than you. Can you let me pass?"

Z hated not being in the lead, but it might make the difference between catching Minns and not, "Go ahead. We'll pull over a little to give you room to pass."

It was Richards. He was probably making a couple of klicks better than he. He slowly passed Z.

The minutes passed in what seemed like a slow-motion chase. The surroundings were flat plains that changed only slowly no matter how fast you traveled. They were gaining on the car but only slowly. They started to see little clumps of houses and knew that they were into the extreme suburbs of Wichita. The car was visible to Z on the occasions when Richards's tank slipped slightly to the left, and the Dodge was on the right lane of the highway.

The driver said, "First exit for Wichita coming up." They all passed it without incident. After a few minutes the tanks had closed quite close to the Dodge. The driver announced, "Next exit coming up."

The Dodge took the exit at an amazing speed, hardly slowing from freeway speeds. Richards's driver was a little slow catching it, but he pulled onto the berm of the off-ramp and skidded off the berm. Trying to correct, he would have flipped if he'd been driving a semi. Instead, he slewed on across the interchange and didn't regain full control until after he'd crossed the intersecting highway and crossed the onramp on the opposite side.

Z's driver did better. He skidded off the ramp but kept control, righted the tank, and had it back onto the ramp. The Dodge was past the toll booth. Z told his driver to go through without stopping. He took the barrier out and the gate and poles. There was a car in front of him. By the time they'd gotten past it, he'd lost the Dodge.

Z went back on the radio and demanded, "Where the Hell's the Dodge?"

The Wendt character answered, "It's too late. He's in traffic. You'll just end up playing demolition derby with the Suburbans out there. We're still following him. You might as well find a place to park and stay in reserve for later."

Z flipped the radio off and expressed his disappointment. Then he flipped it back on and said, "OK. You all heard the man. Let's get a convoy organized and go to that mall up ahead to wait things out."

I watched the Dodge proceed along city streets on a reasonable route to the warehouse.

I said to Griggs, "Get Ballard on the radio."

He did, and Ballard reported first, "We arrived about twenty minutes ago. We've got all the Wichita police and Highway Patrol we could. Both the entrances to the warehouse grounds are surrounded by cars a dozen deep at least. I don't see how anyone could get in. You need to keep surveillance up. He may try for an alternate safe house."

Griggs said, "ETA at the warehouse 10 minutes."

I commented, 'You heard him. Keep following."

To Minerva I said, "I've got a feeling he's not going anywhere else."

Griggs reported, "Minns's next turn will be onto the street which fronts the warehouse on the east side. He's coming straight for you."

Ballard said, "The fence is ten feet tall, topped with razor wire. It's substantial. I don't think he could knock it over with that van. If he does come down this street, we've got him."

Minns did turn down that street, and we got our first view of the blockage waiting for him. It was all of a dozen or more cars thick, parked at angles, seemingly impenetrable. I said, 'Ballard, he's coming at you right now. Be ready."

The Dodge drove at a sedate speed—probably the speed limit. As he got close to the fence, he reached a cross street that fed into the street he was on. He began a turn that seemed like it would take him down that street. Then it turned wide and headed him straight at the fence. Minerva gasped as she realized what he was about to do.

Then the fence disappeared right at that point. It wasn't knocked over. It wasn't holed. It just disappeared and the van drove straight through it.

Griggs exclaimed, "What the fuck! What happened to the fence?" No one could answer him.

Ballard shouted, "What happened?"

Minerva said calmly, 'Minns just bypassed your blockade."

Griggs put the helicopter into a dive, and as our stomachs moved into our throats, he said, "I'm going to land next to them and try to get the kids." But, even as he spoke, Minns herded the kids into a side door of the warehouse. We landed. Griggs jumped out of the cockpit and ran to the door, his sidearm in hand. He reached the door and found it locked. The co-pilot was close behind him. I was fumbling with the door latch. I got it open, and we followed them.

I could see Griggs stepping back from the door and aiming his gun at the door. I shouted, "Stop! There's another . . ." The explosions of the gun firing struck our ears, and I knew it was too late.

When we arrived, he pointed at the door, "Look. I blew the handle and lock off, and it still won't open."

Minerva said, "I wish you had waited. I've got another way to get in."

I said, "Go ahead. It may still work." She nodded and lifted her wand, pointed it at the door and said, "Alo Ahora."

I went to the door and tried pushing and pulling on it. Nothing happened. Just then Ballard reached us. "Come on, the main door to the warehouse is open."

We ran after him to the great sliding door that was at least three stories high entering the warehouse. Inside, we saw the structure that Brahms had figured out by working the parts together like a giant jigsaw puzzle. From ground level it looked like a disc with curved walls, but from Brahms re-construction we knew that it was more like a thick torus. It was well back into the warehouse. In front were some racks of what looked like computer servers but they might have been anything. Partly obscured by the racks were the four men who were behind the complex network of events that we'd been tracing.

Ballard shouted into the doorway, "Minns, if you surrender now, no one need get hurt. We can take this, this. . . whatever it is apart and we can all try to return to life as it once was."

This is the first time that I'd actually heard Minns voice. It was soft, but somehow penetrated the distance and the walls that we'd built up trying to reach this point. "Mr. Ballard, I'm afraid I can't do that. I have an assignment and I have to see it through."

Ballard paused a minute and turned to Harris. He came forward and said, "Let me send my SWAT team in." Ballard was clearly not happy but nodded. Harris gave a nod himself to the SWAT team that was fully suited with body armor, helmets, FBI insignia on all sides. The leader in turn nodded at someone who was apparently second in command. He in turn gave a hand signal to two of his men. One was on each side of the hangar door. They stepped forward and without exposing themselves threw a couple of small canisters through the opening. They began spraying something that I guessed was tear gas in all directions.

After a minute, the two squads carefully entered the now smoking area through which little could be seen. They all had gas masks on. They disappeared into the cloud, and then we heard a series of sounds that made me think someone had tripped over something. The sounds were accompanied by shouts of pain that were cut off sharply. Then someone shouted "withdraw."

Almost immediately, the squads withdrew from the warehouse as cautiously as they had entered. The leader trotted to Harris and reported, "There's some sort of barrier in there. It keeps the tear gas out and seems really solid, although it's clearer than glass. I don't get it. We had brought a battering ram with us. We tried a couple of times breaking through but it was pointless."

Ballard was beside himself. There were few times that I'd seen him angry. He was always speechless at those times as though he couldn't find a single word that would bring his feelings to light. He only scowled and watched his feet for a few minutes.

Harris, unhappy with the situation, brought Ballard back to life, 'Ballard, what's our next step?"

Ballard regained possession of himself and replied, "I want to get in there and talk to Minns."

The SWAT team commander had been listening, "Take my gas mask." He pulled it off his head and made to hand it to Ballard.

"I'll not go in there in a mask and not be able to see or hear what's going on. Can we get that gas out of there?"

No one did anything but shrug. Then an idea occurred to me. "Can we get that helicopter over here and use it to blow the gas out?"

Ballard said, "Let's see." He then got on his radio and asked Griggs to fly the helicopter in front of the main door.

The pilot did and then ran over to us to ask what we wanted. Ballard said, "Can you use the wash from your rotors to clear that tear gas out of there?"

Griggs nodded and said, "I'll try. Get everyone clear." He ran back to the helicopter while we got everyone well away from the door. He revved the engine, lifted off, and hovered a couple of feet off the ground. He moved the helicopter forward as though he would enter the warehouse. Instead, he tilted the helicopter backward so the prop wash blew into the warehouse. Some of the gas was blown out. Then he moved it forward again and repeated the operation. He did that a couple of times, and all the acrid gas seemed to be dispersed. At first, the smell was strong enough where we were to make it uncomfortable being as close to the warehouse as we were, but even that gas dissipated quickly.

Griggs set the helicopter down and came over to us waiting for more orders.

Ballard looked around. No one was anxious to face him. But it was Griggs who had an idea. "Look. I've got that Apache packing more anti-armor ordinance than we'll ever need. Why don't we try using it?"

Ballard looked again at the Apache in a speculative way. He asked, "Those missiles. Is that what you're thinking?"

Griggs said, "No, sir. That would be overkill. That's hyperbaric load that would probably bring the warehouse down over them. I don't guess you want that?"

Ballard shook his head. Griggs went on, "I was thinking about the 30mm cannons that I've got. There are 1200 rounds of depleted uranium shells. I reckon a few of those rounds should knock down that wall—whatever it is."

Ballard agreed. "OK. But two things. I want to warn Minns what we're about to do, and if we go ahead with your plan, I want you in the air and ready to scoot if anything goes wrong—like ricochets coming back at you."

Griggs agreed, "Just give me the word when you want me to light them up."

Ballard turned back to the warehouse and walked partway through the door. "Minns, we're about to blast that barrier of yours down. I don't want anyone hurt. Please shut it down, and no one will get hurt."

Minns didn't say anything, but Reynaldo stepped forward a couple of feet and did. He laughed. Well, that was what I thought the sound that he made was. It had less humor in it than anything I'd ever heard. His words cleared that up completely. They were bitter. "Oh, no. Nobody's going to get hurt. This shield will keep anything out. Gas. Bullets. Explosions. High-power lasers."

I doubted the last but how did I know. I'd seen more than enough wonders to make me doubt.

Ballard replied, "There is a way. You could turn it off."

Reynaldo seemed to open his mouth, and words seemed to be forming on his lips, but they died unsaid.

Ballard turned and said, 'I don't have a choice." As he got into the open, he shouted, "Everyone well back from the entrance. I don't want anyone killed."

When everyone had retreated away from the building, Griggs got into the helicopter and it lifted a foot or two off the ground. He adjusted the position and direction of the helicopter slightly and then shot two short, ear-splitting bursts of fire. No one but he and the co-pilot could tell what had happened. But almost immediately, he opened fire with one long continuous blast that deafened everyone around. It sounded like Gabriel had blown his horn for the last time. We watched stupefied as a small mountain of spent shell casings accumulated below the helicopter.

Just as the unendurable din was about to end, Minerva tugged at my arm. I looked around. She pulled my shoulder down and brought her mouth next to my ear and shouted as loud as she could, "Somebody just *disapparated* somewhere around here."

I was about to object when two people rounded the near corner of the warehouse. Everyone was focused on the interior of the warehouse and didn't notice. But Minerva somehow had known immediately that someone had *disapparated* nearby. She was the first to notice them, but as soon as she did, everyone else was aware as well.

The pair consisted of a man and a woman. The woman ran up to Minerva, threw her arms around her, and shouted, "With all that gunfire, I was sure you must be dead."

The man came up to me and extended his hand.

"Well, Wendt, it's good to see you alive."

I overcame my amazement and shouted (because I was still half-deaf), "What are you two doing here. Why aren't you manning your post back at Hogwarts?"

The Boy Genius just shrugged, "You can't keep Aurora and me out of the fun forever. It was looking like the end was approaching. We both decided—independently—that we had to be here."

Aurora picked up the story. "Yes, we got a port key that took us to Arlington Cemetery."

Minerva interrupted, "A popular destination, eh Wendt?"

But Sinistra was going on, "Then, we disapparated to Nashville. All that rapid traveling brought on Brahms's appetite, so we grabbed something quick to eat and *disapparated* on to here."

While this conversation was going on, the SWAT team had gathered around, and there were lots of guns pointed our way. Ballard broke through the crowd and saw who it was. He wasted no time but ordered them, "Stand Down! These are friends."

He added, "Maybe it's lucky they're here. We're trying to break into the warehouse but we've had no luck. We may need all your skills."

The Boy Genius demanded to know what had been tried, but Ballard just said, "It doesn't matter. I'm going to try to talk them out. I think that Reynaldo may just be a weak link in their team. I think he's not fully committed to what they're doing. I'm going to work on him. But stay close by; we may need help before we're done."

With that, he turned and strode back to the entrance of the warehouse as determined as I'd seen him in quite a while. He walked right up to the invisible shield and stopped—apparently just before it. Minerva asked me how he'd managed that, since nobody could see any trace of it.

"I think he was depending on the reaction of Minns or one of the others. It's hard to resist cringing when you know someone is about to walk into a brick wall."

We'd stepped just inside the entrance, but no one was anxious to get too close to these supermen. Minerva said, "Maybe he knew where the wall was by the pile of bullets in front of it." She smiled smugly as she made the observation.

All I could say was, "Yeh." As a matter of fact there were whole bullets and fragments of bullets piled up all over the floor of the warehouse. We had to be a bit careful walking or we'd fall on our faces.

I turned to Minerva and said, "Can you *disapparate* us past that shield?"

Minerva took my hand and said in a normal voice, "I'm trying to figure out. When you *disapparate*, you always have a 'feel' for wherever you're going. I can't get any feel from the other side of that shield. It's as if the other side doesn't exist in this world."

She looked me directly in the eyes, took my hand in hers, and said, "Dear, dear Wendt, I don't know what will happen—even whether we'll survive the attempt." Her voice caught, and she said, "I love you so very, very much. Are you ready?"

I was starting to nod. Then I heard a sound that stopped me. Ballard spoke softly but somehow his voice carried back clearly to us.

Ballard was saying, "Why do you suppose that your prisoners are all children? And helpless children at that." He looked from one to another waiting for an answer. No one said anything.

He went on, "You know Reynaldo, I know that you'd like to end this thing—whatever it is. You know that it smells to high heaven."

Reynaldo fidgeted and then spoke rapidly. "It doesn't matter what WE want. Nothing gets in the way of THE PROJECT—the almighty PROJECT. If Abadi wants to cheat us, well, he just discovers that he might just be about to slit his own throat.

"And when you, Mr. Ballard, threaten THE PROJECT, you find that you're wandering around the West for however long it takes to keep you out of the way."

At this point, Hadley, seemingly discovering his voice, almost croaked, "Yes. When I was in South America, I left my interpreter alone in the middle of the jungle because we were on a schedule, and I couldn't be late."

Ballard turned to Connover, "I know that you aren't happy about the PROJECT. You're worried about those helpless kids, aren't you?"

Connover was clearly uncomfortable. His lips compressed, and then he burst out, "I have terrible dreams—visions of children tortured."

Ballard seemed to feel that this was the time to make his proposal, "All you have to do Reynaldo is flip the switch. It's your invention, isn't it, this invisible shield. Flip the switch, and we'll do the rest."

With those words, I felt the tension rise around me and felt muscles tense in the SWAT team that was around us.

Hadley encouraged him, "Sure, Reynaldo, do it."

Reynaldo looked over at Connover, who just nodded silently.

Then someone spoke who had remained silent so far, "They're not helpless, you know, just hopeless." The quiet confident voice was that of Lieutenant Minns.

Ballard turned to him, "That's what you say. But what's going to happen to them? You're going to take them somewhere. Alien minds will examine them; alien hands dissect them."

Connover said, "Yes, Lieutenant, what's going to happen to the kids?" He walked over to Reynaldo and said, "I'll help you throw the switch."

Hadley walked over to them and put a hand on Reynaldo's shoulder. "I'm here too."

At that moment, I thought that the tide had turned—that for once, we who'd always been several steps behind Minns and his team were even with them and maybe about to take a step ahead.

I asked, "What promises did you make those kids?"

Minns said, "Why that they were going to heaven."

At that, Ballard finally found the words that he'd been searching for before. "God damn you! Heaven! How can you possibly promise that! There isn't a dungeon in Hell deep and dark enough for you!"

Minns turning to the whole group assembled inside and outside the barrier and simply said, "Why, what is Heaven but the place where the lame walk, the blind see, the deaf hear, and the dumb speak?"

□□ □□
□□ □□

Minns, who had ended by looking at the little group gathered around Reynaldo, turned back to Ballard. "Would you make a deal with me?"

Ballard was wary. He didn't look directly at Minns, and who could blame him. The last time he'd done that had not turned out so well. "Could be. What sort of deal?"

Minns voice, which had seemed thoroughly relaxed and care-free throughout, relaxed a bit further. Just what had changed I couldn't tell, but he definitely seemed to feel that he'd just won some important battle. He answered Ballard, "I'll let you shut down THE PROJECT just as you want."

Here Ballard smiled for the first time that day, but as quickly, his smile turned hard when Minns went on, "Provided that you come see the children first. Interview them. Take as much time as you like. Then, if you still want to shut down the project. . ." His use of the word project had turned casual, no longer capitalized. ". . . We'll let you— even help you."

Ballard's smile had lost some of the rigor that had made his smile look like a death rictus, but it was still stiff. "There must be other conditions. Name them now. I don't want any last minute backing off from your deal with provisos that you think are 'obvious'."

Minns smiled even more broadly. He appeared about to break out in laughter. I certainly didn't feel good about that, and I'm sure that Ballard didn't either. He actually did chuckle once as he said, "No other conditions. You come in and talk to the kids, and if you think we should shut it all down, it's done."

Ballard barked a laugh that had no humor in it at all. "Where's the trick? You take off or *disapparate* or whatever it is that this ship does with us all? No. I don't need to talk with the kids. I know my answer without talk. I know that regardless what happens, I'll want this project shut down forever."

Minns wasn't disturbed. "I made the offer, and I'll not change it. Either you take it or we leave."

Ballard seemed to be on the verge of begging, "Look, how do I know that you will honor your word?"

I was expecting Minns to reply by asking, "How do I know you'll keep your word?" He didn't. Instead, he said, "You're an honorable man." It wasn't responsive to Ballard's question, but somehow, it seemed to satisfy Ballard.

He simply said, "I'll take your offer."

Behind me, I heard the Boy Genius say, "I'm in on this." Almost as quickly, Aurora said, "You're not going without me." The way they said it made me think that they were proposing crossing the gulf of infinite space to some far world.

At that moment, I woke up and said aloud with as much force as I could muster, "I'll go too."

Minns was not perturbed, but glanced at me and nodded in answer.

Minerva added, "I can't believe I'm saying this, but I want to as well." Minns made no objection.

No one else volunteered. Ballard asked, "How do we get in?"

Minns looked to Reynaldo who simply said, "Walk up to the barrier and stand still."

So, the five of us walked up to the barrier, delineated by the scattered 30mm cannon shells. I almost slipped once or twice, but Minerva caught me. I caught her once as well. We reached it, and I discovered that I was holding my breath. The other side of the barrier did seem like a foreign land. Then suddenly without sound, I knew that I was on the same side of the barrier as Minns was AND that the other side that I'd just been on was now infinitely far away—a different world. For just an instant I felt like I would never return to the "normal" side of the barrier.

Minns's smile was the most genuine I'd seen. He was like a proud home owner showing off his new home. He led the five of us to the black buff surface of the torus. I'd once been to a car show where a car was painted black. The coat of paint seemed to reflect no light. There was no hint of sheen or color to it. The surface, which I couldn't resist feeling (despite warnings not to touch the cars), was rough, but even the roughness was not visible. My companion at that car show called the paint job "Murder" and said that the car was a "Murdered Miata". That was the surface of the torus. It was a "Murdered Spaceship".

As I observed this, Minns was saying, "Step back a bit. The hatch is going to open here." We did, and Minns applied pressure on the surface of the torus somewhere. Instantly, the surface that had seemed to be perfectly seamless developed a seam. It was roughly speaking a rectangle. The rectangle separated from the torus along three edges and folded down to the warehouse floor. The inner surface of that section of the torus was a stairway without railings. It was about wide enough for two people to pass on it.

Minns stepped onto the first step and said, "Follow me. Please walk directly on after you reach the top of the stairs."

There was no question. Ballard went first up the stairs and walked confidently into the ship. The rest followed. No one seemed to want to be the first or last.

Once we were inside, we saw that there was at least one additional floor above us, and closer to the center of the torus, there was a cylindrical wall that appeared to extend completely around the ship. The room that we were in seemed to be a common room of some sort. There were conventional tables and chairs that made me think of ones that I'd once seen at an IKEA. They seemed to be injection-molded plastic. The ship seemed to be divided into sectors—perhaps five. The one we were in had a counter along the inner cylinder. There was space behind it, and built into that cylinder were what appeared to be drawers, a refrigerator, and even something that might have been a microwave.

At that point, the children, perhaps attracted by the noise of our entry to the ship ran into the room. Immediately, the blind boy, Tommy Devereau ran up to me and threw his arms around me, exclaiming, "Lieutenant, I can see you!"

I had a hard time forcing my heart—that had risen into my throat—back where it belonged. For a moment, I was only able to shake my head.

In the mean time, Jenny looked over to Minerva and said, "You didn't say that there would be a witch."

Minerva's jaw gaped, and then she said, "Why wouldn't there be a witch where there is so much magic?"

Jenny laughed, and looking around, exclaimed, "Oh, there you are Lieutenant. I didn't see you at first."

Meanwhile, Johnny Subaru had approached Ballard and said, "You visited my house."

Ballard was struck as dumb as Johnny had once been.

Johnny went on, "Did you come to say goodbye to us?"

The other children seemed all to have similar cures. The crutches of a little girl that we'd not seen before were set in a corner, useless. The deaf girl, Jenny Stokes, asked Aurora if she knew how wonderful

268

it was to hear laughter. Jenny said, "I used to watch cartoons and wanted so much to hear myself laugh—really hear myself laugh."

Aurora gulped and said that the funniest thing she'd ever heard was Brahms laughing.

Brahms's mouth gaped. I knew that he wanted to laugh that peculiar, almost soundless laugh, which he had when something struck him as really funny. It was hardly more than a wheeze. I think I would have given all the gold in Gringotts if he'd been able to laugh just then. But we all knew that what we witnessed was far too heart-wrenching to bring laughter. Instead there was no one—not even Minns—who could do anything other than shed tears or shout aloud.

Ballard answered Johnny's question finally, "Yes, Johnny, we all came to say goodbye to you and wish you a good trip." The last he hardly managed to get out of his throat.

Johnny answered, "Don't worry, Mr. Ballard. Everything's going to be all right." He patted Ballard on the back, the way we'd seen his Mom pat him that day that we'd visited them.

Ballard managed to get out, "I know, Johnny, I know."

Minns asked the room in general, "Have you seen everything you need to?"

We all nodded mutely.

Then, Minns swept his hands in a gesture that we all knew was reserved only for the kids. They came around him. When they were there, he said, "All right. You all know that you're going on a long trip. The older ones know how to use the food machines. You must help the younger. You all have friends for the trip. When you arrive, there will be many new friends who will help you finish growing up."

Just then, Jenny blurted out, "Aren't you coming with us Lieutenant? What about your friends?"

Minns seemed on the verge of emotion himself. He controlled himself and said perfectly calmly, "Don't worry about us. We'll be fine. We'll miss you, but we'll meet again in the clearing at the end of the path."

That seemed to satisfy them all. It didn't satisfy me. We filed out of the ship. When we reached the bottom of the stairs, and the stairs rejoined the rest of the ship seamlessly, I turned to Minns and asked, "Why aren't you going with them?"

Minns didn't answer my question.

Minns hesitated and said, "The words that I speak are forming in my mind even as I speak.

"I have an image of a world very very long ago but not so very different from this one. The people had their long ascent from poverty of body, mind, and spirit. Just as they reached the point where all the Universe seemed to open before them, a tragedy struck. Their precious world was about to be lost to them forever.

"There was not another world that they could find—not another—in the whole wide Cosmos in which they could live.

"But they were determined to pass on their Legacy of learning and wisdom to inheritors who didn't exist—whom they could only imagine."

He hesitated, as if to gather his thoughts from some great distance. Then he went on, "It was not difficult for them to imagine that races such as yours—alive with strength and vitality, impetuous and bold—would come to exist. They would strive to dominate the world they lived on and everything in it. Wars would break out using terrible weapons. They thought that something would happen much as it has here."

He paused again and took a deep breath. "Their inheritors would find the hopeless—not the helpless—and give them hope. The very atmosphere of a planet could contain the cure for illnesses. That is where these children are going. They will find a life with creatures who are much like us and much like our predecessors."

At this point, Minns stopped—apparently having given us all that there was. But, at that point, Aurora shouted an exclamation of joy or perhaps ecstasy, "Oh, Yes. Of course, it all makes sense. The meteors are almost as old as the cosmic black body radiation that they have been traveling through for thirteen and a half billion years." She seemed unable to contain her excitement.

"They come from perhaps the first earth-like planet in the Universe. The Universe had only first generation stars—all hydrogen and helium. Then, the very first stars went supernova, scattering heavier elements across the neighborhood. From that mixture the first 2nd generation stars formed and the first earth-like planets.

"Their planet gave birth to life and that life developed intelligence. It must have been the first in the Universe! Their star, being an early generation star, couldn't live longer than a few hundreds of millions of years. They saw the end coming and they tried to move elsewhere."

She stopped a minute and, nodding to herself, went on reflectively, "There wasn't another planet in the galaxy—maybe not in the whole Universe that could support life, was there?" She directed the question at Minns who remained silent. Then she answered her own question, "Of course not. There wasn't another for a billion light years."

She slowed again, "You looked? Of course, you looked.

"When you didn't find one, you devised a way to send your learning forward in time. You coded it in something like RNA and packed it into a metallic matrix. You knew how to make incredibly strong metal crystalline materials that are light because they have huge cavities."

She stopped again and asked herself, "How could you get this RNA into someone's brain unaltered? A bullet made of the stuff would be perfect, but the process of making the bullet would destroy the information."

An inspiration seemed to seize her, "Of course. You devised some crystalline structure that could survive entry into a planet's atmosphere but that would shatter into many fragments when it struck the planet surface."

"You would then have the perfect shrapnel to pack bombs with. Perfect for piercing armor, such as helmets, and carrying information into people's brains."

She began pacing the floor of the warehouse and almost fell a couple of times as her pacing put a foot on a pile of shells. Her loose hair flung around her shoulders with abandon. A vagrant thought occurred to me. If I'd met her first when she was in such a fell mood, would I and Minerva have gotten together? Might this wild, intense woman have overwhelmed my heart? I was glad that I didn't know the answer.

She was still carrying through to the logical conclusions of her thoughts. I dared ask her a question in a gap in her talk. "It seems like a really long-shot that any number of meteors sent into the space would land on any planet – either earth-like or not."

She turned to look at me as though I'd never been there. "Oh, what? Yes. Good question.

"If this race had taken apart all the earth-like planets in the solar system, they could extract a sphere of iron about . . . " I was amazed that she had that number at the tip of her tongue. Perhaps, though, she'd been thinking along those lines for weeks and it took the events of this day to catalyze them into coherent ideas. "4000 kilometers in radius. If you made spheres of iron about a meter in radius, like the one that landed in Iraq, and launched them at a couple of hundred km. per second, they would expand well beyond the local group of galaxies.

"There would be almost ten to the 20th power of them. Sooner or later, most of them would be captured by a solar system. There might be millions of them floating around in our solar system. Most of those would hit a planetary surface sooner or later. The gas giants would capture the vast majority of them. The vast majority of the remaining would hit earth-like planets when the planet didn't have intelligent life and get reprocessed by geologic processes.

"The chances of landing during the right phase of a planet's life and something like this happening must literally be one in a million or less."

She stopped pacing dead away, and her eyes opened wide. "There must be hundreds or even thousands of planets in our galaxy where this has happened. The inheritors would gather together on dozens of planets spread around the galaxy!"

Harris had been watching her closely as she went through this derivation. He asked her, "Do you mean to say, Ms. Brahms, that what Minns said might be true?"

"Not only might be true, but I think almost certainly must be true."

Just then, I felt that weird displacement that happened when I'd been outside the shield and was suddenly inside. This time, I was suddenly outside it again. Everyone else was outside as well.

The room suddenly brightened, and I looked up to be astounded by a view of the sky above us where the roof of the warehouse had been. I felt a tug on my arm and looked to see that Minerva had taken my arm. She whispered, "I don't think this is like the Great Hall at Hogwarts. I think that ceiling is really gone."

Then the ship began to lift off the ground. I grabbed Minerva's arm and started to run out of the warehouse, afraid that a blast of rocket exhaust would cook us alive if we didn't have a wall between us and the rocket engine. I couldn't believe that there was no rocket exhaust, no sound, and really, only a mild ascent. It took a full minute for the ship to clear the roof of the warehouse. Since we were outside, we could see the ship slowly ascending. Then we did feel a blast of air.

Apparently, Griggs had taken off in the Apache and didn't have much trouble keeping pace with the ship for a few minutes. I suddenly had the horrible vision of his trying to fire a missile at the ship, but I didn't have to worry. He only followed it while he could keep pace.

Harris tapped me on the arm and said, "Let's go. I'll see if I can get in touch with NORAD." We got into cars and drove to the trailer that had been the command post for operations here.

Inside, he got in touch with a contact he had at NORAD. They set up a conference call quickly with the Space Defense Command. There was a Major at the SDC and a Colonel at NORAD who did most of the talking— mostly questions.

The Colonel asked, "What do you know about that . . . uh . . . whatever it is?"

The Major repeated the question—in substance anyway, "What the Hell is that thing. It's been rising for the last five minutes and accelerating at a constant one tenth of a G. It's not following a ballistic trajectory, and it's pretty much out of the atmosphere even though it's going slower than Mach 1."

Aurora started to answer confidently but soon discovered that she couldn't say that much. "Well. . . uh . . . it was made here in Kansas but the design came from. . ." She stopped dead at that point. She puzzled a minute while the Major was getting more impatient by the second. Finally, she said, "We don't know where the design came from. But probably from the early Universe."

The Colonel asked, "Did I hear you right? What University did you say? I've never heard of Early University."

It was good that we weren't on video-conference. Everyone was laughing silently where we were. I don't know what the Major was doing, but I suspect it was the same there.

The joviality didn't last long, though. The Major was getting disturbed. "Look, Colonel. This ship is above the atmosphere and it's going at hardly a thousand miles an hour. I've got a bad feeling about this."

The Colonel sounded even more serious. "Are you saying that you want to shoot it down?"

The Major was definitely nervous. "No, sir. It's beyond our range already despite how slow it's going."

The Colonel sputtered, "But it's not going that fast. We've got airplanes that are faster than that."

"It's gone. I'm worried about what happens when it's really above the atmosphere—like maybe a thousand miles."

"What do you think will happen?"

"I don't know."

"When will that happen?"

"Fewer than 20 minutes."

"Well, let's stay on the conference call and see what happens.

The next fifteen minutes were becoming nail-biters. No one said anything. I was glancing at my watch more and more frequently. I finally gave up and just watched it continuously. At eighteen minutes, it happened.

The Major exclaimed, "What the Hell!" That was followed by a profound silence.

The Colonel broke it, "What's going on? Are you there?"

The reply was, "Yes, sir. We've just left the realm of Physics and entered the Twilight Zone."

"What do you mean?"

The Major said, "We're tracking the ship with radar. They don't seem to care. There's no attempt to evade our radar."

In the meantime, Minerva tugged my arm and whispered, "What is this Twilight Zone thingee? Does it have anything to do with vampires?"

I found myself feeling like Aurora must have a few moments before. I opened my mouth to answer and found that I didn't have a good answer either, "Well, . . . uh . . . . the Twilight Zone was a movie. . ." Strictly speaking true, but the TV show was a lot more well known. The trouble was that I didn't want to have to explain about TV as well as the Twilight Zone. "It featured stories that couldn't be explained by normal science."

She nodded wisely, "Yes, that's most of the world for you."

The Colonel broke in, "What's happening!"

"Well, that ship is going at 10% of the speed of light."

Aurora broke in this time. "That's impossible!"

"Right, but it's happening."

Aurora was indignant. "If it were going that fast, the doppler shift would make it impossible to track with radar."

The Major tried to interrupt. "But. . ."

Aurora wouldn't be interrupted. "To get to that speed in 20 minutes, it would have to be accelerating at over a thousand G's! In two minutes . . . nothing solid could accelerate that fast!"

"Right you are whoever you are."

Aurora hadn't been introduced, so she did it herself, "It's Mrs. Brahms."

"Well, Mrs. Brahms. I'll give you something harder to riddle out. We can track it because the Doppler shift says it's going at about 2 Kilometers per second. But the radar range is right now just over

50,000 Kilometers distant."

Aurora just said, "You're wrong."

"God, I wish you were right. Why don't we keep the conference call going? In fewer than 6 hours, it should be going faster than the speed of light." He then chuckled, "Oh, what the Hell. It'll be so far away, we'll loose track of it long before then."

The Colonel had been silent for a long time. That kind of worried me. But he reasserted his presence by reminding everyone that this was all Top Secret, and we could spend a lot of time in prison if we talked about it with reporters or anyone.

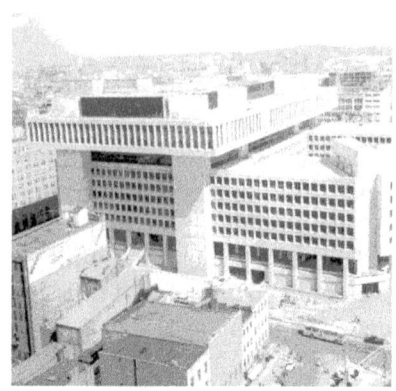

The Difficult Truth

We had a final review of the entire affair. It was conducted by the Head of the Office of the FBI special operations group. The title of the review was, "Lessons Learned."

The Head was not happy with the way the operation had been handled. He was particularly unhappy with the fact that—to his belief—the children had been kidnapped, and we should have prevented it.

No one was ready to admit that it was avoidable. Finally, in desperation, he went around the room and asked each of us individually to give one way that we could have prevented it from happening. He started with Ballard.

Ballard said the truth that none of us wanted to admit, "Any of the people who talked with the children at the end could have stopped it."

The Head was flabbergasted, "The report doesn't say that. You all signed off on the report!"

Ballard started to speak, but the Head interrupted him, "NO! I don't want your answer." He looked around the room and inventoried us, "Let's see. There's you Mr. Ballard from the NSF. Your viewpoint is suspect. You talked me into this mess. There's you Mr. Harris from my unit. Your career is on the line. You have personal motivations. There's you Mr. . . ." He went around the room naming all the government employees involved and declaring them all prejudiced.

He reached Phil Pearson and said, "I don't even know whom you work for. All I know is that you were foisted on me by my boss's boss's boss. I don't trust you at all."

Turning to Sally, he said, "You're a Brit!" Apparently that was enough of an indictment for him.

Then there was Aurora, "You're a Brit too."

For Brahms his analysis was different. "You're a well-known and respected contractor, but you're still a Brit."

That brought him to MY WIFE, "You're a not-well-known contractor and a Brit."

Finally there was me, "That leaves you Mr. Wendt. You're an American and a contractor—which is pretty good in my book." Then he hesitated, and speaking to himself more than anyone else, said, "Wendt . . . Wendt. . . I know your name from somewhere. Several years ago. Was I on a case involving you?"

It didn't take me long to recall what he didn't. I'd been involved with a case that had ended in Nero Wolfe's office. I didn't remember him from the case, so I played dumb and simply gave him the truth, "I have no recollection of you or even of your name."

"Oh, well. Maybe I'm mistaken, but that name is not common and I definitely remember something associated with it. It may come to me yet."

He went on to the question he had now, "Mr. Wendt. You tell me what happened. How did you come to interview the children, and why didn't one of you call a halt to this kidnapping?"

I took a deep breath. I'd half been afraid that that question would come up, and I had an outline of an answer. It was time to flesh it out, "OK. First, let me remind you of the situation.

"The Lieutenant had lifted the kids out from under our surveillance and drove with them to the Wichita warehouse. We had called up all the resources that we had."

The Head interrupted, "Yes, yes. The air cavalry and mechanized cavalry from Fort Riley. They tried to intercept Minns on the way to Wichita but failed.

"By the way, why is it that you all refer to him as The Lieutenant? You all do. He certainly wasn't a lieutenant when you met him."

I scratched my head, "Well, everyone who deals with him seems to. That was what all the kids called him. Even the parents who'd talked to their kids knew him by no other name. I guess it was just easier eventually rather than what we'd started out calling him—his sirname, Minns."

"Go ahead."

"Anyway, he'd gotten the kids past all our barriers and into the warehouse. Once there, we tried various things to get them out. Nothing was successful." I paused here to look over at Minerva. I was about to talk about what might have resulted in our death. She just nodded. I could go ahead. "Well, my wife and I were readying

277

ourselves for a really desperate act. We had an idea for how to get past the shield that they had. It probably wouldn't have worked. and I expected that we'd die, but we were preparing ourselves for the attempt."

The Head interrupted again, "What in the world were you going to try?"

I shook my head. "I'm not going to tell you. It doesn't matter. We didn't have to try it. I just want you to know that that was the level we had reached—being willing to throw away our lives to rescue the kids."

I went on to the real point that I wanted to make. "The thing that saved Minerva and me from throwing our lives at that invisible barrier in the warehouse was that Mr. Ballard found another way. He had been studying the characters of the four men we were opposing. He found that they were driven by an intellect that somehow was shared among the four. All of them except Minns had great misgivings about what they were doing.

"Ballard worked those misgivings. He drove a wedge between the other three and the lieutenant. He hammered away at that wedge and opened a crack and nearly got the three to turn off the barrier that kept us out."

The Head asked, "He didn't succeed?"

"No, he didn't. He was close but not there when Minns offered us a deal."

The Head's voice had gone very quiet, and I was a little afraid when he asked, "You negotiated with them?"

"Yes, sir. The Lieutenant offered this deal: He would let a few of us in provided that we would see the children and only after seeing them decide whether or not to send them back to their parents."

The Head's eyes almost popped out of his head, "I see why you agreed, but why in the world didn't you just glance at them and send them back to their parents?"

I prepared for what I thought would be the hardest part of my story. I closed my eyes and tried to recreate the scene and steel myself to tell the story as straight and without emotion as I could. "The first child that I saw was Johnny Subaru."

The Head's eyes dropped for the first time, "Oh, yes. The Down's Syndrome child. Sad. Very sad."

I came back immediately, "But it wasn't sad. He was transformed. He could speak. He was almost eloquent." I gasped as I struggled to hold back the tears at the memory of him. "How could we send him back? He would have lost all that. It would almost have been murder. And they were all like that."

The Head looked at me almost imploringly, "But to never see his parents again. For them to never see their children again! How could you allow it?"

Here was the point that I hated. How could I communicate what it was like to be in that room with those children, who were full of life, and condemn then to half-life or even death? I shrugged and said, "I don't know." I looked around the room appealing to everyone who had been there. "Would any of you change your minds about what we did?"

There were a few shaking heads, a few spoken "no's", and down-cast eyes.

The Head turned his attention back to me, and he asked a question that I'm sure he thought would be telling. "OK. I know that you went to visit those parents to tell them what happened. What was that like?"

I felt Minerva's hand on my arm. It squeezed, and I went ahead. "We visited the Subaru family."

☐

After the ship had disappeared from the radars of NORAD, we all looked at each other in dismay. We knew that we'd have to visit the families of the children. I didn't want to have to tell the family of Jenny that they'd never see her again. Her disability—deafness—was one that you could live with. I guess everyone's disability—regardless how awful—is one that you can live with. I thought of Stephen Hawking who had somehow survived Lou Gehrig's disease for decades. But how could you tell the parents of a deaf girl that they'd never see her again. No, the coward that I was, I didn't hesitate. I was the first. I volunteered Minerva and me to visit the parents of Johnny.

Minerva surprised me. She said, "I agree. Come on out so that we can disapparate there."

My jaw dropped. Somehow I thought that we'd drive there. I thought I'd have time to think. I thought that Minerva and I could talk during the long drive back to Kansas City. Maybe we'd get caught up in a traffic jam where the tanks had chewed the hell out of I-35.

I didn't say anything until we left the trailer that served as a command post.

Minerva knows me too well. She knew what I was thinking. Her voice was as school-marmly as I'd heard in a long time. "Don't think that you can put this off one minute by insisting on traveling by Muggle means. We're *disapparating*."

I'd been with her long enough to know when resistance was futile. I took her hand even before she offered it and thus took her by surprise for once. After a surprising 10 seconds, the universe spun and I found myself on Mockingbird Drive. Actually we were in an alley that came out on Mockingbird. I strode forward and asked, "You don't want to think about what we say?"

"We've both been here enough. Do you really think it's necessary?"

I didn't comment. She was right. From the moment that I'd had to tell Sally that Fred was gone I'd been in this situation a number of times. Pretending that we didn't know how to break the news was just a coward's reaction to having to give it one more time. But this time was different too. I'd never had to tell someone that her son was still alive but they'd never see him again.

By this time, we'd arrived at the front door. It opened even before we'd reached the porch. The mother was sobbing, and her husband looked me in the eye and stated, not asked, "He's dead."

Minerva said nothing, the coward. I had to say, "He's not dead, but it's complicated."

Mrs. Subaru gasped and threw her arms around Minerva, "He's alive. I knew it! He must be in a hospital. Where is he? And why didn't you just call us and tell us where?"

Minerva was forced to tell part of it after all, "No. Wendt is right. It is complicated. Can we go in and sit down to talk for a few minutes?"

Mrs. Subaru looked mistrustful and said, "No. Let's sit on the porch." She seemed to be afraid that inside the house the truths would be starker, more painful than out in the open. "John, would you go fix our guests some coffee."

I started to object that that wasn't necessary, but Minerva interrupted me, "That would be nice, but would you mind making it hot water for tea?" She gave John a hopeful smile as she asked.

He agreed, and we were stuck while we waited for the tea to come. I certainly wasn't going to do some worthless banter about the weather—even to satisfy some social norm. But Minerva said, "I'm sorry to be such a pain asking for tea, but both James and I find it more . . ." She was stuck and trailed off.

Thankfully, John returned with a couple of coffee cups filled with hot water—no doubt microwaved. He also had several tea bags and sweetener packets. He went back into the house and brought another pair of cups with hot water.

Minerva thanked him, and then she turned to me. So, I was going to have to tell the story after all. "Johnny is alive and well. As a matter of fact, he's more well than he's ever been in his life."

That disturbed Mrs. Subaru more than anything we'd said so far. "What do you mean, better than ever before? There's something terribly wrong, isn't there?"

This was never going to be easy, but now it seemed like I was climbing Mount Everest with nothing more than my bare hands. "You know that I told you before that there were four geniuses who were visiting some children in the area?"

"Yes, and I wanted you to arrest them. Wasn't what they were doing wrong!"

I tried my hardest to keep from sighing, but I did. "Yes. One of the things that they were working on was a cure for some of the worst crippling diseases in the world."

She gasped, "And they were experimenting on our son."

How could I answer that? Yes, they were experimenting. And they apparently succeeded. "When I saw him earlier today, he spoke to me. He walked up to me and asked me if I were the Lieutenant."

John, jumped up, and angrily shouted, "You're lying!"

I noticed Minerva reach into her handbag. I knew what she was reaching for. I wanted to stop her, but I had to keep my attention on him. "No, sir. You can ask Minerva."

She had pulled something out of her handbag ,and I almost threw myself between the two of them.

But, she surprised me. What she pulled out was a cell phone. What the Hell was she going to do with that? She answered me with action. She flipped the phone open and pushed a couple of keys, muttering, "Bloody Muggle invention." Finally, she said, "Yes, there it is. Look." She turned the screen toward the rest of us. On the screen was the small, badly-focused, but unmistakable image of Johnny walking toward the camera confidently. His voice would not have been recognizable to me, but Mrs. Subaru gasped in recognition and sobbed, "Johnny."

John seized the cell phone from Minerva.

I jumped at that. I reached in my pocket for my purse, but Minerva had my hand. "Wait." she whispered to me.

Tears formed in his eyes—the first tears that I'd seen him shed. "That is Johnny! What happened?"

I picked up the story where I'd left off. "The Lieutenant and his friends do have a cure for some terrible diseases. But . . ."

Mrs. Subaru looked up from the phone screen, "But there's a catch, isn't there? What is it?"

Minerva surprised me again by telling the rest of the story. "The cure only lasts as long as he's somewhere that the air has certain gases added." She gulped at the enormity of what she was about to say. "The only place those gases exist in the open is on another planet."

Mrs. Subaru shook her head and apparently had shed all the tears that she had, for there were no more as she said, "I knew it. I knew it from the first time you visited us. Johnny would go, and we'd never see him again. Those hideous aliens have him, don't they? The Lieutenant is just another poor man who's got a Soul in his brain."

Minerva took Mrs. Subaru's hands in hers and said, "No. No. It's not like that. We know that's not true. I can't really tell you how we know, but that's never true."

John sat back down with his wife and asked, "The video. Can we have it?"

Minerva said, "Of course!" She hesitated and turned to me, "Just how do you get this thingee to send him the video."

I took the cell phone and asked for his cell phone number. As I was sending him the video, he asked, "And you are sure that was Johnny."

I was trying to compose an answer as Mrs. Subaru said with complete confidence, "Of course, it is. Didn't you see Johnny patting that Mr. Ballard's back. . ." There she stuck for a moment, trying to hold back a sob, "It was just like when I comfort him."

John didn't seem entirely convinced, but Mrs. Subaru was. She then turned to Minerva and asked, "Would you stay for dinner?"

I started to shake my head, but Minerva kicked my shin and rushed in, "Of course, could I help you fix dinner?" She nodded, and the two went into the house.

It was a long uncomfortable wait for dinner, but Mr. Subaru seemed happy to have some company. We didn't exchange any words but it was like being with Sally when Fred Weasley died. They both just wanted someone to be there.

□□

I concluded the story. The Head shook his head. He looked around at us all and said, "I'd like to fire you all, if I had the authority.

"But I can't fire half of you because you're contractors, and you're gone. I can't fire the rest of you because you're from other departments.

I can't fire you, Mr. Ballard, because you're NSF. That only leaves Harris. How would it be fair if I fired him and nobody else?"

No one seemed to want to answer that question, so he went on, "I'm not going to put a black mark on your record Harris. You probably did better than I would have.

"So, if we're done here. . ."

I interrupted him. "I don't think we're quite done. I want to know what's happened to Minns and the others."

The Head looked over to Harris, "You know more than I do. Why don't you fill everyone in?"

Harris looked around the room once, seeming to assess the group and began. "Well, we took them into custody as soon as the ship had disappeared out of the sky.

"They went directly to the San Antonio VA Multi-trauma unit. We've been studying them there. We've done all the tests that we could think of. The EKG's are more normal looking now. We've been testing intelligence almost daily. They fluctuated up and down some but have evened out, and all of them are sub-genius now." He paused.

Someone asked, "But . . ."

Harris shrugged, "Really, BUT nothing. . . Well. . . Their intelligence quotients are all above what they used to be. The only one that's really close to genius level is Minns at about 145.

"We've decided not to prosecute them for anything. They really haven't broken any laws. They did do some damage to the warehouse property, of course, but they arranged even for that."

The Head was surprised at that and asked, "How in the sand hill can they possibly have done that?"

"Oh, the property management company that leased the warehouse for them has plenty of money to pay for the damages."

At that the representative of the State Highway Patrol of Kansas spoke up, "What about US 77 and I-35. Those highways are pretty much chewed up to gravel by those tanks."

Harris had an answer, "Well, in the first place, it was the FBI that requested the tanks, so it's actually the Federal government that is truly responsible."

The Head was starting to reply with an indignant "NO." But Harris went on. "We've done some research and we think that there's enough money left in the Swiss bank account to cover the costs that we estimate to be around thirty million dollars. Technically, Minns is still the owner of the account, and he's agreed to repay the state of Kansas and even to pay the Federal government some for the expenses of investigating him.

"He's still pretty cagey, though. I think he might want to negotiate. He points out that in a court case, his defense could be that he did nothing strictly speaking illegal. So, if the government chose to spend a lot of money investigating a law-abiding citizen, that citizen is hardly responsible for the costs of the pointless investigation."

At this the Head blew up. "Not illegal! What about kidnapping more than half a dozen kids! They used to hang people for that."

Harris looked forlorn, "Well, sir. I've done a little further investigating. It turns out that none of the parents want to press charges. As a matter of fact, they're all willing to swear that Minns had their permission to take their kids for an outing."

The Head looked heavenward, "An outing. An outing! To who knows where in the Universe."

The Head turned to another possible avenue of prosecution, "What about the fact that he stole half a billion dollars?"

Harris replied patiently, "Yes. He stole a half billion dollars—but from whom? I'll tell you—from ISIS. What court in the US is going to convict anybody for stealing from ISIS? The jury would nominate him for the Nobel Peace Prize."

The Head looked ready to say something, but Harris went on. "No! It wouldn't get that far. The defense would move for a directed verdict of innocent AND they'd get it."

"But what about having fake passports, huh!"

Harris nodded, "The funny thing is that they did nothing illegal. They had valid driver's licenses. They had accurate birth certificates. They did everything by the book."

The Head seemed triumphant here, "BUT! They obtained the drivers license with a false social security number."

"It was a real social security number obtained with. . ."

The Head had almost reached the whining stage, "I know, I know. Valid birth certificate, etc. etc. But that's fraud!"

Harris answered patiently, "Only if they ever applied for social security benefits on both accounts. No one has. And I'm convinced that none of them would ever. You really don't want to prosecute them, do you?"

That question went unanswered. He then turned to the Colonel and the adjutant who'd come along, "What about you. Are you going to prosecute him for being a deserter?"

Colonel Bradley, who was from the Judge Advocate office said, "In the first place, there are precise legal definitions for desertion and none of these men fit into them. They all are Absent Without Leave. But that is not necessarily a prosecutable offense. The Army is taking the position that these men were acting under extreme duress and are not responsible for their actions.

"As soon as they are released from the hospital—and that should be within a month or two—they will be granted honorable discharges from the service. And, of course, they were already in line to receive Purple Hearts. That will happen in a day or two."

I asked, "Not medical discharges?"

"No, we don't want there to be a hint of prejudice against them in the civilian world."

I think that the Head was angrier about that than anything else, but he was stuck without any actions to take.

He growled, "No, I suppose we're finally done."

But it was simply not his day. Aurora had a point to make. "This is supposed to be a session about lessons learned. There's at least one more lesson."

"Oh, what is it?" the Head asked resignedly.

She began slowly. "No one has mentioned that the ship had a faster-than-light propulsion system."

That caused some exclamations of excitement, especially from the military types who were there. The Head, himself, exclaimed, "That's impossible!"

She shook her head. "I'm afraid not."

Bradley urged her to go on.

"Well, I'd have thought it was obvious. The radar tracking of the ship shows that it was not obeying Einstein's laws. Its speed was a substantial fraction of the speed of light, but the red-shift of the radar tracking signal was hardly more than a few Kilometers per second. Even in Newtonian mechanics, the red shift would have been substantial. It wasn't."

People were lining up to object. The Head had apparently had enough. He didn't even make a peep. Bradley asked, "I don't know from Einstein or Newton, but we never recorded the ship going faster than the speed of light. How do you know?"

Aurora promptly answered, "I don't KNOW with certainty, but any ship that can defy both Einstein's and Newton's mechanics and get to nearly the speed of light with very little or maybe no fuel is capable of getting past that speed.

"Beside that, think about where they were going." She paused for reactions. There were none.

She went on, "Well, where do you think they were going?"

Everyone pretty much shrugged. I asked, "What's wrong with someplace in our solar system?"

Aurora nodded, seemingly approvingly, "Well. The only thing against that is that when they described where they were going, it didn't seem much like any place in our solar system. I grant you that they could probably make a lot of odd corners of our solar system habitable, but why lie about it? It's not like we're going out to get them anytime soon."

I agreed. "OK. I kind of agree with you about that. So, then they're going to another star."

She snapped back, "Yes! At sub-light speeds, it would take at the very least several years to get there. The radar tracking showed that they weren't headed toward any close star. For the stars they were generally heading toward, it would take dozens of years, at least, to reach. Do you really think that they were setting those kids up for dozens of years in space?"

At this Ballard asked, "But, close to the speed of light, time slows. It might be only months or even weeks to wherever they were going."

She nodded slowly but said, "You know the problem with that."

He smiled sheepishly after a moment's reflection. "Sure. If Relativity doesn't apply to them, then it really is dozens or hundreds of years—not months."

Harris asked, "But even the Souls who invaded us a few years ago didn't have faster-than-light travel. They depended on long lives, Relativity, and suspended animation at liquid Nitrogen. . . "

Aurora interrupted, "Liquid Helium."

"Oh, yeh, liquid Helium."

"You're right. The Souls were either lazy or not as smart as our boys. Or—my personal favorite—both. If the Souls had been here when these guys showed up, the Souls would have been their dishrags."

Bradley said forlornly, "This is crazy! Is the Universe crawling with super-intelligent aliens?"

Aurora answered, "That's my point. The most important lesson learned out of this is that the Universe IS crawling with super-intelligent aliens."

The Head just dropped his head into his hands that were resting on the tabletop and said, "Why is it always me? Shit."

About the Author

 William Wilkin lived in a small Southern Ohio town until he began his college career. He has a Bachelor's degree in Physics from The Ohio State University and a Master's degree in Physics from The University of Chicago.He has a career in corporate Information Technology.and currently lives in Dallas, Texas.

He enjoys music, both "serious" and "classic Rock". He reads classic Detective fiction and Science Fiction & Fantasy as well as trying to stay current in Physics.

He began writing seriously about 2005. He has a blog, in-mid-world, where he writes about Science Fiction & Fantasy and remotely related topics.

www.ingramcontent.com/pod-product-compliance
Lightning Source LLC
Chambersburg PA
CBHW061946170626
46813CB00006B/2545